MW01253804

An Enigma in Silver

Book 2 in the Mysteries in Metals series

www.spacejock.com.au

Cover images copyright depositphotos.com
Cover 3d models from cgtrader.com

Stay in touch!

Author's newsletter:
spacejock.com.au/ML.html

facebook.com/halspacejock
twitter.com/spacejock

Works by Simon Haynes

All of Simon's novels* are self-contained, with a beginning, a middle and a proper ending. They're not sequels, they don't end on a cliffhanger, and you can start or end your journey with any book in the series.
Robot vs Dragons series excepted!

The Hal Spacejock series for teens/adults
Set in the distant future, where humanity spans the galaxy and robots are second-class citizens. Includes a large dose of humour!

Hal Zero (a prequel)
Hal Spacejock 1: A Robot named Clunk*
Hal Spacejock 2: Second Course*
Hal Spacejock 3: Just Desserts*
Hal Spacejock 4: No Free Lunch
Hal Spacejock 5: Baker's Dough
Hal Spacejock 6: Safe Art
Hal Spacejock 7: Big Bang
Hal Spacejock 8: Double Trouble
Hal Spacejock 9: Max Damage
Hal Spacejock 10: Cold Boots
Hal Spacejock 11: Atmosteal (TBA)
Also available:
Omnibus One, containing Hal books 1-3*
Omnibus Two, containing Hal books 4-6
Omnibus Three, containing Hal books 7-9
Megabus One, containing Hal books 1-5
Megabus Two, containing Hal books 6-10
Hal Spacejock: Visit, a short story
Hal Spacejock: Framed, a short story
Hal Spacejock: Albion, a novella
*Audiobook editions available

The Dragon and Chips Trilogy.
High fantasy meets low humour!
Each set of three books should be read in order.

1. A Portion of Dragon and Chips*
2. A Butt of Heads*
3. A Pair of Nuts on the Throne*
Also Available:
Omnibus One, containing the first trilogy*
*Audiobook editions available

The Harriet Walsh series.
Set in the same universe as Hal Spacejock. Good clean fun, written with wry humour. No cliffhangers between novels!

Harriet Walsh 1: Peace Force
Harriet Walsh 2: Alpha Minor
Harriet Walsh 3: Sierra Bravo
Harriet Walsh 4: Foxtrot Hotel (TBA)
Also Available:
Omnibus One, containing books 1-3

The Hal Junior series
Written for all ages, these books are set aboard a space station in the Hal Spacejock universe, only ten years later.

1. Hal Junior: The Secret Signal*
2. Hal Junior: The Missing Case
3. Hal Junior: The Gyris Mission
4. Hal Junior: The Comet Caper
Also Available:
Omnibus One, containing books 1-3
*Audiobook edition

The Secret War series.
Gritty space opera for adult readers.

1. Raiders
2. Frontier
3. Deadlock (TBA)

Mysteries in Metal series.
Ghostly goings-on in Victorian London!
1. A Riddle in Bronze
2. An Enigma in Silver (2020)
3. A Conundrum in Gold (TBA)

Collect One-Two - a dozen short stories by Simon Haynes

All titles available in ebook and paperback. Visit spacejock.com.au for details.

Bowman Press

V 1.15

This edition published 2020 by Bowman Press
ISBN 978-1-877034-45-9

Text © Simon Haynes 2020
Cover art © Bowman Press 2020
Stock cover images copyright depositphotos.com

Dedicated to my great-grandparents. I hope a small part of your world lives on in this novel.

'Professor, two young gentlemen of the police are here.' Mrs Fairacre's voice was flat and emotionless, as one would expect from a professional housekeeper, and yet she managed to convey a faint air of disapproval.

I glanced towards the head of the table, where Professor Twickham was engrossed in his morning newspaper. The broadsheet was fastened to a contraption of slender brass wires and steel cogs, each page turned by a foot pedal beneath the table. This left the professor's hands free to butter his toast, slice his bacon and enjoy a cup of fresh-brewed tea. It also turned the newspaper into a formidable screen which discouraged interruptions.

Thus, Mrs Fairacre might have donned a feather boa and sung news of the unwelcome visitors in a rich *soprano*, and I doubt the elderly gentleman at the head of the table would have noticed. Roberta, the professor's daughter, was sitting across the table from me, and she now caught my eye and gave me a warm smile. 'Father, the police have unearthed a murder victim in our back garden,' she said, in a loud, clear voice.

'Nonsense,' said the professor mildly, his voice muffled slightly by the newspaper screen. 'The garden is entirely overgrown. One could hide a troupe of circus elephants within its confines with little risk of discovery.'

'In that case, perhaps they are mistaken,' said Roberta, and then she winked at me. 'Should I offer the gentlemen of the police some breakfast?'

That got a reaction. The professor half-rose in his seat, giving her a worried look over the top of his newspaper. Then, bushy eyebrows raised, he cast an anxious glance at the platters of fresh-cooked sausages, cold ham and poached eggs on the sideboard. I could all but read his thoughts, for policemen tended to be burly fellows, and their appetites were legendary.

'Shall I show them in?' asked Mrs Fairacre, casually twisting the dagger. In her youth she'd nursed casualties in the Crimea, and I suspected she knew more than most about the inflicting of such injuries.

'In here? Are you mad?' The professor pulled a small lever, letting the newspaper flop onto the table. Then he leapt up and strode for the door, nimble despite his advancing years. 'I'll see them in my study.' In the doorway, he paused to address Roberta. 'Close this firmly behind me, and do not let them enter under any circumstances! I only hope they do not catch the scent of bacon, else we shall be feasting on crumbs for the remainder of the day.'

'Come on Septimus,' murmured Roberta, once he'd left. 'Quick, or we'll miss everything.'

'He asked us to remain here.'

'I do not aspire to being the dutiful, obedient daughter. Come.'

I *was* the dutiful, obedient type, and the professor's employee to boot. But, as I stood, I reminded myself that the professor had instructed Roberta, and not me, to guard the food. A fine point of law, perhaps, but it was enough. In addition, Roberta was a strong young woman, and was more than capable of dragging me from the room and hauling me all the way down the hall to the professor's study. Experience had taught me it was better to go quietly. So, we waited until the heavy tread of the policemen had passed, then opened the door the merest crack to ensure they had entered the professor's study. Once they closed the door to the study Roberta took my hand with a grip that brooked no argument, and the two of us tip-toed down the hall.

We reached the professor's study, where we took up station either side of the doorframe, backs pressed to the wall. Then Roberta reached out to turn the knob, easing the door open a fraction.

She needn't have bothered.

'Are you insane?' bellowed the professor, his voice carrying halfway across the great city of London. 'You come to *me* with this nonsense? What am I to you? Nothing more than a vulgar crackpot, I'll wager!'

'Sir,' rumbled one of the policemen. 'This is a serious matter, and Inspector Cox—'

'Oho!' cried the professor. 'He takes his revenge on me, does he? The last time Cox darkened my doorway he belaboured my household with the most outrageous accusations, all of them subsequently proven to be false. Much to his shame, I hasten to point out. And,' finished the professor, in an aggrieved tone, 'he and his men ate all my breakfast sausages.'

'I apologise, sir.' The policeman took a deep breath. 'Nevertheless, this is a serious case, and the Inspector feels you might be able to help us with certain aspects. If you would just glance at this report—'

There was a rustle of paper. A moment of silence. An impatient snort. 'I have my speciality, gentlemen. Spirits. Phantasms. Otherworldly shades which have lost their way. This poor devil appears to be the victim of something else entirely, and I do not have the slightest interest in pursuing the matter.'

'But—'

'Unless, of course, the fee is commensurate with my abilities.'

The policeman mumbled something which I did not quite catch. The professor, however, caught it only too well.

'Free?' he roared. 'Are you quite out of your minds? Do you think I am so eager to work with the police that I will abandon all thoughts of commerce and enterprise? Do you know how much I invest in research, and machinery, and new equipment?'

'Sir, we—'

'I'm sorry, but I'm far too busy with *paid* work,' said the professor loftily. 'In fact, I am expecting a shipment this very afternoon, a shipment of scientific equipment which will alter, *completely* alter, the world as we know it.'

'I wouldn't know anything about that,' said the policeman doubtfully, 'but the Inspector—'

'In addition, your precious Inspector has done nothing to earn any favours from me. Now, if you please, I should like to finish my breakfast before it gets cold. Good day to you, sirs!'

Chair legs scraped, and Roberta turned to me, eyes wide with alarm. Discovery was imminent!

Together we turned and hurried up the hall, prancing on tip-toes to avoid making any noise, and in doing so we must have looked for all the world like a pair of pantomime villains. We reached the dining room, but instead of entering Roberta took my hand and pulled me towards the front door. Outside, in the mid-morning sunshine, we took the short path to the front gate, where she led me into the street.

'I think we've run far enough,' I said, quite out of breath.

'We're not running, Septimus. I want to speak to those policemen.'

'But why?'

'I'm intrigued. Are you not?'

I confessed that I was. When I first met the professor and Roberta, I had no inkling they were engaged in the hunting and trapping of other-worldly spirits. At first I dismissed their business as a type of confidence trick, designed to milk rich folk, but the moment I encountered my first phantasm all thoughts of trickery were quickly forgotten. Indeed, that memory would haunt me forever. Now, it seemed the police had a case involving something of the supernatural, and I wanted to know more. 'I'm surprised your father was not more receptive.'

'He may have been, had they offered remuneration,' said Roberta, with a shrug. 'In any case, you and I will decide whether this case merits further attention, while my father reads the newspaper and enjoys the rest of his breakfast.'

'We're going to talk to the police?'

'Not us. Me. And here they come.'

The two policemen were tall and forbidding, and were made even more so by their helmets and dark blue uniforms. Worse, they bore expressions like thunder, and I prayed Roberta did not antagonise them further.

'Sirs, might I speak with you?'

'Not now miss,' grunted one of the policemen. 'We're on urgent business.'

'I know. You were just speaking to my father.'

'Professor Twickham? You're the daughter?'

Well, I thought, you couldn't fault their powers of deduction. But by now Roberta had their undivided attention, and I moved closer, much as they did, eager to see how things might turn out. The older of the two policemen looked Roberta up and down, then glanced at me. His scrutiny was brief but intense, and I felt as though he were peering into my very soul. Then he returned his attention to Roberta, and I let out a relieved breath.

'We can't talk in the street, miss,' growled the policeman. He indicated a waiting cab, the horse flicking away flies with its jet-black tail and with sudden shakes of its mane. 'You'd better come down the station.'

I could see his point, for we were already attracting attention. Barrow-boys and labourers afforded us curious glances as they strode by, and any conversation was sure to be overheard.

'Mr Jones and I will make ourselves available later this afternoon, provided you send a cab for us,' said Roberta. The policeman opened his mouth to argue, but she forestalled him. 'My father has an appointment with his bank manager at two o'clock, and his absence will give me the opportunity to speak with you in private. In the meantime, perhaps you would care to leave that report with me so that Mr Jones and I might acquaint ourselves with this mysterious case of yours.'

'Impossible. This is an official police document,' said the constable, tucking the report under his arm.

'Very well,' said Roberta calmly. 'In that case, I wish you all the best with your investigation.'

The policemen could only stare as Roberta whirled around and strode purposefully towards the Professor's house. She did not look back, and after a moment or two the older constable relented. 'You win, miss!' he called. 'You can study the report.'

'Give it to Septimus,' called Roberta, and she vanished inside.

The policemen turned to me, and the older constable held out the report. 'I leave this with you because I have no choice,' he growled. 'Lose a single page, and—'

I drew myself up, standing taller than either of them. 'You see before you a respected bookkeeper, accustomed to dealing with important papers,' I said grandly. 'Your report will be perfectly safe in my hands.'

'Don't get high and mighty with me,' growled the constable. 'Look after the report, or I'll have your head.'

With that he thrust the precious report into my hands, and both policemen turned and strode to the waiting cab. The vehicle creaked as it bore their solid bulk, and then the driver flicked his whip and the horse set off with alacrity.

Indoors, I found Roberta waiting impatiently. Indeed, she was practically dancing from one foot to the other, with no trace of her casual withdrawal. 'Well? What's in it? Quick, give it here!' she exclaimed.

'Is that you, Roberta?'

The professor had just emerged from his study, further down the hall, and Roberta muttered a coarse oath under her breath. She turned to face her father, hiding the report behind her back. 'Indeed it is, father. Tell me, what did the police want?'

'Oh, that was nothing to do with us.' The professor waved dismissively. 'Nothing at all. No cause for alarm.'

'Your sausages are safe, then?' asked Roberta mischievously.

'Yes, my dear. And I intend to finish my repast this instant.'

I was about to join him, for I'd barely started my breakfast when the police put in their appearance. Roberta, however, had other ideas. She gripped my elbow all-too-firmly, and I almost yelped at the sudden pain. 'You don't mind if Septimus and I retire to his office? I would like him to cast his eye over some designs I've been working on.'

At this point the professor gave me The Look. Soon after hiring me, he'd revealed his hopes for his daughter's future. These included a wealthy suitor, with good prospects and a steady income. Professor Twickham himself had risen from modest beginnings, to say the least, and he explained that he did not want his only child to suffer the same fate. He even had tears in his eyes as he told me so, although I was unsure whether that was emotion or the noxious chemicals he was working with at the time.

In any case, the professor made it clear that a match with a penniless bookkeeper such as myself would not be in Roberta's best interests. I would consign his lively, intelligent daughter to a life of near-poverty, whereas he only wanted the best for her.

Roberta, of course, might go ahead and do whatever she wanted, but the professor clung to his hopes nevertheless. And thus, whenever she declared her intention to spend time in my company, the professor turned his special expression upon me. It blended a stern warning, beseeching entreaties and threats of violence all at once, and I'd promptly named it The Look, complete with ornate capital letters.

'Father, are you unwell?' asked Roberta, who was oblivious to his meaningful looks, capitalised or not. 'You bear the most pained expression.'

'It's merely hunger,' mumbled the professor, and after another warning glance in my direction he turned and entered the dining room.

'Come, Septimus. Your office has a lock on the door, does it not?'

I gulped. If the professor discovered the pair of us behind a locked door, he wouldn't only be applying The Look. No, it would be The Poker followed by The Horsewhip and then summary dismissal...if not execution. 'Maybe we should wait for him to depart on his appointment?' I asked timidly.

'Which appointment?' asked Roberta, frowning.

'He was to visit his bank manager. You told the police so.'

'Oh Septimus, you poor muddled fool. When will you learn to doubt everything I say?' Roberta brandished the report in my face. 'I merely wanted to get my hands on this. The juicy tidbits within weren't enough to tempt my father, but I am more than ready for adventure!'

I was still blinking with astonishment as we climbed the stairs to the second floor, where my study was situated. I was shocked that Roberta had deceived the police so casually, although I had to admit it was not out of character. Since our first meeting I'd been forced to constantly revise my opinion of her, and I was slowly learning to accept that, with Roberta, the unexpected was *status quo*.

As soon as we reached the second floor Roberta threw open the door to my modest study. Before I could stop her she swept all the carefully-arranged paperwork from my desk. Ignoring my strangled cry of protest, she scattered the police report on the worn surface, carelessly spreading the pages here and there with no regard to the proper order. 'Be a dear and turn the lamp up,' she commanded me.

I was still distraught at the cavalier treatment she'd meted out to my work, but I did as instructed and the spluttering mantle glowed white hot.

'Good heavens,' remarked Roberta.

I looked down at my desk, and immediately recoiled in disgust. Amongst the sheets of hand-written notes were two large photographs, and the contents were appalling. The first depicted a forest clearing, with a twisted figure stretched out on the ground in the centre. The second was a close-up of this figure showing a savagely mauled corpse, barely recognisable as a human male. The eyes were wide open, glazed, and what remained of the face was contorted with pure horror. One arm had been torn clean off, the appendage lying in the dirt nearby. Half the flesh was missing, and a white, blood-streaked bone protruded from the remains. To my eye, it looked like a grotesque Sunday roast, and I turned away, sickened. 'Who is that poor fellow?' I asked, fearing I might know the man. Why, it might be an old friend from school, or–

'Not a local. It seems it was a seasonal labourer looking for work.' Roberta did not quail as she studied the photos closely, and then she took up a page of the report and began to read.

'W—was it wild dogs that left him in that terrible state?' I asked her. To me it seemed certain that only the most vicious of animals could have done so.

'The body shows ample evidence of bite marks,' said Roberta, quoting from the report. She eyed the grotesque photo. 'Well, it would be hard to fault that particular conclusion, wouldn't it?'

I nodded, keeping my eyes averted.

'How old would you say the victim was?' she asked me.

I shuddered as I recalled those blank, staring eyes. 'No more than twenty-five years of age.'

'Hmm.' Roberta worried her thumbnail as she read the dense writing, squinting now and then at an ill-formed letter or an ink blot. Then she tossed the page aside and took up another. After a minute or two of careful perusal, she gave a start. 'Oho! Here's something.' She indicated the paragraph. 'Listen to what the coroner has to say. 'Upon measuring these bite marks, one can infer that the mandibles were far greater in size than those found in even the largest species of *canis lupus familiaris.*"

I vaguely recalled my schoolmaster berating the entire class during

Latin prep. 'Lupus? Is that not ...a wolf? Are they suggesting such a creature yet exists, right here in England? Why, it's been hundreds of years since—'

'I agree. Wolves are extinct in this country.' Roberta eyed me over the top of the loose page. 'However, while your Latin is sound, you should know that *canis lupis familiaris* is the scientific term for a domesticated hound or dog.'

'And yet the coroner states that the bite marks are too large. Does that not suggest an exotic creature such as a lion or a tiger? Perhaps a jungle beast has escaped from a travelling show, and is even now mauling innocent victims.'

'If you would only take up a page of the report and read for yourself, my dear, there would be no need for such guesswork,' said Roberta, a trifle tartly.

Nothing would have induced me to examine the photographs, but I acquiesced with respect to the handwritten pages. Soon, I too was squinting at the laborious writing, until we both had a grasp on the facts of the case. 'There are no reports of escaped circus animals in the vicinity of the crime,' I said, gathering the pages into a neat pile.

'And in any case, these bites were not made by any species of feline, whether big cats, domestic cats or something in between,' said Roberta, holding the photograph out to me. 'Compare the victim's wounds to the diagrams on page nine.'

'I shall take your word for it.'

She gestured impatiently. 'If we are to investigate this case, you will have to overcome such squeamishness.'

I took the photograph and placed it face-down on my desk. 'Roberta, what are we to investigate? This poor man was killed by a wild creature, which has nothing to do with the, er, specialised work that you and the Professor are known for.'

'My dear Septimus,' said Roberta quietly. 'Spirits and phantasms are not the only paranormal entities inhabiting the hidden planes of this world.'

The gas lamp spluttered as she spoke, and I felt icy cold fingers crawling up my spine. Barely a week had passed since the professor, Roberta and I had saved England, if not the entire world, from an onslaught of evil shades and malicious spirits. I still experienced nightmares, and the thought of as-yet-unknown terrors roaming this fair land was chilling. 'There are...worse horrors?'

'Oh yes indeed.' A mysterious smile. 'Had father and I revealed the full spectrum of spookiness lurking the shadow realms, you might have decided against working with us.'

'When you employed me, you neglected to mention the existence of any spirits whatsoever,' I pointed out.

'Well yes, that's true. But you coped admirably, did you not?'

I was silent. During recent events, I'd betrayed the professor and had almost got him killed. If Roberta considered that an admirable outcome, I was in no hurry to experience something she rated a genuine disaster. 'So,' I said, changing the subject, 'do you have any notion of the type of creature involved in this savage crime?'

'None whatsoever. This report does not even hint at the supernatural, but the police would not have come to my father unless they suspected something out of the ordinary.' Roberta smiled at me. 'And since father isn't interested, you and I will have to solve this mystery on his behalf.'

'We shall have to go armed,' I said. 'We must have weapons if we are to face such dangers.'

'I don't wish to alarm you,' said Roberta, in a tone of voice which I did indeed find most alarming, 'but this creature may fall to neither sword nor gun.'

Silently, I picked up the photograph. 'Where did this poor fellow meet his end?' I asked, studying the woods whilst avoiding looking at the victim. 'This could be one of several parks in London.'

'The report did not mention it, and I suspect that was by design. It seems the police intend to keep such details secret, even from my father.' Roberta put her hands on her hips. 'I am quite decided, Septimus. You and I will visit the police as arranged, and I will not leave until they reveal everything.'

I smiled as I imagined Roberta interrogating the tall, stern-looking policemen, but then I saw her expression and I decided that even the much-feared Tomás de Torquemada would have quailed before that look. My smile vanished, and I nodded meekly.

'Now, I must go and research before the police send a cab for us,' said Roberta briskly. Then she looked down at my desk. 'Perhaps you might spend the time studying these photographs, in order to prepare yourself. The police are sure to reveal further horrors, and I do not want you exhibiting weakness in their presence.'

Before I could protest this rather brutal assessment of my character, she was gone. I tidied the report once more, ensuring the pages were sorted into their proper order, then placed the photographs at the back, safely out of sight. Once that was done, I gathered up the paperwork which Roberta had so casually swept from my desk, and spent the next hour rearranging documents. As I worked, my imagination ran away with itself, dreaming up ever-more-horrifying creatures, with slavering jaws and unearthly howls and claws that could tear apart a human being in mere seconds. It seemed to me that, research or no, Roberta was leading the both of us into uncharted waters. Perhaps the professor, already knowing something of the savage, murderous creature, had been wise to send the policemen packing.

However, at this juncture Roberta and I had only agreed to speak with the police. At most, we would be asked to tour the crime scene in broad daylight, accompanied by several burly police officers. I consoled myself with the thought that, if this mysterious adversary proved dangerous in the extreme, we could decline the case and still be home in time for afternoon tea. We had no reason to put ourselves in mortal danger, other than a sense of civic duty and Roberta's curiosity. In vulgar parlance, we did not have a horse in this particular race, and were therefore free to walk away at any time.

In light of events to come, this turned out to be particularly naive, even for me.

3

'Do you think the police have forgotten about us?'

'That would be most unwise on their part.' Roberta was standing on tip-toes beside me, craning her neck to look along the busy road. She carried a parcel under her arm, wrapped in brown paper and tied neatly with string. From the size and shape I guessed it contained one or more books from her father's collection, their age and value the reason for the careful packaging. Given her scant regard for my own belongings, I was surprised she hadn't wrapped the books in used greaseproof and fastened the whole by hammering three-inch nails through the covers.

As for myself, the police report advertised itself with an uncomfortable bulge inside my coat, and I confess I was not looking forward to the interview at the station. I'd already expressed my doubts to Roberta, but she appeared determined to see it through. Then I brightened, for it was possible the police *had* forgotten to send transport, in which case we could forget the whole matter. Mrs Fairacre had hinted at scones and jam for tea, and I knew for a fact she had secured a jug of fresh cream.

'If they don't arrive soon, I swear I'll flag down a cab,' muttered Roberta, dashing my hopes.

Then I saw it. A black maria sped towards us, and as I regarded the sinister contraption I hoped the compartment was not already occupied. What would the professor say if Roberta and I were transported to the police station in the close company of footpads and pickpockets?

The carriage drew up, the horses snorting and stamping impatiently. The driver was a young constable, and when he saw Roberta he leapt down from the seat and offered his hand. 'You'll have to sit with me, miss. I got a customer in the back.'

I glanced at the seat, which barely had room enough for one. 'And me?' I enquired.

The constable gestured at the running board which ran the length of the carriage. 'Hop up, sir. You'll be right as long as you hang on good and proper.'

After a moment's hesitation, I obeyed, hauling myself up by dint of a vertical brass handrail affixed to the side of the carriage. Once perched on the running board, I discovered to my consternation that it was barely four inches wide, the wet, muddy surface slick and treacherous under the soles of my shoes. The carriage's front wheel was close enough to touch, the skinny mudguard barely wider than the iron-shod rim. I turned to look at the rear wheel, and I imagined what might happen to me if I fell under it whilst the carriage was in motion. I had heard stories of people all but sliced in two as a result of such accidents, and I gripped the brass pole until my knuckles whitened.

Just behind me there was a barred opening in the side of our carriage, little more than a foot across. I could not see inside, but my imagination supplied details aplenty. I imagined callous murderers hunched within, and I hoped they were securely chained. Meanwhile, our driver was ensuring Roberta was comfortable, perched as she was on the driving seat. When he was satisfied he sent the carriage on its way with a loud crack of his whip.

The sudden lurch caught me by surprise, my feet slipping on the running board, and as the carriage swerved towards the middle of the road, joining the throng of traffic, I dangled from the side like a drunken sailor. Only my death-like grip on the handrail saved me from disaster, and I could hear the big, heavy wheel behind me, rumbling ominously on the cobbles. My heart raced as I hauled myself back onto the running board, and I renewed my grip with fanatical fervour.

I looked up, expecting to see Roberta gazing upon my acrobatics in horror, but instead she was sharing a joke with the constable. Her hair streamed back in the headwind, and she appeared to be urging the man on. Encouraged, he drove the horses to greater efforts with a flick of his wrist, and we had to swerve suddenly to pass a slow-moving carriage. I pressed myself flat as the gilded side flashed by, but despite my avoiding action the other vehicle's lantern caught my elbow with a bruising blow. 'Have a care!' I shouted, my anger rising. While the two of them were enjoying their joyride, I was in mortal danger!

Roberta looked down at me. 'Hold on, Septimus. Do not fall!'

'Oh, what excellent advice,' I muttered. Then I raised my voice once more. 'Please, I beg you. Ask the constable to moderate his pace.'

'Come, my dear. We're barely moving.'

The cobbled road was a blur, belying her words, but we did slow a little. Unfortunately, this was not out of deference to my safety, but rather due to the steeper grade, for we now approached Blackfriar's Bridge. After clattering across, scattering angry labourers and pedestrians, our speed increased even further on the downward slope. To secure my position, I took my right hand from the rail and grasped one of the bars in the small window nearby.

Suddenly I felt a hand gripping my arm, and I almost fell off the carriage in my surprise. Someone inside had just reached through the bars, snatching at me with grimy fingers, the nails cracked and broken. 'Let go of me!' I cried. 'Let go this instant.'

My attacker laughed, and with a savage tug they broke my grip on the metal bars. I was now holding on with but one hand, grasping at the brass handrail, and as the man dragged me closer to the barred opening I saw his eyes glittering from the darkness within. Those eyes! Savage, vengeful, determined.

The man got a second hand onto my arm, pulling until the side of my face was pressed to the bars. He must have been using the side of the carriage for leverage, because he overpowered me easily. My fingers slipped from the brass handrail, and I was quickly at the mercy of my attacker. His grip was now the only thing holding me to the side of the carriage. 'What do you want?' I cried. 'What do you hope to gain?'

'Give me the key for these cuffs,' he growled, and I would have recoiled from his foul breath had I been able to.

'I—I don't have a key!'

'Don't lie to me, copper. Give me the key or I'll—'

'I'm not with the police, I swear it! They're just taking me to the station.'

'If you was a crook you'd be in here with the likes of me.' The glittering eyes studied me from up close. 'Mind, you do look like a dandy,' he allowed. 'You a detective, is that it? Sneaking around in ordinary getup, fooling people?'

19

'I'm a bookkeeper!' I shouted, as I dangled from the side of the carriage, my arms trapped by the man within. 'I add up figures. I calculate profit and loss. I do not work for the police, I assure you. Now please, let me go!'

Even as I said it, I realised it was a mistake.

'Fine,' said the man, and he promptly released my arms.

Immediately, I found myself falling backwards, into space. I grabbed for the barred window, but it was too late. Far, far too late. The world revolved around itself, a whirling confusion of cobbles and leaden sky, until I slammed into the road and tumbled end over end. Almost immediately, I saw the black maria's iron-shod wheel upon me. Dazed and winded, it was all I could do to roll aside, the superhuman effort doubtless saving my very life.

I came to rest in the gutter. Vaguely, I heard shouting, and then I passed out.

4

It appeared that Roberta was first on the scene, for as I returned to consciousness I discovered she was cradling my head in her arms. 'Septimus? Can you speak?'

Speak? I could barely breathe! 'Uh,' I remarked, which encompassed my thoughts on the means of transport, the constable's lack of care and the man who'd attacked me.

'Oh good, he's come round,' said the constable, visibly relieved. 'For a moment there I thought he was a goner. Come on sir, up with you. We don't want to keep the Inspector waiting.'

I was hauled to my feet and roughly brushed down, protesting feebly all the while.

'You, er, won't mention this to anyone, will you sir?' asked the constable anxiously. 'I got three nippers at home, you see, and I need the wages to keep 'em fed.'

'Of course he won't say anything,' declared Roberta. 'Come on, Septimus. Take a hold once more, and let us be on our way.'

Many would be outraged by such a callous reaction to my fall, but that was Roberta all over. She was in possession of a stony exterior several miles thick, and rarely did she exhibit sympathy. It was only a few days since we'd engaged in a passionate kiss, the sheer power of which had curled my toes within my socks, but there had been no mention of the embrace since, nor, sadly, a repeat. I did not know whether she was afraid of upsetting her father, or whether she'd found the kiss repulsive, and therefore an experiment never again to be attempted. Either way, her manner towards me had become more businesslike, and this did little to lighten my mood.

By the time I staggered to the carriage, Roberta was already in the driving seat with the constable. I took hold of the handrail once more, my knuckles grazed and bruised, and as we set off I heard a cackle of laughter from the prisoner within the carriage.

Our pace was more sedate, at least, and not long after we drew into the courtyard at the police station. While the horses were cared for, the prisoner was taken from the back of the carriage and hauled away, and despite his dire situation he still managed to give me a twisted grin. 'What did that man do?' I enquired, curious as to the nature of the man's crimes.

'What *didn't* he do?' muttered the constable. 'Now, come this way if you please.'

He led us inside, where we navigated a series of gloomy passages. Eventually we found ourselves in a waiting room with a dozen other civilians, the atmosphere as dark and oppressive as the gas lighting. Nobody spoke, and silence lay heavy on the room.

Roberta took my arm. 'Are you all right, Septimus?'

'Fine and dandy,' I said curtly. 'There is nothing I like more than falling off a speeding carriage, bouncing along a cobbled street on my head, and lying unconscious in the gutter. Nothing, aside from sitting in a police station, awaiting an interview with an inspector with whom I have had earlier, most unpleasant, dealings.'

'Excellent,' said Roberta, seemingly oblivious to my sarcasm.

A constable looked in. 'The inspector will see you now. Follow me.'

'Oho, it's all right for some,' muttered a woman sitting nearby. 'It's 'oo you bleedin' know around here.'

Ignoring her, the constable led us through another maze of ill-lit corridors, until we arrived at a plain wooden door. He knocked, and a voice within bade us enter.

Sitting behind the worn desk was a ginger-haired man in his early thirties. Inspector Cox, my nemesis. Recently, he'd all but blackmailed me to secure my help, threatening me with jail, or worse, if I did not comply with his wishes. And now I was supposed to help him? Willingly?

He looked up as we entered, glanced at Roberta, then fixed me with a piercing, all-knowing gaze. Then he did a double-take. 'Good heavens, man. Did you not think to tidy yourself up before putting in an appearance?'

I opened my mouth, intending to land the blame for my ragged, mud-stained clothing at the feet of his irresponsible constable, but before I could speak Roberta landed an elbow in my midriff. 'I, er—' I managed, before falling silent.

'Well, I suppose it's no business of mine.' The Inspector held his hand out for the report. 'That is our property, I believe. I have already had words with the constables involved, and you can rest assured they will be disciplined for their part in this matter.'

'They were only trying to secure our help,' said Roberta. 'I left them no choice.'

'I will bear that in mind when I'm considering their punishment.' Inspector Cox took up a folder and tucked the report inside. 'Now,

I will ask the sergeant to show you out, as I'm exceedingly busy and I don't have time to waste chatting with civilians.'

Roberta and I stared at him. 'Are you saying you do not need our help with this case?' demanded Roberta.

'That's a fair deduction, miss, and one worthy of a police detective.'

'But you sent a carriage!' I said. I was still aching badly from my tumble, and would not soon forget that hellish ride.

'A miscommunication. The constable was supposed to collect the report, nothing more.' The Inspector nodded towards his sergeant, a slab-sided man with grey sideburns who I'd also encountered recently. 'See them out, Parkes, and be sharp about it.'

'Yessir!' growled the sergeant smartly, and he fastened a meaty hand about my upper arm.

'Now wait just a minute,' protested Roberta. 'Inspector, I promise you, our assistance with this case is imperative. There will be more victims, I guarantee it, and your men cannot hope to prevail against the horrors they will face!'

As she spoke I happened to glance at Sergeant Parkes, who was big enough to knock an alehouse down with his fists. His grip tightened upon my arm at Roberta's slight, and I prayed she did not continue in the same vein lest he nip my limb off at the elbow with his huge, vice-like fingers. 'Perhaps we ought to leave,' I suggested.

'Nonsense,' snapped Roberta. 'The police begged for our help, and they're desperately going to need it.' She turned to the inspector and brandished the parcel of books. 'In this package I have research pertaining to your investigation. An extract of Petronius in which he wrote of fantastical creatures. Commentary by Gervase of Tilbury dating from the twelfth century. A reproduction of artwork by Lucas Cranach de—'

'I am not interested in artworks or commentary,' interrupted Cox. 'I have a murderer to catch.'

'Inspector, your men are no match for a creature such as this. They are ill-equipped to deal with such a beast, and there will be many more deaths if you do not heed my warnings. Surely you cannot be so ignorant and stubborn as to—'

Moments later we were heaved through the front doors by the burly sergeant, with the Inspector's final, shouted rejoinder still ringing in our ears.

'Well,' muttered Roberta. 'Of all the cheek!'

I thought we got off lightly, under the circumstances. In truth, I was glad the police had turned down our help, for I was in no hurry to confront the beast which had murdered the man in the photograph. 'Should we make our way home for tea?' I asked hopefully.

'Are you giving up so easily?'

'The police don't want us.'

'So you're content to leave this investigation to Cox's muddle-headed foolery, despite strong evidence of the paranormal? You are confident they will be able to track down this creature and capture it without losing their own lives in the process? You are happy that other innocents may die while the police flounder and fumble around?'

'The answer to all of those questions is no,' I said, once I could get a word in. 'But what would you have me do? Should I march into the police station and snatch the report from Inspector Cox's grasp? Do you believe I ought to threaten him?'

'So you're going to let the matter rest.'

'We have no other choice. We cannot snoop around for clues when we have no idea where the crime even took place.'

'Didn't you notice the details on that folder the Inspector was waving around?'

I'd been recoiling from Cox's pointed finger and angry shouting, and had paid no attention to the folder. 'I was nursing my bruises,' I said, somewhat aggrieved.

'Tell me, Septimus. You hail from the village of West Wickham, is that not so?'

'Indeed I do. It's a sleepy place where nothing ever happens, which is one reason I made for London as soon as I was able.'

'Knowing that, I shall give you three guesses as to where this savage crime occurred.' Roberta gave me a calculating look. 'I shall be astonished if you need more than one.'

My stomach sank like a stone, for West Wickham wasn't just the place of my birth. 'My parents!' I cried, horrified by the implications. 'They live there! They...their lives may be at risk from this monster!'

'Perhaps *now* you are willing to help me catch it,' said Roberta, with an air of triumph.

5

Unsurprisingly, the police did not lay on a carriage for our trip home. Roberta and I were forced to catch the omnibus, which was sheer torture. We were crammed shoulder to shoulder with workers and clerks in the heavy, double-deckered contraption, and were thus unable to discuss the case until we finally alighted a few streets from the professor's home. By then I was bursting with worry, and it was all Roberta could do to stop me running for the nearest train station.

Once on foot, however, the dam broke. 'If I catch the evening train I can be there by nightfall,' I said, the words running together in my haste. 'And if I cannot catch a train, I will hire a carriage, and if I cannot hire a carriage—'

'Septimus—' began Roberta.

'—then I shall walk. It's not much more than a dozen miles to West Wickham, and—'

'SEPTIMUS!' Roberta grabbed my arm and tugged so hard I feared it would come away in her hands. 'Running into danger is likely to get you killed. This will take careful planning, and forethought, and preparations. We must speak to my father, and if he still refuses to help us, then you and I will travel to West Wickham without him and begin our own investigation.'

I stared at her. 'But—that's impossible!'

'Why?'

Why indeed? How could I explain the innocent web of lies I'd spun for the benefit of my parents? Several months earlier I'd arrived in London seeking employment with a respectable bookkeeping firm. Instead, I'd wound up in Professor Twickham's employ, keeping his books in exchange for a modest wage plus room and board. I could not reveal this arrangement to my parents, since they believed I was furthering my career with a large accounting company. A belief that I had fostered with my regular letters. In them, I'd fabricated this mythical company, adding little touches such as the names of people I worked with, a description of the man in charge of my department, the managing director, and so on. All of it, naturally, was completely false. If I introduced the professor and Roberta to my parents, the truth would be unmasked. My parents would not be upset nor angry. Far worse. They would be disappointed, and that was something I could not countenance.

And so I reached for the first excuse I could think of. 'It would not be proper, you and I travelling together.'

'Then we shall call ourselves Mr and Mrs Jones,' said Roberta promptly.

I was quick to point out the flaw in this argument, even though it appealed to me greatly. 'My parents would be surprised to learn of their new daughter-in-law.'

'Septimus! Have you not mentioned me in your letters to them? Am I of so little consequence?'

I hastened to reassure Roberta that she was indeed of great importance to me, and that, after a fashion, I had mentioned her in my letters home.

'After a fashion?' Roberta eyed me doubtfully. 'What do you mean by that?'

How could I explain that I'd called her Robert, and given her a bushy beard and a cane, the latter required thanks to an injury sustained in some remote war? Oh yes, I'd truly let my imagination run free in those letters. Now, as far as my parents knew, this 'Robert' was a close friend at work. You see, my mother clung to the hope that I would marry Cecilie Carmichael, the daughter of a successful local merchant, and Roberta's sudden appearance in West Wickham would trouble her no end. The merchant's daughter was a pleasant enough girl, although rather dull, and escaping her modest charms had played a large part in my decision to leave my home for the sights and sounds of London. Had I remained, my mother and Mr Carmichael would have ensnared me for certain. 'I have not told my family a great deal about you,' I said, prevaricating somewhat.

'I see,' said Roberta primly. 'Is that because of your arranged marriage?'

'There *is* no arranged marriage!' I said heatedly. 'A few months ago my mother tried to match me up with a local girl, but I assure you I have no interest whatsoever.'

'Well, if we can't travel together we shall just have to travel apart. Surely there's an inn or a tavern I can stay at?'

For a moment I was tempted to agree. After all, the professor would forbid it as surely as night follows day, and then Roberta could lose her temper at him instead. But no, it was my place to break the bad news. 'Roberta, we really can't—'

'Oh, very well,' she snapped. 'Go and investigate the killing by yourself! See if I care what happens to you!'

'But—'

'No, my mind is quite made up. It is clear you do not want me with you, and I respect your wishes.'

'But—'

'Go, Septimus. Attempt to capture this savage monster on your own, but don't come crying to me when it has torn out your insides and ripped off your limbs.'

I found the prospect of seeking help after my limbs had been ripped off both distasteful and highly unlikely, but said nothing. In truth, I was surprised she'd yielded with relatively good grace. On the other hand, I suspected that leaving her behind would shatter whatever remained of our budding relationship. So, I took the easiest path and fabricated a lie. 'Roberta, I don't have to go. I can send a telegram to my parents asking them to be careful. With the police involved, I'm sure that will suffice.'

She looked surprised. 'Really? A moment ago you were set to catch the first train out of London.'

I still had every intention of visiting my parents that very evening, but I adopted an innocent expression and lowered my voice. 'I was not thinking straight. It was the shock of the revelation, you see. I reacted too quickly.'

'You'd stay here in London, even though your parents might be at the mercy of this savage beast?'

'I, er—'

But before I could reply, or change my mind once more, she stopped before me, taking my hands in hers. 'I'm sorry, Septimus. You're worried about your parents, and I'm heaping further troubles on your shoulders. Of course you should go and visit them, and as soon as possible.'

Relieved, I gave her a warm smile.

'That is, assuming my father will let you go anywhere,' continued

Roberta, promptly crushing my newfound hope. 'He has strong views on the matter of staff taking leave of absence, but it should be all right as long as he's in a good mood.'

My heart sank as I tried and failed to remember a time when the professor was in good humour. The elderly gentleman was intemperate at the best of times, and downright acerbic for the rest. However, I decided it would be a little tactless to mention this to his equally fiery daughter. 'We could still find time to research the creature together,' I said, offering Roberta an olive branch.

'I think not,' she replied coldly.

We walked the rest of the way home in silence, with Roberta taking to her room the instant we reached her father's house. I made my way to the dining room, hoping to find afternoon tea laid out, but instead of scones, jam and cream I encountered the professor himself. 'Good afternoon, sir.'

'Why do you claim such, when all evidence points to the contrary?' he demanded sourly.

I groaned inwardly. The professor and Roberta had been hewn from the same block of stone, thus exhibiting similar characteristics when angry. A slight pinching of the nose, a clipped speaking voice, and large quantities of steam jetting from the ears. I debated whether to excuse myself, to beat a hasty retreat as a resident of Pompeii might have done, given the opportunity, but it appeared the professor was not letting me go that easily. In addition, I needed to beg leave of absence to visit my parents, although the chances of obtaining such permission now looked remote in the extreme. 'What troubles you, sir?'

'First the infernal police show up, disturbing my latest research. Then I discover that those clowns at the docks, the halfwits at Her Majesty's Customs, are holding up my shipment of vital equipment for some trumped-up reason. They accuse me — me, sir! — of importing items contrary to the national interest. But get this, young Septimus. They are willing to release my goods if I pay five times the usual customs rate. It's extortion, plain and simple!' The professor slammed the flat of his hand on the table, shaking the newspaper in its brass page-turning contraption and almost knocking a teacup off its saucer. 'They know I cannot obtain this equipment within our fair shores, and must therefore deal with the Americans. They know I must import the equipment, and they've guessed how important it is to me. Therefore, they have raised an invoice which Queen Victoria herself, God bless her soul, would balk at!'

The professor was famously tight with the purse strings, as evidenced by my own wages, and I guessed this invoice was made out for no more than a modest sum.

'Septimus, I would like you to handle this matter,' said the professor. 'You must use every resource at your disposal to ensure my equipment is delivered no later than tomorrow morning. Mind, though! I refuse to pay a penny more than the usual rate.'

My heart sank. Was I to emulate Odysseus of old, caught as he was between Charybdis and Scylla? To one side of me, the irate professor, refusing to budge an inch. On the other, H.M. Customs, determined to extract blood from every passing stone. I could spend weeks on this insurmountable task, getting precisely nowhere, but the professor had given me less than a day. 'Do you have the requisite paperwork, sir?'

'On the desk in my study. You'll find everything you need inside the Manila folder,' remarked the professor, and he resumed his perusal of the newspaper.

6

After a hopeful glance at the sideboard, in case the much-needed refreshments had magically appeared behind my back, I left the dining room for my office, there to commence work on Professor Twickham *versus* H.M. Customs. On the way I obtained the folder from the professor's study, and the heft and weight of documents within caused my heart to sink. This was no simple matter, nor one that could be resolved in haste.

As I sat in my worn leather chair, making space on my crowded desk for the customs paperwork, I came to a decision. No matter the professor's demands, or the outcome of this dispute, I resolved to leave for West Wickham that very night. If necessary, I would resign my position with the professor. I quailed as I imagined both he and Roberta haranguing me as they attempted to enforce the terms of my employment, but my mind was quite made up.

I simply had to see my parents, to ensure their safety. I might be ill-equipped to deal with a vicious, supernatural monster, as Roberta had pointed out, but even so I was prepared to put my limited experience to use in their defence.

With this decision made, I felt a certain calmness of spirit. Indeed, rather than turn immediately to the professor's knotty problem, I took out a form and wrote a telegram to my parents, asking them to prepare my room as I would be arriving that evening. I reached for the bell-pull, intending to summon the Twickhams' maid, but paused with my hand on the tassel. The housekeeper, Mrs Fairacre, occasionally undertook the maid's duties when the latter was absent, and the thought of causing that worthy to ascend three flights of stairs to collect my telegram was enough to still my hand. This, because the matter of rank in the Twickham household was cloudy at best. Clearly, the professor and Roberta occupied the upper tier, as was befitting. In any other household the professor would have stood above all, but his daughter had long ago joined him on the top step. I, as a qualified bookkeeper in the professor's employ, should have been next, with Mrs Fairacre at my beck and call. In practice, the housekeeper was a *confidant* of the professor, and both Roberta and I suspected the pair would one day be married. I could no more order Mrs Fairacre around than I could the kitchen cat.

That left Elsie, the maid. Aged fourteen or fifteen, she was a thin, nervous girl who blushed whenever I spoke to her. Little wonder, then, that I carried the missive downstairs myself, leaving it neatly folded on the stand near the front door. Next to the stand was a brass button, connected to one of the professor's contraptions somewhere deep inside the kitchen. I pressed it and fled, hoping that whoever came to despatch the telegram did not realise it was mine...and a personal message at that. Then, as I ascended the stairs to my bedroom on the uppermost floor, a thought hit me. What if someone in the household glanced at the contents of my telegram? The words I'd scrawled were unassailable proof that I had lied to Roberta's face. Should she learn of my deception...

I turned around and raced downstairs, and my heart sank as I hurried towards the hall stand. Elsie, the maid, was ahead of me, already holding my telegram. 'My apologies Elsie,' I said quickly. 'I discovered I must add further instructions to my message.'

'Yes sir.' Nervously, she held out the folded piece of notepaper. 'Please call me when it's ready.'

'No, no, I will tend to it myself,' I promised.

'I'd rather you didn't, sir.' She looked at me anxiously. 'If you do all my work, I'll be out of a job.'

'I, er—'

A bell rang, and Elsie started. 'Mrs Fairacre! I forgot she wanted my help. She was muttering something chronic when you drew me away, sir.'

'On this occasion, perhaps I ought to deliver the telegram.'

She nodded quickly and hurried away. As soon as she had disappeared, I dashed to the front door, letting myself out. I was on my way to the nearest telegraph office when I spotted a runner, and so I paid him tuppence to deliver the missive on my behalf.

With the matter of my parents now resolved, for the time being at least, I returned to my study.

It was time to devote all my attention to the professor's case.

'This will not do,' I muttered, as I perused a page from the professor's customs documents. 'No, this will not do at all!'

The page in question was filled with columns of figures, the ink smudged and the numbers clearly having been formed with an unsteady hand. One did not expect fine penmanship in such documents, never that, but the standard here was atrocious. It was an accounting of the many charges and imposts the professor was supposed to pay, although I was only able to make out the author's intent by angling the page to the light and squinting fiercely.

Having ascertained the document's purpose, I discovered a troubling issue: many of the sums were incorrect.

In addition, if you will excuse the pun, it soon dawned on me that the mistakes were deliberate. Oh, they would have fooled the casual reader, but in my experience numbers did not transpose themselves so readily, and the author had employed various other tricks to ensure the total the professor was being asked to pay bore little relation to the charges themselves. The total, in fact, was ten or fifteen percent higher than it should have been.

I doubted whether this was a lone incident. Why would you stop at cheating one person if you could cheat hundreds? And if this were part of a wider scheme, why, the entire branch of H.M. Customs might be rotten to the core! For the money had to be going somewhere, and it was certainly not into the Treasury coffers.

I sat back in my seat, beset by both triumph and worry. On the one hand, this feat of creative accounting was evidence of wrongdoing, and with it I could cause a great deal of trouble for those involved. On the other, if I took it to the authorities there would be an investigation, and the professor would be lucky to see his scientific equipment before Christmas. Christmas twenty years hence, I suspected.

The only alternative was to use the customs document as leverage, and I shuddered at the thought. I could barely countenance the idea of marching into the customs office and confronting the staff therein. Blackmail servants of the Crown? I'd be putting my own neck into a noose! Recently I'd read that convicts were no longer deported to Australia, but I suspected they'd find a place for me on some rotten-hulled collier that would barely clear the shores of England before sinking like a large, unwieldy stone. Failing that, the crew might toss me overboard once out of sight of land. Sea-going types were a close lot, and it was possible the rot was not entirely confined to the Customs office.

A small, insistent voice made itself heard. *Why not tell the professor?* it whispered. *Go tell the professor, and he will rant and rage at the Customs men in your stead!*

I was sorely tempted, for the tongue was honeyed indeed, but I knew it would be unwise in the extreme. The irate professor might cause a pitched brawl with a dozen naval types, and I could only imagine how Roberta might feel about my part in an *imbroglio* of that nature.

I examined the page again, cursing at the dilemma I faced. However I tackled the problem, I could see no favourable outcome. My mood darkened, and I heartily wished I could be transported to my parents' sitting room in West Wickham, with high tea on the table and a fire burning merrily in the grate.

I was still lost in gloomy contemplation when there came a knock upon the door, and to my delight it opened to admit Roberta. The last time I'd seen her thunderclouds had been gathering upon her brow, but now the look she gave me was almost kindly. 'Septimus, I'm sorry.'

'Why, whatever for?' I enquired lightly.

'I was unpleasant towards you, and it was churlish of me. My only excuse is that I wanted to accompany you to West Wickham so that we might investigate this crime together, and your refusal was hard for me to accept.'

'There is no need to apologise. I quite understand.'

She smiled, then gave me an enquiring look. 'Have you decided what you will tell father? Your excuse for leaving, I mean?'

I looked down at the Customs documents on my desk, and I suddenly realised I had no alternative. I would have to visit the offices of H.M. Customs, confront the man in charge, and attempt to blackmail him into releasing the professor's goods. A successful conclusion would put the professor in a good mood, and then he might release me from my duties. The alternative–an utter failure to secure the professor's shipment–would lead to outcomes too awful to contemplate. In that moment I decided not to bother Roberta with the customs problem. After all, I was employed to deal with such matters. Indeed, I decided to set her mind at rest quickly so that I might complete the work with all haste. 'I'm not going to West Wickham,' I said quietly, keeping my gaze averted. Roberta had an uncanny knack of seeing through me, and I had no wish for her to ascertain the truth.

'What?' she cried in surprise. 'Not going? Whyever not?'

During my formative years I'd had the good fortune to act in one or two theatrical productions. Nothing grand, of course, but after each play several members of the audience took it upon themselves to compliment me on my acting abilities, some of them without prompting from my mother. Now, perhaps, was the time to employ some of those hard-earned skills. I leapt up, exclaimed loudly and slapped myself upon the forehead with the flat of my hand. 'Because I am such a fool!' I cried, in my best stage voice. 'As it happens, I forgot a prior engagement!'

Roberta regarded me steadily.

'Why, this very evening there is a lecture on the intricacies of bookkeeping.' I placed one hand on my breast and swept the other towards the ceiling in a dramatic gesture. 'By attending, I shall further my knowledge and make myself even more useful to your father.' At this moment I was still regarding a distant, imaginary horizon in the most noble fashion, but I risked a quick glance at Roberta to see how my performance was being received.

'If you go to my father with that overblown nonsense,' she said, in a bright, clear voice, 'he will assume you've been quaffing his precious brandy.'

I deflated like a pricked balloon, sinking back to my aging chair. 'It's true enough, all the same,' I mumbled. 'Thanks to my lecture I cannot possibly leave London this evening.'

'Septimus, that is quite the weakest story I've ever heard, but it might be salvaged with a little polishing.'

'But–'

Roberta laid a hand on my arm. 'You see, my dear, your problem is that you do not possess a knack for fabricating tales.'

If only she knew! I thought, as my letters home came to mind. As I recalled those intricate webs of lies, and the likely effect on my parents of Roberta's appearance in West Wickham, I drew upon all my reserves of honesty and integrity. At the same time, I crossed my fingers under the desk. 'Roberta, I promise you...it's the truth!'

She was silent for a moment, and I sensed that my words had finally convinced her. When she spoke again, my feeling turned out to be correct. 'Very well, Septimus. As far as I am concerned the matter is now closed. Attend your precious meeting, improve your accountancy, and let us hope your parents get all the help they need from Cox and his band of stone-headed policemen.'

A burden lifted from my shoulders. All along I had been worried that Roberta might hatch a plan of her own–joining me at the station to board the train with her own *valise*, for instance–but now that risk had finally passed. All that remained was to hint gently that I had urgent work to perform, so that Roberta might leave me alone to perform it. 'Now that we have resolved our differences...' I began.

'Oh, is that father's customs matter?' asked Roberta, taking up the file. 'Did he saddle you with this millstone despite knowing of your precious accounting course?'

'I couldn't very well bring that up,' I said. 'The professor was in a fine temper, and my duties—'

'You're a good man, Septimus.' Roberta's expression softened. 'Tell me, is there anything I can do to help?'

I was sorely tempted. If Roberta accompanied me to the Custom's office, her presence might deter any physical retribution once I confronted the manager with evidence of his fraud. But I quashed the idea quickly, for I could not willingly put her in such danger. 'This I must do alone,' I said, with all the enthusiasm of a soldier tasked with capturing an enemy fortification entirely by himself.

'You don't seem sure.'

'I must. The customs office is in the dockyard, and that's no place for—for—' I gestured vaguely.

'A woman?'

I reddened. 'I did not mean it as a slight. But aboard those vessels are men who haven't seen female company for a year or more, and I would feel the urge to respond to any catcalls or ribald comments with a challenge.'

'Don't be silly, Septimus,' said Roberta dismissively. 'We shall make our way to this customs office immediately. We must convince them to release papa's goods on the spot, so that you might set off for West Wickham before nightfall. If there *is* a dangerous creature roaming the countryside, you do not wish to encounter it in darkness.'

I recalled our earlier argument, during which Roberta had expressed a hope that this monster might tear off my limbs, but that apparently had been forgotten. Then I became aware of her mistake. 'You meant the accountancy lecture,' I told her.

'Yes, of course. The vitally important lecture that you will not miss for anything.'

Deep down, I wondered whether she were toying with me, as the kitchen cat did with the occasional mouse. Her face, however, was open and innocent, and I could detect no hint of subterfuge as I gathered my papers.

Twenty minutes later we were sitting in a hansom cab, bound for the docks.

Despite my fears, we were not set upon by bands of sailors starved for female company the moment we alighted at the docks. This was chiefly because the larger ships were moored on the far side, while the smaller vessels nearby had but one or two hands aboard. Fortunately, these men were far too busy with their work to pay us any attention.

There was a genuine urgency to the place, with workers scurrying everywhere and goods being loaded and unloaded. The whole was seen through a haze of coal smoke, which drifted across the water from three large steamships. Far below the waterline, men stripped to their waists would be stoking the boilers, and I wondered which exotic lands the enormous vessels were bound for. I myself had never left these shores, and I felt a stirring deep within as I gazed upon the ships. What would it be like, disembarking in a foreign land, with exciting new customs and a completely unfamiliar language?

Before I could dwell on the thought, my attention was drawn back to the task at hand. Upon asking for directions, we were pointed towards a grand three-storey building overlooking the water. The building was impressive, but despite its size it was almost lost amidst a forest of dockyard cranes. Ducking under a creaking cargo net that bulged with large bales of wool, Roberta and I made our way to the entrance. Here, I announced our business, and the clerk began leafing through pages in a ledger. 'Would Tuesday week be suitable, sir?'

'Suitable for what purpose?' I enquired.

'Why, to speak with the manager.'

'You don't understand,' I said patiently. 'I am here on urgent business.'

'Around these parts there is no other kind,' said the clerk evenly. Then he glanced around before lowering his voice. 'If you wish to advance your position in the queue, however...'

He left the words hanging, and I gazed upon him with some

confusion. I was about to protest that of course I wished to advance my position, for it was imperative I see the manager that very afternoon, but then I recalled the grease which was employed to keep the wheels of this particular establishment running. A bribe. Of course.

However, as I reached into my coat, Roberta took my wrist with an iron grip. 'Shall I fetch Inspector Cox from the Kensington police station?' she asked me. 'You know how keen he was to resolve this matter.'

Fortunately, I caught her intent right away. 'Is that wise? He was in a foul temper the last we saw him.'

'Hold up, hold up,' said the clerk hastily. 'We don't need the police in. Take a seat, both of you, and I'll see what I can do.'

Hiding a look of triumph, I sat on a nearby bench with Roberta. For her part she kept a neutral expression, as though manipulating hapless clerks were part of her usual day's work.

The man hastened up the central staircase, his shoes clattering on the concrete steps. Five minutes passed before he returned, and when he did so he looked nervous. 'Mr Bransen will see you right away. He's on the top floor, just across from the stairs.'

Roberta and I stood, and after ascending three flights of stairs we found ourselves standing before an imposing wooden door. A brass plaque announced Mr Bransen, Manager, but as I raised a hand to knock the door swept open.

Bransen was a portly man with sparse hair combed across the top of his head. He was patting his mouth with a napkin as we entered, and I spied the remains of a lunch tray hastily placed on a nearby cupboard. 'I'm sorry to interrupt your lunch,' I began.

'Think nothing of it. Now, what's all this about an inspector from the police? What's going on?'

'Are you familiar with this shipment?' I asked, holding out the professor's customs documents.

Bransen snorted. 'Familiar? That old goat has been pestering me for weeks. Where's my shipment? Why is it late? Why is it so expensive? I've had every complaint in the book, and then some.' Then he frowned. 'How is this a police matter? Are they to arrest him?'

'The police are not involved...yet.' I held up the sheet of paper filled with figures, which I had carefully removed from the file before passing it over. 'This, however, is enough to have you jailed for fraud.'

'You're with him!' growled the manager, as realisation dawned. 'That professor. He sent you to clear his goods!'

'I–'

'Get out!' roared Bransen, pointing a quivering finger at the door. 'Get out this instant, or I'll have you thrown into the Thames with anchor chains around your necks!'

8

Stunned at the outburst, I could only stare at the Customs man. Confronted with proof of his wrongdoing, he should have been grovelling before me, not hurling threats like the victim of a common pickpocket. There was something behind his angry expression, though. A hint of fear which he was trying to conceal with his bluster. Before I could speak again, probing gaps in his armour, the door crashed open and a burly man hurried in.

'Sir, you gotta...' The man's voice tailed off as he became aware of Roberta and me...especially Roberta. 'Beg pardon, ma'am,' he muttered, touching his forelock.

'They're leaving. Don't pay them any mind,' growled Bransen. 'Now speak up, man. What is it?'

'There's somefink you gotta see. It's in warehouse six...it's...it's not natural, sir.'

At his words I glanced at Roberta, who also happened to be looking at me. Both of us were intrigued by the mention of something unnatural.

Bransen was not intrigued in the least. 'Have you been drinking again?' he demanded sourly.

'No sir. The men seen this thing before, but only on their own, like. We made fun o' them, but this time...well, they won't go inside that warehouse no more, not for love nor money. They say it's—it's haunted.'

'I shall investigate, but if this is a jape it'll go ill for everyone,' muttered Bransen. He strode towards the door, ushering us ahead of him with outstretched arms.

'Our business is not yet concluded,' I said, attempting to stand my ground.

'Oh, it's concluded all right, and if I see the pair of you in my dockyard again...' He left the threat hanging, and Roberta and I were bustled into the corridor, where Bransen paused to lock his door before accompanying the burly man downstairs.

'We must follow them,' murmured Roberta.

I was about to argue the folly of her suggestion, but she'd already set off in pursuit. So, I tucked the sheet of figures into my coat and descended the stairs in her wake. Outside we saw Bransen at the head of a dozen workers, all striding towards a nearby warehouse. Truth be told, Bransen was striding purposefully whilst the men lagged behind. They were rough, hard-bitten types, powerfully-built from years of back-breaking labour, but they looked more like timid schoolboys as they trailed Bransen. None of them paid Roberta or myself the slightest attention.

The warehouse was one of many in a row, unremarkable in every way. It had huge double doors, one of them with a smaller wooden door for easier access, and it was the latter which stood ajar. Bransen hauled it open without hesitation, and after glaring at the men, who were hanging back, he vanished inside.

I was content to watch and await developments, but Roberta grasped me firmly by the hand and all but dragged me into the warehouse after the angry manager.

The interior was dark, with the only illumination provided by grimy skylights high above. Everywhere I looked I saw goods piled to the rafters, and if there was any order to their arrangement I could not ascertain it. Bransen was nearby, lifting a workman's lantern from the wall. He lit it with a match, which he extinguished carefully under his boot, and then he became aware of our presence. 'What do you think you're doing?' he demanded angrily.

Unmoved, Roberta nodded towards the interior of the warehouse. 'Is that where the men claimed to have seen something?'

'Whether they did or not, it's no concern of yours.'

'You'd be wise to accept our help. My father and I have extensive knowledge in these matters.'

'And what matters would they be? Superstitious fools frightened by a stray cat? A foreman who drinks himself to sleep every night?'

'Phantasms. Shades. Spirits of the departed.'

The manager snorted. 'I can only think of one kind of spirits affecting my men. As for ghosts and ghoulies, you're as cracked as that mad old professor of yours.'

'I have witnessed apparitions that would have you screaming from sheer terror.' Roberta spoke calmly and evenly, but Bransen merely snorted again, this time in disbelief. Having delivered this well-reasoned argument, he turned and strode deeper into the warehouse, lantern held high. 'I dislike that man intensely,' muttered Roberta, as a frown creased her brow.

'At least he's not ordering us out,' I murmured.

There was no reply, for Roberta was busy rummaging in her purse. She took out a curious pair of spectacles which had one lens as dark as night, and another of deep ruby red. I had seen the eyepieces before, and indeed, I had used them myself on more than one occasion. They were of Roberta's own design, and they allowed the wearer to peer into the spirit realm.

With the spectacles in place, Roberta cast her gaze around the darkened warehouse.

'Hmm,' she remarked.

'Do you see it?' I whispered. The tension was unbearable, for I knew a large and dangerous spirit might be advancing on me at that very moment.

Silently, she removed the glasses and handed them to me. I donned them with shaking fingers, looping the arms over my ears with some difficulty. Once they were firmly in place I peered around the warehouse, and a gasp escaped my lips at the sight thus revealed.

Dozens of spirits whirled around the cavernous interior, leaving ghostly green trails in their wake. They sailed between the neat rows of cargo, occasionally passing right through a crate or a bale. The apparitions were moving aimlessly, rather than with sinister intent, and not one was larger than my fist. 'What are they?' I whispered.

'I have not encountered their like before,' replied Roberta. 'From my reading, I would say they are sprites. Mischievous at times, but not particularly dangerous.'

I saw movement, something larger, but it was Bransen advancing further into the warehouse. Seen through the glasses I noticed he had a curious aura, with dark flames seeming to writhe and dance on his skin. 'Why does he–' I began.

'Mr Bransen is not long for this world,' said Roberta calmly. 'He carries the first signs of death about him.'

I snatched the glasses from my nose, staring down at them in horror. 'Are you saying these spectacles foretell death? But we must warn him this instant!'

Roberta shook her head. 'He's ill, that is all. His spirit prepares to depart.'

The thought sickened me, and I vowed never to look at another human being with the glasses. Why, if I caught sight of myself in a mirror...

'These sprites did not just manifest out of thin air,' said Roberta, untroubled by the manager's fate. 'Father and I have detected little in the way of spirit activity over the past few days, and so it's likely these guests arrived with some cargo from distant lands.'

'I thought spirits could move between their world and ours at will?'

'Occasionally, but these lack the power for such a journey. Far more likely they're attached to a specific object.'

Roberta donned the spectacles and looked around her. I, meanwhile, could see nothing but shadows. Occasionally a trail of dust would rise from the floor, whirling around before settling again. This, despite the heavy, leaden air in the warehouse. I could hear rustles and creaks as well, as though the cargo itself were alive. They were only small signs, but it explained why the workers had thought the interior to be haunted.

'There's nothing here!' shouted Bransen. He was at the far end of the building, and I could hear his heavy footsteps as he navigated the stacks of cargo. 'Nothing but superstition and wits addled by an excess of drinking!'

'Do you see?' murmured Roberta. She handed me the spectacles and pointed. 'The sprites are concentrated in that area.'

I saw for myself that she was right. Although the glowing spirits flew freely around the warehouse, they appeared to be orbiting one particular stack of cargo. There was nothing unique about it, not that I could tell, for it was merely crates, chests and boxes like the rest. As I watched the sprites whirling around in their busy dance, glowing like fireflies in the shadowy warehouse, I was taken by the scene. 'They're quite beautiful,' I murmured.

'Don't drop your guard,' advised Roberta. 'Pretty they may be, but they might be dangerous all the same.'

I wanted to enquire further, but I heard Bransen's footsteps approaching, and without thinking I turned in his direction. The creepy aura was evident, as before, but now I saw the raised lantern was attracting sprites like moths to a streetlight, with the tiny sparks orbiting the flame, getting closer and closer. More and more of the glowing sprites approached, trailing the manager by the dozens.

'I've wasted enough time on this nonsense,' growled the manager. 'You two, out of here, and don't let me see you again!' Angrily, he opened the lantern and blew out the light. At that moment, the sprites eagerly circling him froze. Then one darted straight at him. *Through* him. 'Hell's bells!' shouted the manager, slapping at his neck. 'I've been stung!'

Roberta snatched the glasses from me, pressing them to her nose. 'Relight your lantern!' she cried. 'Light it this instant, or our lives are forfeit!'

'What do you–'

'Light it, man!' shouted Roberta. 'We'll never make it out if you don't!'

I glanced towards the warehouse entrance, which was fifty feet away. Daylight seeped through the timbers, with safety lying on the other side. I had no doubt these sprites, should they turn nasty, would finish us long before we reached it.

The manager slapped at his neck again, then clutched at his shoulder in pain. As he did so, the lantern fell from his grip and landed on the concrete floor, the glass shattering with an air of finality.

9

'Don't move!' shouted Roberta urgently. 'Stand as still as a statue. You must freeze as though your life depended upon it.'

The manager began to raise his hand, but restrained himself with an effort. Within seconds, the bright sparks circling him shot away to swirl around the fallen lantern instead. In the half-darkness I could see the sheen of nervous sweat on the manager's face, and his eyes were wide as he cast a look towards the exit. Then he looked down at the circling, ever-moving sparks of light, and I realised he was weighing up his chances of escape.

'Do not even think about it,' Roberta urged him. 'You'd be dead before you covered three paces.'

The manager swallowed fitfully. 'What in God's name are those th-things?' he stammered. Earlier he'd been overbearing and unpleasant, but now he reminded me of nothing more than a frightened child.

'Some kind of stinging insect, probably transported here in goods from a foreign land.' Roberta shot me a warning glance, lest I correct her. 'Once captured, they will be harmless.'

'How will you trap them before they attack again?' demanded the manager, his voice rising. 'With your bare hands?'

'It would help if you remained calm. And silent, if at all possible.'

The manager opened his mouth, then closed it again.

'Good,' murmured Roberta. Carefully, she reached into the satchel at her side, withdrawing a sheet of paper and a short brass tube. She then extended her hand towards me, offering me the sheet of paper. 'Hold this,' she whispered, and then she flicked at the brass tube, causing it to emit a tiny, flickering flame.

'Wh-what do you think you're doing?' hissed the manager. He gestured at the stacks of goods, freezing again as one of the sparks came to investigate his sudden move. 'You can't light a fire in here! If this lot goes up we'll burn like torches!'

Roberta ignored him. 'Septimus, from where did these...insects...first appear? Do you recall?'

I raised my hand cautiously, pointing into the shadowy depths of the warehouse.

'One step at a time, then. Come now, and do not lose that piece of paper!'

We set off, taking small steps across the rough wooden flooring whilst keeping our arms at our sides and the rest of our bodies as still as possible. To an observer we must have looked like stiff, unnatural automatons, but it appeared to work because the glowing sprites paid us no attention.

'These spirits would have been trapped in a small vessel, likely fashioned from metal,' whispered Roberta. 'Someone broke the seal and released them, probably one of the dockworkers thinking to help themselves to what they hoped were valuable contents.'

'How shall we return them to captivity?' I glanced over my shoulder to see the manager frozen in place, one of the glowing sparks already circling him inquisitively. 'If we attract them, won't they attack us?'

'At first, perhaps, but our suffering will be short-lived.'

Needless to say, her words did not reassure me in quite the way she intended.

We were halfway to the rear of the warehouse when there was a hair-raising groan. I froze, thinking there was another terror concealed in the darkness ahead of us, then breathed out once more as I heard a rattle overhead. It was nothing more than a breeze finding gaps in the wooden shutters.

My heart still pounding, I continued my slow progress.

By now we were approaching several stacks of goods, one of them with a battered wooden crate on top. The lid was on the floor, leaning against the stack, and I realised we had found the source of these dangerous sprites.

We approached, slowly, and together we peered inside the wooden crate. The interior was in near-complete darkness, but I made out a jumble of what looked like ordinary household objects. Metal platters, tankards, cutlery...there was nothing supernatural or even particularly unusual about the contents.

Then Roberta gave a cry of discovery, and she reached into the crate to withdraw a polished metal jar. The sides were engraved with curious symbols, and as she held it aloft I heard a curious, low-pitched ringing which caused the hairs on the back of my neck to stand on end. I glanced round fearfully, expecting to see the cloud of glowing sprites arrowing towards us, but most were still circling the broken lantern. Half a dozen surrounded the manager, and I prayed he was not foolish enough to swat them away.

'Find the lid,' whispered Roberta. 'Quickly, now. And be silent!'

I did my best, but rummaging around in a box full of metal objects in the darkness was never going to be a hushed affair. In the end I laid the sheet of paper on a nearby bale of fabric, and then I began to remove items one by one, placing them on the floor to one side.

By the time I found the lid the floor around me was covered in metal objects, with knives, forks and platters laid out as though a dozen guests were about to feast off the scarred wooden planking. I passed the lid to Roberta, who inspected it closely before nodding to herself. Then she held out her hand for the sheet of paper.

At that moment the wooden shutters rattled, and I heard the building creak as it stood up to a gust of wind. Dust swirled, and I watched in horror as the sheet of paper was whisked away. I leapt forward, so intent on capturing it that I forgot all about the obstacles in my path. There was an ear-splitting clatter as I landed amongst the silverware, a noise that only intensified as I sprang back again with the precious sheet of paper clutched in one hand, scattering objects far and wide. The sound seemed to go on and on, with plates skidding this way, cups spinning that, and cutlery spreading far and wide. I was still holding my breath as the last metal cup rolled across the floor to fetch up against a wooden crate, coming to a stop with a final, mocking ping.

I felt a prickling between my shoulder blades, and at first I thought it might be Roberta's angry glare burning holes through my coat. But when I turned I realised it was something far worse. The glowing sparks had abandoned the lantern, and the manager, and were flying straight towards me.

'Septimus, the paper!' shouted Roberta. 'Crumple it, and hold it out!'

My fingers were shaking, but I did as I was told. By now the mass of sprites was only feet away, and I braced myself for the agonising pain followed by the quick end Roberta had promised.

Then Roberta struck a match, and I saw the sprites change direction at the sudden glow. I was frozen with horror, for I realised she was to be struck down before my very eyes. Not for long though, because Roberta touched the match to the crumpled paper in my hand, and as the material flared up the creatures again changed course, once more heading towards me. Vaguely, I was aware of the manager sprinting for safety, his boots raising dust clouds that sparkled in a shaft of sunlight.

'Come on, Septimus! Now!'

I looked down to see Roberta holding the jar towards me, the mouth gaping wide. Without thinking, I popped the burning paper inside, and barely had I done so when the cloud of glowing sprites tore past me, chasing it down like baying hounds on the scent of a fox.

The jar leapt in Roberta's hands as the sprites poured in, and then she slapped the lid on, twisting it firmly into place.

I slumped against a stack of goods, spent. As I raised my eyes to the heavens, scarcely able to believe we'd survived the ordeal, I saw a tiny flash of light. I squinted, but in that instant it vanished between the slats of a wooden shutter. Was it one of the sprites, now free to roam at will? Or just a speck of dust in a thin beam of sunlight?

Roberta was busy with the crate, and I helped to gather the goods I'd scattered far and wide. She was silent as I placed the items inside the wooden box, and when I was done she added the sealed jar and took up the crate's wooden lid.

'Surely we cannot leave them here?' I asked, when I realised she was about to fasten the crate once more. 'If someone is importing deadly creatures from the other world, we must put a stop to it! Why, this lunatic...this unknown madman–'

'Oh, he's not unknown. In fact, he's familiar to the both of us.'

I stared at her. In my short time with the Twickhams, I had

encountered two wicked, lawless adversaries, and I was in no hurry to resume their acquaintance. 'You don't mean...'

'I'm afraid so.' Roberta held the lid towards me. 'Septimus, this crate is addressed to my father.'

10

'How is that possible?' I stared at Roberta in surprise. 'Your father described these goods as scientific equipment!'

'I suppose he was avoiding any awkward questions from the authorities.'

I shook my head in despair at the professor's lax approach to safety. 'If we hadn't arrived in time to recapture the dangerous sprites, they might have caused untold harm across the city.'

'But we did, and they didn't,' said Roberta calmly. 'Now be a dear and bring the crate with you.'

There was no arguing with her, and as we left the warehouse we spied Bransen surrounded by his workers. They were plying him with questions, which he was doing his best to deflect, and when he saw us emerging from the interior he looked both ashamed and angry. I guessed he was angry at himself for running, and ashamed at leaving us to perish. 'Well?' he demanded.

Roberta smiled disarmingly. 'Insects, as you suggested. Most likely a nest inside someone's goods. I believe they will soon perish in our colder climate.'

'They won't return?'

'Oh, of that you can be certain.'

Bransen noticed the crate in my arms. 'Where d'you think you're going with that?'

'It's addressed to my father,' said Roberta. 'Surely you won't object to us collecting his goods? After all, that's why we troubled you in the first place.'

'Troubled is right, but there's paperwork to clear and inspections to organise. You ain't taking that nowhere without my say-so.' The manager rounded on his workers. 'And as for you lot, I've never seen such a bunch of lily-livered cowards. Get back to work this instant, or I'll have you in the poorhouse before midnight!'

The men hesitated, then departed for the warehouse somewhat less than enthusiastically. The manager then approached me to take the professor's crate, which was still clutched in my arms. Before he could do so, Roberta stepped in front of him. 'Mr Bransen, this will seem like an odd request, but would you do me a great favour?'

'I'm not sure I'm disposed to–'

'It will be to your benefit, sir.'

Roberta's polite manner, as much as her words, gave Bransen pause. Finally, he nodded.

'Please make an appointment with a physician at your earliest convenience.'

'What? Why?'

'I–I cannot be specific, but you have an air of malaise about you. A relative of mine passed recently, and she exhibited the same–'

'Out!' roared Bransen, pointing a shaking finger towards the exit. 'Take your thrice-damned goods and get out right now! I never want to see or hear the name Twickham for as long as I live!'

Suddenly, I predicted Roberta's likely response to his words, and I knew it would only add fuel to the fire. So, I took the heavy wooden crate under one arm and placed my left hand in the middle of her back, propelling her away from Bransen before any more could be said. The manager had taken Roberta's warning as a personal affront, which was bad enough, but as he calmed down he might finally put two and two together, deducing all of a sudden that the crate was the source of the supernatural appearances within the warehouse.

Thus, I held my breath in case he recalled his workers and ordered them to set about my person. Thrown into the Thames, my body would likely wash up on some distant shore days hence, if it were ever found at all. As for Roberta, I shuddered to think of her likely fate at the hands of such rough types.

By the time we reached the street my arm ached from the heavy crate, but there had been no shouted challenge from the manager, and I would have gladly walked another dozen miles with that box under my arm if it led to our safety. 'Did you have to rile him so?' I demanded.

'I tried to warn him of his sickness,' said Roberta. 'That he felt it was such an insult is entirely his own fault.'

'But–'

'Enough. I will write him a note this afternoon, and that will end our concerns over Mr Bransen's health. One can lead a horse to water and all that.'

'But the way you angered him–'

'It had the desired effect,' said Roberta, nodding towards the crate. 'He ordered us to leave, with no further arguments over the release of my father's goods.'

To that, I had no reply.

She hailed a cab, and as I settled on the seat with the deadly cargo on my lap, I finally breathed a sigh of relief. Not only had we survived, but I'd secured the professor's goods, as requested, and had therefore fulfilled my obligations. Now I could ask for leave of absence, and I hoped he would be so grateful for the safe delivery of his precious shipment he would grant permission on the spot.

The cab struck a pothole, and the metalware inside the box clattered. 'Why do you suppose he ordered the cutlery and plates?' I asked Roberta. 'The jar and its contents I understand, but these other items–'

'Did you not see?'

I had barely seen anything in the gloomy warehouse. Little more than our own doom, at least. 'See what?'

'All of the metal objects were engraved in a similar fashion, with symbols matching the runes on the jar. They were all of the same origin, whatever that might be.' Roberta looked thoughtful. 'It's likely they were recovered from a tomb, or a burial mound. Every month brings fresh discoveries in distant lands, with explorers digging up relics and treasures. Most of them are amateurs, and none of them truly understand what they're bringing into the cold light of day.'

I looked down at the wooden crate sitting in my lap. What if the strange jar with its deadly contents was not the only danger within? The cutlery might cause wounds that would not heal, the plates might poison those who ate from them, and the bowls might have been used in human sacrifices! Quickly, I removed the box and placed it on the floor at my feet.

Roberta snorted with laughter. 'Oh Septimus, your face is truly a picture.'

'You won't be laughing if your father unleashes those monstrosities on the city,' I said, somewhat aggrieved. 'You can be certain it will fall to you to round them up again.'

Roberta indicated the box at my feet. 'No doubt I'll manage to do so with a lot less noise than you did.'

I laughed at that, and in return she gave me a sunny smile. Finally, it felt like our earlier disagreement had been settled.

'Would you deliver that crate to my father?' asked Roberta, once we were safely home.

'Don't you want to come with me? The professor will be delighted with the outcome of our expedition, and you ought to share in his good mood.'

Roberta smiled. 'I know you think otherwise, but it's not that rare to witness my father's sunnier side.'

I wisely said nothing, instead bidding her goodbye before carrying the heavy wooden crate directly to the professor's study. The door was closed, and so I set the box down and knocked twice.

There was no reply.

I glanced up and down the hallway, unsure whether to leave the deadly delivery outside, or risk entering the study. If I left the crate in the hallway someone might trip over it, or worse, open it to investigate the contents. On the other hand, if I entered the professor's study without permission, only for him to spy me within, there would be little chance of witnessing this sunny disposition which Roberta assured me he did, in fact, possess.

I knocked once more, louder this time, and again there was no response. In the end I decided to place the crate inside, since a few harsh words from the professor could not possibly be worse than the risk of unleashing several dozen malevolent, otherworldly sprites on the city.

I opened the door and peered in cautiously, but to my relief the study was deserted. There was a large wooden desk piled high with equipment and paperwork, and two or three bookcases held thick, leather-bound volumes, glass jars containing all manner of anatomical specimens suspended in murky liquids. To my right was the professor's workbench, scorched and seared from earlier experiments, which was currently home to delicate metal stands holding glass beakers and flasks, all of them interconnected by a tangled web of tubing. A Bunsen burner was playing its flame on a particularly large flask, and the purplish contents were bubbling away merrily.

Since there was no room on the desk or the workbench, I set the crate on the floor and turned to leave. Then I hesitated. What if the professor rummaged through the box, disturbing the metal jar? It would be best if I left him a note explaining that the contents were dangerous in the extreme.

Crossing to his desk, I looked around for a sheet of paper, then took up a quill and wrote my warning message. As I blotted the sheet, I happened to notice a telegram lying on the professor's desk. Now, I am not prone to prying, but the contents were so short I managed to read them at a glance, before I even realised what I was doing.

Professor, I must see you immediately. 3 p.m. Drover's Arms.

Inspector Cox.

Cox! The same inspector who had thrown Roberta and me out of the police station, refusing our assistance! So why was he now demanding help from the professor? Then my face cleared as I realised the truth of the matter. This telegram had most likely arrived the day before, and the professor had simply ignored it. The professor having missed the appointment, the inspector had then sent his two constables round, only for the professor to once again rebuff them.

But where was the professor now?

'Mr Jones, are you looking for something?'

I jumped about a foot in the air at the unexpected voice, and turned my guilty, startled face to the doorway. Standing there was Mrs Fairacre, who had arrived, as usual, in complete silence. 'N-no,' I said quickly. 'I am writing the professor a note about his delivery.' Here, I indicated the crate. 'Roberta and I collected the shipment, but there's something dangerous inside and I needed to warn the professor.'

'Miss Twickham had no business visiting the docks,' said Mrs Fairacre sternly.

I was about to point out that 'Miss Twickham' had made it her business, and I had as much chance of stopping her as I had of holding back the tide. But Mrs Fairacre now had my note in her hand, and the words therein confirmed my story.

I indicated the crate. 'If you see the professor before I do, please tell him to be careful. There is a metal jar inside, and the contents...well, they're not from this world.'

'I'm sure Professor Twickham is more than capable of dealing with the contents,' said Mrs Fairacre, in a tone of voice that suggested I wasn't. 'Now, if your business in here is finished...'

'Yes, yes. I am leaving.'

She looked me up and down. 'Perhaps you might tidy yourself before dinner. Elsie dusted the dining room only this morning, and she will have to clean it twice over if you present yourself in those clothes.'

'Right away, Mrs Fairacre.'

The housekeeper stood aside to let me by, then followed me out, firmly closing the door behind the two of us. Then she departed for the kitchens, and I went upstairs to attend to some bookwork before dinner.

Dinner was a wonderful spread, with a large roast chicken, boiled potatoes with sprigs of mint on top, and a large bowl of garden peas. A rich golden gravy completed the meal, and there was plenty of fresh, crusty bread to mop our plates with. It's no wonder we ate in silence, and with great relish.

Finally, as the plates were cleared away, I told the professor of my intended absence. 'It's a refresher course for bookkeepers and accountants,' I explained. 'As you know, sir, I'm always looking to improve my skills.'

There was an element of truth in my words, for there *was* a refresher course and I'd already put my name to it. Only it was for the following week.

'But my dear boy, there's no need to waste your money on courses!' cried the professor. 'My bookkeeping needs are simple enough, and you have ample skills already.'

'One should never stop learning, sir.' I hesitated. 'I would only be away this evening, tomorrow and Sunday, if you can spare me.'

'Father,' put in Roberta. 'Septimus should be allowed to attend his course. It's important for him to remain current with the latest practices.'

The professor smiled. 'Very well, young Septimus. I cannot refuse you after your success with my delivery. Attend your course, but I shall expect you back on Sunday evening.'

'Thank you, sir. I appreciate it.'

He nodded at me, then positively beamed as Elsie entered the dining room with a large, elaborate trifle in a patterned glass dish. The upper layer consisted of whipped cream at least two inches thick, with coloured jelly and sponge layered beneath. 'Excellent, my dear. A most welcome sight!'

'I made it myself, sir.' Elsie flushed. 'Mrs Fairacre's b–been teaching me.'

'Really? But that's wonderful! One day you'll be running the kitchens in a great house, I'm certain of it.'

Elsie looked secretly pleased as she placed the bowl on the table close to the professor, and she was still smiling happily to herself as she departed.

There was a lengthy silence as we served up portions of trifle, and a longer one as we sampled our desserts. The trifle was truly excellent, and I resolved to tell Elsie so the next time I saw her.

'Father, I have news to share,' said Roberta suddenly. 'You remember Hetty, don't you? I went to school with her, but we lost touch when her family moved north, to Yorkshire.'

'Er yes, of course I remember, er, Hetty.'

'Well, I received a telegram from her this afternoon.' Roberta lowered her gaze. 'Sadly, it seems her mother has taken ill.'

The professor tutted and shook his head. 'I trust she recovers quickly.'

'It's not certain by any means. The poor dear is quite sickly, and the family is not coping well.' Roberta had tears in her eyes as she spoke, and she now dabbed at them with a lacy handkerchief. She was clearly overcome by her friend's troubles, and my heart went out to her. She'd lost her own mother at a young age, and I could see how the situation would have special significance to her. 'Hetty asked me to stay,' continued Roberta. 'She seeks moral support in her time of need, but I know you need me here–'

'My dear girl, of course you must go!' declared the professor, equally moved by Roberta's rare show of emotion.

'But, father...your work...' began Roberta haltingly.

'You must bear it no mind!' cried the professor. 'Indeed, I insist you go to your friend in her hour of need.'

'Then it's settled,' said Roberta, suddenly businesslike. 'Fortunately, I have already organised my fare.'

'You shall need another. Elsie will accompany you.'

Roberta lowered the handkerchief, taken aback. 'Elsie? Whatever for?'

'She will prove most useful if the situation is as fraught as you say.'

I caught the merest hint of an emphasis on the word 'if', and with a shock I realised the professor held suspicions about his daughter's tale of woe. How could he doubt Roberta's word, when she was clearly in such distress? Did he believe she was going north for some other, less altruistic, reason? I felt a tinge of unease. Was it...could it be...a romantic dalliance?

'Father, you cannot ask that of the poor girl,' argued Roberta. 'She has never left London, I'm sure of it.'

'All the more reason,' said the professor, and he was unmoved by her further entreaties. 'It's settled. Find her a valise, tell her to pack some things and the two of you shall travel together.'

I returned to my dessert, troubled by this development. Roberta was not keen to have Elsie accompany her, not in the slightest, and that meant there was more to her trip than she was revealing.

'But Mrs Fairacre...' began Roberta, not yet ready to wave the white flag of surrender. 'The housework...'

'Mrs Fairacre will be perfectly happy on her own,' replied the professor. He served himself a second helping of trifle, then glanced at us, noting our surprise. 'Yes, I too have an expedition planned for the weekend, although one far less tragic than yours, Roberta. Earlier, I learned of a thrilling lecture taking place in Brighton. An American is touring with his theories on the possibility of crossing over to the shadow realm. He's a charlatan, of course, but in his amateurish way he's hit upon some fiendishly clever ideas. The lecture is quite unmissable, and a treat I'm very much looking forward to.' He smiled. 'It seems, therefore, that all three of us will be going our separate ways this weekend.'

It was a pity the professor had not made his plans known sooner, for I would not have had to beg my leave of absence. I could have waited until he left for Brighton, then departed on my own errand without anyone being any the wiser! Still, with the professor and Roberta both engaged in their own expeditions, I could devote my full attention towards the murderous creature that was stalking my parents' village.

12

It was after ten at night, and my travels had not proceeded as smoothly as I could have wished. Indeed, the entire trip had been one disaster after another.

Upon leaving the professor's, I had taken a cab to the station, where my train had been uncharacteristically late. After a short trip I disembarked with my trunk at an out-of the way station, where I was meant to board a connecting train to Croydon. The station was little more than a platform in the woods, the ticket office boarded up with no sign of either the stationmaster nor any porters. Neither was there any sign of a train, connecting or otherwise.

The only other passengers to alight with me were a military gentleman and his wife. She wore a travelling outfit, with a cloak over her dress, while he was in uniform with a sword buckled at his side. I recognised his uniform as that of an officer in the Royal Navy, and I guessed his rank at that of lieutenant. He paced the platform as we waited, stopping now and then to scowl along the railway line, which remained stubbornly bereft of trains. Each time he stopped he took out a silver hip flask, the contents sloshing and gurgling as he up-ended it for a quick tot.

'Well this is a damnable thing,' muttered the man irritably, after we had waited with growing impatience for ten or fifteen minutes.

'These lubbers can't even run the trains on time!'

The lady placed a hand on his arm. 'Calm, Bertie. You're not aboard your precious ship here.'

'Just as well, or someone would get a flogging,' growled the officer. He cast a glance at me then looked away again, instantly dismissing me as someone of no importance. I was only glad he hadn't decided to start his floggings with me.

'Perhaps we could arrange a carriage?' suggested the lady.

'Do you expect me to fashion one from those trees yonder?' demanded the lieutenant. 'Perhaps pull the blasted thing all the way to Lewes myself?'

I cleared my throat. 'Would you like me to make enquiries? There must be a village nearby, and I may be able to rouse someone to help.'

'There's a good man,' said the lieutenant. 'Run along quickly, eh? My ship awaits, and there'll be hell to pay if I miss the tide. It's going to be too damn close as it is.'

'Would you watch my trunk?' I asked him. 'I have no valuables, but I shall need my spare clothes and–'

'It will be quite safe, I'm sure,' interrupted the officer. 'No more delays, I beg you. Go! Secure a carriage!'

His wife was clearly used to her husband's brusque nature, for she gave me an apologetic smile as I turned to leave. I nodded briefly to acknowledge her gesture, then made my way past the ticketing office and descended a dozen concrete steps to the road below. It was almost completely dark, with the moon hidden behind heavy clouds, but there was just enough light to make out the branches of overhanging trees. I could spy the muddy, rutted road, and I looked to my left and right as I tried to decide which way to go. Then I saw a wooden signpost opposite, with half a mile to a village on my left and two miles to another on my right. Neither was known to me, and so I chose the closer.

My shoes were not made for such conditions, with one quickly springing a leak, and the legs of my trousers were soon spattered with mud. The road itself was churned up and muddy, but walking alongside meant pushing past weeds and bushes, all of them coated with filth thrown up by carriages passing during the day.

As I walked, I kept an ear out for distant whistles. It would be just my luck if the connecting train pulled into the station while I was seeking alternative transport, and I was certain the naval gentlemen would not ask them to wait for me.

I couldn't help noticing the deep silence in the woods, and all of a sudden I recalled the gruesome photographs I had seen earlier that day. I wondered whether the victim, a man of about my own age, had been walking along a road much like this one as he'd been grabbed and savagely mauled. All of a sudden, the silence around me was not so much deep and peaceful as sinister and forbidding.

I shivered and lengthened my stride, less concerned about a few spots of mud on my clothes than I was about the possibility of an attack.

Ten minutes later I heard a branch snap. It was away to my left, somewhere beyond the hedgerow encroaching on the road, but the sound carried easily in the night air. My blood chilled, and I froze in place, listening for all I was worth.

Silence.

I swallowed fitfully, then hurried onwards, stumbling on the uneven ground, slipping in muddy puddles, and yet trying to keep the noise of my passing to the absolute minimum. At every loose pebble, every splash of my foot in yet another puddle, my heart threatened to burst from my chest. Every shadow seemed to conceal hidden horrors, and when the moon finally burst through, lighting the road with stark, ghostly white, the shadows only grew deeper and even more menacing.

A few minutes later I saw a flickering light ahead, and with an overwhelming sense of relief I discovered I had reached the village. As I drew closer I saw half a dozen houses alongside a modest green. The dwellings had steep gable roofs, and I could see firelight gleaming through thin curtains. Nearby, shaded by a huge oak tree, was a modest stable, and beside that was a lean-to shelter containing a farm cart. The ends of the shafts lay on the ground, but as I approached I could see the vehicle within appeared to be old but in serviceable condition.

Buoyed by my good fortune, I strode to the cottage abutting the stable and knocked firmly on the front door. It opened, and a man stood silhouetted against the candlelight. He was stooped, middle-aged, and his bald pate was surrounded by a fringe of grey hair. He was wearing a threadbare dressing gown and carried a battered tin from which steam rose in gentle wisps. My first impression was of a farmer, tired from the day's work, who was about to turn in for the night.

Meanwhile, he was studying me cautiously, but as he took in my city clothes and somewhat bedraggled appearance I saw comprehension dawning. 'You'd be a passenger from the station what missed your train.'

'Good evening,' I said, nodding politely. 'You surmised correctly, sir. Myself and two other passengers have been left stranded at the nearby station. One is a naval officer whose ship is sailing with the next tide, and the other is his wife.' I hesitated, for I was reluctant to ask this tired-looking man for help. Who knew how many hours of labour he'd already endured that day? And at what hour would he have to rise the following morn? But before I could ask, he posed the question himself.

'You'd like me to drive you to the closest town, wouldn't you?'

Gratefully, I nodded. 'We shall pay you, of course.'

He gestured dismissively, but I saw a pleased look upon his face. 'I'll get dressed,' he said. 'Come in and take a pew, and there's tea on if you want a mug.'

'Thank you.' I looked down at my muddy shoes, then glanced around for a boot scraper. Seeing none, I undid the laces, removed my sodden shoes and placed them next to the door.

'That's good of you, sir. Most wouldn't have bothered.'

I followed the farmer into a small but tidy living area, where a fire was giving its last in the grate. A kettle hung near the flames, the metal blackened from use, and nearby a teapot sat on a tray. There were two high-backed armchairs, much-repaired, and a simple, pallet-style bed took up one corner of the room.

'Mugs are on the mantlepiece,' said the farmer, pointing them out. 'Have a seat, and I'll be back in a jiffy.'

I poured myself a mug of black tea, added a generous dash of fresh milk, then sank back into the nearest armchair. The fire warmed my feet, and before long I saw steam rising from my damp woollen socks. The tea was strong enough to sting my tongue, but its warmth quickly spread through me, counteracting the chill night air that I'd experienced on my walk from the station.

As I sat there in the cosy warmth, I felt a growing reluctance to brave the night airs once more. If it weren't for the lieutenant and his wife, I might have asked the farmer for the use of his armchair, that

I might rest until morning before resuming my journey. Something about the woods had troubled me greatly, but whether it was an ancient evil or a gang of highwaymen lying in wait, I knew I'd have to brave them once more in order to rescue my travelling companions.

13

The farmer soon returned, now wearing rough trousers tied with a cord, and a much-darned woollen jumper. He donned a sheepskin cap, pulling the flaps down to cover his ears, and then nodded towards the door. 'We'd best be off, young man. T'is a cold night, and naval gentlemen are not the most patient of souls.'

Outside, I waited as he led a docile mare from the stables, and before long she was secured between the shafts. I clambered aboard, adding old straw and dried mud to my clothes in the process, and when I was seated the farmer took his position and commanded the mare with a click of his tongue.

The horse shook her mane, perhaps in protest at the late hour, but set off without further ado. The old cart squeaked, rattled and groaned as it swayed over ruts and splashed through puddles, and while it wasn't very fast, it was many times better than navigating the rough track on my own two feet.

I wondered how Roberta would fare on her own journey to the north of England, and I prayed her voyage would be less of a trial than my own. I consoled myself with the thought that she would be heading away from danger, at least of the supernatural kind, but I could not help wishing she were with me. Before long I experienced a daydream of sorts, in which I travelled to West Wickham with

Roberta at my side, there to introduce her to my parents. They would be taken with her, I was certain of it, and after seeing us together there would be no more talk of the match my mother was hoping to make for me with Cecilie Carmichael.

But it was a foolish daydream, no more. The professor had made his wishes clear, and I would not be free to court Roberta unless I made a tidy sum for myself, securing both her and my own futures. Sadly, the only sums a modest bookkeeper such as myself was likely to make were in other people's ledgers.

Above all else, of course, there was the matter of Roberta's feelings towards me. One moment she could be as sharp as one of Mrs Fairacre's knives, the next tender and caring. But the tenderness, the fondness, seemed to be that of a sister tasked with the supervision of her foolish and somewhat naive younger brother rather than that of a partner, or a lover.

My brain having tied itself in knots, I shook myself and took a deep breath of cold night air. This had the intended effect, and as I took stock of my surroundings I discovered we were drawing up to the station.

The lieutenant must have heard the cart's approach, for he now appeared at the top of the stairs. As he took in the rickety hay cart with its hunched-up driver and passive mare, the look on his face was a veritable study. Lost for words, at first, he eventually found his voice. 'I thought you were fetching a carriage,' he said at last. 'Do you expect my wife to sit in that contraption?'

I felt a stab of annoyance. Did the ungrateful fool truly believe I had been given a choice of luxurious carriages, and had instead chosen the farm cart? 'The farmer has kindly agreed to carry us to the nearest town, where I'm sure you will find more suitable transport. Or, if you prefer, you can wait here until morning.'

'Out of the question. I refuse to stay here one moment longer!' The lieutenant frowned at the farmer. 'And I suppose this good samaritan expects a hefty fee for his modest services?'

'He offered to drive us for nothing,' I said quietly. 'I thanked him for his kindness, but assured him we would be more than happy to pay.'

The lieutenant's wife now appeared at his side, and she smiled warmly at the farmer. 'Sir, you are an angel. The hour is late and you must be tired, yet you come to our aid without a second thought.' She gripped her husband's elbow. 'Of course we shall offer recompense, and we shall be most generous at that.'

The lieutenant winced, though whether from the thought of paying the driver or the sudden pain in his arm I could not tell. A little of both, I suspected. He recovered quickly, and switched his attention to me. 'The luggage. With your help, we shall move it ourselves.'

I climbed down from the rear of the cart and took the stairs to the platform, where I followed the lieutenant to our things. As we picked up the first of the trunks, he spoke to me in a low voice. 'I apologise for my lack of civility, but I am under severe pressure. The ship that awaits me is my first command, and there will be nobody to blame but myself if we miss the tide. All eyes will be upon me, from the crew to my superior officers onshore, and once gained, a reputation for slack discipline is devilishly hard to shake.'

'I understand, and in your position I would be in a similar state.' I could smell the alcohol on his breath, and his red-rimmed eyes spoke of exhaustion, worry and lack of sleep. 'Let us hope the rest of our journey proceeds without incident.'

He smiled briefly, nodding his thanks, and then we lifted the trunk and carried it to the waiting cart. The lady was already positioned next to the farmer, on the raised driving seat, and she gripped a small handrail as the cart swayed under the sudden load.

'I thought your lady wife was best sitting up here,' explained the farmer. 'It's raised, see? Should keep her dresses clean.'

'Thank you,' said the lieutenant. 'That was most thoughtful of you.'

We returned for the second chest, my own this time, and the lieutenant grunted as we lifted it. 'Do they not have house bricks where you are going, such that you must take your own supply along with you?'

'I do have a number of books,' I admitted. Roberta had raided her father's library, taking down volume after volume and packing all which she felt might help. This, despite my protests that I would be away for barely two days, and could not hope to read more than three or four of the dozens of valuable books.

Roberta had also packed several items which she assured me I would find useful. There had been no time for her to explain their purpose, and I would have forgotten or mixed up the instructions in any case. So, she had scrawled notes and included one with each mysterious piece of equipment, which included intricate devices of brass and copper wire, and polished wooden boxes with rows of lenses, folding blades and several other items for which I had no words.

We got the heavy chest to the road, navigating the steps carefully lest we overbalance and injure ourselves. Once placed in the rear, the old cart leaned to the left with a loud creak, and I eyed the wheel critically, wondering whether it would shatter in the first hundred yards. If that happened, the short-tempered lieutenant would likely explode like one of his own guns.

The officer, though, climbed aboard without a second thought. I joined him, somewhat gingerly, and the two of us sat on the rough wooden boards. The farmer clicked his tongue, and after some to-ing and fro-ing he managed to turn the cart and set off along the muddy track.

'How long to reach Croydon?' called the lieutenant.

'Not goin' all the way to Croydon,' replied the farmer, without looking round. 'It's much too far.'

I felt the officer's angry glare upon me, as though this news were entirely my own fault. For my part, I studiously avoided meeting his gaze whilst awaiting the inevitable outburst.

But before the irritable lieutenant could express his displeasure, the farmer reassured him. 'Thornton Heath is close by,' he said. 'There you will find a fancy carriage to take you the rest of the way.'

The lieutenant appeared to be in two minds over this news. On the one hand, it meant breaking our journey once more, thus involving another delay. On the other, should we secure a coach-and-four, or a ride with a rapid mail service, we might arrive in Croydon in half the time. From there, I would finally be able to resume my journey to West Wickham, whilst the naval gentleman and his wife could speed their way towards Lewes on the south coast.

'Very well,' said the lieutenant at last. 'Proceed with all haste, and let us hope a carriage awaits us.'

14

The village of Thornton Heath was typical of those changed forever by the arrival of the railway. A station had been built in the middle of a field some ten years earlier, its construction based on little more than speculation and hope. Now, over two thousand souls lived and worked in the area. New houses had sprung up, seemingly overnight, and on the outskirts the farmer pointed out a brickworks where moonlight revealed row upon row of clay bricks stacked six feet high and at least twelve deep. From what I could deduce, there were enough building materials in that yard to house half of Surrey. Clearly, progress was marching towards England's sleepy villages, and I wondered whether the woods, moors and lush green fields would one day be replaced with houses from coast to coast.

There was an inn halfway along the deserted high street, and a coachman was roused from his bed to help us. Despite the late hour, he seemed pleased at the unexpected business, and I guessed the railway had eaten considerably into his livelihood.

By now our helpful farmer was all but done in. We thanked him profusely for his help, and I saw a flash of gold in the lamplight as the lieutenant rewarded him with a half-sovereign. I added a few shillings of my own, all I could comfortably spare, and then our saviour clicked at his mare, turning the shabby old hay cart in the street before guiding it back the way it had come.

Our new driver helped me to load the trunks onto the luggage platform at the rear of the carriage, while the lieutenant and his wife took their places within. It was a large vehicle, once painted a gleaming black picked out with gold leaf, but the gilding was mostly missing, and the bodywork was scratched and faded after years of heavy use.

But still, it afforded protection against the elements, and I knew the next leg of our journey would be a comfortable one.

I climbed into the carriage and took a seat as the coachman closed the door. The naval gentleman and his wife sat opposite, facing the front of the carriage, and the three of us were bathed in the gentle candlelight from a lantern affixed to the door frame.

I heard a muted whip crack behind me, and the carriage moved off, swaying and creaking. Glancing at my fob watch, I discovered it was now after eleven at night, and I wondered how long it would be before I finally reached my childhood home. Across from me, the lieutenant and his wife sat shoulder to shoulder, the latter nestled against her husband, barely able to keep her eyes open. I met the officer's gaze and he nodded, thanking me for my help. I smiled politely in return. We had faced adversity together, however minor, and having overcome the challenge there now seemed to be an unspoken bond between us. All of a sudden he put his hand out towards me. 'Lieutenant Bertram Ware,' he said, in a clipped voice. 'This dear lady is my wife, Martha.'

'A pleasure to meet you both,' I said, and we shook hands. 'Septimus Jones, at your service.'

'I only wish we could have met under better circumstances,' said the officer.

I nodded, but said nothing. Under better circumstances, I doubt he would have noticed me. After a few moments I moved to the side of my seat, propping myself up against the padded wall of the carriage, and as the vehicle made its way towards the town of Croydon I allowed my eyes to close so that I might have the strength and energy to face the rest of my late-night journey.

I awoke with a start, aware that something had changed. For a moment I though we'd arrived, but then I spotted the wooded banks on either side of the road. We were still on the road, and yet the carriage was slowing. 'Do you know why we're stopping?' I whispered to the lieutenant, keeping my voice low lest I wake his sleeping companion.

He was staring out the small window set into the door, but he heard me and shook his head at my question. Outside, moonlight filtered through the trees, bathing the scene in a dappled light that left more shadows than it dispelled. The candle in the lantern had burned low, but it was just light enough to see the officer had taken a firm grip on the hilt of his sword.

I heard the horses whinny nervously, followed by soothing words from our driver, muffled and indistinct inside the coach. At this sound, the carriage came to a complete halt.

The officer seated across from me looked as though he'd like nothing more than to jump down and give the driver a piece of his mind, but Martha was leaning against him, fast asleep with her head on his shoulder. So, he turned to me. 'Would you go ask the blasted fellow what he's playing at?' he hissed.

I nodded, got to my feet, and in that instant all hell broke loose. There was a roar that made the hairs on the back of my neck stand up, an uneven, unearthly sound that grew louder and louder as whatever was making the horrible sound raced towards us. The driver gave a shout of alarm, and then, before I could grab for support, something slammed into the carriage with the force of a cannonball. The vehicle rocked on its springs and I was thrown to the floor, the lieutenant and his wife also hurled off their seat to land on top of me.

I heard a tormented scream outside, barely human, that pierced me to my very soul. More growling, the sound of ripping fabric, and screams that grew fainter by the second.

Then...silence.

Shocked, we regained our feet. The attack had lasted but a moment, and was over before we had even realised what was happening.

'W–what in heaven's name was that?' demanded Martha, her face pale and her eyes wide and staring.

'A wild animal,' replied her husband. 'A savage hound, most like.'

He reached for the door, but she gripped his arm with both hands. 'Dear, you–you cannot go outside!' she said. 'That creature is still out there!'

'I must see to our driver,' said the lieutenant. 'The poor fellow may be lying nearby, injured. In any case, no wild animal can stand against cold hard steel.' So saying, he patted the hilt of his sword.

'But–'

'Sir,' said the lieutenant, addressing me. 'Take this dirk, and defend my beloved with your very life.'

He offered me a murderous-looking dagger, pommel-first, and I saw the long, slender blade gleaming in the candlelight. It was honed to a razor-sharp edge, and I wondered how many lives it had claimed in the officer's grip. Even so, it seemed to offer scant protection against the creature that had just attacked our driver. Already, I'd guessed that this was no mere hound, and I had little doubt we were facing the very same monster that had savagely mauled the victim in the police photographs. 'It might be best if we waited in here,' I said, and to my eternal shame I heard a tremble in my voice.

'Out of the question,' said the officer sharply. 'You would leave our driver out there with this beast, alone and wounded?' He pulled out the silver hip flask and thrust it at me. 'Here sir, partake of some liquid courage, for you are sorely lacking.'

Embarrassed, I shook my head. How could I tell him that I suspected our driver had already breathed his last? Judging by the bloodcurdling screams and the way they had faded to silence during the attack, I imagined the monster was already feasting on the poor unfortunate's remains. But to say so aloud would be callous in the extreme, and I knew the officer was right, despite the danger.

Martha was aware of the danger also. 'Bertie, you cannot go out there,' she said firmly.

'But I must. It's my duty.'

'Hang your duty!' she cried. 'What good is your duty to me if you lose your life?'

The lieutenant didn't stop to argue. With a look that spoke volumes he pressed the hip flask into my free hand, almost daring me to ignore it. Then he wrenched the door open, leapt down and drew his sword with a *rissk* of metal. The blade gleamed, and I saw the officer moving cautiously towards the front of the carriage, brandishing his sword and ready to defend himself at a moment's notice. Once he was out of sight I pulled the door to, ensuring it was latched. Then I crouched beside it, dagger in hand, prepared to haul the door open at the first hint of the lieutenant's return.

15

Several minutes passed, with no sign of the lieutenant nor any sound of the beast. My hand began to ache from the deathly grip on the dagger, but despite the discomfort I would not have released that weapon for all the gold in England.

Martha was sitting behind me, anxiously peering through the opposite window. 'Oh, where is he?' she demanded. 'Where has he got to?'

'My lady, you must draw the curtain and stay clear of the window. We must give no sign that this carriage is occupied.'

She looked at me, puzzled. 'Mr Jones, a wild animal could not possibly open these doors.'

'Perhaps not, but a large hound might leap at the carriage, gaining access by breaking the glass.'

Martha retreated to the middle of the coach, having hurriedly drawn the curtain, and I rose to blow out the flickering candle that had been illuminating the interior. In the sudden darkness, the scene outside took on a ghostly, moonlit appearance, and I strained my eyes for any signs of movement. I could feel my heart hammering in my chest, and my breathing was shallow and rapid. The tension was unbearable, and I almost wished the creature *would* attack. Anything would be preferable to the nervous wait.

Suddenly a face loomed before me, and I fell backwards in fright. The door opened, and to my relief I discerned the lieutenant's uniform, gold buttons gleaming in the moonlight. 'H–how goes it with the driver?' I asked, struggling to keep my voice even.

'No sign of the man, but there's blood a-plenty,' commented the officer. 'A trail leads into the woods, but I lost it in the darkness.' He glanced at his wife, then studied me once more. 'Are you able to drive this carriage?'

'I have seen it done before, of course, but–'

'Good man. Up top with you then, and let's be on our way.'

I thought of the exposed driver's seat, and recalled the horrifying screams as our coachman had been taken by the beast. Would I be next? But I knew I had no choice, as the lieutenant would need his hands free to wield his weapon. So, I got to my feet, and was about to step down from the carriage when there was a blood-curdling roar from my right. The lieutenant spun to meet the threat, but barely had time to raise his sword before a huge, hairy beast cannoned into him, snarling and growling and snapping its huge teeth. The horses whinnied and reared, and were it not for the darkness and the enclosing trees, I felt certain they would have bolted. Perhaps, like me, they were frozen with shock and fear.

Martha screamed, her cry rending the air. 'Help him! *Help him!*'

I was still stunned by the suddenness and ferocity of the attack. In the dappled moonlight it was hard to make out any detail, but as man and creature fought desperately, I realised the lieutenant was having the worst of it.

'Mr Jones!' grunted that worthy, as he strove to fend off his attacker. 'Your assistance...if you please?'

Having watched the melee for no more than a second or two, I snapped out of my fugue and leapt from the carriage. 'Leave him, you foul beast!' I shouted, brandishing my dagger. 'Flee, or it'll go badly for you!'

I don't know what effect I expected my words to have, for the creature was not to be reasoned with. I suppose I hoped that antagonist and defender would cease fighting. Naturally, they didn't.

I stood there with the dagger, undecided. Before me on the ground was a tangle of hairy limbs and navy uniform in constant motion, and by stabbing wildly I risked plunging the long, slender blade into friend as much as foe. But then the beast got the upper hand, or more accurately, claw, and it crouched over the lieutenant with its long, curved fangs at his throat. The gnarled, hairy back was presented to me, as wide as a dining table, and I took one step forward and plunged the foot-long dagger right into its shoulder with both hands.

I felt the blade grating on bone, and then the handle was torn from my grip as the beast arched its back, howling with pain. I snatched at the knife, pulling it free, then gazed in horror at the creature's distorted, hound-like face, with elongated snout, hellish red eyes and gleaming, bloodied fangs. Slowly, I began to back away as the creature left the lieutenant and instead began to advance on me. Behind it, I could just see the other man scrabbling in the dirt and leaves, seeking his fallen sword.

Despite the mortal danger, I found myself analysing the creature, for a small part of me knew that if I survived the encounter I would need all the knowledge I could gain. The beast walked in a hunched fashion, though still upright like a man. It was taller than myself, and the arms and legs were knotted with muscle and sinew. Hair covered every inch of its body, and it looked exactly like a cross between man and wolf. Indeed, it was strikingly similar to some of the woodcut images Roberta had shown me in her father's books.

So terrifying was its appearance that I felt my legs weaken, and it was all I could do not to turn and flee. Deep down, I knew this would be a fatal mistake.

The creature got closer, and I brandished the dagger. It seemed an ineffective gesture, but I was hoping to keep the monster at bay until the lieutenant recovered his sword and ran the nightmare creature through with it. Alas, I could see the officer behind the creature, and although he was casting around for the weapon, his movements were slow and uncoordinated. I realised he'd been dazed in the attack, and with sinking heart I realised there might be no help at all from that direction.

The monster snarled, baring its fangs. There was a determined gleam in its eyes, one that spoke of imminent revenge upon my person, and I felt myself weaken further. Was this how my life ended? I should not have been surprised, for Roberta all but predicted it.

'Away, you foul creature! Leave him alone!'

The shout came from the carriage to my left, and with a start I realised it was Martha. The creature turned to look at her, and I felt a chill in my guts. She was in the doorway, unarmed! If it leapt at her, I would not be able to save her!

The creature raised its snout to sniff the air in a most distasteful fashion. Then, without warning, it leapt towards Martha. She shrieked in alarm, suddenly aware of her predicament, and I sprang after the beast with my dagger, intending to do my best whatever the risk to my person.

The monster was barely six feet from Martha now, and rapidly outstripping me. By the time I caught up it would have torn out her throat, or snapped her neck. I drew back my arm, intending to throw the knife, but in that instant Martha snatched her husband's discarded hip flask from the carriage and hurled it directly in the monster's face, screaming incoherently all the while.

There was a hollow *thunk* as the metal flask connected with the beast's nose, followed by an unearthly, pain-stricken howl that set my teeth on edge. The beast came to a sudden stop, clutching at its muzzle and shaking its head, and I, still in full flight, promptly stabbed it in the back with my dagger. Up close, I could smell burnt flesh and hair, but the significance did not strike me until much later.

My desperate attack finally seemed to break the creature's spirit, for it whirled around and bounded for the trees, whimpering and howling in pain. I stood there with blood dripping from my dagger, whilst Martha collapsed against the side of the carriage, overcome by the narrow escape.

The lieutenant managed to find his feet at last, retrieving his sword and straightening the tattered remains of his dress coat. Half the buttons had been torn off, and there were streaks of blood on his white shirt.

'Are you badly wounded?' I asked him.

'Luckily, t'is no more than a scratch.' Still dazed, he shook his head once or twice, clearing the fog, then approached and clapped me on the shoulder. 'That was brave of you, Mr Jones. Uncommonly brave.'

'Your lady wife was braver,' I remarked. 'She distracted the beast, and–'

Before I could finish the sentence, Martha ran up to us, embracing the lieutenant so hard I swear I heard his ribcage creak. He put one arm around her, still holding the sword in the other. After a moment or two, he broke the embrace. 'Come dear. We only wounded that foul beast, and it may return to exact vengeance.'

'What of the driver?' I asked.

The lieutenant shook his head. 'I will not risk our lives one minute longer. Martha, take a seat inside the carriage and secure the doors. Mr Jones and I will sit up top, and the two of us will attempt to drive this contraption together.'

As I turned to comply I spotted the hip flask lying amongst the churned-up dirt and dry leaves. I picked it up and offered it to the lieutenant, who took it with thanks. 'Treasure that always,' I remarked. 'It may have saved all of our lives.'

Permit me to gloss over the embarrassing scenes which followed the attack. Suffice to say it took me a good ten minutes to determine the workings of our carriage, and a further five minutes of clicking my tongue and vainly waving the coachman's whip in mid-air before our wary horses deigned to move off. I suspect that, in the end, they proceeded along the road in the hope that, upon reaching our destination, someone would rub them down and feed them large quantities of oats and hay. I sincerely doubt it was due to my ineffectual efforts at driving them.

Of the hideous creature that had attacked us in the woods, there was neither sight nor sound.

Our progress was slow, the horses ambling along with little regard to the dire peril that might befall us at any moment.

'Will they not go any faster?' demanded the lieutenant, who was growing ever more impatient beside me.

'I dare not raise my voice,' I whispered, with a meaningful nod towards the nearby trees. 'It might attract attention.'

'The whip, then. Apply it, and we–'

'If I spook the horses they might bolt into the darkness, taking us with them. Then, rather than arriving late, we would not arrive at all.'

The lieutenant saw reason in my words but he accepted them with bad grace, crossing his arms and harrumphing under his breath.

For my part, I had no confidence in my skill with the whip. It was designed to make a noise directly above the horses, encouraging them to greater effort, but with my inexpert handling it was more likely to strike one of the magnificent creatures in the rump, or perhaps nick an ear, and the results would be catastrophic.

So we ambled on at little more than walking pace, with the impatient naval gentleman fuming at my side.

After thirty or forty minutes he rose suddenly in his seat, pointing ahead. 'There!' he cried. 'Street lamps! Civilisation!' He clapped me on the shoulder, almost causing me to drop the reins. 'We made it, Mr Jones. We made it!'

I felt a flood of relief, for I'd been expecting an attack by the wounded creature at any moment. I could still recall the fury in its gaze, and I shivered as I relived the moment when it had faced me. There had been intelligence behind those reddened eyes. Intelligence and malice and a thirst for revenge. Had Martha not distracted the foul beast, I would have been torn limb from limb.

Croydon was a large town, and despite the late hour there were still people about. Our horses, who seemed to know the place, led the way to a coach stop, where we were met by a stable boy. He took hold of their halters, speaking softly to them, then cast a puzzled glance at myself and the lieutenant.

The lieutenant turned to me. 'I apologise, but I must leave the matter of our missing driver with you. Make a report to the police, and by all means mention my name. But you must impress upon them the urgency of my journey, which is vital to the safety of this country.'

I was not surprised, for I'd already guessed he would leave me to deal with the police. From the very first, the officer's overriding concern had been for leaving port on time with his precious ship, and I did not expect him to deviate from his goal. 'You may leave the matter with me,' I said quietly. Then I offered him the dagger, which I'd kept beside me for the duration of our voyage lest we be forced to defend ourselves once more.

But the lieutenant refused it. 'That dirk has served me well throughout my naval career, and I hope it brings you similar luck. Please allow me to bestow it upon you as a small measure of my thanks.'

I accepted the gift with much gratitude, since my own journey was far from over.

'You there!' called the lieutenant, addressing the stable boy. 'Find me a driver, and quickly. I must get to the station this instant.'

The boy ran off, and the officer turned to me once more. 'When he returns, he can assist you with your trunk. I apologise for leaving you like this, but–'

I gestured dismissively. 'I understand. You have your duty.'

'Good man.'

I climbed down from the driving seat and strode towards the rear of the carriage. As I passed the door, Martha opened it and looked out. 'Mr Jones, I must thank you for your help.'

'There is no need, ma'am.'

'Oh, but there is. You saved my husband's life, and that is a debt I shall not forget.'

'Thank you, my lady. But in turn, you saved mine.'

She smiled at me. 'I will remember your name, Mr Jones. One day we shall meet again, I am sure of it.'

I nodded politely, and made my way to the rear of the carriage. My trunk was lashed to the luggage platform, stowed above the lieutenant's, and I set about undoing the buckled leather straps.

Before long I was joined by the stable boy and a tall, thin man with hollowed-out cheeks. I turned to meet them, and saw concern and suspicion writ large across their faces. 'What happened to Masters?' demanded the man. 'What you doin' with his carriage?'

'We were attacked on the road from Thornton Heath,' I said grimly. 'I'm afraid our driver is missing, and I fear for his life.'

'No!' whispered the man, drawing back in horror. 'Was he taken by...by a beast?'

'You know of it?' I demanded.

'Y–yes, sir. This is not the first such attack, but none have been this close.'

'I must report the matter to the police. They will organise a search party, I'm sure, and with luck they will find the driver safe and sound.' I did not mention the trail of blood the lieutenant had discovered in the woods. That news I would save for the police. 'Can you take this trunk and stow it somewhere safe? Once this matter is resolved, I must resume my journey to West Wickham, and I will gladly pay for its safe delivery.'

'We'll send it on sir, but as to resuming your journey...' he shook his head. 'T'is only a few hours until dawn, and the creature has yet to attack in daylight.'

I yearned for the safety of my parents' home, and could not stand the thought of a night in a strange bed. 'The beast will be licking its wounds for some time yet,' I said, with more confidence than I felt.

'You fought it?'

'My travelling companions and I gave a good account of ourselves,' I said modestly. 'The creature will carry the scars of our battle for the rest of it's blighted life, however short that might be. With luck, it might retreat deep into the woods, there to expire of its own accord.'

My audience gazed upon me with rapt attention, and their eyes only widened as they saw the bloodstains on my sleeve. I had not noticed the blood before that moment, and guessed it had been deposited upon my person as I plunged the dagger into the creature's back.

'Where is the new driver?' called a voice from the carriage, and I recognised the impatient tone of the lieutenant. The driver and the stable boy sprang into action, grabbing my trunk and carrying it inside, before returning at the double. The driver now wore a tall hat, and was hastily donning a coat as shield against the cold night air. He clambered onto the seat and took up the whip, wielding it expertly with a loud crack. The horses set off at speed, and the last I saw of the carriage and its occupants was a brief wave from the lieutenant.

16

After organising the delivery of my trunk I made my way to the police station, following the directions given to me by a passerby. Situated on Park Lane, I was lucky in that it lay upon the route to the particular station I would need to use in order to resume my journey.

The lieutenant had presented me with the ornate leather scabbard for his dirk, and I could feel the sheathed weapon bumping against my chest as I walked, concealed as it was under my coat. The feeling gave me reassurance, even though I was not the combative sort. Having already survived one perilous encounter, I felt confident I would be able to give a good account of myself if required.

There was a lantern outside the police station, and within I found a sleepy-looking constable taking the night watch. He perked up considerably as I recounted the events in the nearby woods, and soon had runners dispersing to summon his fellow policemen. He showed little surprise at my description of the attacker, and I realised this was not the first such attack to be reported.

'We must locate this unfortunate fellow Masters with all haste,' said the constable, now fully alert. 'My guvnor will want to question you about the attack, but that can wait until the morning. Where are you staying?'

'I am travelling onwards to West Wickham,' I told him, and wrote down my parents' address. 'I am happy to answer questions, but–'

'Surely it would be safer to find lodgings for the night?'

He was the second person to advise me so, and I was about to explain that my parents were expecting me, and would be extremely worried if I failed to arrive, when there was a commotion behind me. Half a dozen police poured in, most still fastening buttons on their coats. Their boots thudded on the wooden floor, and there was a cacophony of voices as they organised themselves. I was all but forgotten, and I confess I made myself scarce at the earliest opportunity. The search was now in the hands of the police, and I felt my duty had been carried out to the best of my ability.

Outside, I got my bearings before heading towards the nearby station. It was one of several in the town, albeit smaller than the rest as it only serviced a regional line. From here I would travel a few miles to Elmers End, before embarking on the final leg of my journey. Unfortunately there was no train line to West Wickham, but it was only two miles by road and I was more than familiar with the area, having roamed the countryside far and wide in my youth. Thus, I was willing to risk the walk, even with the monster abroad. After all, what chance the creature would skirt Croydon and make its way to the very part of the countryside I had to walk through? So small as to be impossible, by my estimate.

That left the matter of the train to Elmers End, which was by no means guaranteed. It was well past midnight, and I suspected the last passenger train had long since departed. However, I was not in a position to be choosy, and would gladly bribe a porter or stationmaster for a ride aboard a mail or goods train. So desperate was I to reach West Wickham that I even considered hiding near the end of the platform, and boarding a train illegally as it pulled out of the station.

In the end there was no need. I spoke with the porter at length, recounting the sorry tale of my journey to that point. He was apologetic with regards the missed connection, sympathetic when I detailed my journey along dark, muddy roads to organise the hay cart, and breathless with excitement when I described the savage, life-or-death struggle in the woods. He had me show off my dagger, his eyes wide as I demonstrated the fashion in which I had stabbed the beast, and I suspected my tale would grow and grow with embellishment as he spoke of it to his acquaintances, no doubt earning himself many a free beer in the local inn.

'Well,' said the porter at last. 'You've 'ad a right old night, and no lie.'

'But is there a train?' I asked him. So wrapped up had I been in the telling of my tale, I had not thought to ask until now. How foolish would I look if he told me there was no train due until morning? Would I have to repeat the theatre at every station in Croydon, even those which led to villages far from my destination?

'There's a goods train coming at half past the hour,' said the porter, to my great relief. 'They're not supposed to carry passengers, mind, but I'm sure we can make an exception. Not supposed to stop at Elmers End, neither, but they'll see you right.'

I thanked him profusely, and handed him a small token of my appreciation.

Fifteen minutes later I heard a distant whistle, and soon after a train pulled into the station in a cloud of steam and smoke. The porter went to speak with the driver and engineer, and I saw him pointing me out before gesticulating energetically, obviously recounting the juicier portions of my tale. Then he turned and beckoned, and I joined the men in the cab.

The driver and engineer wore overalls, much begrimed with coal dust and soot. We shook, and then one of them handed me a tattered rag to wipe my hand on. 'Just 'ang on over there,' said the driver, pointing out a spot at the rear of the cab. 'We'll 'ave you in Elmers End in two shakes of a lamb's tail, you see if we don't.'

Standing aboard the big, heavy train as it pulled out of the station, I felt invincible. Let the creature attack now, I thought. Let it confront the train head-on, and we'll see who survives *that* encounter!

The noise was immense, and there was no opportunity for conversation. I did not mind in the slightest, because my only thoughts were for a comfortable bed and few hours of peaceful, dream-free sleep.

It seemed like no time at all before the brakes squealed and the train came to a halt, stopping neatly beside a concrete platform. The sign proclaimed this to be Elmers End station, and I thanked the men profusely before dipping once again into my rapidly-diminishing funds. I consoled myself with the thought that I would not have to pay anyone for the last two miles of my journey, as I would be walking that part alone. Then I remembered my trunk, which would be delivered the next day, and I muttered under my breath as I thought of the payment that would also require.

I turned my back as the train departed the station, and was promptly enveloped in whirling clouds of steam, smoke and grit. By the time I opened my eyes, the train was vanishing around a bend in the track, the red tail-lights flickering once or twice before disappearing completely from view.

Silence descended upon me. It was dark, and somewhere nearby an owl hooted. With one hand on the dagger under my coat, I left the station and strode towards the high street, keeping to the shadows. Unlike Croydon, Elmers End was little more than a village, and it appeared everyone was tucked safely into their beds. I saw not a soul as I passed the blacked-out houses, with only the moonlight to guide me. Street lamps had not yet reached this part of the country, and in my dark clothes I was all but invisible.

Soon, cottages and roads gave way to fields and tracks. I lengthened my stride, for although I was weary to the very core of my being, I knew my journey was almost at an end.

I was only half a mile from home when the moon vanished behind gathering clouds, and soon after the weather added to my troubles. Rain fell in little more than a fine drizzle, but over time it drenched me as efficiently as a brief but heavy downpour.

By the time I reached my parents' street I was bedraggled, exhausted and all but done in. Therefore, you can imagine the lump that appeared in my throat when the front door was flung open and my mother enveloped me in a warm and welcoming hug. For a moment I was transported to my childhood, and I revelled in the brief respite from my trials and tribulations. Then I realised I was transferring half a rainstorm onto her person, and I broke the embrace and stood back.

'Oh Septimus,' said my mother, in her kindly, sympathetic voice. 'You are a sight!'

I had not seen my parents for some months now, and yet my mother looked exactly the same. A head shorter than myself, her greying hair was tied back in a bun, and warm smile was exactly as I remembered it. She was a portly, good-humoured woman, with rosy apple cheeks and a personality that spoke well of everyone, deserved or not. But she also had a core of solid steel, and took no nonsense from any quarter.

'I'm sorry about the late hour,' I said. 'My journey was eventful, to say the least.'

I took my coat off, hanging it from the stand in the hall, and then we entered the sitting room, where the embers of the evening fire were barely glowing in the grate. To my surprise, the only evidence of my father were his pipe and slippers.

'He went out to look for you hours ago,' explained my mother.

Shocked, I stared at her. Then I glanced towards the bay windows. They were curtained, but I could hear the rain outside, and worse, I could vividly recall the howls of the wounded creature. My father was out there? Alone? 'I must go to him,' I said quickly, and I dashed to the hall to put my coat back on.

'Septimus, do calm yourself,' said my mother, following me. 'Your father will be fine.'

'You don't understand!' I cried. 'There are...creatures in the woods. Things that...' my voice tailed off as I realised that revealing the full horror of the situation would not reassure my mother in the slightest.

'And what are we to do if you go to find him, and he returns in the meantime?' asked my mother. 'He will then have to tramp the countryside looking for you once more, and when you return and he does not, the whole sorry tale might repeat all night long.' She took the coat from me, shook it emphatically, and hung it up. 'No, you will take a seat and have a bowl of hot stew, for there is some left over from dinner. By the time you've finished your repast your father will be home safe and sound.'

There is the steel, I thought. I knew from long experience that arguing was pointless, and so I allowed myself to be led back to the sitting room. Here, I removed my shoes and stretched my feet to the fire, and soon after my mother placed a supper tray on my lap with the promised stew as well as a hunk of crusty bread. I was famished, having travelled the best part of the day and night, and I fell upon that meal like a starving prisoner.

'Slow down, else you'll choke yourself to death,' remarked my mother.

'Apologies.' I smiled up at her. 'It's good to be home.'

'And it's nice to have you home, but I don't want you leaving feet first so soon after arriving.'

I finished the rest of my meal in a more leisurely fashion, albeit still under her watchful eye, and then my mother brought seconds without my having asked.

'Does your landlady not feed you properly in London?' she asked. 'You're looking a little peaky.'

I had described this 'landlady' several times in my letters home, which, as I have already explained, owed more to the fiction of Verne and Dickens than the scientific accuracy of, say, Pasteur and Koch. Fortunately, I had based my fiction on reality, which made it easy to keep the facts straight. 'Mrs Fairacre provides ample food, although not up to your standards, of course. If I am looking a little pale, I assure you it's the result of my lengthy travels.' I glanced towards the window, for there was still no sign of my father. 'How long has he been gone?' I asked.

'He left after tea.'

'In which direction? Did he say?'

'Don't bother your head about it. You must get out of those damp clothes and into a warm dressing gown, and then you and I will sit before the fire and–'

She stopped at a commotion from the hall, then gave a cry of alarm as my father stumbled into the sitting room. A tall man, he was in a bad way, with bedraggled clothing splashed with mud and one hand pressed to the side of his face. 'Stanley!' cried my mother, rising from the armchair. 'Were you set upon? Are you injured?'

I too had sprung to my feet, for it seemed to me that my father must have encountered the same beast I had. If so, he was lucky to be alive!

'It's nothing,' said my father, waving us feebly away. 'Like a fool, I tripped in the darkness and fell into a stream.' Then he fastened me with his one good eye, the other being covered by his hand. 'Septimus, my boy!' he cried in delight. 'You made it safely!'

'Unlike you, you old clot,' growled my mother. 'Come! A hot bath before you catch your death, and I won't hear a word against it.'

I was temporarily forgotten as she all but dragged my father from the room, bustling him away against his protests. As he left the room I glanced down, and I felt my heart stop as I saw a pinkish stain spreading on the wet floorboards. Blood? Exactly how badly was he hurt?

I dashed into the hallway, catching sight of my father leaning heavily on my mother, who was helping him into the kitchen where there was, I knew, a large bathtub. 'Should I rouse a physician?' I called.

'Don't trouble yourself,' my mother replied. 'A few scratches won't put paid to your father.'

I was not convinced, as I could see further droplets of blood spreading on the puddles of water my father had left in his wake. But then my mother closed the door firmly behind her, and there was naught to do but return to the sitting room, there to await news.

17

When I awoke the next day it took me several minutes to recognise my surroundings. Then everything came flooding back. My mother had sent me to bed the night before, after finding me napping in front of the fire. She had still been warming a copper of water for my father's bath, and I only agreed to retire after she reassured me that he was not badly injured.

Upon reaching the spare room, which had once been mine, I had tumbled into bed and fallen into a deep, restful sleep.

Judging by the sunlight flooding through small gaps in the curtains, it was now close to midday. I felt the first stirrings of hunger, and then a sudden twinge of anxiety as I realised the village policeman might call on me at any moment. I had not done anything wrong, yet I felt a stab of guilt over the fate of the carriage driver, whom we had abandoned in the woods. One could argue that stumbling around in the dark with a wounded creature on the prowl might have led to more deaths, my own included, but in the bright light of day it would be hard to explain just how perilous the situation had been. The events had a hint of cowardice about them, and my only defence was that I had taken my cue from the far more capable lieutenant. If a seasoned military man called for retreat, who was I to argue?

I got up and donned my clothes, which had been laid out on a nearby armchair. They were dry and smelled clean and fresh, and with a fond smile I realised my mother must have brushed them down and aired them earlier that morning.

Then I remembered my father's injuries, and I opened my door and strode towards the kitchen, from whence I could hear voices.

'Septimus! Good morning, my son.'

I smiled at my father, who was seated at the kitchen table with a substantial bowl of porridge before him. 'Good morning, sir. How are you today?'

'Quite recovered, thank you.'

I noticed a mark high upon his cheek, somewhere between a graze and a bruise, and he laughed ruefully as he noticed my gaze. 'When I fell into the stream I made a hell of a splash,' he remarked. 'Almost put my damned back out, too!'

'Language,' cautioned my mother. She came over to peck me on the cheek, then directed me towards an empty place at the table. 'Sit yourself down, and I'll bring you some breakfast.'

'Thank you.' I saw a newspaper near my father's elbow, still folded in half. 'Anything of interest in the paper?' I asked him.

'Nothing to bother us,' he replied. 'Usual nonsense.'

'Any mention of an attack in the woods near Croydon?'

He frowned. 'What do you know about that?'

My mother also turned to study me, and I quailed under their questioning gaze. 'I–I was passing by,' I stammered, suddenly ten years old once more and struggling to explain the farmer's missing apples. 'The, er, police might come round to interview me.'

My mother tutted, shaking her head. 'The police! Whatever have you been up to now?'

'Let him be, Emma,' said my father gently. 'The lad's done nothing wrong, you know that.'

'But the police! There'll be gossip and rumours all over the village.'

'Let them talk. About the only thing they're fit for in any case.'

My father helped many of those in the village with their taxes, and few paid him on time, if at all. Fortunately, he kept the books for merchants and landowners, which was lucrative enough to support both himself and my mother. This was one of the reasons I'd moved to London, firstly to gain more experience, and second because a small village like West Wickham did not have enough work for *two* bookkeepers, and my father had no intention of retiring.

'Cecilie was asking after you the other day,' said my mother, changing the subject.

I must have looked alarmed, because my father smothered a sudden grin. As I have already stated, Cecilie Carmichael was the other reason I'd moved to London. Not her, exactly, as much as the match my mother hoped to foster between us. Cecilie's family was one of my father's most important clients, and on paper it would be a convenient marriage for both parties. Cecilie would have a professional young gentleman for a husband, and I would be marrying a rung or two above my own station, with a view to a management position in her family's business.

Unfortunately, one did not marry a piece of paper but rather a living, breathing human, and Cecilie was not a patch on Roberta. She was a decent sort, friendly and kind, but she lacked a certain spark. Roberta was fiery and unpredictable by comparison, and all the more interesting for it.

If I was completely honest with myself, there was another, all-too-human element to consider. One always desired the things that were just out of reach, rather than being content with those more easily obtained. Imagine my bitterness and disappointment should I marry poor Cecilie, only to have Roberta reveal that she would have accepted a proposal had I but asked her, her father's wishes notwithstanding.

'Penny for your thoughts,' said my father, with a mischievous grin. He already knew upon which lines I was thinking, and with my mother nearby he also knew I could not reveal them.

'Let us make it a sovereign and I'll tell you,' I said, with a grin of my own.

'That's too rich for my blood.'

'Then I shall keep my secrets,' I remarked, and I devoted myself to the bowl of steaming hot porridge before me. Once I had scraped the bowl clean I looked around for more, the first helping barely having touched my appetite, but my mother shook her head.

'We've been invited to high tea with the Carmichaels,' she said.

I suppressed a groan. Mr Carmichael, Cecilie's father, was a bombastic windbag who would venture an opinion on any subject matter, however modest his knowledge of the topic. He would advise farmers on the tilling of their land, my father on the matter of bookkeeping, and politicians everywhere on the subject of ruling the country, while his wife was a long-suffering woman who barely got a word in edgeways.

I hope, therefore, you can understand my lack of enthusiasm. I suspected the elder Carmichael would take me aside at some point to corner me in his study, where, spluttering in a choking fog of cigar smoke, he would demand I reveal my intentions towards his daughter.

'At what time are they expecting us?' I asked casually.

'Four o'clock.'

I resolved to make an appointment with the village constable for ten to the hour, so that my interview, when it ran over, would give me an excuse to be late. So late, in fact, that it was barely worth attending the tea at all. Then another thought hit me, and I smiled to myself. If I chose the moment well, I could reveal before all comers that I had just been questioned by the police, and the Carmichaels would have a fit. It would not put them off forever, but might afford me a little breathing space before I returned to London a free man.

Then came a knock at the door, revealing a visitor who ruined my carefully thought out plans.

My father returned to the kitchen with the village constable in tow, resuming his place at the table while the tall young man stood awkwardly nearby. I knew Sam Tyler well, having spent several years at school with him, and indeed, we'd both been responsible for many stolen apples over the years. Not that he'd admit it these days, of course. Not without thumbscrews.

He nodded to my mother, who gave him a grim, forbidding look, then begged leave to sit down. 'Sep, it's about this attack in the woods,' he said. 'The Croydon police asked me to follow up for them.'

'I know. I gave them my address, and they said you'd be round to interview me.'

'What can you tell me?' He took out a lead pencil and a notebook. 'All the details, mind, but not too fast eh?'

'There's not much to tell. I was travelling by carriage with Lieutenant Bertram Ware and his wife, after the three of us missed our connecting train. On the way to Croydon, from Thornton Heath, we were set upon by a wild creature of some kind.'

Tyler scribbled in his notebook. 'Did you see it?'

I nodded.

'How close?'

'As close as you're sitting now.'

Tyler blanched. 'In that case, you're lucky to be alive!'

I wished he'd keep these asides to himself, as he would only worry my parents needlessly. 'I was armed with a dagger, and the lieutenant had his sword. We drove the creature off, but unfortunately we could find no sign of our driver.' I hesitated. 'He was taken in the original attack.'

'Taken?' demanded Tyler. 'How big was this wild animal?'

'Taller than you or I. Muscled like a circus strongman. As hairy as a wolf, and with snout and fangs to match. Its eyes blazed with rage, and yet there was intelligence and cunning also.'

My mother gasped, and I turned to see her staring at me in horror. 'You said nothing of this last night!'

'Father was missing, and I did not mean to worry you,' I said evenly. Then I noticed Tyler had stopped writing. 'Are you not taking notes?'

'I can't write that nonsense down,' he said, defensively. 'The sarge would have my guts if I went back with a horror tale that might have been penned by Shelley herself! Why, from the way you describe it, you might have been attacked by a circus bear.'

'You asked for all the details,' I pointed out.

'How dark was it in the woods?'

'The moon was full.'

'And this Lieutenant Ware will back you up?'

'He was rushing to meet his ship, which was due to sail on the tide. The navy will know where he is, of course.'

Tyler said nothing, and I guessed what he was thinking. The police were very much newcomers on the scene, while the Royal Navy had centuries of tradition and proud service on their side. Thus, cooperation was unlikely.

For the next few minutes I recounted the events in full, elaborating where possible. When I got to the fight, and the way I'd defended myself with my dagger, Tyler whistled. 'That took guts.'

'I was fighting for my life,' I said quietly. Then I covered the rest of the tale, including reporting to the Croydon police station.

'So, broadly speaking...' began Tyler. 'Your carriage was attacked in the woods, you fought off one of the assailants who you describe as a large, hirsute fellow, and then you hunted for the driver who you suspected was wounded, or deceased. Unfortunately, in the darkness, you could not find him, and fearing for Mrs Ware's safety, you drove the carriage to Croydon yourself.'

I nodded. The summary bore little semblance to my tale, but there was no point pounding the table with my fist and raising my voice. After all, the reason I was visiting West Wickham in the first place was because a vicious monster was on the loose and the police refused to accept my—or more accurately, Roberta's—help with the case. Let the police hunt their 'hirsute fellow' as much as they liked, for in the meantime I would be free to track and capture the real culprit myself.

'Well, I think that's everything,' said Tyler, getting to his feet. 'I'm glad you're all right, Sep. You had a narrow escape, my friend.'

I showed him to the door, and upon my return I faced a battery of accusing looks from my parents. 'Please!' I exclaimed, hands raised. 'I have endured the most terrible events, and I wish to forget them. I have done my duty and shared the details with the police, and you heard everything that happened. Now I just want to put everything behind me, so that I might enjoy the rest of my stay.'

My parents exchanged a glance, and then my mother nodded. 'Very well. The matter is closed. Now, do you have suitable clothing for tea this afternoon, or would you like to borrow something of your father's?'

'My trunk will be arriving soon, and it contains everything I shall need.'

'In that case, you can spend an hour chopping wood for the fire. The exercise and fresh air will do you good.'

I knew this was meant to be a punishment of sorts, but once outside, axe in hand, I found the task enjoyable. The *thunk* of the heavy axe, the splitting and stacking of the blocks, and the feel of the sunshine on my back served to clear my mind, and for the first time since leaving London I felt a certain spring in my step.

Even the forthcoming tea with the Carmichaels did not sour my mood. After all, they could hardly bind me hand and foot and carry me into a church to be married. I would just have to let it be known that I was still making my own way in the world, and was not ready for family responsibilities.

On that promising thought I resumed my chore, chopping wood until my arms ached.

18

My trunk arrived barely thirty minutes before we were due at the Carmichaels', and my father helped carry it to my room. He winced with pain as he picked it up, and again when he set it down, and I couldn't help noticing his stiff, awkward movements. He shook these irritants off without comment, though, and seemed in good spirits as he left me to unpack.

Unlocking my trunk, I proceeded to hang my clothes and set three dozen thick, leather-bound books on the shelf in the wardrobe. Most had obscure, wordy titles, some in Latin, and I wondered whether any of them would help me track and capture the beast I'd encountered in the woods. The thought of confronting the creature again, let alone trying to subdue it, made my heart beat faster. How could I, a lowly bookkeeper, hope to defeat such a monster with nothing more than dusty old books and a dagger?

But before I faced that life-threatening event I knew I must confront another: high tea at the Carmichaels'.

I turned to survey the bundles of cloth still sitting in my trunk. Roberta had packed several pieces of equipment, carefully wrapping each one before placing them inside, and as yet I had no idea what she might have supplied me with. I hoped for a shotgun, or a small cannon, but suspected they might be lures or traps of some kind. I only hoped they weren't lanterns and magnifying lenses with which to illuminate and read the contents of the books.

I hefted one of the parcels, then, on a whim, unwrapped it. To my horror, I found myself staring down at the metal jar engraved with curious symbols...the very same jar with which Roberta had trapped the glowing sprites in the warehouse the previous day. What madness possessed her to wrap it up and pack it into my trunk? And what was I supposed to *do* with the things? Slowly, I turned to stare at the other parcels. Were they just as dangerous as this one? Or were they even worse?

Quickly, I wrapped the jar and placed it back in the trunk. I could not afford to inspect the rest of the items then, as I would barely have time to dress before we departed for the Carmichaels' place. They lived at the top of the village, on a hill near the church, and it was a good ten minute walk at the best of times. With my father in pain, I guessed it would take longer.

So, I locked my trunk, checking twice to make sure it was absolutely secure, then donned a suitable outfit. It consisted of a tweed jacket and matching trousers, and it had been a favourite of mine before moving to London. There, I'd had little opportunity to wear it, dressed as I usually was in more businesslike attire, but now it was like encountering an old friend.

By the time I slipped on a pair of brogues and ran a comb through my hair, I could hear my mother calling. After a final look at my trunk with its dangerous contents, I left my room and pulled the door to behind me.

There were polite smiles all round as the Carmichaels' maid showed us into a large, sunlit drawing room. Mr Carmichael was a tall cadaverous fellow with short, iron-grey hair and old-fashioned mutton-chop sideburns. He had a piercing, authoritative gaze and his voice was a deep bass that carried easily. His lady wife was a short, slender woman who disguised her unbending will behind a mousey, nondescript appearance. As for Cecilie, she had bloomed since I'd last seen her, and she looked radiant in an expensive dress. Her hair was made up in the latest fashion, and she met my eye with a level, unwavering gaze. In those eyes I caught an echo of her parents' attributes, with her mother's will and her father's self-confidence, and my heart sank. It was bad enough battling Cecilie's parents, but now I faced a third opponent, equally formidable.

As we stood there, exchanging pleasantries, it seemed to me that my fate was all but sealed.

'Cecilie, you simply must show Septimus around the gardens,' said Mrs Carmichael, the moment my parents were seated on the overstuffed sofa. I was on the point of sitting down myself, but stood again as Cecilie approached me, one arm outstretched. Politely, I crooked my elbow, and she linked her arm through mine, patting my hand. She stood so close I could smell her expensive perfume, and at that moment I wished with all my heart that Roberta would bestow me with similar attention. Then I chided myself, for I was determined to be a polite and attentive companion to Cecilie during my visit. I may yearn for another, but that did not give me the right to sulk, nor to act like a boorish cad. So, I smiled warmly and indicated the french doors nearby. 'Shall we?'

'I'd be delighted,' breathed Cecilie.

Once outside, strolling across the manicured lawns in the glorious afternoon sunshine, I have to admit that I felt a romantic stirring. Cecilie spoke brightly of the plants and flowers, pausing so that I might admire one glorious display after another, and the heady scent from the blooms combined with her happy chatter infused me with a feeling of euphoria. In that moment I knew we could be happy together, raising a family and eventually living in a magnificent house such as this, with gardens and flowers and barely a care in the world.

'Do you remember the Hall sisters of Ravenswood house?' Cecilie asked me suddenly.

I did indeed. The two spinsters lived alone in the fabulous residence, although recently it had fallen on hard times. I used to pass the house regularly before I moved to London, and it had been depressing to see it gradually overtaken by neglect. I guessed the sisters would be in their late fifties by now, and perhaps not as energetic as they'd once been. 'Are they still in good health?' I enquired.

'Oh yes, I'm sure they'll live forever. But there's news, Septimus! Recently they opened the house to guests, most likely to make ends meet, and there's someone staying there at this very moment. I have yet to find out much about this person, but they too have travelled down from London. They might have news of the latest fashions, or plays they've seen, or...'

I smiled to myself as she continued to speculate, amused at the excitement caused by little more than the arrival of a stranger. In a small town like West Wickham, such an event was headline news indeed. Then Cecilie mentioned something that wiped the smile from my face.

'–of course, both of them have been a little bit doolally ever since they lost their poor dear father in that horrible murder. It was before we were born, but mother and father discuss it still, especially with that poor man killed just last week in a similar fashion.'

I stopped and faced her. 'Cecilie, wait! Are you saying old Mr

Hall was murdered?'

'Oh yes. It was hushed up at the time, though.' She shuddered delicately, but I could see the excitement in her eyes. 'They said wild animals attacked the corpse,' she whispered, gazing around her as though said wild animals might overhear her. 'I heard daddy talking to Sam Tyler a few nights ago, and they said old Mr Hall was torn limb from limb!' she finished, with some relish. 'And the man in the woods ended up exactly the same way!'

I knew exactly how the man in the woods had ended up, because the photographs gave me nightmares still. But this piece of information about Mr Hall was extraordinary, because it meant the evil creature I'd confronted might be far older than I guessed. What if it had lived in the area for a generation or more, taking victims without warning? Were there parish records I might peruse? Police files, perhaps? In that instant I vowed to quiz Sam Tyler, the local policeman. During my interview earlier that day he'd scoffed at the idea of a monster, and had adapted my story to fit some bland official version. But Tyler loved a drink or three, and I knew I might loosen his lips with the aid of a few pints at the inn.

'What are you thinking?' asked Cecilie. 'You are uncommonly quiet today.'

I should have kept quiet and said nothing. I should have, but Cecilie had fastened me with such an adoring gaze that I was quite incapable of resisting. Her eyes shone in the sunlight, and her breathless excitement was infectious. In my defence, whenever I recounted a tale of derring-do for Roberta's benefit, she would usually call me a headstrong fool and point out where I'd gone wrong. It was refreshing to have a rapt, attentive audience, and I'm afraid I played to that audience without shame or restraint. 'I fought the very same monster last night,' I said modestly. 'We were attacked in the woods near Croydon, and I stabbed the beast twice with my dagger.'

The effect on Cecilie was even greater than I expected. 'Oh my!' she exclaimed, putting a hand to her mouth. Her eyes were as round as saucers, and a pink flush appeared upon her cheeks.

Much gratified, and feeling ten feet tall, I continued in a similar vein. 'The creature took our driver, who has yet to be found,' I said. 'We followed a trail of blood into the woods, but lost it in the darkness. In the end, I was forced to drive the carriage to safety myself.'

'Gosh,' breathed Cecilie. She was standing close, her face tilted up to mine, and she looked delectable in her slim-waisted dress. I felt a yearning to put my arms around her and draw her close, and I don't know what might have happened if we had not been interrupted by the tinkle of a bell, calling us to tea. I only know that both sets of parents exchanged knowing glances as we entered the drawing room. I cannot speak to my own expression, but Cecilie's bright eyes and flushed cheeks spoke volumes.

'Here come the lovebirds!' exclaimed Mrs Carmichael. 'Come, you two. Have a seat together, and pray don't let us intrude.'

Inwardly, I cursed my foolishness. A few moments in the sunshine and a little female attention had all but undone my resolve. Thinking back on the encounter, I wondered whether Cecilie hadn't been a little *too* attentive, as though she'd been casting bait on the waters to snare her prize fish. The perfume, the expensive dress, her immaculate appearance...were they all props in a theatre production?

I accepted a cup of tea and a toasted crumpet, buttering the latter in silence with my head bowed. I would be the first to admit I am far from a man of the world, with little experience in the ways of women. Witness the way in which Roberta could bend me to her will, and if that weren't evidence enough, I now had an embarrassing encounter with Cecilie to add to my catalogue. How could I have boasted so, especially when I was supposed to dissuade her from pursuing me?

I groaned at my idiocy, the sound a little louder than I intended. I looked up to see my mother frowning at me. 'My apologies,' I said. 'My arm aches, and it gave a twinge.'

'Septimus was in a fight!' proclaimed Cecilie.

'Was he now,' said her mother, her expression hardening all of a sudden. 'Is this a common occurrence?'

I was tempted to say yes, but my own mother would never forgive me.

'His carriage was set upon in the woods last night! He fought off the attacker all by himself, stabbing them again and again with his knife!'

Mr and Mrs Carmichael exchanged a glance, volumes passing between them with that single look, and I realised the issue of my marriage to Cecilie might have just resolved itself. Let me just state that they did not appear to be thrilled at my bravery, rather they were horrified that their daughter might be partnered with a young man who indulged in common brawls at the drop of a hat.

'He was attacked without warning,' said my mother stoutly. 'Of course he defended himself!'

'Did you get a good look at this attacker?' asked Mr Carmichael. He was casually studying his teacup, but as he asked the question his deep, intense gaze met mine.

I felt the room closing in on me, and all of a sudden the bright sunshine spilling through the french windows appeared to dim. The gaze was hypnotic, intense, and I struggled to voice a reply. 'N–no, not really,' I said. 'It was dark, but I'd say he was a large fellow.'

'And you stabbed him? Twice, right in the back?'

'Yes sir.'

'Was he armed?'

I looked around the table. How could I mention the wolfish fangs? The claws? I would be laughed out of the drawing room, if not despatched to the nearest lunatic asylum. 'It was dark,' I repeated lamely.

Mr Carmichael sniffed. 'Doesn't sound a fair fight to me. Most likely you attacked some tramp who was going about his business. You'd better hope he survived, or the police will be after you for murder. As it is, there might be reparations.'

'We were attacked in the woods,' I said, my voice low. My parents were staring at me, and I felt the heat in my face. 'I gave a good account of myself, and my actions helped save the life of a lieutenant in the Royal Navy. His report will confirm my version of the events, and I assure you there will be no mention of tramps going about their business.'

'That may be so, but let me give you some advice,' said Mr Carmichael pompously. 'Forget all about this attack, and in future keep such wild tales to yourself. People will think ill of you, believe me, and once a poor reputation is gained it's hard to shake.'

My father opened his mouth to protest, but my mother silenced him with a glance. Then, as though nothing had happened, my parents spent the next hour exchanging pleasantries with the Carmichaels. I glowered in silence, while poor Cecilie endured ten minutes or so before excusing herself with a headache. She did not look at me as she left, her enthusiasm for my heroics having been quenched by her father's version of events.

Eventually the afternoon drew to a close, and we uttered pleasantries before departing.

'Well,' said my mother, the moment we were out of earshot. 'Septimus, if I thought you did that on purpose I swear I'll–'

'Oh, leave the boy alone,' growled my father. 'Can't you see the old devil took against Septimus of his own accord? You and Mrs Carmichael can plot and scheme all you like, but–'

'Plot and scheme?' protested my mother. 'You saw them together, Stanley! They're made for each other, and they'd be so happy.'

The argument continued, but I wasn't paying attention. During tea, something had been troubling me, and all of a sudden it struck me like a bolt of lightning. Mr Carmichael had asked me to confirm whether I'd stabbed the creature twice in the back, but I had not mentioned the number of times the dagger had gone in, nor the location of my attacks.

So how had he known?

19

As we approached my parents' house I realised they had stopped speaking to each other. I myself was lost in thought, and only looked up when I heard my mother exclaim in surprise.

'Who do you think that is?' she asked.

She was pointing west, in the direction of Station Road and the distant Ravenswood House where the Hall sisters lived. I squinted into the setting sun, and just made out a young woman in a colourful print dress, striding along with a wicker shopping basket dangling from one arm. Her dark hair was tied up in a loose bun, and she strode along in a most purposeful manner.

'She's not a local,' said my mother, who knew everyone in West Wickham by name.

Suddenly I remembered. 'Cecilie told me the Halls are taking in paid guests. Perhaps she's staying there.'

My mother frowned, although I was not sure whether it was the mention of Cecilie or the fact the Halls had fallen on hard times. 'A young woman on her own like that,' she muttered. 'It wouldn't happen in my day! These modern girls are just too much with all their gadding about, I swear.'

'She looks happy to me,' I said.

In return, I got another frown.

The young woman vanished from sight, and my father unlocked our front door, holding it open for my mother. She swept inside, and, after an apologetic look in my direction, my father followed. I went straight to my room, because now, at last, I could make a start on my investigation. I would be returning to London on Sunday night, just two days hence, and could ill afford to waste time on high teas, wood chopping or idle chat about guests who may or may not be staying with the Hall sisters.

The first order of business was to write down everything I'd learned so far. I started with a description of the beast, reliving the confrontation and the subsequent fight so that I might recall every detail. The pen scratched on the page as I wrote furiously, barely pausing to think.

Next I made a note about the much older murder, when Mr Hall from Ravenswood had apparently fallen to the beast. Alongside I jotted Sam Tyler's name, complete with question mark. The matter needed investigating.

And speaking of the police...why had Tyler scoffed at my tale, when Inspector Cox's report into the recent murder openly speculated on animal bites and teeth marks? It was almost as though the London police were investigating a completely different case. Or rather, the local police were keen to play down the stranger, less-believable aspects of these attacks. I wrote 'Cover up' and added two question marks, underlining the whole.

Next I detailed my conversation with Mr Carmichael, who had somehow learned of the precise blows I had landed on the vicious creature. I went back to my conversation with Tyler earlier that day, recalling as much as I was able, but I could not remember whether I had told him about stabbing the monster twice in the back. Even so, Carmichael was showing an uncommon interest in the case, especially if he was reading official police reports on the matter. Although to be fair he *was* something important on the village council, as my mother never hesitated to remind me.

I continued with my labours, and ten minutes later I was satisfied I'd written down all the salient facts.

Putting away the pen and paper, I glanced towards the wardrobe, and then the locked chest. My next task was to learn what I could of this creature, so that I might track it. For that I would need the books. And once I had the knowledge I needed, I could only hope that Roberta's equipment included a means of attracting the beast, and then trapping it.

Here I paused. I could read books all night, for they were my lifeblood, but when it came to laying snares and trapping vicious, murderous creatures I would be the first to admit I was out of my depth. In Wild West novels, the town sheriff would gather a posse who would set off as one to round up some evildoer or other. A large group of allies sounded like the ideal solution to me, but my father was clearly in pain and Sam Tyler had not believed a word of my tale. Mr Carmichael had barely spoken to me after tea, and I could not imagine Cecilie or her mother traipsing through the woods with pitchforks and flaming torches. That left my mother, and she, like Carmichael, was barely speaking to me.

They say that you should approach a large task by breaking it into smaller ones. For the time being I would concentrate on research, which should result in a plan for tracking or luring the creature. Only then would I think about the final part of the plan, which also happened to be the most challenging and dangerous: capturing and subduing the hellish beast.

By dinner time I'd read several dozen passages on the subject of supernatural monsters, and they left me with a firm conviction. Should I face this creature on my own, underprepared and armed with little more than a dagger, the outcome was inevitable: a lonely, gruesome and very painful death.

There was one ray of light, which was a treatise on the effects of silver upon such creatures. Apparently a small amount would cause untold pain, even burns to the flesh, and all of a sudden I remembered the monster's reaction when struck in the face by the lieutenant's hip flask. The lieutenant's *silver* hip flask. There had indeed been a smell of burning, although at the time I had not understood the cause, nor felt an overwhelming need to approach the creature so that I might inspect its wounds more closely. In fact, I'd felt an overwhelming need to flee in the opposite direction.

Encouraged by my findings, my mood improved considerably. Silver would be easier to obtain than, say, gold, and if the creature were vulnerable to an ordinary hip flask, imagine how it might react to a weapon fashioned from the metal? I did not have the first idea how to forge something from silver, but Roberta and the Professor were both experts, and given my evidence, might they not return to West Wickham with me a week or so hence?

I started at the sound of the dinner gong, and jumped up to return my books and close the wardrobe door. After checking my appearance in the small, oval mirror on the dressing table I left my room and strode along the hall to the dining room.

On the way I heard voices raised in conversation, but they were coming from the sitting room. I looked in, and was surprised to see my parents standing with their backs to the fire, smiling down at a visitor who was sitting in a nearby armchair. The armchair faced away from me, and all I could see of the visitor was the top of her head, her long black hair tied up into a loose bun. As I got closer I noticed the floral print dress, now with the addition of a light woollen cardigan, and I released this must be the young woman staying at Ravenswood.

'Ah, Septimus,' said my mother, seemingly recovered from her bad temper. 'Let me introduce Isabella Makepeace, who is staying in the village for a few days. She was kind enough to bring a basket of eggs and garden vegetables from the manor.'

'Oh, rest assured the gifts were compliments of the Hall sisters,' said the woman, before rising and turning to meet me.

The world tilted on its axis, and I could only smile foolishly as I shook the woman's hand. Blood thundered in my ears, and it was impossible to make out a single word being said.

Let me be clear. These were not the symptoms of some romantic thunderbolt, the likes of which you may have read about in penny dreadfuls. I was neither smitten nor tongue-tied by wild beauty.

No, I was shocked beyond measure because the young lady shaking my hand, the lady my mother had introduced as one Isabella Makepeace, the young lady staying at Ravenswood–

–was none other than Roberta Twickham.

20

'Now then Septimus, there's no need to stare,' said my father, much amused at my open-mouthed, slack-jawed expression. 'I'm sure you've seen many a pretty lass in London.'

Roberta was facing me with her back to my parents, and having given me a polite smile and a handshake, she now closed one eye in a wink. Then, as though she were born to the stage, she turned away and continued to charm my parents. 'It's the old house, you see,' she was saying. 'Ravenswood has seen some famous names over the years, and I'm keen to write its history. Why, Pitt himself was a resident once!'

I realised my mouth still hung open, and I closed it with a snap.

'It has a rich history, yes,' said my mother. 'But I fail to see why–'

'Oh, the reason for my calling upon you is twofold,' continued Roberta. 'The sisters are in quite a muddle with their accounts, and they told me you have a son who dabbles in that line. I happened to be passing, and I thought I'd drop in and ask for his assistance on their behalf.'

Dabbles! Of all the cheek!

'Well yes,' said my mother. 'Septimus there is a learned bookkeeper, and he happens to be visiting at this very moment. But my husband is a bookkeeper also, and in fact, it's my husband who looks after the books for–'

'Dear,' interrupted my father, and I noticed a mischievous twinkle in his eye. 'I think Septimus is the man for this particular job. I suspect it's along the lines of a volunteer effort.'

My mother eyed me thoughtfully, then studied Roberta. In particular she looked down at Roberta's hand, noting the lack of a wedding band. I could all but hear my mother's thoughts, for poor darling Cecilie wasn't a patch on Roberta, and my mother had already caught me staring so hard at Roberta that my eyes were threatening to fall out of my head. Of course, the stares I'd been directing at Roberta weren't for the reason my mother thought they were, but nevertheless she sensed something in the air. Thus, she was unwilling to let me accompany Roberta. On the other hand, she was a kindly soul, and she'd known the Hall sisters her entire life. With the tiniest of sighs, she relented. 'Septimus will be glad to help the sisters out, my dear.'

'That is good news indeed,' declared Roberta. 'It's a fair walk to the manor, and this basket is heavier than I thought.'

My mother eyed Roberta's sturdy frame, then the near-empty basket. It contained a handful of items, and could have been carried easily by a child of three. 'We were just sitting down to our evening meal,' she said. 'Perhaps tomorrow?'

'Emma, for shame!' said my father, again with that mischievous glint. 'Miss Makepeace must stay for supper, and if there isn't enough to go around she can have my share. I am still full after the splendid repast at the Carmichaels'.'

'Our son is to marry Cecilie, their daughter,' my mother explained to Roberta. 'It's all but arranged.'

I thought Roberta would be shocked, but she took this earth-shattering news in her stride. Indeed, she appeared to be amused by it. 'How marvellous,' she remarked. 'Will it be a big church wedding?'

'We're not that far along yet,' said my mother.

'Oh? How far along *is* Ce–'

'It was warm today wasn't it?' I said, desperately cutting Roberta off. During a recent war on the continent both sides had employed hand grenades, which were small bombs pitched amongst the enemy so as to cause as much damage as possible. Now, it seemed, Roberta was trying to achieve the same effect with a few well-chosen words. To ward off the inevitable explosion, I prattled aimlessly about the weather.

It seemed to work, because after a few pleasantries we moved to the dining room, where my parents' part-time cook served a delicious dinner of pork sausages, mashed potato and green beans with gravy. Roberta behaved herself during the meal, conversing on a wide range of subjects with which I had no idea she was familiar, from recent theatre productions to politics and everything in between.

My father particularly enjoyed the conversation, and under any other circumstances I would have been overjoyed to see them getting along so well. My mother tended towards silence, casting glances first at Roberta, then at me, and then at Roberta again. For my part, I held my tongue and concentrated on the excellent food, determined to avoid any suggestion that Roberta and I were already known to one another.

After dessert, Roberta regaled us with a story about a well-known author, who had imbibed a little too much and fallen headlong into the Thames, only to be fished out with a boathook. My father roared with laughter, and I even saw my mother smiling warmly.

The meal was a great success, and the contrast with high tea at the Carmichaels' could not have been more stark. Roberta was lively, friendly and intelligent, and she had clearly made a favourable impression upon my parents. As I watched her smiling and laughing at my parents' dining table, I imagined future meals, with the four of us gathered under one roof as a family, and I wished with all my heart that one day it might be so.

'Oh, look at the time!' exclaimed Roberta, having spied the clock on the mantelpiece. 'I must be on my way, but thank you so much for a wonderful dinner.'

My father glanced towards the window. 'It's getting dark,' he said. 'Septimus, will you walk the young lady home?'

'Septimus can help with the dishes,' said my mother, giving him a meaningful glance. 'There's no need for him to trouble the sisters, not at this hour.'

'Nonsense,' said my father. 'I'll do the dishes. The poor lad has hardly spoken all evening, and I'm sure he can use some fresh air. Anyway, we cannot send this young woman out alone, not after recent events.'

'Ooh!' said Roberta, in mock surprise. 'What recent events?'

'Septimus will tell you on the way.' My father grinned at me. 'If he can find his voice, that is.'

Roberta and I left the house together, and I swear the curtains twitched as my mother watched over us. I said nothing until we'd gone fifty yards or more, lest we were overheard, and then I let everything out. 'What are you playing at?' I demanded. 'What addle-brained insanity drove you to fool my parents into–'

'Nice to see you too, Septimus darling,' said Roberta calmly.

'But your sick friend!' I protested. 'You were catching a train to the north!'

'Have you *seen* the north?' asked Roberta mildly. 'Anyway, it wasn't a sick friend, it was my friend's sick mother.'

'But nobody was sick!'

'They might very well be,' Roberta pointed out. 'But if they are, they didn't tell me about it.'

'But the lies! The subterfuge! You said you had a letter!'

'A letter as genuine as your course on modern accounting methods,' she said.

A thought occurred to me, and I came to a sudden stop. 'Your *father!*' I said, staring at her in wide-eyed horror. 'If he learns of this, he'll suspect–'

'Don't worry, Septimus. I'll tell him you're getting married.'

'You will do no such thing,' I declared hotly. 'Just because my mother and the Carmichaels are plotting my future, it does not follow that I will go along with it.'

'Is she pretty?' Roberta asked me.

I was still facing her, and in the gathering dusk I saw a change come over her expression. Previously confident, teasing, she now looked vulnerable, and I moved quickly to reassure her. 'Roberta, I have no interest in Cecilie Carmichael. You may have that in writing if you wish.'

The instant passed, and the expression was gone. 'No thank you. I've had enough of letters for the time being.' Abruptly, she changed the subject. 'Have you discovered anything about the creature?'

That's when I realised she had not yet heard of my encounter. She walked in silence as I revealed the events of the previous night, and when I'd finished she was silent a while longer. Eventually we reached the rusty, slightly skewed metal gates leading to Ravenswood House, and I came to a halt. 'Don't you have anything to say?' I asked her.

'Yes, Septimus, I do. First, you're lucky I'm here, because together we shall be more than a match for this beast.' All of a sudden, she leaned in and kissed me on the cheek. Before withdrawing she whispered in my ear, her breath warm on my neck. 'Second, my dear, I'm very *very* glad you survived.'

Then she took the basket from my hand, turned away and strode up the drive towards the house.

I watched her go, dazed, and once she was out of sight I turned and walked home. My heart sang the whole way, but as I opened the front door, still floating on a cloud of euphoria, I encountered an opponent almost as dangerous as the murderous creature of the night before: my very inquisitive mother.

I had barely closed the front door behind me when I was met by my parents. My father appeared to be in good humour, but it was clear my mother had something on her mind.

'Septimus, dear,' she began. 'You know I keep all your letters, don't you?'

'Do you, mother?'

She brandished a handful. 'Indeed. And barely a week ago you repeated a tale that your good friend Robert told you at work. Now let me see...'

My heart sank as she leafed through the close-written pages. The author-falling-in-the-river story! Roberta had told it at dinner, but in one of my letters I had ascribed it to Robert, my fictional co-worker with the war injury and the walking-stick. 'Mother, there's no need to—'

'Ah, here it is.' My mother read silently, then looked up at me in triumph. 'As I thought, it's identical in every particular. Well dear? Would you care to explain?'

'He *is* a very famous author,' I said lamely. 'The story was widely reported.'

'Septimus!' growled my mother.

I realised the game was up, but that did not mean I had to reveal all my secrets. 'I'm sorry to have deceived you, mother. Yes, Robert is a fiction, but I was trying to spare your feelings. I know you wish to pair me with Cecilie, and I knew you would be concerned if I told you I worked alongside a charming young woman such as Ro–, I mean…Isabella.'

'Is there anything between you?' asked my mother. 'If so, it would be wicked to let Cecilie believe otherwise.'

I flushed as I recalled the way Roberta had kissed my cheek and whispered in my ear. 'We are not involved romantically.'

'But you wish to be?'

Mutely, I nodded.

Suddenly, my mother took me in her arms, enfolding me in a warm hug. 'Septimus, my dear, there was no need for deception. Above all else, I want you to be happy.' She stood back, her hands at my shoulders, holding my gaze. She still clutched the letters, and they rustled against my coat. 'A marriage to Cecilie would have improved your position, but what good is money if you spend the rest of your life pining for another? You must follow your heart, Septimus, no matter where it might lead you.'

I admit I was quite overcome, both by the hug and the words.

Nearby, my father cleared his throat. 'The Carmichaels are stuck-up toffs,' he muttered. 'You're well out of it, son.'

'Stanley!' protested my mother.

'Come, Emma. You know it's true.'

'Well, perhaps a little,' allowed my mother. 'But enough of this. After all these twists and turns I'm in need of a strong cup of tea. Goodnight Septimus, and I pray you sleep well.'

'Good night, mother.'

I went to follow, but my father stopped me. He stood in his shirtsleeves, having removed his coat after dinner, and I realised he wanted to say something out of earshot of my mother.

'Isabella is a fine young woman,' he began.

'I am in complete agreement.'

'And she works alongside you, at the bookkeeping firm?'

'She works with me, yes.'

'I see.' My father was no fool, and he spotted the omission. 'It's lucky your mother was set on uncovering the truth about your friend Isabella, and did not enquire further as to your employment status.' He hesitated. 'I do not know what exactly you are doing in London, and as long as it's legal and above-board, it's none of my business. Just do me one favour. Assure me you have enough money, and that you are eating well and taking care of yourself.'

This was a long speech for my father, and I was touched. 'Sir, I promise you, I am gainfully employed. As to money and the rest, I have more than I need.'

He smiled, reassured by my words. And then the smile broadened. 'About Isabella...I'm no expert in these matters, my son, but I would say she likes you. She likes you a great deal.'

I reddened.

'But she'll keep you on your toes, that one. Mark my words.'

And with this parting advice, he gave me a hug. It had been many years since he'd shown such affection, and I was moved by the gesture. In fact, it was so many years that I had not realised I was now taller than he was, and as we hugged I happened to look down. Imagine my surprise when I saw a spot of fresh blood on the back of his shirt, seeping through the fabric at the shoulder. I stepped back, looking at him in concern. 'Father, you're bleeding!'

He winced. 'When I fell into the stream last night, there was broken glass from a bottle some fool had discarded. The cut was a deep one, but your mother patched me up.'

'Are you sure? If it–'

'I will go to her now and ask for a fresh poultice. Believe me, Septimus, it will heal in no time.'

He bid me goodnight and left before I could protest further. As he strode down the hall I could see the small patch of blood like a rose bloom in a field of snow, and I vowed to call a physician the very next morning if he did not report an improvement in his condition.

I awoke the next morning from a most disturbing dream. In it, the woods had been illuminated by the light of numerous flaming torches, and a group of familiar people had gathered in a clearing. Overhead, the moon shone with a baleful, forbidding light.

Amongst those gathered were my parents, the Carmichaels, Roberta and Cecilie, and a mysterious figure in a hooded cloak. They stood in a rough circle around me, holding their torches aloft whilst chanting in unison in some foreign tongue.

As for myself, I was dressed in a flimsy nightgown, with bare feet and legs. The ground was cold and wet, and when I looked down I discovered to my horror that I was slowly sinking into a muddy bog. Already the slime had reached my knees, and without help I knew I would soon be dead.

I reached out to those around me, but my mouth would form no words, and the more I tried the louder the chanting became. When I tried to drag myself free, those watching would thrust their burning torches at me, driving me back.

Deeper and deeper I slipped, the ooze rising first to my waist, and then to my shoulders. The more I struggled the faster I sank, but even when I forced myself to remain still, the slime continued its inexorable claim on my being.

I tilted my head as the mud reached my chin, striving to keep my mouth clear. Desperately I forced my toes downwards, reaching for a bottom that simply wasn't there. Would that I could touch firm ground, and save myself!

But no, it was hopeless. I sealed my mouth firmly as the ooze closed over it, and now that it was impossible to speak I saw that my tormentors were holding boat hooks. They had also ceased chanting, and were standing together in idle chatter. Snatches of conversation came to me, even as the slime reached my ears, and with disbelief I heard Roberta telling Cecilie that I was a poor fish.

'Trust me, my dear. You're well out of it.'

Then the mud claimed my ears, and seconds later it closed over my eyes, hiding the scene from view. I struggled mightily in the suffocating darkness, striving one last time to save myself, but once my nose went under I knew all was lost.

The last thing I recall was a low menacing growl and glowing red eyes full of malice.

I awoke from the nightmare with arms and legs thrashing, thoroughly tangled in the bedsheets. My heart pounded like a steam hammer, and I took several gasping breaths before I realised I was safe and sound under my parents' roof.

I got up, still breathing heavily, and dressed quickly. Today I would speak with Roberta, and together we would investigate the terrible beast that roamed the nearby countryside, killing at will. With her guidance, and the books and equipment she had packed for me, I had little doubt we would ascertain the monster's true nature.

Then a thought struck me. We could not discuss murderous monsters and matters of a supernatural nature in my parents house, not when they might overhear every word. No, we would have to meet elsewhere. Somewhere secluded, where we would not be disturbed. Somewhere like–

I all but clapped myself on the forehead when I realised that, as usual, Roberta was several steps ahead of me. No wonder she had invited me to Ravenswood, to help the sisters with their books! It was just a pretext! The manor would be ideal for our purposes, with its many rooms and large grounds.

I glanced towards my trunk, and then at the wardrobe. What equipment, and which books, should I take with me? I could not hope to carry a quarter of them on my own, and it would raise eyebrows all over the village if I hired a cart to take my trunk to Ravenswood.

Still puzzling over the matter, I went in to breakfast. There was buttered toast and hot tea, and my parents and I enjoyed a pleasant breakfast during which I recounted a few tales of my time in London. Not, you understand, the more life-threatening ones!

When I enquired after my father's injuries, my mother responded with an airy gesture. 'He's healing just fine, the old warhorse. Don't trouble yourself!'

'Not so much of the old,' muttered my father, who was perusing the morning paper. Suddenly he started. 'They found that driver of yours, poor fellow.'

I paused with a piece of toast halfway to my mouth. 'Really?'

'Yes. A terrible scene by all accounts. Near torn to pieces.'

'Stanley!' protested my mother. '*Not* at the breakfast table!'

I prayed silently for the unfortunate soul, and hoped that he had passed to the next world without incident, for it would be a tragedy indeed if he ended up in one of the professor's traps.

'Ma'am, there's a note for Master Jones.'

We looked to the door, where the cook stood with a folded piece of paper in hand. She smiled at me as I approached, for we had known each other for years and she knew I was particularly fond of her. 'It's good to see you looking well, sir.'

'You too, Eda. How is your family?'

'Middlin' sir. Just middlin'.'

She left, and I unfolded the note. As I expected, it was from Roberta.

11am at Ravenswood. Bring Tanner, Weatherall and Simpkins. Also cherrywood box with brass corners.

I turned the note over, but there was no clue as to who these mysterious fellows might be. Since I'd never heard of them I deduced it was a secret code, and one I must tackle straight away. 'I've been called to Ravenswood,' I told my parents. 'Thank you for a fine breakfast, and I will likely return later this afternoon.'

'Be seated this instant,' said my mother, indicating the half-eaten toast. 'I don't know how you do things in London, but around these parts we don't like to see good food going to waste.'

Chastened, I took my seat, and within seconds I had finished my toast and drained my cup.

'Give yourself ructions you will,' grumbled my mother.

I got up, kissed her forehead by way of apology, then smiled to my father and left. Once in my room, I located the wooden box first, since that was the easier of the instructions. As to the rest of the note, I racked my brains with letter transpositions until I felt the beginnings of a headache, but no matter how I jumbled those names I could not discern their hidden meaning.

Of course, by now I suspect you're well ahead of me, and so you can imagine how I reacted when I realised those names were not a code, but rather the authors of several of the leather-bound books I'd placed in my wardrobe. Combined, the three had penned seven weighty tomes, and when I'd taken them down and added the cherrywood box to the top, it took all my strength to lift the collection. Before doing so, I carefully folded my handwritten notes on the case and tucked them inside one of the books.

I escaped the house without being seen, which was just as well because the books bore lurid titles that would have raised many awkward questions. Animal sacrifices were mentioned, as were lycanthropes and vampires and the sexual practices of paranormal beings. Those were the tamest, and the others I forbear to repeat.

Suffice to say that fifty years earlier, possession of such books might have led to a public drowning in the village pond.

As I walked to Ravenswood, my arms filled with books and my chin holding the cherrywood box in place, I felt the warmth of the sun on my back and revelled in the birdsong from the nearby trees. The scene was idyllic, and it was hard to reconcile the terrors I'd experienced in my dreams. In addition, my heart was gladdened by the thought of spending the day with Roberta - especially given her father was attending a lecture in Brighton, and would not be there to cast warning looks in my direction.

Walking along Beckenham Road I passed the magnificent Wickham Court, a manor which would not have looked out of place in the wealthiest part of London. Then there came the hammering of iron from across the road, and I spied the blacksmith hard at work. A large, muscled fellow, he appeared to be working on a horseshoe, shaping the red-hot metal with repeated blows from a heavy mallet.

I stopped at the bakers for some sticky buns, thinking they might be a nice treat for Roberta and myself. Alas, I had not thought about carrying them, and I left the shop with a brown paper bag balanced on top of the wooden box, which was in turn balanced on top of the valuable books.

I jumped as a carriage clattered past, heading back towards Wood Lodge. Fortunately the road was dry, and I was only assailed by dust and not a fountain of mud.

Ahead lay Ravenswood at last, and as I passed through the iron gates I adjusted my grip on the books. They were extremely uncomfortable, and I would be glad when I could finally put them down. As I strode along the gravel path I noticed many weeds in evidence, in places completely choking what had once been a neat, expansive driveway. A fly settled on my cheek, but I managed to dislodge it by blowing hard out of the corner of my mouth.

The house came into view, and I felt a tinge of regret as I studied the faded, weathered facade. Just a few years ago Ravenswood had been a jewel of sorts, and while it was a modest place compared to the grandeur of Wickham House, it was still a shame to see it fallen so.

Two storeys high, the gabled roof was pierced with a dozen attic windows, or dormers, where once the servants had their quarters. Now several panes were broken, and as I got closer I could see cobwebs and other signs of neglect. Little wonder the Hall sisters were taking paying guests.

As I approached I spied something out of the ordinary to my right. There was a stand of trees some three or four hundred yards away, and in the shade stood a solitary figure in a dark, hooded cloak. I could not make out the person's face, since the hood left nothing but shadow, but from the stooped appearance I guessed them to be elderly. With a start I recalled the hooded figure from my nightmare, but when I stopped on the gravel, turning to stare at the distant figure, I discovered to my surprise that the mysterious, cloaked shadow had vanished without trace.

A shiver ran up my spine, for I had the distinct impression the sinister figure had been watching me. Had they been lying in wait, or had they followed me from my parents' house?

Or was some local going about their innocent business?

My questions had no answer, and so I proceeded along the drive to the house. Here, the front door was ajar, and although I knocked twice there was no sign of a maid or butler. I called out, but my voice echoed around the empty hall. Peering inside, I saw wood panelling and polished flooring, the former with lighter, rectangular patches where, I assumed, family portraits had once hung. No doubt they had been sold to meet some debt or other.

'Hello?' I shouted.

I heard footsteps, then saw the welcome sight of Roberta as she appeared through a pair of tall oak doors. She smiled, and beckoned. 'I'm in here. Come through.'

I traipsed across the hall, and discovered she was using the library. The shelves were filled with books, most of them faded and dusty, and with no small relief I put my burden on a fragile-looking side table.

'You brought them!' exclaimed Roberta. 'These will be tremendously helpful.'

'Where are the sisters?' I asked her.

'Oh, they're tending the kitchen garden,' said Roberta, as she took up one of her father's books and leafed through the contents. 'They won't intrude, trust me. They grow their own food, and they're greatly troubled by weeds.'

'And Elsie, your father's maid? He was most insistent she travel with you.'

Roberta smiled. 'I paid her handsomely, and asked her to remain at her own home until called. She was mightily relieved, for she was not keen on travelling so far from London.'

'She could lose her position over this.'

'Father wouldn't dare,' said Roberta, and I knew she meant it. 'Now, let us turn to the task at hand.'

I took out my handwritten notes and passed them to her. 'This is what I have discovered so far.'

Scanning the pages, she made one or two noises under her breath. Then she looked at me. 'Mr Carmichael bears investigating. And we must interview this policeman, Sam Tyler.'

I was about to agree, until I remembered how Tyler had always been popular with the ladies. Far more popular than I, there was no denying it. In my younger years I had attended many a village dance alone, often because the girl I asked to accompany me was, in turn, hoping Sam would ask her. I do not think I could have survived the mortal blow should he and Roberta become close. I knew it was foolish, this jealousy, but why tempt fate by introducing the two of them? 'I should speak with Sam, as we attended school together, and thanks to certain escapades we have in common, I may have some hold over him. And I think Mr Carmichael would react well to you, if you sought an appointment to discuss local history and the like.'

Roberta hid a smile. 'Tyler is your age, I take it, while Mr Carmichael is old and crusty.'

'You will charm him, I'm certain of it, while I would not be welcome.'

'Then the matter is settled.' Roberta indicated my notes. 'This comment about the silver. There is no need to forge an entire weapon out of the material, as it will suffice to plate something with the material. I shall need bellows, and–'

'There's a smithy in the village,' I said.

Roberta shook her head. 'Too many questions would be asked, and in any case I doubt the smith would allow me to use his forge.'

'But what sort of weapon is needed?' I asked, thinking of swords and maces and the like.

'Honestly? A crossbow and bolts, or failing that, arrows. Why approach a monster when you can shoot it down from afar?'

'What about a shotgun?' I asked her. 'If we emptied the pellets from several cartridges, and refilled them with silver–'

'That hardly seems fair on the monster,' objected Roberta.

'Why should it be fair? This is not a boxing match!'

'Have you fired such a weapon before?'

I had to admit that I hadn't. 'But it must be easier than firing a crossbow, or loosing off an arrow in the middle of the night.'

'Very well. We will secure two such guns, and cartridges to suit. There may be weapons right here at Ravenswood, if the sisters have not yet sold them.' Roberta took up the small wooden box and opened it. Inside was a glass pipette with a hollow bulb in the middle, and a small vial of dark liquid.

'What are those for?' I asked her.

'It's a concoction of my father's. You add one drop to blood, and it will glow in the presence of the supernatural.'

'You intend to prove whether the creature is supernatural or not?'

'Yes. From your description it seems to be the case, but in the darkness, in a violent melee...you would not be the first to be mistaken.'

'You sound like Sam Tyler. He suggested I'd fought a circus bear.'

'Well, we can verify the truth of the matter easily enough. Do you have the knife with which you wounded the beast?'

'It's at home, in my wardrobe.' I saw her waiting expectantly. 'Would you like me to fetch it now?'

'Right away, please. And Septimus, in future you should carry it with you at all times. Whether this beast is supernatural or not, it would reassure me greatly if I knew you could defend yourself.'

'I shall return immediately.' So saying, I left the library at Ravenswood and hurried home. On the way I kept a weather eye out for the figure in the dark cloak, but saw no sign of them. Before long I was heading back with the dagger concealed in my coat, and on my way I came across Sam Tyler, the policeman. He was chatting to the blacksmith, who stood in a sheen of sweat from his hard work. The pair of them were admiring a chestnut mare standing patiently in the yard, no doubt having her shoes replaced, and I nodded to them both before continuing on my way.

Roberta took the dirk from its scabbard, tilting the blade to the sunlight streaming through the tall windows. 'You cleaned it,' she said, disappointed.

'I could not return it to the scabbard dripping with blood,' I said defensively.

'Oh well. There may still be a dried fleck or two.'

'Will that be enough?'

'We shall see.' Roberta took the pipette and dipped one end into the tiny bottle, drawing up a small amount of fluid. Then she passed the tip over the dagger's honed blade, allowing the liquid to flow across the shiny metal.

I moved closer, eager to see the results, and neither of us was disappointed. There was a reddish gleam, just enough to cast a weak shadow, and I turned to Roberta in triumph. 'You see? A circus bear, my foot!'

22

We now knew for certain the creature was of supernatural origin, but there was still much to work out. For example, it was all very well securing weapons and silver shot, but before we confronted the creature we would need to find it.

Using a sheet of paper, I drew a rough map of the area, indicating the location where I had been attacked and the spot where the first victim from Cox's report had been photographed. It encompassed several square miles, much of it heavily wooded, and for the first time I began to appreciate the magnitude of our task.

'It might go into hiding after each attack,' said Roberta. 'If it's taking refuge in a den or a lair of some kind, we'll never find it.'

'If the Hall sisters are willing to speak of the matter, perhaps we could ask them about their father? If we could find out where he was killed...'

'Triangulate the location of the attacks, you mean?' Roberta nodded. 'That might narrow the search down, although it's unlikely the beast has used the same spot for its lair over all these years. Someone would surely have discovered it.' She paused. 'Poachers.'

'I'm sorry?'

'Who are the poachers in these parts? Do you know?'

I suspected several locals, but it was dangerous to speculate. When a family fell on hard times, there was sometimes no recourse but to take game from the woods. Others supplemented their income by selling whatever they might hunt and kill. In either case, if someone were caught, punishment was swift and severe, and one learned to remain tight-lipped about the matter. 'They do not advertise their activities,' I said, playing for time.

'If not poachers, who else is likely to be out in the woods at night?'

'His lordship's gamekeeper, for one,' I pointed out. Sir Lennard oversaw the village from Wickham Court, the impressive mansion I had passed earlier that day, and his keeper was a canny sort with a nose for trouble.

'Poachers or keepers, it's all the same to me. If they've seen or heard something out of the ordinary, it would help us tremendously.'

'Safer to approach the gamekeeper,' I said. 'For one, if you and I are going into the woods at night with shotguns, I would sooner he knew of our plans beforehand. Otherwise, we might end up on a charge.'

'Very well. You speak to this gamekeeper, and I shall ask my hosts about weapons. If I am successful, then later this afternoon we will need a few items of silver to melt down. If *you* are successful, then tonight we will seek this beast.'

'And hopefully shoot it dead,' I declared.

'No, Septimus. We must capture it alive.'

'Why? It's killing without mercy!'

Roberta opened a book and turned it towards me. On one page was a slavering beast threatening a woman in the forest. On the facing page was a naked man, curled on the ground with his clothes nearby.

'Is that supposed to be the victim?' I asked.

'No, my dear. A transformation. If this beast is what I think it is, then it might pass amongst us by day as an ordinary man...or woman.

Only by night, and perhaps under moonlight, does it transform into the monster you encountered.'

'But that's preposterous!' I exclaimed. 'What sort of magic trick turns a man into a beast?'

'Magic?' Roberta indicated the dagger sitting on the nearby table. Even now, there was a faint reddish glow. 'Supernatural forces may seem like magic to the uninformed, but I thought you'd learned more than that by now.'

Chastened, I nodded. Even so, the idea that the creature might walk amongst us, undetected, was troubling indeed. It could be someone I knew! Then a thought struck me like a thunderbolt. My *father*...last night he'd been wounded in the face, right where the silver hip flask had struck the beast, burning its flesh. And the wound on his back...did it correspond with the location into which I had plunged my dagger? *No, it was impossible!*

'Septimus, you have turned quite pale. Are you all right?'

'Y–yes,' I said quickly. 'A brief dizzy spell, that is all. I am quite recovered.' My words were confident, but my insides were in turmoil. Sick with anxiety and dread, I imagined the outcome if my father were the one responsible for these gruesome murders. Why, we might trap the beast, locking it inside a woodshed or a stable for the night, only for my father to emerge some hours later, as naked as the day he was born! But how could it be my father, when the creature had tried to kill me in the woods? Surely he would have recognised me? 'When in beast form, is there any conscious thought? Any access to memories or awareness of who they might be?'

'If we catch the monster I shall ask it,' said Roberta lightly. 'Oh, the books have theories and speculation aplenty, but no solid information.'

'And what is the prevailing theory?'

'That the creature, once transformed, is no more than a savage, bloodthirsty beast. No trace of its humanity could possibly remain, judging by the way it treats its victims.'

I did not comment on this pronouncement, for history was replete with monsters of the human kind who had slaughtered, tortured, dismembered and even partaken of their victims, and none had needed to transform into hairy beasts to commit such atrocities. It seemed to me that evil might lurk in the most ordinary-looking person, outward appearance to the contrary.

'Before we venture into the woods tonight, we shall speak to Sam Tyler and Mr Carmichael,' declared Roberta. 'They appear to be concealing information and I'm determined to find out what it is.'

I concurred. For a moment I wondered whether Mr Carmichael, or even Sam Tyler, were the beast. Somewhat uncharitably I hoped they were, for that would absolve my father. As I thought on the matter, I simply could not reconcile the gentle, caring man who had helped to raise me with the snarling beast I had stabbed the previous night.

It could not be true. It could not.

If Roberta noticed any sign of my turmoil, she did not remark on it further. 'Our first port of call ought to be the weapons,' she said. 'Without those, the rest of our plan will collapse. Let us speak with the sisters now, and see whether they have a gun or two locked away. An estate like this is sure to have a shotgun, even if just to shoot pests.'

I shook myself, putting aside all thoughts of my father as some kind of slavering beast. 'Even if they have guns, which is by no means assured, will they allow us to use them?'

'I shall tell them we wish to hunt rabbits for dinner.'

I nodded, for this seemed plausible, and so we put aside the professor's books, packed up the pipette and the vial of dark liquid, and went outside into the sunshine. Here, we entered a large kitchen garden, where all manner of vegetables and herbs grew. I heard voices, and when Roberta and I peered behind a trellis of runner beans we saw the sisters engaged in weeding. They were similar in appearance, middle-aged with greying hair, and they were both outdoor types who loved gardening. The sisters stood at our approach, both smiling warmly as they recognised me. 'Septimus!' declared the taller sister, Ellen. 'Why, it's been years, young man. To what do we owe this pleasure? And I see you've met our guest, Isabella.'

'Good afternoon, Miss Hall,' I said, with a grin.

'Less of that, Septimus. It's Aunty Ellen to you.'

'Yes, aunty.'

Emily, the second sister, was still smiling at me fondly, and now she came forward to give me a hug, gardening gloves and all. 'My, you've grown since you went away!' she declared. 'I remember when you barely came up to my knee!' Emily had always had a kind word for me, and I returned the hug with warmth. Then she stepped back, and her smile widened as she switched her attention to Roberta. 'Oh, it does my heart good to see a happy couple in the bloom of youth.'

'Now then,' said her sister Ellen. 'Don't leap to conclusions dear, or you'll embarrass the pair of them.'

'But anyone can see—'

'You must excuse Emily,' said Ellen quickly. 'She reads far too many romantic novels. Now, I assume you've not come to help with the weeding, so what can we do for you?'

'I wondered if you'd like some rabbit to go with these fine vegetables,' said Roberta. 'Septimus told me the woods are quite overrun.'

Emily cackled. 'When I was a gel, young gentlemen took their ladies off to the woods for *quite* a different purpose. Why, there were rumours...'

She would have continued, but Ellen nudged her, none too gently. 'Hunting, is it? Well, father kept guns of course, but they've not been used for many a year.' She pointed to a window. 'You should find something in his study, on the first floor.'

'Are you sure that's all right?' asked Roberta. 'I don't want to intrude on a private area.'

'Oh, don't bother yourself over that,' said Ellen, with a gesture. 'It's been so many years now, and yet one never had the heart to sort through his things.'

'It's not like you'll find anything of value,' remarked Emily. 'In that, it's much like the rest of the house.'

I smiled and thanked them, and Roberta and I returned to the house and climbed the stairs to the first floor. Since we could not see the windows, thus rendering the directions vague in the extreme, we eventually found the study by opening doors in turn and peering inside. The first three rooms were empty, but the fourth had a large wooden desk, and piles of paperwork and books scattered around as though the occupant had only just risen from his work. In fact, it had been two decades or more since Mr Hall had passed away, as evidenced by the thick layer of dust on every surface.

Roberta crossed to a glass-fronted cabinet, which had been designed to store and display various guns. The racks were all but empty, apart from a lone weapon at the extreme left. It was a shotgun, and when Roberta took it down I saw the barrel was pitted with rust. The varnish on the stock had worn, and the weapon looked like it had not been used for many a year. And yet the barrel was oiled, which meant the gun had not deteriorated recently. 'It must be an heirloom,' I said. 'Perhaps a Purdey belonging to Mr Hill's father, or even his grandfather.'

'It's a museum piece,' remarked Roberta. She cracked the weapon and sighted down the inside of the barrel, then blew into it. There came the sound of wind across the neck of a glass bottle, and a puff of dust emerged from the other end. 'Can you search for shells?' she asked me.

I opened the cabinet's lower doors, and immediately spotted two boxes containing ammunition. One had shells of brass, while the other held similar items, but with paper casings. I took out several of the latter and discovered the casings had swollen in the box, perhaps due to damp. The brass shells, on the other hand, looked new, and so I took two large handfuls, placing them into my pockets.

'We should confirm they match the weapon,' said Roberta, putting her hand out. I passed her a shell from the box, and she slotted it into the barrel and closed the weapon with a loud, metallic *snick*. Then she aimed through the large window, keeping her finger clear of the trigger.

'Where did you learn to use a shotgun?' I asked her.

'Septimus, you have witnessed complex machinery designed and built with my own hands. Do you think I need instruction on a child's toy such as this?'

Chastened, I knew this to be the truth, for I'd seen not only her intricate diagrams and blueprints, but the working models built from them. Her father was no mean slouch when it came to engineering, but he often deferred to his daughter.

'Even so,' she continued, 'we shall both have to practice. The mechanics of the thing are one matter, but shooting a target is another entirely.'

'Not rabbits,' I said hastily, for while I was fond of meat, I was equally fond of animals.

'Agreed. We shall hunt nothing more than tree trunks, and the sisters can tell themselves we are the worst shots in the country.' Roberta unloaded the shotgun once more, and we left the study together.

23

Ravenswood's extensive gardens were hemmed in by public woods, and it was here that we went for our shooting practice. First, Roberta inspected the shotgun in the sunlight, trying to determine whether the barrel would burst when put to use. Unfortunately it was not possible to be certain, so I volunteered to fire the first shot.

'Once you have taken aim, close your eyes and avert your face from the breech,' suggested Roberta. 'In this way, an unexpected blast may not take your sight.'

I was holding the loaded weapon gingerly, at arms length, half-expecting it to detonate of its own accord. But I could sense Roberta's growing impatience, and so I brought the faded stock up to my cheek, pressing my face against the rough wood. I sighted along the rusty barrel, aiming directly at a tree which stood no more than six feet away. The trunk was twelve inches across, and there was a six-inch bole at eye level which made for the perfect target. It was so close I could almost have reached out and touched it, and once I was happy the weapon was pointed in the right direction I did as Roberta had advised: I closed both eyes and turned my head away. A heartbeat or two as I prepared myself, and then I squeezed the trigger.

The gun went off with a tremendous thunderclap, the wooden

stock bucking against my shoulder. Cautiously I opened my eyes, expecting to see the bole obliterated by my shot, but to my surprise it was untouched. I frowned at it through a cloud of smoke, wondering whether it was far tougher than imagined, and the spread of shot had merely bounced off it. Then I heard a crack, and I shifted my gaze to a branch fully six feet above my target. Slowly, it toppled and fell, the wood blasted where my shot had torn into it.

'That would have served as a useful warning shot,' remarked Roberta, trying to offer encouragement. 'After all, we do not want to shoot the monster in the face.'

'The creature might have been twelve feet tall, and my shot would still have passed overhead.'

'At least we know the gun is sound. Now reload and try again.'

I opened the barrel, and the empty brass shell tumbled to the ground, trailing smoke. Taking a fresh shell, I slotted it into the warm barrel and closed the weapon up once more. I raised it to my shoulder, sighting with extra care, and when I was certain the target was directly in view, I pulled the trigger.

The weapon bucked, the sharp report like a physical blow to my ears. This time I saw smoke and fire jet from the barrel, and I quickly lowered the weapon to survey the results of my shot. Again, the bole was untouched, but three feet to the left a bush at knee level had been completely stripped of its leaves. Even now, fragments rained down, and there was a green mist where the rest had simply vaporised. 'How could I possibly miss something that close?' I demanded, gesturing at my target with the gently-smoking weapon. 'From this distance I could throw stones and hit it!'

'Perhaps the weapon is defective,' suggested Roberta. 'If the choke is worn, it could be throwing shot in every direction.'

I was silent as I loaded the shotgun with a fresh shell. Already, I could see the outcome of our little practice session, and I found it somewhat humiliating. Worn chokes, defective weapons or ill-timed breezes, I knew for certain that Roberta would take the gun and blast the very middle of the bole with her first shot. That was not the humiliating aspect, not in the slightest, for I would be the first to admit I had all the mechanical skill of a lead ingot. No, the part I dreaded was when Roberta made excuses on my behalf, in a vain attempt to salve my pride.

Raising the gun, I aimed and fired in one quick motion, hoping to overcome my nerves and let my instincts take over. But if anything, my third shot was wider of the mark than the first two. I saw a ragged hole torn through a tree twenty feet behind my target, followed by another rain of shattered twigs and torn leaves. As I lowered the gun I thought I saw a hooded figure in the distance, moving quickly out of my line of sight. It was hard to be sure, especially through the gunsmoke, and I decided it must have been a shadow.

Without a word, I passed the shotgun to Roberta. Our roles were now fixed for the night, because when we confronted the monster, I knew I would be the bait while she would be the hunter.

Bang!

The shotgun went off while I was still nursing my pride, and Roberta staggered backwards, stunned by the recoil. I glanced towards the tree, expecting to see torn bark and shredded wood where the bole had been. Instead, the bole was intact. I looked around, and eventually spied a bush to the right missing half its leaves. 'Definitely a worn choke,' I remarked, without actually knowing what a choke was.

'Do not distract me when I'm aiming,' growled Roberta.

'I barely moved!'

'No, but your breathing was enough to put a trained marksman off his aim.' She reloaded and fired again, and this time the upper half of a three-inch sapling leapt into the air before slamming onto the leafy ground, its trunk bisected by her shot. She tried again, the recoil again driving her backwards. Her foot caught on a root, tripping her, and before I could leap forwards to catch her she landed flat on her back in the dry leaves, gun pointing at the sky and a most annoyed look on her face. I helped her up, keeping a straight face all the while, and when we both looked towards the target there was no evidence that she'd fired at all.

Roberta dusted herself down, shaking dry leaves and twigs from her hair, and then we looked at each other, standing there in a cloud of gun smoke with sunlight filtering down through the trees. In that instant we started to laugh. Here we were, planning to confront a murderous beast with our one and only weapon, and neither of us could hit a tree trunk six feet in front of us.

'Well,' said Roberta at last. 'If nothing else, the noise might startle the beast.'

Still laughing, I pointed towards the ruined bushes. 'We ought to search underneath,' I said. 'We might have taken half a dozen rabbits by mistake, and that would fulfill our promise to your hosts.'

'Rabbits don't live in trees, Septimus.' Roberta handed me the weapon. 'Come, let us return to the house. We must hope that the next portion of our plan does not end on such a sour note.'

Despite our singular lack of success with the shotgun, Roberta was determined to craft special shells for the weapon. She intended to make them more dangerous to the creature by removing the lead shot and coating it with silver. I suspected the new ammunition would be a waste of time, given our inability to hit a large, unmoving target, let alone a beast moving at speed in the dark, but I humoured her for two reasons. One, we had time to spare, and I could think of no better way to spend it than in her company. And two, because I suspected she wanted to tackle a task for which she was better suited. Melting and pouring silver, unpacking and repacking the shells...these were engineering tasks of which she was more than capable, and employing her strongest skills would go some way towards erasing the embarrassing sight of her being knocked backwards by the gun, to land with arms and legs waving in the soft bed of leaves.

'What are you laughing at?' demanded Roberta, fixing me with a glare.

'It is nothing, I assure you. Now, where do you think we can obtain enough silver?' I asked, hastily changing the subject.

Roberta reached into the neckline of her dress and drew out a thin silver chain.

'But that's yours,' I objected.

'I've had it since I was a little girl,' she agreed. 'But if not this, would you care to steal something from your parents? Or do you perhaps carry a bar of silver about your person?'

'Not a bar, but...' I hesitated, feeling in my pocket. Drawing out a small selection of coins, I selected five florins from amongst them and passed them to her. 'Will that be enough?'

'Plenty. We shall only need one or two.' She frowned. 'In order to melt them I shall need a crucible and a source of intense heat, either a furnace or a blowtorch.' She turned the coins in one hand, deep in thought. 'Oh, if only we were home! I could have this done in an instant in my workshop. But it's not worth going all the way to London, so we shall have to make do.'

'We *could* ask the blacksmith,' I suggested. 'I know you said he might not let you use the forge, but–'

'A jeweller would be better.'

'There are none in these parts, but there ought to be in Croydon.'

Roberta shook her head. 'Let us try the smithy first. This will not take long, and should not be too much of an imposition.'

'As you suggested earlier, he will ask questions,' I warned her.

'Then I shall give him answers, though they may not be accurate ones.'

24

The blacksmith was a man of few words and many muscles, and he loomed over us like a Greek hero of old as Roberta explained what we needed. Bare chested, with an open, honest face, he did not appear surprised in the slightest at her request. Perhaps, I thought, it was not uncommon for villagers to melt down valuables when hard times struck.

'Two shillings per hour,' he said, and directed us to the rear of the smithy. Here, next to a sooty wooden workbench and a rack of tools I did not recognise, was a furnace and bellows. There were coals in the furnace, and when the blacksmith applied his huge strength to the bellows these coals glowed white hot. Finally, he indicated a row of crucibles on a nearby shelf, ranging from small to large.

Roberta nodded her thanks, and the smith returned to his work at the front of the workshop, where he plucked a red-hot horseshoe from a bed of coals and began to strike it repeatedly with deafening hammer-blows. The noise rang out again and again, making it all but impossible to speak.

Roberta took down three crucibles, including the largest, the smallest, and one from the middle of the row. She placed them on the workbench, then turned to me. Holding her hands up as though firing the shotgun, she then pointed to my pockets. I took out both handfuls of shells and she indicated the largest crucible, into which I placed them with much care.

Next, she took one of the shells and, using pliers from the tools arranged on the wall, opened up the narrow end. She set aside a small piece of wadding, then tipped the lead shot into the middle crucible, being careful not to tap out the second piece of wadding and the powder it held in place.

After a few minutes work, a row of opened cartridges sat along the rear of the workbench, lined up in two neat rows. Now Roberta indicated the bellows, and then me, and I did not need to hear the directions in order to understand her meaning. In the meantime, she placed my silver florins inside the smallest crucible and took down a long pair of tongs, which she laid on the workbench. Finally, she donned a pair of thick leather gloves which reached almost to her elbows, before taking up the tongs and gripping the crucible with the business end.

With a nod of her head she indicated the forge, and I opened the door quickly, careful not to touch the handle too long lest it burn me. A wave of heat struck me in the face, and the moment the crucible was placed amongst the coals and the tongs withdrawn, I closed the door and applied myself to the bellows.

The blacksmith had operated the bellows with ease, but I quickly discovered they were very hard work. They required far more effort than expected, and I soon felt sweat on my brow. Roberta gestured at me, exhorting greater effort, and I did my best to comply. It was no wonder the blacksmith had such a large build, if he had to labour as I was day after day!

At last, with sweat dripping from my brow and running down my neck, Roberta bid me pause. She opened the door with a gloved hand, wincing at the extreme heat, then took up the tongs and withdrew the crucible just enough to look inside. She checked the contents with a swirling motion, but was not yet satisfied for she immediately returned the container to the coals. With the door closed once more, she nodded to me, motioning with her free hand to indicate I should apply myself with even greater effort.

I pumped the bellows for all I was worth, and I began to see spots and flashes in my vision. The heat was overwhelming, and my heavy tweed jacket did not help the situation. I could not pause to remove it though, as Roberta was still gesturing at me, indicating I should go even faster. My breath came in ragged gasps, and I feared I might collapse in a dead faint at any moment.

As I laboured away, Roberta sought something amongst the tools on the wall, then went to speak with the blacksmith. My heart sank as I watched the pair of them in conversation, for I was not certain I would still be on my feet by the time she returned. Fortunately their conversation was short-lived, and Roberta returned with a small piece of mesh made from woven metal. She also carried a pail of water, which she stood next to the forge to which I was devoting all my efforts.

She placed the mesh over the mouth of a fourth crucible, then pressed it down to form a hollow. Next, she took a small amount of lead shot, spreading it carefully across the mesh. Then she approached me, tongs in hand. 'We must work quickly!' she shouted, raising her voice over the wheeze of the bellows, the roar of the furnace and the clanking of the blacksmith's hammer. 'The lead will melt in an instant!' She placed a hand on my arm and I stopped working the bellows, grateful at the respite. Then she handed me a pair of pliers and pointed towards the mesh. 'You must tip the shot into the water the instant I give the signal. Understand? Do not let the mesh touch the water, or the shot will stick to it and we shall have to start all over again.'

I was still incapable of speech, and merely nodded. My arms and shoulders ached like the devil, but this fresh task would be easy compared to the working of those bellows.

Using the tongs, Roberta extracted the crucible with the molten silver from the furnace, and rested it briefly on the workbench. The crucible glowed red, illuminating her face in a most fetching manner, and I smiled at the intense look of concentration thus revealed. She took up a short iron rod and stirred the silver with it, raising sparks, and then she set aside the now silver-coated rod and nodded to me.

I gripped one corner of the mesh with my pliers, and Roberta poured a small measure of liquid silver over the lead shot. It spattered and sparked, splashing hot droplets, but she kept her hands steady until the entire surface was coated, a little excess silver having run into the crucible beneath the mesh. 'Now!' she shouted, nodding towards the pail of water.

I lifted the mesh with the pliers, transferred it to the pail and tipped it over. Most of the shot fell into the water immediately, raising a cloud of steam, and I tapped the mesh on the rim of the pail to dislodge the rest.

'Back to the crucible!' shouted Roberta. 'Add more shot, and keep them apart.'

I complied, placing the silver-coated mesh on the open mouth of the crucible sitting on the workbench, steam or smoke rising from the small amount of molten silver gathered in the bottom. I added shot, careful not to touch the mesh, and then Roberta poured another measure of silver over the whole.

After repeating the process two or three times, Roberta placed the crucible with the molten silver in the furnace, then added the larger crucible we had used to gather the excess. As the contents of both were reheated, she bent to scoop shot from the pail of water. Most of the shot was misshapen, but all gleamed from the coating of silver we had applied. Upon inspecting the result, she nodded in satisfaction.

There remained but two tasks. The first was to repack the cartridges, sealing the ends once more with the pliers. This, Roberta left to me.

The second was to pour out the remaining silver from both crucibles, so as not to waste it. For this Roberta used a small metal cup, creating a flat metal disk of pure silver which she quenched in the pail.

Our task complete, I returned the newly-packed shells to my pockets, and we went to thank the blacksmith. Roberta paid him with the silver disk she had just minted, which I felt was generous in the extreme given it was worth two or three times the amount the man had asked for.

He seemed pleased, which did not surprise me in the least, and he thanked us profusely as we left.

Having manufactured silver shot with which to subdue the beast, we decided our next task was to seek information from the gamekeeper at Wickham Court. Much of the land in the area was owned by the Lord of the Manor, Sir Lennard, and his keeper would be more familiar with the woods than most. Aside, that is, from poachers, and I had already voiced my objection to approaching such shadowy, dangerous fellows.

Given that the monster could likely transform into human form and back again, we agreed there was little point seeking its lair. After all, as a human it would not need one. Therefore, we decided to ask the keeper about sightings of the beast, before seeking permission to look for it that coming night.

Wickham Court had a separate lodge, distant from the fabulous main residence, and it was here we were directed by a maid. We found the gamekeeper in a workshop of sorts, surrounded by racks of guns and tools of his trade. He was cleaning a weapon which probably cost more than my parents' house, carefully applying oil to the gleaming, engraved barrel with a folded rag.

The gamekeeper was a man of middling height, perhaps in his fifties, with white hair and a thick, luxurious moustache. He had piercing blue eyes which regarded us with suspicion from beneath equally bushy eyebrows, but when he saw Roberta he smiled in a welcoming fashion. 'Good afternoon to you miss,' he said, with a polite nod. 'To what do I owe this honour?'

'Miss Davinia Fotherington-Hay at your service,' said Roberta, in a plummy, upper-class accent. 'Father sends his warmest regards.'

It was all I could do not to stare at her. First Roberta had dreamt up the name of Isabella Makepeace, and now she was pretending to be landed gentry! Not only that, she'd chosen the name of one of our clients, a name that had achieved some notoriety in the London papers. If the keeper was current with the goings-on of high society, he would see through Roberta's subterfuge in an instant.

'A pleasure to meet you, ma'am, although I'm not entirely certain–'

'One read about these horrible murders in the papers,' said Roberta breathlessly. 'It seems they're taking place on Sir Lennard's estate.'

'Not all of them,' said the gamekeeper, with a frown. 'One poor soul lost his life in the woods, but the other was out Croydon way.'

'And Mr Hill, from Ravenswood?' demanded Roberta. 'Such a tragic loss.'

'That was over thirty years ago,' said the gamekeeper. 'Nothing to do with the current ruckus. Nothing at all!'

During this exchange I had kept my silence, but now I felt it was time to intervene. It seemed to me that Roberta's approach, whilst well-intentioned, was setting the gamekeeper against us. Why, the man was getting more defensive by the minute, as though Roberta were personally accusing him of the deaths! 'Miss Davinia is by means of an amateur sleuth,' I said to the gamekeeper. 'She investigates notorious cases most enthusiastically,' I added, and I hoped the man got my meaning. Investigates, yes. Discovers anything of importance? An emphatic no.

It seemed to work, for the keeper relaxed somewhat. 'I suppose you want all the gory details?' he said.

'Ooh, how thrilling!' gushed Roberta, who, as I suspected, had taken her cue from my words, and was now playing the brainless socialite to perfection. 'Was there a *lot* of blood?'

'Buckets,' said the keeper. 'The poor fellow was spread about like a dog's breakfast, and some parts of him have never been found.'

'Oh my! Just *wait* until one tells Hetty! The poor gel is investigating a murder in Spitalfields, but that was just a common stabbing and the police already have a suspect. This is *so* much more interesting!' Roberta gripped the keeper's arm. 'But you must be wondering why one sought you out. Well, one wanted to ask about sightings of this beast. Have you seen it yourself?'

'I've seen all kinds in the woods, my lady, and there's always a feeling of being watched.'

'No hard evidence? Tracks, perhaps?'

He shook his head.

'In that case,' said Roberta, with the air of someone who was never refused, 'one simply must see the crime scene.'

'There was no need to trouble yourself by asking permission, miss. The woods are public access. You can go there now.'

'Oh, but one wishes to experience the full horror at night.'

The keeper looked startled. 'You do?'

'Indeed!'

'I would caution against it,' said the keeper, with a frown. 'This beast killed again only yesterday, and–'

'My man here will protect me,' said Roberta.

The keeper looked me up and down, doubt written all over his face.

'But one hears the woods are rife with poachers,' continued Roberta, 'and if you spotted the pair of us prowling around, you might open fire. Imagine the fuss if you shot me dead!'

'Not *rife*, exactly,' protested the keeper. 'One or two, maybe, and rarely at that.'

'Even so, it seemed wise to seek permission, since Septimus will be armed and you might mistake *him* for a poacher.'

Again, the keeper looked me up and down. 'I'm fairly certain I could tell the difference,' he said at last. 'But in order to be certain, we shall agree on a password for the night. If I challenge you, you must reply with the word 'animal'.'

'Oh thank you,' said Roberta, beaming with joy. 'One is *so* looking forward to this adventure, for it will make such a stir when one returns to London!'

25

I could not escape the gamekeeper's croft quickly enough, for it seemed to me Roberta had overplayed her hand. I expected the man to quiz her at any moment, asking for particulars of her father's estate for example, but fortunately he erred on the side of caution. I suppose he had little to lose by allowing us to roam the woods at night, whereas he stood to lose a great deal if he upset the daughter of a wealthy family.

'That went better than I expected,' said Roberta happily, as we strolled towards Ravenswood.

'I feel one almost overdid it,' I remarked in a plummy accent, and was rewarded with a laugh.

We had decided to peruse the Professor's books for more information about the creature we would be hunting, and also to devise a means of trapping it. However, we had barely gone two hundred yards when Roberta stopped. 'Look, a bakery! Let us find something to build up our strength.'

'There are sticky buns in the library,' I said, indicating the road to Ravenswood. 'I bought them up with me earlier.'

'We shall give those to Emily and Ellen in lieu of fresh rabbit. It's the least we can do.'

I saw the sense in this, and we left the baker's some minutes later, each with a pair of hot muffins. We ate them on the way, and I was grateful for the sustenance since I had expended most of my energy on the blacksmith's bellows.

Once at Ravenswood we returned to the library, where Roberta laid out her father's books on a large table. I took up the wooden box containing the pipette and vial, and as I did so, a thought occurred to me. A plan I was unwilling to share with Roberta. 'I will take this with me when I leave, and return it to my trunk,' I said.

'Oh, there's no need. You can leave that here with the books.'

That did not suit me at all. 'I thought to run another test on some blood, just to familiarise myself with the process.'

'I see.' Roberta hesitated. 'Well, I suppose that will be all right, but please use the vial sparingly. My father went through hell to obtain the ingredients.'

'No more than a single drop,' I promised.

She merely nodded, distracted by the books laid out in front of her. Then, having selected two, she passed me one of them and took the other for herself. We then spent an hour or two in silence, with only the occasional turning of pages to be heard. My book covered a range of supernatural topics, but while I learned a great deal I did not find much on the subject of men turning into beasts and then back again. I confess my mind wandered for much of the time, for I was conscious of the testing kit sitting beside me inside the wooden box, and deathly afraid of what it might reveal when I eventually put it to use later that same day.

The shadows in the library were getting quite long by the time

Roberta closed her book. I followed suit, and waited expectantly. Since my own reading had failed to turn up much in the way of useful advice, I hoped her own had been more productive.

'We shall need strong rope to tie the beast up,' she said. 'If my hosts don't have anything suitable, we shall have to buy some in the village.'

This seemed obvious to me, and I felt I could have suggested rope without having first read the weighty tome at my elbow. 'Was there any practical advice on capturing the creature?'

'The scent of fresh blood might prove useful in attracting it. Naked flames, on the other hand, would tend to drive it away. As to the trapping of the thing, see here.'

Roberta leafed through her book, then showed me a drawing within. In it, a group of men were standing around a pit dug into the ground, from which a savage beast glowered at them. The pit was still half-covered with branches, through which the beast had fallen, and a haunch of some animal dangled from the tree above. The ache in my arms redoubled at the sight, for digging such a pit would require a great deal of hard work. 'No doubt we could borrow a shovel from the Hill sisters?' I asked, without much enthusiasm.

'Better to pay a man or two to help,' said Roberta. 'You look quite worn out, my dear, and it would not do for you to fall asleep later, whilst we maintain our watch.'

'But how will we entice the creature towards this trap?' I asked. 'It might have an unparalleled sense of smell, but even so, the woods are extensive and–'

'Before stringing our bait from a suitable tree, we shall drag it through the undergrowth,' said Roberta. 'If you imagine a straight line with the trap in the very middle, we can lay our trail for a mile in each direction to ensure we cast as wide a net as possible. In the meantime, our workers can be digging the pit.'

I decided the plan was a good one, for not only did it reduce the danger to all involved, but it also meant I would not have to dig the pit myself. If the monster followed the trail and attempted to grasp the bait, it could not fail to plunge into the hidden pit. And if the hole were deep enough, it would not be able to leap out and assail us. And lastly, if it tried to escape, a charge or two of silver-plated shot in its hide would soon put paid to the attempt.

For the first time that day I felt a surge of hope. To that point we had only tinkered around the edges, gathering equipment and preparing ourselves, but now we had come up with a solid plan to capture the creature. Even more promising was the fact I would not have to face the monster at close range. I had suspected Roberta might ask me to sneak up behind the beast and place a noose over its head, and so I was greatly relieved at the idea of a pit trap which could achieve our purpose without loss of life nor limb.

'Night will not fall for a while yet,' said Roberta. 'You should take the opportunity to interview Sam Tyler, and also to seek two or three men willing to dig our trap in the woods. In the meantime I will ask the sisters for some rope and then go to interrogate your prospective father-in-law.'

I ignored the jibe. 'Where in the woods? Have you a location in mind?'

'Underneath the overhanging branch of a tree, of course. I shall leave the rest to you, but ensure it's deep in the woods. To date, the monster has steered clear of civilisation, and it would be a waste of time setting our trap close to the village.' She frowned. 'We shall need a haunch of meat for the bait. Can you secure one? It does not have to be fresh, which may reduce the cost.'

'I will speak with my parents' cook.'

'Excellent.' Roberta stood. 'Well, my dear, we both have our tasks laid out before us.' She glanced out of the window, where the sun was yet above the trees, albeit dropping quickly. 'We shall meet after sunset at your parents' house.'

As she stood there in profile, with the sunlight illuminating her features, her hair aglow, I felt a quickening of my heart. Roberta sensed my gaze, and she turned and smiled in a most beguiling fashion. 'Are you admiring the view?'

'I, er...' Turning away in confusion, I fumbled with the brass-bound wooden box, eventually picking it up and tucking it beneath my arm. 'After sunset,' I mumbled, and I hurried from the library.

Aside from the errands I had agreed to with Roberta, there was one more on my list. A secret task that I had kept to myself, and one that I faced with a great deal of apprehension and dread.

Instead of confronting Sam Tyler or tracking down a joint to be used as bait, my chosen path carried me towards my parents' home. I carried the wooden box under one arm, and the closer I got to my destination the heavier it weighed on me. I knew that the tiny vial within might uncover a truth that would shatter my life, as well as that of my parents.

A sensation came over me, as though I were being watched, and I stopped to look over my shoulder. A few people were abroad, going about their business, but none were paying me the slightest attention. I glanced back at the gates of Ravenswood, but there was no sign of anyone and the house was hidden from view.

I shook myself to dispel the feeling, and continued onwards. At home I greeted my mother, who was reading in the sitting room, and made my way to the rear of the house. I passed through the kitchen, where a large pot was simmering on the range, and peered outside the back door, where the wicker laundry basket usually stood for collection. After looking around to ensure I was not observed, I quickly lifted the lid.

Empty.

That ruled out my father's bloodstained shirt of the night before, and I confess I was not disappointed. I had done my best, and now I could safely continue with the rest of my errands, free from nagging guilt and worry. I left the kitchen and strode towards my room, in order to conceal the test kit within my trunk. But on the way I noticed the discoloured floorboards, still a little damp from the evening before when my mother had led my father, dripping wet, to the bathtub.

I recalled the drops of blood that had fallen on the boards, diluted by the puddles of water, and then I looked at the small wooden box clasped in my hand. Would they suffice to give a reading? There was only one way to find out!

I crouched, setting the box on the floor, then inspected the floorboards closely. I was certain they had been mopped the night before, for my parents were not the sort to leave a spill in their neat house, but would there be any residue? I bent double, my nose almost to the floor as I inspected the woodwork in the semi-darkness, paying particular attention to the section running under the skirting boards.

Still uncertain, I took up the glass pipette and drew a tiny amount of liquid up from the vial. Then, holding my breath, I released a single drop onto the floorboards, right where they met the skirting. At first there was no reaction, but then I saw a wisp of smoke, curling gently in the all-but-undetectable air current. The smoke increased as the liquid spread out, until the droplet covered a good two inches square. The floorboard so covered turned a dark colour, and as the smoke continued to rise I was suddenly concerned that the timber might burst into flames. Roberta had used the liquid on metal, not wood, and I had no idea of the kind of chemicals I was toying with.

Then the smoke cleared, and I withdrew in horror as the dark patch began to glow with a faint, baleful red.

26

I left my parents' house in a highly disturbed state of mind, scarcely able to believe the truth I'd uncovered. I simply could not reconcile my gentle, caring father with the savage beast that had already killed several times, but the test I'd performed had all but proven his complicity.

Now I faced a terrible dilemma, for I could not allow the beast to roam unchecked, but neither could I allow my father to be imprisoned, or punished, or even killed. I was tempted to present the facts to Roberta, but I could not betray my father, even to her.

I resolved, therefore, to continue with the plans I had made with Roberta, but with one small alteration. I would persuade my mother to keep my father home that night, using whatever pretext she found necessary. Safely ensconced with my mother, we would not be able to trap him in our pit in the form of the slavering, murderous beast. And if we did manage to trap the creature, despite my father being kept out of the picture, I would know for certain that my father, though his blood exhibited supernatural properties, was *not* the monster.

This compromise soothed my conscience, for the time being at least, and so I turned my attention to the next part of the plan, making a beeline for a row of modest cottages nestled at the foot of a nearby hill. These houses were small but well-kept, with freshly painted woodwork and tended patches of garden. Most were occupied by staff employed at the great houses nearby, and the residents took as much pride in their own homes as they did those of their employers. Mrs Green, my parents' cook, had retired from full-time service some years ago, but still helped out some of her regulars on occasion. They appreciated the assistance from time to time, while she, in turn, appreciated the income.

I found Mrs Green in her garden, tending to a large rosemary bush. 'Good afternoon, Eda!'

She glanced at me, her face lighting up. 'Septimus!' she cried in delight. 'Whatever are you doing in these parts?'

'Your garden is looking splendid,' I said, and I meant it. Then I hesitated. 'Might I ask you a favour?'

'Come in, do. The snails don't bite, although my poor lettuce would argue otherwise.'

I opened the wooden gate and entered the small garden. There was a neat path made from broken flagstones, with moss growing from the cracks. On either side was a profusion of vegetables and flowers, and contrary to Mrs Green's remark about the snails, her lettuce seemed to be doing very well indeed.

Mrs Green was wearing a wide-brimmed straw hat against the sun, and as I approached she handed me a small pair of pruning shears. 'Take the tops off while you speak with me, would you dear? You're so much taller than I.'

I reached up and began snipping at the rosemary bush, which had grown up the cottage wall to a considerable height. There was a basket on the ground, and I dropped the cuttings into it to join those already present.

'Now, what's all this about a favour?' asked Mrs Green.

'I need to buy a haunch of meat. Mutton, perhaps, or whatever's cheapest.'

Mrs Green laughed. 'Septimus, I know you've been living in the city for some months now, but I'm sure you don't need my help to find the butcher.'

'It doesn't have to be fresh,' I explained. 'In fact, it would be better if it were not.'

'Cheaper, you mean.'

'Exactly.'

'Well, I won't be asking why you need a haunch of spoiled meat, but I do know they're not hard to come by.' Mrs Green sniffed. 'On occasion that butcher has tried to sell me one! As if I, Eda Green, would be fooled by his shameless patter.' She gave me a curious look. 'But why would you want such a thing? You might add all the rosemary in this basket to the pot, and it would still taste foul.'

'Oh, it's not for eating,' I assured her. 'It's by way of an experiment.'

She laughed. 'You always was getting up to mischief, young Septimus. I remember the time you tried to build a fireplace out of your father's books, and then–'

'Yes, quite,' I said quickly, for I had no wish to delve in to my past at that particular moment. 'But this is entirely different. I've become interested in science, you see, and–'

Mrs Green raised one hand, silencing me. 'I have no wish to know what experiments you might be performing on a spoiled haunch, but it turns my stomach just thinking about it and I'd ask you to spare me the details.'

'It's not–'

'Enough, Septimus. I have a wholesome supper planned, and I am looking forward to it.' She thought for a moment. 'Mrs Landers had a joint that was getting on a bit last time I was over. If she still has it, it'll be too far gone to eat by now.'

'Thank you, Eda. That could be just what I'm looking for.' I cut some more rosemary, then broached the subject of labourers. 'Do you know of two or three strong men who would dig a hole for me? I need it completed before sundown.'

Mrs Green hooted with laughter, surprising me. 'You hoping to plant that joint and grow a mutton bush, Septimus? Oh, you city folk!'

'No, I–'

'The things you come up with, I swear!' Mrs Green doubled up, cackling with laughter so hard I thought she'd have a fit. 'Planting a joint!' she said, through gasping breaths. 'Have you ever heard such a thing?'

'No, of course I haven't.' But others soon would, because I knew the tale would go around the village in no time, and from today I would forever be known as the city fool who tried to grow his own lamb tree. 'I assure you, the two requests are not connected. Now, I need two or three labourers, complete with shovels,' I said, in my most businesslike fashion. 'I shall pay them for their time, naturally.'

Mrs Green straightened, wiping tears from her eyes. 'So it's a hole you want dug, is it?' Then she nodded, still smiling. 'My boys Alfie and Ted will dig your hole, Septimus, especially if there's a drink or two in it for them.'

'Excellent!'

'They're working Pilson's farm until five, but I'll send 'em to your parents' house when they're done. Shovels and all. Give 'em sixpence each, and if they ask for more tell them I'll clip them around the ears.'

'Thank you, Mrs Green. I really appreciate it.' I stepped back and offered her the clippers. 'You've been most helpful.'

Instead of taking them, she surveyed the rosemary bush, eying it critically. 'A little more off the top, I think.'

I left Mrs Landers' house with the haunch of mutton under one arm. It was wrapped in two layers of hessian, and yet the unpleasant smell followed me home like a lost puppy.

I had given her a shilling for the haunch, although I suspect she would have offered it up for nothing. When she opened the meat safe, waving away the buzzing flies, I had recoiled from the strong smell.

'I was going to disguise the taste with rosemary and thyme,' Mrs Landers had said, 'but I think it's too far gone even for that.'

Never had a truer word been spoken. My only problem now was where to store the thing before it was needed, because it seemed to be getting riper by the minute. In the end I placed it inside the wood bin at the back of my parents' house, closing the door firmly after I had done so. That at least would keep any stray dogs away, and I told myself it would only be there for an hour or two at the most.

Having completed two of my errands, I then set out to tackle the third and final one. I had to spend some time asking around after Sam Tyler, for he was only a part-time constable and there was no police station in the village, but once located he readily agreed to accompany me to the inn for a drink or two.

As we strolled along the high street he put a brotherly arm around my shoulder. 'Septimus, my friend, do you need me to explain where babies come from?'

I drew back in shock. 'What?'

'Only I hear you've been planting mutton in the woods, and that's not how...' he tailed off, laughing long and hard at the expression on my face.

Meanwhile, I sighed. 'As I explained to Mrs Green, I am conducting a scientific experiment. And I have yet to dig a hole, let alone bury anything.'

'Well, if you do manage to grow a lamb tree I want to be the first to know. We shall go into business together and make our fortunes!'

I endured his ribbing until we reached the inn, where several elderly men were gathered at the tables and public bar. A few glanced up as we entered, most looking away quickly as they saw Tyler. As the local representative of the law, he was not entirely trusted.

I requested two pints of ale from the publican, and once served we took our drinks to a table near the door, which was at some distance from the other patrons. It was reminiscent of many a lazy afternoon I'd spent in the village before leaving for London, with the gentle murmur of conversation and the setting sun filling the pub with shafts of light upon which dust motes danced.

'Out with it then,' said Tyler.

'What do you mean?'

'You're not usually this free with a pint, so I take it my ale is by means of a bribe. So tell me, what have you been up to?' He snorted. 'Aside from burying things in the woods, that is.'

I hesitated. Sam had barely touched his pint, and I suspected I would not get the answers I sought until he'd downed three or four. On the other hand, it was only natural that I ask about the events of the night before, and he would be far more suspicious if I started to discuss the weather. 'How goes the investigation into my attacker?'

He looked wary. 'That's police business, Sep.'

'Maybe so, but I was in the middle of things. I must know what happened!'

Tyler took a healthy swig of ale. He was a heavier drinker than I, which was why I'd suggested the pub in the first place. An hour of conversation, a few rounds, and he'd be telling me all that I wanted to know. 'They found the driver,' he said at last.

'Really?' My father had already told me so, for the details had been in the morning news, but I feigned surprise because I wanted to keep Sam talking. 'Did he survive the attack?'

Tyler shook his head.

'The poor devil,' I muttered. 'I suppose he was stabbed by the attacker,' I said casually. 'Not that you would know, of course, unless you were privy to the official report.'

'Croydon police are keeping me informed,' said Tyler loftily, tapping the side of his nose. 'I'm an important member of the investigative team. The sarge told me so himself.'

'Do you still think it was a tramp?'

Tyler drained his pint and signalled for another. 'We have a number of suspects. The Croydon lads are rounding them up for questioning, and after that it's only a matter of time before someone cracks.'

I imagined they would crack indeed, for the 'Croydon lads' would no doubt beat these suspects until they obtained a confession. 'Excellent news. That will certainly put paid to any more attacks.'

Tyler looked at me, unsure whether I was teasing him. Then his pint arrived, and he took a long drink before sighing happily. 'There's one thing better than ale, Sep, and that's ale someone else is paying for.'

So far Tyler had revealed little of use, and my hopes of a nugget of real information were disappearing as quickly as his drink. So, I decided to ask him about the older murder before coming back later to the more recent deaths. 'Old Mr Hall—' I began.

'Now you're really dredging up the past,' said Tyler with a frown. 'What of him?'

'I learned, only recently, that his body was found in a most disturbing state.'

Tyler gestured. 'Before my time. I wouldn't know.'

And yet, I thought, Cecilie had reported her father discussing the matter with Tyler only recently. In addition, Tyler was no longer meeting my eye, and he seemed uncomfortable to boot. 'Are there no records?' I asked.

'Ancient history like that...it's best to leave it well alone, Sep. You don't know what you might dig up.'

Now Tyler *did* look at me, and there was a warning in his glance if ever I saw one. However, Tyler was my only link to the police aside from Inspector Cox, and the latter was not only in London, he'd also made it clear he would have nothing to do with me. So, valiantly, I sallied forth once more. 'Come on, Sam! When we were children together we lived for mysteries like this! Now you're like one of the adults we used to deride for hiding all the juicy details.'

'I am sworn to secrecy.'

I called for two more pints, and Sam hesitated before taking his. 'I know exactly what you're up to,' he said, with a wry smile. 'I'm betting I can hold my tongue until your purse is empty.'

'I don't know what you're talking about,' I said, and I sipped my ale.

He shrugged. 'It's your money.'

Inwardly, I cursed. Tyler was proving a tougher nut than I

expected, and I would need a great deal of luck to break through his defences.

So, it was fortunate indeed that Roberta happened to enter the pub at that very moment.

27

Tyler stood as Roberta approached our table, and belatedly I followed his lead. Roberta smiled at us, and I introduced her to Sam. 'This is...Isabella Makepeace,' I said, recalling her *nom de plume* at the last second. 'I–I work with her father in London.'

'Miss Makepeace!' exclaimed Tyler. 'Is it just me, or does the sun shine twice as brightly all of a sudden?'

I expected Roberta to brush off this gauche compliment, but instead she smiled in a most fetching fashion. 'Septimus, who is this dashing rogue, and why have you waited so long to introduce us?'

I swallowed. 'Sam Tyler. He's the village police constable.'

'But not a constable for long, I take it,' murmured Roberta. 'It's clear to me he's destined for greater things.'

She could not have laid on these compliments any thicker with a builder's trowel in each hand, but Tyler lapped them up like a man in a trance. Roberta took a seat at the table, and Sam and I did likewise. Then she rested her elbows on the table and nestled her chin in her cupped hands, fastening Tyler with an adoring gaze that would have rendered me speechless had she applied it to me instead. The effect on Tyler was impressive, all the same, for he turned a fetching shade of pink and stammered his words. 'S–Septimus and I grew up together,' he said. 'We've known each other for years, but to my eternal disappointment he has never mentioned you to me.'

'Let us not speak of Septimus,' said Roberta, with an airy gesture. 'He is but a clerk in my father's employ, and he spends all day talking of dreary accounting matters. Speak to me instead of your thrilling life in the police force!'

I knew Roberta was putting on an act – or at least, I hoped she was! – but I was stung nevertheless, and I wanted to remind her that I was sitting right there, not two feet away, while she disparaged me. But then I caught sight of Tyler, and I hid a smile. The poor fool seemed besotted, beside himself, and all it had taken was a winning smile and a few well-chosen words! What sort of weakling fell so easily under a spell?

'I–I cannot discuss my cases,' said Tyler.

'Septimus, will you order drinks?' asked Roberta, without even looking at me. 'A brandy punch for me, I think, or failing that, gin.'

I got up and crossed to the bar, where the publican served me two ales and a small glass of gin. As I gathered the drinks and turned from the bar, I was astonished to see Roberta holding one of Tyler's hands in both of hers. She gazed at him in rapt fascination as he spoke, and my heart plunged to my boots. Play-acting it might be, but the sight of them together was distressing to me in the extreme. After all she had never held *my* hand nor gazed with longing into *my* eyes, and she'd only met Tyler a few minutes earlier!

Quickly I turned back to the bar, placing the drinks on the scarred timber. Then I took a large swig from the nearest ale, before emptying the contents of the gin glass into it. Next, I nodded to the barkeep, holding up the empty glass. He refilled it and I carried the drinks to the table once more, being careful to place the doctored ale at Sam's elbow. Get a couple of fortified drinks inside him, I thought, and he'd be incapable of sitting upright, let alone holding Roberta's hand.

Tyler took a deep draught from the pint mug and smacked his lips. 'Now that's the good stuff!' he declared, before helping himself to another healthy dose. While his head was back, his gullet bobbing in a most distasteful fashion, Roberta glanced at me and rolled her eyes. This gesture, small though it was, gave me great joy, for it proved she was suffering almost as much as I was. I was still smiling to myself when Tyler set his glass down, his actions already somewhat unsteady.

'The police have a very important job,' he said, slowly and deliberately. 'We must protect the public, but also shield them from the w–worst details of crimes committed. Why, if only the general public knew of the horrors we had to witness in the l–line of duty!'

Such as? I wanted to shout, perhaps taking him by the shoulders and giving him a good shake into the bargain. But Roberta had her own methods, and they were far less crude.

'Not all are as thoughtful as you are,' said Roberta. 'A close friend of mine in London has a suitor in the metropolitan police force, and she's always sharing sordid details of his investigations.' She sighed. 'Sometimes I'm at a loss, for it would be nice, just once, to share some little tidbit with her.'

I held my breath. The hook was baited, and I wondered whether Tyler would take it.

'Well,' he said conspiratorially. 'I shouldn't be telling you this, dearest Isabella, but there's a case right now which would turn your friend's stomach.'

Still holding my breath, I waited desperately for his next words. Surely he could not be involved in two gruesome cases, and would now be forced to reveal the details we sought on the attacks in the woods? Or was he about to make up a complete fiction?

'I'm sure Septimus here has regaled you with his brief encounter in the woods, when he was attacked by a savage, deformed creature under the light of a full moon?'

'Indeed he has.'

'Well, it's all lies,' breathed Tyler. 'He was actually confronted by an angry cook, who was looking for the place where dear old Sep buried her Sunday roast!' Releasing Roberta's hand, he sat back in his chair and hooted with laughter, slapping his thigh. 'Oh, you two are a pretty picture!' he said at last, and he laughed again at our puzzled looks. 'A few glasses of ale and the attentions of a pretty girl,' he said, amidst further laughter. 'Did you really think I would fall for such obvious play-acting? Why, I only went along with the charade to discover whether Isabella here might propose marriage in order to loosen my tongue!'

I was stunned, for it seemed Tyler was more than a match for Roberta's subterfuge. He'd not only seen through her, he'd fooled her into the bargain! I glanced at her, fearing her reaction, but she seemed unperturbed. Indeed, she appeared to be...waiting for something?

I turned to Tyler, just as his eyes rolled backwards into his head. He lolled to one side, then the other, before falling forwards across the table. His forehead connected with a solid *thunk*, and as his glass went flying Roberta stuck out a hand and caught it neatly.

'Your friend is quite overcome,' she remarked, replacing the glass. 'We had better help him outside for some fresh air.'

I was still gazing at Tyler. I knew he liked to drink, but I had never seen a man collapse so quickly.

'Septimus?' said Roberta. 'Now, if you please.'

I got up, still in a daze, and with Roberta's help I guided Tyler outside. He appeared to have kept some of his wits about him, for he mumbled under his breath all the way, but the words were jumbled and made no sense.

There were two wooden benches outside, and Roberta indicated the furthest from the door. Here, we propped Tyler up, and then Roberta and I sat either side of him. We were well out of earshot, but I kept my voice low as I quizzed Roberta. 'What happened to him? Was this your doing?'

'Of course,' she said calmly. 'I doctored his beer when he was distracted.'

'So did I,' I remarked. 'In my case it was gin, but I suspect you employed something a little more exotic.'

Roberta displayed a tiny glass vial, half-empty. 'A concoction of my father's. I carry it always, and it has proven useful on more than one occasion. But come, his state will not last long. We must set to work.'

'What do you intend to do with him?' I asked.

'In this condition, he will answer our questions without too much protest.' Roberta leaned closer to Tyler. 'Sam, my dear. Why are the police concealing information on the killer?'

'O–orders from above,' murmured Sam. 'Powerful.'

'Tell us everything,' I said.

'Pretty girl,' muttered Sam. 'Nice hands.'

Roberta frowned at me. 'You must be specific, Septimus. His brain is too addled for anything so vague.'

I turned to Tyler. 'Whose orders?' I demanded.

'Septimus ordered ale,' replied Sam promptly, and he giggled.

'Who ordered you to ignore my report?'

'Sarge.' Sam burped. 'Don't scare the civilians, he says. We'll catch this monster, but until then we...we gotta...keep it under our hats, son.'

'Do the police really have suspects?' Roberta asked him.

I swallowed, hoping my father's name did not come up. As it turned out, I needn't have worried.

'Not a one,' said Sam blithely. 'Mishtery mam in the woods.' He frowned. 'Man, I mean. Or monster.'

'I hope you extracted more information from Carmichael,' I muttered to Roberta.

She shook her head. 'He told me to ask the Hall sisters. Wouldn't even let me into the house.'

'No wonder you happened by so soon.'

'Big house,' said Tyler. 'Dangerous.'

'What did you say?' I demanded. 'Which house? Why is it dangerous?'

But Tyler's head was dropping, and before I could extract any more information he was snoring lustily.

'Your gin must have interacted with the concoction I gave him,' said Roberta. 'Normally they remain conscious far longer.'

'What did he mean about a dangerous house, I wonder?'

'There are many mansions in these parts,' said Roberta with a shrug. 'It could be any of them.'

I indicated Tyler. 'What do we do with him?'

'Leave him to sleep it off,' she said, getting up. 'Come, let us walk together. You can tell me how you got along this afternoon.'

I told Roberta about the stale mutton joint, now concealed in the wood bin, and also the labourers who would be calling upon my parents at five p.m., complete with shovels and a willingness to use them.

She, in turn, revealed that she had borrowed a clothesline with which to string the joint from a tree, and expanded upon her attempts to interview Mr Carmichael. 'I presented myself as Isabella Makepeace, amateur historian, for he would have surely seen through me should I have claimed to have been a member of the aristocracy.'

'I'm surprised you did not drug the man over a cup of tea,' I said.

'I would have, only there was no offer of refreshment.' Roberta hesitated. 'To be honest, he seemed eager to be rid of me, as though he had urgent business elsewhere. He spent more time looking at the clock than at me.'

'Clearly a gentleman of little taste,' I said gallantly.

She smiled.

We were walking aimlessly, for it still wanted an hour until five o'clock, and I did not want to wait awkwardly in my parents' sitting room with Roberta on one side and my mother firing questions from the other. As for my father, I did not believe I would be capable of meeting his eye without betraying my fears.

After a few minutes we found ourselves strolling along the edge of the woods, revelling in the birdsong and the last rays of the setting sun. All of a sudden I remembered something which I had been meaning to ask her. 'Roberta, the equipment in my trunk...what on earth possessed you to pack the jar with those devilish sprites in?'

She gave me a curious smile. 'Have you heard of fighting fire with fire?'

'You mean to fight one supernatural being with another? Will that work?'

'Septimus, there are no rules or laws in our business. One can only muddle along, learning along the way.'

'And what if we learn that the creatures trapped in the jar are even more dangerous than the monster prowling the woods?'

She shrugged, unconcerned. 'In that case, we shall chalk it up to experience and try a different approach.'

I fell silent. Since joining the professor's employ, I had encountered one paranormal phenomenon after another, most of them deadly. In each case, I had reassured myself that Professor Twickham and Roberta knew what they were doing, and it was somewhat disconcerting to discover that they too were in the dark much of the time.

Suddenly I felt Roberta's hand in mine, and as our fingers interlaced I felt my heart skip a beat.

'My father is a difficult man at times,' she said, in a low voice. 'But you must understand that he means the world to me.'

'Of course I do!' I said valiantly, as this was apparent even to the most casual observer.

'I would not willingly hurt him, and thus we come to a matter that concerns both you and I.'

My heart began to beat most painfully, for there was only one subject she could be referring to. The professor had endured very modest beginnings, to say the least, and he did not want his daughter to suffer the same fate. He was not so crass as to direct his daughter to marry this young gentleman or that, as many fathers would, for Roberta would then have disobeyed him and married whomever she wanted. Instead, he had let it be known that he would not be happy unless she married someone of means. As his only child he wanted her to make a 'suitable match' as he worded it, and long before she met me, Roberta had given her word.

'Perhaps I should discover a gold mine,' I said, only half joking. 'In Australia they report one find after another, and a willing young man could easily make his fortune there.'

'I most certainly do not want you to leave for Australia,' said Roberta quietly. She stopped, looking up at me. 'I only want you to know that my heart is yours, as I hope yours belongs to me.'

'Of course it does,' I breathed, barely able to get the words out quickly enough. 'You know that, Roberta!'

She smiled, and then her arms went around me and our lips met. I would have remained in that embrace all afternoon, happily oblivious to the passage of time, but a sudden noise from the woods nearby caused me to start in alarm.

Roberta turned, breaking free, and we both spotted a hooded figure fleeing between the trees. I was about to give chase, but Roberta took my wrist. 'Leave them be,' she said. 'It's not important.'

'They were spying on us!' I declared hotly. 'And it's not the first time, either. I have seen that fellow on more than one occasion!'

'Well, he's halfway to Croydon by now, and he saw little of consequence. A gentleman sharing a kiss with his beloved, nothing more.'

I smiled at this description of our embrace, but alas the mood was quite spoiled. 'I'd like to know why he's watching us,' I said darkly. 'You do not think it might be the monster in human form, gathering information on his next victims? Why, he might be preparing to spring a surprise on us later tonight!'

'If he falls into our trap he won't be springing anywhere,' remarked Roberta. She glanced towards the sun. 'Come, it must be getting close to five. Let us wait near your parents' house and meet these labourers of yours. They might even know of a suitable tree, and while they're digging you and I can lay a trail with the joint.' Then she snapped her fingers. 'The rope! I will fetch it now, then meet you near your home.'

'And the gun,' I reminded her.

She smiled. 'For some reason I have lost all my senses. Of course we shall need the gun!'

'I shall come with you.'

'No, you must wait for the labourers. We do not want them to depart, thinking we had forgotten them.'

'Be careful,' I muttered, as she hurried away. The sight of the cloaked figure had been troubling, and now that Roberta and I were on a new footing, so to speak, the thought of losing her caused me even greater concern. I turned for home, and despite my worries I am certain there was a foolish grin on my face the whole way, reliving as I was the moment Roberta and I had kissed. Soon I was in such high spirits that I spared barely a thought for that cloaked stranger in the woods, being much more taken with matters of a romantic nature.

Given events later that night, this would prove to be a huge mistake.

28

Alfie and Ted, Mrs Green's sons, arrived just after five as promised. They were stout, barrel-chested young men of few words, tanned by long hours in the sun, their muscles forged by lives of hard labour. Each carried a shovel over one shoulder, and they followed Roberta and me without comment as we led the way into the woods. Even the sight of the old shotgun which Roberta carried, and the coil of rope slung over my own shoulder, and the bulging satchels at our sides, did not elicit any queries as to the nature of our little expedition. They did, however, maintain a respectable distance, not out of social propriety but because of the leg of mutton. The joint had ripened further since I'd stored it in the wood bin, and despite being wrapped in two layers of cotton there was an unpleasant aroma which assaulted the senses in a most distasteful fashion.

As we strolled up the hill beyond the village, Roberta leaned closer to me, speaking in a low voice. 'We shall set our trap near the scene of Cox's victim. Beasts will often return to the scene of prior killings, and it's as good a place as any.'

'Do you know where that is?' I asked her.

She nodded. 'I discussed the case with Miss Emily, in a roundabout fashion, and she gave me directions. She was less willing to talk about her father, poor dear, but I gather his murder also took place in the same general area.'

I heard a murmur behind me, and looked round. Alfie and Ted were also walking close together, and they seemed concerned at the direction in which we were walking. 'It's gettin' on a bit,' said Alfie, the older of the two brothers. He had a mop of dark hair and a narrow face, and that face now bore a look of concern. 'Sun's going down, and twilight is no time to be out. Why don't me and Ted dig this hole of your'n tomorrow?'

'Come, gentlemen!' I said, adopting a jolly, chiding tone. 'It's just a hole in the ground and you'll be done in no time! A shilling each for half an hour's work.'

The two men exchanged a glance. Ted, fair-haired and slightly shorter than his brother, muttered something, and then the two of them turned to me. 'Two shillings each. Digging is one thing, but this is danger money, like.'

I was about to explain that Roberta and I would be guarding the trap ourselves, all night if necessary, and if the pair of us weren't afraid of a little darkness, then the two powerfully-built labourers had nothing to fear. Then I saw Alfie eying the shotgun, and I realised my argument would carry little weight.

'Two shillings it is,' agreed Roberta, with all the ease of one spending another person's money.

It seemed to me that the birds grew quieter the deeper we progressed into the woods. We saw evidence of rabbit tracks, criss-crossing our path in every direction, but no sign of the ubiquitous creatures themselves. In the gathering gloom before sunset, the woods seemed eerie and forbidding.

'Well this is a jolly jaunt,' remarked Roberta, still keeping her voice low. 'I confess I keep turning about to ensure that our unwilling workers have not deserted us.'

'They do seem ill at ease,' I agreed.

'A feeling I share.' Roberta opened the gun and checked the load, closing it again with a loud click. 'Perhaps we should have gathered a large group to storm the woods and flush the monster from hiding.'

I shuddered as I imagined the woods echoing to the sound of angry voices, with flaming torches and pitchforks and guns. A wild melee was sure to eventuate, and I had an upsetting vision of my father breathing his last on the tines of a fork.

Earlier, I had taken my mother aside, and after some casual questioning on my behalf she had confirmed that my father had no plans to leave the house that evening. Even so, I feared he might slip away and prowl the woods as the monster, and so I was relieved beyond measure that only Roberta and I would be there to confront him with our leg of mutton and our pit. As long as I held the shotgun, per our agreement, then no real harm should come to my father.

It was another twenty minutes before we happened upon a large clearing, and despite the gathering twilight it was easily recognised as that of the police photographs. The torn, mangled body had lain in the centre, not ten yards from where I now stood, and I felt a shiver up my spine as I imagined the final minutes of the terrified victim. A farm labourer from a nearby village, he had been walking home when set upon by the monster, and it did not take a vivid imagination to hear his screams echoing amongst the nearby trees.

'Let us scout the area,' suggested Roberta. 'We are looking for a tree with an overhanging branch perhaps ten feet from the ground, and the dirt beneath should be clear of rocks and large stones in order to make digging an easier task.'

I looked around to see little else but trees with overhanging branches, many of them ten feet or so above the ground. Thus, it was necessary for our small party to divide up, and we set about inspecting the dirt beneath each tree surrounding that clearing until we eventually found one suitable for digging.

The two men did not tarry. They had their shovels in the soft earth in an instant, first cutting the turf in a neat rectangle before really digging in, throwing gouts of dirt over their shoulders as the pit took shape.

Roberta and I set our equipment against a nearby tree, then gathered fallen branches with which to cover the pit. We laid several longer ones in parallel, then wove shorter ones across them, forming a lightweight cover. Next we gathered armfulls of twigs that could be used to disguise the resulting holes, and finally we made a pile of dry leaves that would blend the surface with the surroundings.

The men were still digging, and I eyed the growing pile of earth with alarm. 'We shall have to move that,' I told Roberta. 'I shall ask them to spread it out beyond the tree, and we'll cover it with more leaves.'

'I hope you have another shilling or two,' she replied.

I took out a small lantern borrowed from my parents, setting it on a stump before lighting it. By now it was getting dark, and I could already see a star or two in the sky above. We still had to drag our bait through the woods, string it from the branch and cover the pit, and I realised we should have started a little earlier.

Alfie's head appeared above the edge of the pit, the light from the lantern reflected in his eyes. 'How much deeper?' he asked.

'At least eight feet,' I suggested. If the monster fell in, I did not want it to climb straight out again. As for the men, they assured me they would be able to climb out if we lowered a sizeable branch into the pit.

To his credit, Alfie did not argue. Instead, he vanished, and soon fresh gouts of dirt flew out of the hole.

'I should make the first trail with the bait,' I told Roberta. 'Can you watch over them?'

'Of course.'

She took up the shotgun, again checking the load, while I tied one end of the rope to the leg of mutton. It was slimy to the touch, and once free of the cotton bags it stank worse than ever. 'If the creature's sense of smell is half as good as ours, it will still detect this from a mile away,' I remarked.

'Don't delay, my dear,' Roberta urged me. 'And if you hear the slightest noise, you must abandon the bait and run back here as quick as you can. Be certain I will not think less of you!'

I promised I would flee at the first sign of the monster, and then I left the clearing, dragging the leg of mutton behind me. I had decided to count off four hundred paces, keeping the clearing at my back, and then turn right for another fifty before returning to the start.

I hoped that the lantern, though small, would guide me with its flickering light, for the only other way to locate Roberta was for each of us to cry out, and I feared our raised voices might alert any creature lurking in the woods.

Afterwards I would set out in the opposite direction, repeating the pattern. By spreading the scent over such a large area, the monster could not fail to detect it. Of course, with my father safely at home there was a chance that all our efforts – and my shillings – would be wasted, but what alternative did we have? I would have to return to London the following evening, for I had given the professor my word, and so tonight represented our one and only chance of success.

In that instant I vowed that, should we fail, I would find a way to confide in Roberta, revealing my suspicions about my father. After much experimentation and study, she and the professor might even concoct a cure. But first I had to satisfy myself that the creature we hunted was *not* my father, for it was still possible that the test I had administered to his day-old blood had given a false result.

I realised I had neglected to count my steps, and so I cleared my mind to concentrate on the task at hand. Navigating the rough ground, I clambered up and down banks, stepping over tiny streams and rivulets which would eventually combine to form a river. Several times my bait snagged on roots, meaning I had to go back and free the foul thing, working by feel in near-total darkness, and by the time I turned for the clearing I was wishing we could have thought up a better plan.

It was some time later when I began to suspect I had missed the clearing. I paused to listen, scanning the trees around me for any signs of life, but heard and saw nothing. Then, to my left, I heard the snap of a twig. Instantly, I felt the hairs on the back of my neck rise, and a chill ran through my veins like iced water. I was gripped by terror, certain I would be set upon at any moment, and yet I did not know in which direction to run. Run? I could barely see my hand in front of my face, and was more likely to dash my brains out on a rock or a tree than lose my life to a marauding beast!

So, I began to move once more, creeping along with the end of the cord wrapped around my hand, the leg of mutton tugging upon them painfully as it bumped over one obstacle after another. There! Was that a flicker of light? Squinting, I felt my spirits soar as I saw a glow between the trees. Moments later I emerged in the clearing, trailing my foul burden behind me. Then I stopped, for Roberta was talking to someone, and he had a gun over his shoulder.

As I approached Roberta and the newcomer I felt a surge of relief, for it was none other than Sir Lennard's gamekeeper. He turned at the sound of my footsteps, the gun casually slung over one shoulder. 'Your partner in crime, my lady?'

'Indeed, indeed,' said Roberta, once again employing her upper-class accent. 'Septimus is laying a trail for our prey.'

'Are you certain you know which is the prey and which is the hunter?' enquired the keeper. His tone was light, but the gaze with which he fixed me was anything but. He was willing to humour Roberta, whom he saw as a slightly mad young woman, but he clearly expected me to know better.

Behind him loomed the pit, and even now I saw a shovel of dirt fly out to land on the large pile alongside. The pace had slowed considerably, which was not surprising.

'I trust you will be filling that in once your exciting little game is done?' the keeper asked me, indicating the pit with a jerk of his head. 'It wouldn't do for someone to fall in and break their neck.'

I had not thought of it, and I cursed inwardly as I saw more of my dwindling savings evaporate before my very eyes. 'We shall indeed, although it might have to wait until tomorrow.'

The keeper nodded, and after a last look around, including a small, disbelieving shake of the head, he departed.

'He thinks me a lunatic,' remarked Roberta.

'We both are,' I muttered.

'The men are all but finished. Will you pay them before you set off with the bait once more?'

I shook my head. 'Ask them to wait until I return. In fact, you might ask them to spread the dirt pile and cover the pit for us.' I did not say so, but I did not want to leave Roberta alone in that clearing. She might be armed, but we had already proved to be less than proficient with the shotgun, and the sturdy young men with their shovels would be far more capable of defending her.

She nodded, and I set off with my burden once more, heading into the woods for another thousand laborious paces.

29

It was two hours later, and I was uncomfortable, tired and chilled to the bone.

We had finished preparing our trap more than an hour earlier, with the mouth of the pit covered up and the bait strung from the tree. Alfie and Ted had been paid, leaving me with barely two pennies to rub together, and upon their departure we had doused the lantern, hidden our equipment under a bush, and cast about for somewhere to conceal ourselves. In the end we chose a tree with low-slung branches, which made for easy climbing.

Now, having been perched in our tree for what seemed like half the night, my rump was numb and I was in danger of nodding off. Roberta sat nearby, on a branch slightly higher up and on the opposite side of the trunk, but we dare not communicate–even in whispers–lest the creature hear us.

From our position the pit was invisible, blending in perfectly with its thick cover of dried leaves. The pile of dirt had been spread about to disguise it, and the leg of mutton hanging from the tree was a barely-discernible shadow against the deeper darkness of the undergrowth beyond.

Some starlight filtered through the trees, leaving faint patches of light on the ground, but most of the canopy was in pitch darkness.

As an experiment I raised my hand, waving it in front of my face, and could only be certain it was there at all because I felt the wind of its passing.

The thought of fighting for my life in such conditions had me doubting my sanity. The only thing that prevented me from giving up and going home was the thought that the monster might be out there, waiting, and Roberta and I might walk straight into its gaping jaws.

All of a sudden I heard a sharp noise, and I stared into the woods. It was little more than the snap of a twig, but I knew that such a sound required a large, heavy being, rather than a passing rabbit or badger. Tense, with my nerves at breaking point, I strained my ears for further evidence.

There! Eyes wide, I saw a shadow in the undergrowth, no more than twenty yards away. It was indistinct, just one dark patch against another, but it was clearly moving in our direction. I saw it pause, and briefly lost it against the surroundings, then spotted it again even closer. Oh, how I wished the moon would rise!

I heard an indrawn breath behind me, and realised Roberta had also spotted the beast. I prayed she would remain silent, for a supernatural being might have supernatural sight and hearing, and both would leave us at a disadvantage. I was not as worried about the creature's sense of smell, for the foul stench of our bait would most certainly confuse that.

The figure drew closer, its shape altering as it tilted its head back to study the leg of mutton. I heard a low sniff, repeated once or twice, and I prayed the thing was not overly fussy about its diet.

Come closer, I thought. *Come just a little bit closer.*

Almost on command, the creature took one step, then another. All of a sudden the ground gave way with a succession of loud cracks as the thin branches snapped. I expected the creature to hurl itself backwards, using its reflexes and inhuman strength to save itself, but the floor vanished so suddenly it had no chance. With a rustle of leaves our prey dropped into the eight-foot pit, landing at the bottom with a loud thud. My skin prickled at the unholy roar of pain and anger, and then Roberta and I were clambering down the tree hand over hand, ready to fire upon the monster should it try to escape captivity.

Roberta and I had prepared ourselves for this moment, and she quickly took up the lantern, lighting it from her small brass tube. In her other hand she held the engraved metal jar containing the lethal, glowing sprites. At the first sign of the monster emerging from the pit, she would remove the lid and hurl the jar at the thing, and then I would cover our retreat with the shotgun.

Cautiously, we approached the pit. There was a ragged hole in the surface where the creature had gone through, and I fastened my unblinking gaze upon it like a mouse confronted by a snake. At any second I expected the huge creature to spring out, all but laughing at our inadequate pit, but as we got closer there was nothing but silence.

Finally we reached the lip, and Roberta cautiously extended her arm, allowing the lantern's light to spill into the darkness. As she did so there came a groan, and we both stepped back hurriedly.

Then, instead of a roaring monster, we heard a stream of foul language that turned the very air blue. The ranting and raging was of a particularly human nature, and as we approached once more we spied our captive. There, in the bottom of the pit, lay an elderly gentleman dressed in a hooded robe. He was clutching his ankle, and the swearing continued as he writhed in pain.

'Could the creature have turned back into a human so quickly?' I whispered to Roberta. Despite my shock, I was still aware of an overwhelming joy, for the figure at the bottom of the pit was not my father.

Roberta tilted the lantern to spill more light onto the scene. Below, our victim had finally noticed the light shining down from above, he glared up at us with a most aggrieved expression. 'I do not think it turned at all,' said Roberta at last.

I recognised the man below us, and I was so surprised I almost fell into the pit on top of him. For the man in the hooded cloak, the man who had been spying on me, the man who had fallen into our trap...it was none other than Roberta's father, Professor Twickham!

'I thought you and my daughter had departed London on some dalliance,' growled the professor. 'Gadding about together, running off to the same place in the countryside...what did you expect me to do?'

We'd helped him out of the pit, and the elderly gentleman was now trying to brush himself down. Roberta went to help, but he waved her away impatiently. 'All that nonsense about accounting courses and friends with sick mothers...your lies were so transparent a child might have seen through them!'

'What about your lecture in Brighton?' demanded Roberta hotly. 'You told us an American was presenting some fascinating new facts, and instead you've been sneaking around, spying on Septimus and myself!'

'Sir...Roberta,' I said urgently. 'Please keep your voices down, I beg you!' I glanced around nervously, for we were standing in the woods with a flickering lantern and the ripe smell of our bait in our nostrils. The pit was exposed and useless, and we would make a welcome meal if the monster happened by. 'Let us discuss matters later. Right now we are in mortal danger!'

'*And* you raided my study!' cried the professor, completely ignoring me. 'When I began to gather the supplies and equipment I required for my expedition, I found many of my most vital items missing!' He snatched up the engraved metal jar, waving it under Roberta's nose. I feared the lid might fall off, redoubling our woes, but fortunately it held fast. 'Do you have any idea how much this cost me?' he roared. 'Do you?'

'You've ruined all our plans!' shouted Roberta, who was getting riled up herself. 'All day we've been preparing, and you blundered in and destroyed everything!'

'Forgive me for saying so, but you cannot dig a pit in the woods and then express surprise when some innocent passerby happens to fall into it!'

'Innocent passerby? You were following us!'

I gazed from one to the other, desperate to intervene but also fearing the consequences. In my experience these fierce rows tended to blow over fairly quickly, but if I interrupted again, both were likely to round on me. Unfortunately, they were shouting so loudly I would not have heard the monster if it approached us at the head of a marching band playing for all they were worth.

'I cannot *believe* you, father,' shouted Roberta. 'Do you have so little trust in me?'

'You and Septimus spend far too much time together,' said the professor defensively. 'I wanted to be certain that–'

'Certain of what?'

The professor looked uncomfortable. 'Now, Roberta. You're a sensible girl, but when it comes to matters of the heart–'

Incensed, Roberta advanced on him. 'If you say another word I shall throw you back in the pit, there to remain until you starve.'

I thought he might counter that thirst came before starvation, but wisely, the professor remained silent. Roberta, having won the argument, contented herself with gathering our equipment, muttering under her breath all the while. For my part I had no desire to speak, for I had just realised that the monster's absence only heaped further suspicion upon my father.

30

We walked towards the village in a most dispirited mood, heading downhill with myself and the professor side by side and Roberta following close behind. A discussion had been held around the gaping pit, and in the end we had decided to abandon our plan. Collecting branches, weaving them into a new cover, and disguising the whole with twigs and leaves once more would have been a lengthy task, and then there was the matter of hiding in the trees once again, perhaps until dawn. There was no guarantee the second attempt would be any more successful than the first, and consensus was reached quickly. Now that the professor had joined us, we were sure his superior knowledge of the supernatural could be put to good use. Once he and Roberta had calmed down, he explained that aside from keeping an eye on us, he'd also agreed to look into the recent murders on Cox's behalf, since the local police did not seem to be getting anywhere.

We'd left the pit exposed, the bait still dangling above, but I carried the shotgun in the crook of my arm and was ready to use it. The professor was using my other arm for support, since he was having trouble with his ankle. Behind us, Roberta carried the lantern, using the light to guide our way. As we walked together in silence, stumbling now and then on the uneven ground, the professor gave me a sidelong glance. 'I assume my daughter forced you to go along with her plans?' he asked, keeping his voice low.

I opened my mouth to confess that I had travelled to West Wickham of my own volition, lying to him in the process, but Roberta forestalled me. Clearly, the professor had not spoken quietly enough.

'Of course I did,' she said stoutly. 'This plan was entirely of my doing, and Septimus is blameless.'

I was silent, for I understood her tactics. I might easily be dismissed from the professor's employ for my actions, but Roberta was immune.

'I see.' The professor eyed me from under his bushy white eyebrows. 'You and I will discuss this later, my boy,' he said, with the air of a schoolmaster promising a visit to the head's office.

'Why not discuss it now?' demanded Roberta. 'The monster is long gone, after all, and a spirited conversation will help to pass the time.'

At that instant I saw a flash out the corner of my eye, and a split second later there was a loud crack. Not five feet away, a large piece of bark was ripped from a tree, leaving a white gash. I stared at it, stupefied, then realised the professor and Roberta were already ducking for cover, the former moving as quickly as a sprinter despite his ankle, and the latter having already doused the lantern.

'Septimus, get down!' shouted Roberta.

I turned and ran, hearing the crack of another shot as I did so. It was not the boom of a shotgun but the sharp report of a rifle, and even as I ran for the trees I felt something pluck violently at my clothing.

I reached the tree and crouched behind it, using it for cover. Another bang, and I felt the trunk shiver as a bullet slammed into it. Heart thudding, I took hold of the shotgun and peered around the trunk, sighting along the barrel. I saw a flash in the woods, felt the wind of a passing bullet, and then I pulled my own trigger. The searing flash left after-images in my eyes, and the sound was enormously loud. I thought I heard a cry, but it was indistinct and I could not be certain.

'Just one, do you think?' demanded the professor.

'So it seems,' I muttered, desperately reloading in the darkness. A shell slipped from my fingers, and I gave up trying to find it and took another from my pocket, slotting it home and closing the gun with a snap.

'Why the devil are they shooting at us?' demanded the professor.

I wondered whether it was the gamekeeper, but he'd been carrying a shotgun, not a rifle. Also, he knew we were in the woods that night, and would not have fired upon us without warning. 'I don't know, sir,' I said urgently, 'but I suggest we keep quiet.'

We remained there for several minutes, crouched behind trees with our hearts in our mouths. My shotgun was only a short-range weapon, whereas our attacker's rifle was deadly for three hundred yards or more. In daylight we would have been helpless, but cloaked as we were by darkness, we had a chance. Perhaps, also, the attacker had not realised we were armed, and the return fire had driven them off.

'We can't stay here all night,' whispered the professor.

'I agree. They might be flanking us right now.'

'Don't be so sure. If they get close enough, they know you will shoot them.'

I recalled our comical attempts with the weapon the day before, but decided against mentioning it. The professor had already fallen into a pit, damaged his ankle and endured a stand-up shouting match with his daughter, and the knowledge that neither she nor I could hit a brick wall at three paces would only sap his spirits even further.

I heard footsteps approaching fast, from my right, and all of a sudden Roberta thudded down beside us, scattering dry leaves. We kept our heads down, expecting another shot, but there was none. 'We should leave right away,' she whispered. 'Back to the village as quickly as possible. They won't follow us there, and we'll be safe with people around.'

It seemed like an excellent plan, so we rose from our hiding place, moving off slowly in a half-crouch. I was not accustomed to walking in that manner, and my thighs soon burned from the effort. After a few minutes, with no sign of our attacker, I reverted to walking upright. I kept the gun level, the muzzle pointing towards the woods from which the earlier shots had come, but it was as though our attacker had melted into the darkness.

Thus we emerged at last on the outskirts of the village, and our mood immediately improved. Nobody had fired upon us, and it seemed we were safe at last. 'Where are you staying, father?' Roberta asked the professor.

'I am lodging with a farmer and his wife.'

'At this hour, perhaps you should accompany me to Ravenswood. The manor has rooms aplenty, and I will find you suitable bedding. The sisters are dears, and I'm sure they won't mind another guest.'

The professor looked pleased, and I guessed his current accommodation was modest, to say the least.

Upon reaching my parents' house I bid the professor goodnight, then handed Roberta the weapon. 'Are you sure you'll be all right on your own?'

'It's barely three hundred yards, Septimus. We shall be fine.'

The last I saw of them they were walking along the main street together, the professor limping slightly due to his injured ankle.

I let myself in and crept towards my room, avoiding a floorboard which I knew would emit a loud creak at the lightest of touches. I undressed in the darkness and sought my bed, drawing the covers up and relaxing in the luxurious comfort. As I lay there, tired and sore, I recalled those rifle shots in the woods, and I wondered again whether it had been a deliberate attempt to kill us. But who would do such a thing, and why? In the end I decided it must have been a poacher who had mistaken one of us for the gamekeeper. They had fired the shots to cover their escape, nothing more. It was only lucky nobody had been wounded, or killed.

I dwelled on the events a while longer, but the hour was late and as the bedding warmed around me I fell into a deep, untroubled sleep.

31

I rose early the next morning, dressing quickly before meeting my parents in the dining room for a light breakfast. I knew my mother wanted to ask me about the night before, to explain why I'd asked her to keep my father home, but he was sitting at the table with us and she was forced to save her questions for later.

'Don't eat so quickly, Septimus,' she grumbled. 'I swear you'll choke.'

'Sorry, mother. I have urgent business this morning.' I finished off my boiled eggs and toast and gulped the rest of my tea, then excused myself and left for Ravenswood. I took with me a burlap sack containing the rest of the items and equipment Roberta had packed into my trunk, for I was sure the professor would find a use for them.

I kept up a punishing pace as I strode along the high street, suspecting the professor and Roberta would already be making plans. It was vital I be there in case the professor came to the conclusion that the beast must be hunted down and killed, because if that happened I would register my opposition in the strongest possible terms.

If he insisted death was the only recourse, I decided I would reveal my fears about my father's involvement. The professor was possibly the only person in England who would be able to help him, and once he knew my secret he might perhaps devise a cure, or failing that, a special concoction to suppress the curse.

So, I was in quite a state as I hurried between the rusty metal gates, my shoes crunching on the gravel with every step.

'Septimus!'

The voice came from my right, and I looked round to see Miss Emily tending a garden bed. She was holding a dutch hoe, and had just been attacking thickets of weeds growing amongst the roses. 'Good morning, Miss Hall,' I said, with a polite nod. I turned to leave, but she stopped me.

'Can we speak a moment?'

I glanced towards the house. Even now, the professor might be designing some trap or weapon with which to kill the monster, and the sooner I made my case the better.

'I shouldn't worry, my lad,' said Emily, with a laugh. 'I was in the dining room barely ten minutes ago, and your friends had yet to come down for breakfast. They were out very late last night.'

'As was I.' I hesitated, unsure how much to divulge. 'The truth of the matter is–'

'The three of you came to West Wickham to hunt our werewolf, did you not?'

Her manner was so matter-of-fact that I was quite taken aback. Emily had also used a specific term for the beast which I'd seen in one or two of the professor's books, a name that Roberta and I had avoided using ourselves, since we were not certain exactly *what* we were hunting. Emily, though, seemed absolutely certain. 'How...how do you know of werewolves?'

'When my father was killed, oh, almost thirty years ago now, the police investigation lasted no time at all. They declared he was killed by an unknown hand, his body subsequently mauled by a wild creature. They said it was a robbery, yet his purse was untouched. Later, they claimed a fight may have broken out, even though my father was a gentle soul loved and admired by all. Soon, even these patently false theories dried up, and no further questions were asked. The case was closed.' Emily gave me a wry smile. 'My sister and I were not satisfied, and so we began to investigate by ourselves.'

'What did you find out?'

'In the end, nothing of note,' she said simply. 'There is knowledge aplenty if you know where to look for it, but while we became acquainted with these hideous werewolves and their ways, it was as though the creature had disappeared. People stopped speaking of it, as though my father never existed. No trace was seen of it for years, not until the recent murders.'

'Do you think it left the area? Hunted elsewhere?'

'Most like, or perhaps its wilder nature was somehow suppressed.' She glanced at me. 'Why do you hunt this beast? You have never struck me as the adventurous type, so what is your sudden interest?'

'The professor is experienced in these matters. Along with his daughter Roberta–'

'Roberta? Do you mean Isabella?'

I improvised hurriedly. 'She was travelling incognito. It's a necessary precaution at times.'

'How thrilling! But please, do continue.'

'Well, together with my own modest contributions, the three of us help people troubled by...by otherworldly phenomena.' Under the bright morning sunshine it sounded a little foolish, and I stumbled as I tried to explain further. 'We capture spirits and...and ghosts and the like.'

'My word!'

'The London police sought the professor's help with the recent murder. Unfortunately, the professor refused the case, being busy with other matters, but Roberta and I accepted the challenge. Upon reading the official report, we travelled to West Wickham to do our part.' I did not add that my own interest had only been piqued when I learned that my parents' safety was at risk.

'If only the professor had been available when my father was killed,' murmured Emily. 'He might have stopped the beast, and others would not have lost their lives.'

'Let us hope we can stop it now.'

Emily gave me a smile. 'Now, let us talk of happier matters. I don't mean to intrude, but I beg you to humour my romantic heart.'

'Oh?' I asked warily. 'How might I do such a thing?'

'Why, you and Roberta of course! Ellen told me I was being foolish, but I'm sure I detected a certain *frisson* when I saw the two of you together. Oh, *do* tell me you're a couple, even though you act otherwise! How my heart would sing for you!'

Had I been speaking to anyone else, I would have immediately bid them a stiff good day and departed at speed. But I'd known Miss Emily for years, and I knew she had a penchant for romantic tales. 'We are very fond of each other,' I said, in a low voice.

'Will you marry? Do say you will!'

'I'm afraid that is impossible.' Briefly, I explained the professor's objection, and as I did so I felt an unburdening of sorts. It felt good to recount my woes, especially to an appreciative audience. 'So you see, as a lowly bookkeeper–'

'There is nothing lowly about you, my lad,' said Emily, frowning. 'You're a fine catch for *any* young lady.'

I blushed at the compliment. 'It would seem so, for my mother is encouraging a match with Cecilie Carmichael,' I said dispiritedly.

'Oh, that will never work,' said Emily. 'She is most unsuitable. No, you are quick-witted and intelligent, and you need someone to challenge you. I speak from experience, for my sister and I received a number of proposals over the years, and we turned every one of them down. Dull, for the most part, or foppish sorts with no interests aside from their London clubs and the scantily-clad young ladies therein.' Emily all but wagged her finger at me. 'No, the professor is entirely wrong in this. Take my word for it.'

'I beg you, do not speak to him about this matter!' I said, alarmed.

'I would not dream of it.' She smiled. 'It seems you had better seek your fortune, my lad. Only then will you achieve the happy union you desire. Now, these weeds are not going to pull themselves up, and my sister will soon rouse your friends with the breakfast gong, so I suggest you hurry along to the house.'

I said goodbye and resumed my walk along the gravel driveway, feeling thoroughly deflated. I'd been hoping for inspiration or advice from Miss Emily, but in the end she'd merely confirmed what I already knew.

As a solid, reliable bookkeeper I was destined for a solid, unremarkable life.

When I entered the hall there was no sign of the professor or Roberta. I looked into several empty rooms, my footsteps echoing from the bare walls, until I eventually took the stairs to the first landing. I heard voices from further along the corridor, male and female, and as I approached a half-open door I knew I'd found my quarry.

'Ah, Septimus!' cried the professor. 'Do come in, my boy, but mind the wires!'

I stood in the doorway, stunned by the scene before me. At first glance it looked like a huge spider had spent the night spinning a copper web, joining every part of the room with fine strands. Here and there, this tangled mesh was anchored to small brass devices with intricate gears and cogs, which looked like the workings from a number of clocks. In other places the wires were held by wooden coat stands, an umbrella tied to a chair leg, and even a broomstick wedged behind an empty bookcase. It seemed the professor, in his enthusiasm, had raided the Hall sisters' belongings to construct this large and very complicated device, and I hoped they would not object.

I noticed small squares of paper attached to many of the strands, each containing numbers. These ranged from single digits to much larger figures, but there did not appear to be any order to their arrangement. Others had lettering such as N, ESE and SW, from which I deduced they were meant to represent compass headings.

Roberta stood near the window, where she was looping a strand of copper wire over a nail affixed to the wall. Nearby, an old portrait in a wooden frame leaned against a wardrobe. Between the two of them they had half-dismantled the room, and I wondered what Emily and Ellen might say if they walked in to see the state of their belongings.

I turned to the professor to voice a mild objection, but his eyes had lit up as he spied the sack I carried over my shoulder. 'Is that the equipment Roberta purloined from my study?'

'It's the equipment from my trunk, sir, but I do not know the origin.'

'As long as it's here, that's all that matters.' He ducked under a strand of wire to take the sack from my hands, depositing it on a nearby table before removing and unwrapping mysterious items one by one, in the manner of an excited child with a Christmas stocking. At each fresh discovery he exclaimed in delight, and once he'd revealed all the equipment he began to connect the pieces to wires at various locations around the room. 'You were on the right track, my dear,' he said, addressing Roberta. 'These items might have proved useful to you, in a limited fashion. But see how much more effective they will be in this vastly improved configuration!'

'Did you ask permission for...' I gestured helplessly around the room, '...for all this?'

'To make an omelette one must first break the egg,' said the professor loftily.

'Septimus, do not be concerned,' said Roberta. 'Everything will be replaced when we are done.'

I gestured again, this time more emphatically. 'When you have done what exactly?'

The professor looked up from his work. 'I call this machine my Paranormal Prognosticator.'

'I still say detector would be more apt,' called Roberta, who had taken out a small piece of paper and was now fastening it to the wire she had just attached to the wall.

'Accuracy is not everything,' replied the professor. 'When marketing our services it is important to catch the eyes and ears of prospective customers.'

'You are liable to catch their necks with this device,' I said, feeling a strand of copper wire stretched before me.

'This is merely a prototype. I've been working on the plans for weeks now, but until recently I lacked the final part of this wondrous machine.'

'What part is that?'

The professor spun round, picking something up from a nearby bookshelf. He held it aloft with a triumphant gesture, and my heart sank as I recognised the engraved jar containing the deadly sprites. 'With the aid of these little beauties, my device will be complete!'

'Please tell me you are not planning to release those horrible things!' I cried. 'Why, the last time they escaped, they all but killed the manager at the docks!'

'Escaped is the operative word,' said the professor. 'In a controlled environment, with careful, professional handling, these sprites are no more dangerous than gunpowder. Witness the truth in my words!'

He began to unscrew the lid on the engraved jar, and had the room not been criss-crossed with wire I would have leapt forward and restrained him. As it was, I barely had time to duck under the closest strand before those evil little sprites began to flow from the mouth of the jar. Glowing with a baleful, ghostly light, they swirled around the professor in a fast-moving cloud. Once they got their bearings I expected them to attack, passing through his body, repeatedly shocking him until his heart gave out.

Instead, they separated. A third of their number orbited the professor, illuminating his features with their glow. Another third made a beeline for Roberta, who watched their approach with some trepidation. And the final third raced directly towards me. I strove to maintain my composure as I braced for imminent death, for I was determined that Roberta's last memory of me be something noble and brave, not cowardly and craven.

32

I was tempted to turn and flee as the sprites raced towards me, weaving and gleaming with their unholy light. Had I been alone, or perhaps only in the professor's company, I might have done so, but Roberta was there too, and I knew I had to make every effort to save her, no matter the cost to myself.

So, instead of escaping through the nearby door, I leapt *into* the room, directly towards the approaching danger. At the last moment I dived towards the floor, rolling over and over on the polished wooden boards, passing beneath the maze of copper wires strung about the room. At any moment I expected the first stab of pain as the sprites attacked, but my sudden movement must have caught them by surprise, for no such attack came.

Vaguely, I heard shouting, but was far too caught up in my rescue attempt to pay it any mind. I had but one goal, for I was determined to reach Roberta if it were the last thing I did on this Earth. Failing all other options, I was prepared to shield her body with my own, protecting her until my final dying breath.

Some of the supports holding the web copper wire went flying as I crashed into them, and the centre of the professor's contraption promptly collapsed, tangling me head and foot. I struggled mightily, shouting at the top of my voice and kicking and waving my arms like a madman, but within seconds I was trapped as securely as a spider's winged prey.

I made one final effort then gave up in despair. I was trussed like a turkey, and I couldn't even turn my head to witness Roberta's final moments.

All of a sudden the vague shouting ceased, and I heard footsteps approaching at speed. There was a bout of muttered cursing nearby, and then firm hands took hold of me, rolling me over none too gently. I found myself staring up at the professor's face, and he did not look happy.

'You impetuous fool!' he thundered. 'What in the world did you think you were doing?'

'R–Roberta,' I stammered. 'The danger!'

'There was no danger, you blithering idiot,' raged the professor, who was easily the most angry I had ever seen him. 'Get up this instant, so that you might gaze upon the sorry state of my machine!'

Dazed and disoriented, I was hauled to my feet. My first glance was in Roberta's direction, and to my astonishment she was standing in her original location near the wall, perfectly safe. I looked around for the marauding sprites, expecting to see them circling prior to a surprise attack, but discovered that instead they were running back and forth along the few wires that I had not quite managed to bring down, almost as though they had become attached to the copper. Spread out, they followed the web of wiring, flowing around the room in peaceful harmony. The only place they avoided was the section I had torn down with my fruitless struggles, a section which the professor now gestured at.

'Just look at it!' he shouted. 'It will take me an entire hour of work to repair this damage. Perhaps two!'

'Father,' called Roberta. 'Perhaps if you had explained the process before releasing the sprites in the manner of an amateur magician performing parlour tricks on Blackpool pier–'

'What possessed you to panic so?' the professor demanded of me. He was no longer shouting, and instead he now looked hurt. In a way, this was even worse. 'Do you not trust me, Septimus?'

I was still gazing at the glowing sprites, which were moving rhythmically around the wires. The effect was hypnotic, and despite the gravity of the situation I found them quite beautiful. 'I–I had witnessed the danger those sprites represented once before,' I said. 'I was convinced they were about to attack us sir, and my first instinct was to save your daughter.'

'That's very noble of you,' said the professor gruffly. 'It is to your credit, even though it came at the expense of my work.'

Roberta now approached, giving the wires with their slow-moving lights a wide berth. 'Father, do not fuss so. The detector is not badly damaged, and with our help it can be mended in no time.'

'Prognosticator,' muttered the professor automatically. He glanced around at the tangled wires, then nodded. 'Very well, we shall set to work together, but you must follow my directions precisely! With a machine of this nature, calibration is critical.'

At that moment there came the sound of a gong from below, and I recalled my conversation with Miss Emily. 'That will be breakfast,' I said.

The professor rubbed his chin. 'I cannot pause for such trivial matters. Septimus, you will fetch me a tray, and while you are gone my daughter and I will undo the damage you wrought upon my invention. Hurry now, for a light breakfast will speed the work.'

'Yes sir,' I mumbled.

'Three eggs, mind, and ensure the tea is hot and strong! And toast aplenty, for hard work leads to a healthy appetite.' The professor paused. 'Perhaps you might bring a sausage or two, and bacon if they have some. I have a fancy for kidneys also, and–'

'Father, Septimus has but two hands to carry this light breakfast of yours,' remarked Roberta.

I left before he could add to my burdens, and upon my return, breakfast tray in hand, I was pleased to see the wires in the centre of the room had already been restrung. The small paper squares had been replaced and the glowing sprites travelling back and forth along the copper, passing right though the tickets as though they did not exist.

'Aha!' cried the professor, as he spotted the tray. 'Breakfast at last!' He sat down, tucking a napkin into the collar of his shirt, and silence fell as he availed himself of the spread. Roberta sipped a cup of tea and ate a slice of toast or two, but neither was paying much attention to their breakfast. Indeed, father and daughter watched the copper wires with much anticipation, as though expecting some miraculous revelation at any moment.

'How does it work?' I asked. I had intended to remain silent after the professor's earlier outburst, but I guessed his mood might have improved now the machine was up and running again. He also had a weakness for expounding on his accomplishments and explaining his inventions to me. This, because he was secretive with his peers, most of whom he suspected of plotting to steal his ideas. As for Roberta, she designed most of the devices in the first place, and when the professor did come up with some new invention on his own she would usually point out a flaw within minutes.

'You will note that the wiring is arranged in a particularly clever fashion,' began the professor. Having finished his breakfast, he got to his feet and began pacing a small area that was free of wires and obstacles. 'A lesser inventor might have employed regular spacing,' he said, pausing to indicate a nearby strand of wire, 'but the effectiveness is increased exponentially by random juxtaposition.'

'I see,' I murmured, even though I did not. 'But the function of this machine...a detector, I believe you said?'

'No no! Prognosticator!' He gestured, encompassing the room, the web and the glowing sprites. 'These wonderful little workers are attracted by paranormal entities, but the wires prevent them from sallying forth. Instead, they arrange themselves in certain patterns, and from those patterns we can deduce the approximate location of the entity we seek. From there, it is just a question of surrounding the area and closing in upon our prey!'

I realised the implications immediately. This machine of the professor's was about to pinpoint the location of the werewolf! Sick to the stomach, I guessed where it might send us: to my parents' house! I decided to speak up right away, before the professor and Roberta obtained their results and shared the findings with the village. If word got out, they might raise an angry mob who would descend on my father like a pack of wild animals, administering their own brand of justice before I could save him. 'Sir, there is something I must tell you,' I said urgently.

'Not now my boy,' said the professor, as he inspected the wires. 'The sprites begin to settle, which means we're getting close! Roberta, the notebook if you please. Stand ready!'

'It's important. I–'

'Father,' called Roberta. 'They've stopped!'

'Quickly, dear. Read off the range and heading. Carefully now, for we must be accurate!'

Events were getting away from me, but aside from tearing the web of copper wire from its mountings, for a second time, I could do little to interfere. Detection was imminent, and afterwards it would be too late.

'The heading is east by south east,' called Roberta. 'Perhaps a few degrees further south.'

'Excellent, excellent! And the range?'

Roberta studied several wires, adding up the numbers on the pieces of paper hanging from those with glowing sprites attached. 'Eight hundred and seventy-five yards.'

'We have it!' cried the professor. Ducking under the maze of wires, he hurried to the window. 'This wall faces south, so we'll be seeking our werewolf in *that* direction,' he said, pointing to the left. 'Septimus, your parents' house lies yonder. How far would you say it was?

'Not that far,' I said. Then, with a rush of relief, I realised the implications. 'Professor, it's nowhere near that far!'

'Something beyond, then.'

'Yes, yes. Beyond! Far beyond!'

'My dear boy, you are babbling.'

I could not help it, for the relief was indescribable after all my worries. My father was in the clear!

'Range nine hundred and ten,' called Roberta. 'Father, the creature is moving away from us.'

With a sick feeling I realised I had celebrated too soon. I had assumed my father was home, but what if he were out and about?

'We shall have to wait for it to settle,' said the professor grimly. 'Let us hope it remains within range, or else we will lose the scent.'

There was a lengthy silence, broken only by Roberta's reading of the ever-increasing range. When she reached a mile or thereabouts, she paused. At that moment the sprites began to move once more, sliding aimlessly along the wires without settling. 'We've lost it,' she said at last.

'Damn and blast!' cried the professor. 'But no matter! As long as the prognosticator is up and running, the foul creature will be caught eventually. Septimus, Roberta and I will remain here while you fetch the police. They must be appraised of our findings, so that they might bring reinforcements from Croydon.' He rubbed his hands together gleefully. 'What a coup this is,' he crowed. 'What a coup! A first trial of my wonderful machine, and already it pays dividends.'

I was in despair, but knew I could not refuse the errand he had charged me with. With a heavy heart and a great deal of reluctance, I turned for the door.

'Septimus, what did you want to say earlier?' the professor called after me. 'The urgent matter you wished to raise. What was it?'

I hesitated. Part of me wanted to share the burden, but I knew that my father's dark secret, once revealed, would be impossible to hide once more. In addition, I did not know how the professor and Roberta would react to the news, and I was not prepared to risk the consequences.

In the end I took the easy way out, which was no decision at all. 'It's not important now,' I said quietly, and I left to find Sam Tyler.

33

On my way through the village I stopped an elderly passerby to enquire as to Sam Tyler's whereabouts. The man looked me up and down, then snorted. 'Wouldn't bother, son. He'll find you soon enough.'

'What do you mean?'

He shook his head and turned away, pretending not to hear me when I called after him. Frowning to myself, I hurried along the high street, wondering at the odd conversation. Why would Sam Tyler be seeking me? Well, it didn't matter as long as we met up sooner rather than later. Indeed, it would make my errand all the easier.

I rounded the next corner and saw Tyler barely ten yards away, striding towards me with the blacksmith at his side. 'There he is!' shouted Tyler, pointing in my direction. 'Stay where you are!'

I glanced round, thinking some pickpocket or ne'er do well might be fleeing behind me, but the only person in sight was the elderly man I'd already spoken to, and he was ambling along in a most relaxed fashion. Before I could move, strong hands grabbed me as the blacksmith took me in an unbreakable hold, my arms bent painfully behind my back. 'What are you doing?' I protested.

'What have *you* done,' growled Tyler. 'That is the question.' He gestured to the blacksmith. 'Come, bring him to the pub. The coach with the Croydon police will be here any minute, and we can hand him over without fuss.'

I stared at him in shock. 'Croydon police? Sam, what's happening?'

'It's Constable Tyler to you,' snapped Sam. 'And if you know what's good for you, you'll shut up until you're told to speak.'

'Sam, whatever you think I've done, I assure you Professor Twickham and Roberta will vouch for me.'

'Who's Roberta? And what professor?'

'You met Roberta yesterday.' I recalled the conversation. 'She was, er, calling herself Isabella Makepeace then. The professor is her father.'

Tyler shook his head. 'You'll have to do better than a girl with a false name and a man I've never met. Now get moving.'

'But–'

'Want me to dot 'im one?' demanded the blacksmith. 'That'll shut him up good and proper.'

'Not yet, but if he opens his mouth again you can thump him with my blessings.'

I was manhandled towards the pub in a daze, my arms forced behind me and my shoulders crying out from the strain. I did not say a word the whole way, for the blacksmith was a large man and I did not want to provoke him. Tyler seemed angry as well, although his was a cold, hard anger that frightened me more than the blacksmith.

The whole situation was incredible, but from the men's demeanour it was obvious they thought me responsible for a serious crime. Overnight, something must have happened that I was unaware of, and as they half-dragged me towards the pub I decided the wisest course of action was to go along with events until I could clear my name.

We rounded the next corner and I saw a gleaming black coach already waiting outside the pub, the horses' flanks flecked with foam. Someone had ridden here in a hurry, and my heart sank as no fewer than four policemen emerged from the inn.

Tyler gave a sharp whistle, and all four men looked in my direction. 'This here is your suspect,' he said proudly, as they crowded around. 'Septimus Jones, a local who now resides in London.'

There was a sergeant amongst the four policemen, a hard-bitten man with a pockmarked face and the nose and ears of a bare-knuckle fighter. He sized me up at a glance, then jerked his thumb towards the coach. Immediately, two of the constables restrained me, while the third applied handcuffs to my wrists. 'We'll take it from here,' growled the sergeant. 'You did good, constable.'

'Thank you, sir.'

I was bundled into the carriage, none too gently, and we set off immediately with the policemen surrounding me on every side. The sergeant sat opposite, and he regarded me steadily as we bumped and swayed along the road, as a scientist might view a particularly venomous specimen.

'W–What have I done?' I asked him, in a low voice. 'Am I being arrested?'

'What have I done?' he said, mimicking my words but employing a fluting, high-pitched tone. 'Oh lumme, what have I done?'

The constables seated beside me laughed.

Then the sergeant leaned forward, pushing his face close to mine, menacing me. 'You've committed murder most foul, you horrible little coward,' he growled. 'A murder you'll swing for, you mark my words. An' if we have a little word with the hangman he'll make sure you dance for a bit on the end o' that rope, 'stead of snapping your neck clean like he's meant to.'

I felt like I was trapped in a deadly nightmare, and I could only stare at the man, speechless. Why did everyone believe me to be a murderer? All of a sudden I recalled the gunfire in the woods the night before, where an unknown assailant had shot at myself, Roberta and the professor from the darkness. I had returned fire, just once, and at the time I thought I might have heard a faint cry. My blood ran cold at the memory, for although I had only acted in self-defence, it seemed my shot might have done far more damage than I thought. I had thought little of it at the time, for the shotgun was a short-range weapon and my antagonist would have been hit, at the very worst, by no more than a tiny pellet or two.

But what if the man I'd struck had bled to death, somehow mortally wounded by my shot? What if one of those tiny pellets had nicked a major artery in his neck, or his thigh? That would explain why the rifle fire had stopped soon after!

I felt a crushing despair as the carriage bore me towards the police station. If I had taken a life, then the only honourable thing to do was to explain the circumstances, calmly and rationally, before confessing to the crime. But before any confession, I would insist the police interview Roberta and the professor, so that they might lend credence to my version of events. Once they confirmed I acted to save their lives, then the charges against me might be lessened, if not withdrawn altogether.

Somewhat encouraged by this thought, I almost looked forward to my interview with the police. The sergeant was against me, that was clear, but I was certain his superior would be more rational, and together we would soon thrash out this thing.

I was unceremoniously hauled out of the carriage to stand blinking in the bright afternoon sunshine. We'd stopped in a courtyard beside the Croydon police station, the same station where I had reported the attack on the Lieutenant, his wife and myself only the night before last.

This time, I was not an upright citizen but a wanted criminal.

I was barely aware of a horse tied to a nearby hitching rail, not until I saw Mr Carmichael preparing to mount. He was dressed in immaculate riding gear with a leather crop under one arm, and the horse was a magnificent stallion of at least sixteen hands. He paused as he became aware of me, and then he marched across the yard to meet me face to face. 'To think you might have married my daughter,' he spat, his eyes blazing with fury. 'You, sir, are a cad of the very worst kind! The shame of it. The shame!'

I mumbled a reply, unwilling to speak aloud in case the sergeant silenced me with his fist. Failing that, I worried the police might abandon me in the yard so that Mr Carmichael might administer some violent punishment of his own. He certainly looked angry enough.

'Sir, we must get the prisoner inside,' said the sergeant politely. 'If you would stand aside–'

Carmichael ignored him. 'I have just given my statement,' he growled at me. 'I hope it serves to convict you, for only then I will have done my duty!' He turned on one heel and mounted the horse, and at his nod the groom loosened the reins and passed them up. With a deafening ring of horseshoes on cobblestones, Carmichael rode off.

'My, you *do* have friends in high places,' mocked the sergeant. 'Now git in there, before I speed you along with my boot.'

I was led along a series of cramped, dreary passages which echoed to our footsteps. Eventually we emerged in a small, windowless area with a wooden counter. The police had looked inside my coat before placing me into the carriage in West Wickham, mainly to check whether I carried any weapons. This time the search was more thorough, and my effects were taken from me and placed into a wooden tray. I still carried half a dozen of the brass shotgun cartridges Roberta and I had packed with silver-coated shot, and these elicited raised eyebrows and meaningful glances between the policemen.

After giving my name and particulars, which were noted in laborious handwriting, I was led to a small stone cell with a barred window and a solid wooden door. There was a slatted wooden bench along one wall, with a filthy-looking bucket pushed underneath, and before I could turn to ask for an Inspector, or station sergeant, or whomever was in charge, the handcuffs were removed and the door was firmly closed and securely bolted behind me.

I sat on the bench, as far from that bucket as possible, and put my head in my hands. Events had moved so quickly I could scarcely believe my predicament, and I confess I pinched myself once or twice to ensure this was not, after all, some vivid nightmare dreamt up by my guilty subconscious. The sharp pain, and the reddened skin at my wrists, told otherwise.

I thought of my parents, and wondered how they were taking the terrible news of my arrest. My mother would be distraught, poor thing, and I was certain my father would board the next coach to Croydon, determined to confront the police and demand my release. A lump arose in my throat, and I felt a stab of guilt at my earlier, uncharitable thoughts. How could I have suspected him of being this hideous werewolf creature?

And what of Roberta and the professor? I had left them tending to that fabulous machine, awaiting the arrival of armed police in order to finally capture the beast and ensure peace for the inhabitants of West Wickham. They too would be concerned, perhaps already asking questions as to my whereabouts.

After sitting quietly, mired in woe and self-pity, my thoughts turned to the man I had supposedly killed. Was it someone from West Wickham? One of the shadowy, secretive poachers, perhaps? Had we interrupted their night's work, perhaps by scaring away the game they were trying to hunt?

Then I had a most troubling thought. What if the werewolf had tracked us in *human* form, complete with a rifle? After all, if the beast lived in the village, it might have got wind of our trap and decided to protect itself! And one or two pellets, coated in silver, might have been enough to kill the thing, where a mortal would only have been wounded.

Then I realised it was impossible. Given the professor's machine had detected the creature barely an hour ago, it could hardly have fallen to my silver shot the previous night.

But what if the werewolf had an accomplice? A supernatural creature might have powers of persuasion, especially if it were long-lived...ancient, even. An impressionable soul could easily fall under its spell, doing its evil bidding without question. All of a sudden I had a wild idea, imagining a cult of sorts that might have arisen with the werewolf at its centre. Ordinary-looking villagers holding dark masses, worshipping the beast, and despatching any threats to its well-being. Sam and the blacksmith, for example, who had captured me and turned me over to the Croydon police without asking for a word of explanation. Mr Carmichael, who had gone out of his way to make a statement, and had burned with anger as he confronted me in the courtyard. Were they *all* protecting the werewolf?

'Oh Septimus,' I groaned to myself. 'Now you truly are going mad.' For a moment I imagined Emily and Ellen Hall in dark hooded robes, lighting blood-red candles and chanting curses from forbidden books, and despite the gravity of my situation I laughed out loud. It was inconceivable!

Then I heard the bolt being pulled back, and I turned to face the door. Now, at last, I would be able to put my side of the story. I only hoped the officer in charge was more willing to listen to my tale than the sergeant with the battered, pugilistic face.

34

A pair of constables entered my cell, one of them standing nearby with his wooden truncheon at the ready while the second applied the handcuffs once more, this time in front of me.

'I–I want to know what I'm being charged with,' I said. I felt ashamed at the quaver in my voice, even though it was forgivable in the circumstances. 'You can't drag me away and lock me up like this, not without reason.'

'Save it for the sarge,' snapped the constable with the truncheon.

Once secured, I was marched out of the cell and down the flagstone passage outside.

We stopped at an unremarkable wooden door. One of the constables knocked, and upon hearing a voice from within, he opened the door and ushered me inside. The room was of medium size, with a battered wooden table in the centre and three or four chairs arranged around it. One of the chairs was occupied, and my stomach sunk as I recognised the sergeant with the battered face. Please no, I thought, suddenly afraid. Please don't let this man be my only interrogator!

He gave me a nasty smile as I was pushed down onto one of the chairs, my back to the door, then slowly and deliberately cracked his knuckles. He had large hands and thick wrists, and I imagined the pain and damage he could cause with a few well-aimed punches. I could lose several teeth, have my jaw broken or suffer life-threatening internal injuries. I felt sweat upon my brow, and when I saw the constables leaving I almost beseeched them to stay. But what could they do against their sergeant, a superior officer? Why, if he so ordered, they would most likely hold me down while he beat me!

'I–I want to give my side of the story,' I said quickly. 'I'm just a bookkeeper, an accountant, not a vicious murderer. If someone has been killed I assure you it was not a deliberate act.'

The sergeant grunted. 'Save the pretty speeches until the guv'nor gets here.'

I felt a flood of relief at his words. There *was* a senior officer! The prospect of a civilised discussion with an Inspector or the like was so welcoming that I felt my knees weaken.

We were kept waiting for another ten minutes, although it felt like an hour. During this time the sergeant did not take his eyes off me, and I quailed under his unblinking gaze. If it was a tactic to soften me up prior to interrogation, it worked admirably, because by the time the door opened I was ready to tell everything I knew...if not more.

'What have we here, Wallace?' demanded the newcomer, in a deep voice. I turned to gain an impression of the senior officer, and was relieved to see a reasonable-looking man, middle-aged, with grey hair and a stern but somewhat kindly face.

'Septimus Jones,' said the sergeant, hastily rising to his feet. 'He's suspected of the West Wickham murders, sir.'

Murders! I blinked at this startling turn of events, for surely the police could not think me responsible for *all* of the deaths? Why, the lieutenant and his wife could give a cast-iron alibi for the coach driver's killing, and I had been living in London when the first victim had been found! 'I–I think there's been a mistake,' I said quickly. 'I thought you had brought me into the station because of an accidental death in the woods last night, but–'

'I didn't ask you to speak,' said the senior officer sharply. He turned to the sergeant. 'Organise a tray of tea, will you? Two cups, there's a good man.'

Wallace frowned, then glanced at me. 'Sir–'

'At the double.'

Unwillingly, the sergeant left us alone. As the door closed behind me, I felt an oppressive weight lifting from my shoulders. 'Sir, I have not been charged,' I said quickly, 'and yet the sergeant has already threatened me with execution. He said the hangman–'

'I still haven't asked you to speak, Jones.' The officer sat down, and I saw he carried a Manila folder overflowing with paperwork. He placed it upon the scarred wooden surface and opened the cover, inspecting the first page. Then he regarded me steadily. 'I am station sergeant Edwards, and despite the sergeant's enthusiasm, for the time being you are currently the suspect in only the one death. Additional charges might be laid, of course, depending on the outcome of this little interview.'

I swallowed.

'During this interrogation, you will speak only when I ask you a direct question. Is that understood?'

I nodded. 'Yes, sir.'

'Good.' Edwards turned over several pages, then paused to study one in more detail. I strained my eyes, hoping to gain a clue from the upside-down writing, but from where I was sitting I could not make out the words. 'What were you doing in the woods last night?' he asked me suddenly.

From the start I decided to be completely honest with the man, no matter what kind of lunatic he thought me. I reasoned it was better to be thought a complete idiot than to be caught in a lie.

'I took leave from my position as a bookkeeper, travelling down from London on Friday night with the intention of hunting and trapping the creature which has been terrorising people in the area. My parents live in West Wickham, you see, and I feared for their safety...as well as that of friends and others in the village.'

'I repeat my original question,' said Edwards. 'What were you doing in the woods last night?'

'We...I had a plan to trap the killer. I hired two locals, Mrs Green's sons, labourers both, to dig a pit. Then I arranged a bait above this pit in order to attract the, er, creature.'

'Do you own a shotgun?' he asked me suddenly.

'I borrowed one from the Hall sisters, of Ravenswood. I did not feel comfortable venturing into the woods at night unarmed. You see, on my way to West Wickham–'

'Let us stick with last night's events, Mr Jones. You fired that shotgun, did you not?' He gestured. 'There is no need to answer that question, as we have already examined the weapon.'

'We were fired upon first. Several bullets struck the trees, fired from a rifle I believe, and when we took cover they kept shooting. I fired back at one of the flashes, purely in self-defence. In my presence were Professor Twickham, an elderly gentleman who had injured his ankle, and his daughter Roberta. My thoughts were for their safety.'

'How far away was your target when you opened fire?'

'I can't be sure, but the flashes of gunfire seemed to be thirty yards away, at least. I believe I can find the spot again, and your men could then see the damaged trees for themselves. Perhaps some of my own pellets might be found also, and there ought to be blood from the victim.'

Edwards made a note. 'What made you think you could roam the woods with a shotgun?'

'I sought out Sir Lennard's gamekeeper earlier that day, and he gave me permission. If you ask him, I'm certain he will confirm it.'

'We'd like to ask him, Mr Jones, but unfortunately it's Sir Lennard's keeper we found dead.' Edwards leaned closer. 'And the way I see it, you're the main suspect.'

I sat there, stunned, as the door opened behind me. Sergeant Wallace came in with a tray, which he set on the table. The old china teapot and chipped mugs seemed completely out of place in that room, but I barely noticed. The keeper, dead! It was staggering! But why had he fired upon us?

'Sir, why don't you give me five minutes alone with 'im?' suggested the sergeant. 'He'll talk then, I'm sure of it.'

'You may leave us, sergeant.' Edwards waited until the door closed, then inspected another page. 'You made a statement here on Friday night,' he said, changing his line of questioning without warning. 'An attack in the nearby woods.'

I swallowed, still shocked at the keeper's death. Was I truly responsible? If so, it was an absolute tragedy! But why hadn't the man challenged us instead of firing without warning? Why, he'd even given us a password! 'That...that is correct, sir. A naval lieutenant, his wife and myself were travelling in a carriage, having missed our connection.' As I recounted the events, I found the words coming a little easier. 'The driver was taken without warning. We heard growls and roars as though from a wild creature, and then the beast attacked the lieutenant. I wounded it twice, and the lieutenant's wife succeeded in scaring the beast off by means of a silver hip flask. Somehow, the silver appeared to scald it, burning the flesh and hair. It appeared highly distressed by the touch, and fled into the night.'

Edwards said nothing.

'Sir, I work with Professor Twickham, a renowned expert in

paranormal phenomena.' I thought renowned was taking things a little far, but I needed to impress upon the officer that I was familiar with the other-worldly. Only then might my story find a sympathetic ear. Then I heard the door open again, and I felt a prickling between my shoulder blades. Was it sergeant Wallace, back to suggest beating the so-called truth out of me? Quickly, I continued, hoping to prolongue the interview for as long as possible. 'On Friday morning, I spoke with the metropolitan police about this matter, Inspector Cox having already sought the professor's help with the case.'

Edwards rose to his feet, astounded. 'Inspector Cox!' he cried.

'Er, yes, that is correct,' I said. 'Inspector Cox of the Kensington police. It was his report that...' My voice tailed off as I noticed Edwards standing to rigid attention, and slowly I turned to look over my shoulder. Instead of Sergeant Wallace, hovering behind me with fists at the ready, imagine my surprise when I saw the neat, red-headed figure of Inspector Cox himself.

35

Cox entered the room, and then the bulky figure of Sergeant Parkes squeezed through the doorway behind him. A huge man, Parkes usually had to duck when entering a room, but despite his imposing physique he could not quite match Cox's air of authority.

'Well? Has he confessed?' demanded Cox. I thought I saw his lips twitch, but it might have been the poor light.

Edwards shook his head. 'We're just going through the preliminary questions, sir.'

'I shouldn't waste your time. This man is working for me.'

The effect on Edwards was electric, and I was only slightly less shocked myself.

'That may be the case, sir,' began Edwards, 'but we have witnesses placing Mr Jones in the woods with a shotgun at the time of the killing. He's already admitted to firing it, too.'

'You have three unexplained deaths in the area. I'd be surprised if anyone *wasn't* carrying a weapon.'

'I can't let the suspect go sir, not without clearing him first.' Edwards seemed to regain a little of his composure. 'In any case, the metropolitan police has no authority in these parts. I won't release him without word from my commanding officer.'

'I should like to speak with Mr Jones in private.'

'Of course, sir.'

'I was not asking your permission.'

Edwards left, and, at a nod from Cox, Parkes stepped out after him, closing the door firmly behind himself. Then Cox turned to me. 'I told you not to interfere in this case,' he said sharply. 'What do you think you're doing?'

'My parents live in West Wickham,' I said simply. 'If the police weren't going to do anything about these deaths, I decided it fell to me.'

'No doubt the professor and that daughter of his are sniffing around as well.'

I did not deny it.

'What have the three of you found out? Quickly now, before Edwards returns. He's a good man, but we've had dealings before and I know him as a bit of a stickler.'

'The professor is convinced there's a werewolf in the area,' I said.

'I want the truth, son. Don't waste my time with fairy tales.'

'It *is* the truth. Roberta tried to warn you at the station, and she brought books to support her theories. A werewolf is a man that can transform into a wolf, and vice-versa. We believe he lives amongst us by day, then hunts his victims at night.'

Cox simply regarded me, expressionless. It was lucky he'd had dealings with the professor before, else he might have stood up and walked out in disgust. Even so, my stating the facts so baldly, without preamble, was almost too much for him.

'The professor and Roberta have constructed a device at Ravenswood,' I continued. 'We tested it just this morning, and it detected the creature, or the human host, on the outskirts of West Wickham. Unfortunately it quickly moved out of range, and I was sent to inform the police.' I gestured, making the handcuffs clank. 'At that point I was arrested and brought here, protesting all the while. But if you could only gather a force of men, and lie in wait in West Wickham, the professor's machine could once again seek the beast out, and you would quickly have your murderer in chains.'

'Let us not rush ahead,' said Cox evenly. 'I will not make a fool of myself in front of Edwards, for if I request a large force of men and the professor's machine turns out to be a useless frippery, it will be the last help I shall get. And what of the gamekeeper? They found him shot in the back at close range, you know. Near cut in half, the poor fellow, and you can't tell me this werewolf of yours also carries a twelve-gauge.'

'But that can't have been me!' I declared, realising the implications immediately. 'I fired upon my attacker from thirty yards, at least, and he was firing at me at the same time, using a rifle. There is no chance I could have hit him in the back. In any case, what possible reason would I have for killing the gamekeeper? He gave me permission to enter the woods at night, and indeed, he gave me a password to call out if we were challenged, for he feared we might be mistaken for poachers.'

'That does set a different complexion on things,' admitted Cox. 'Did you not tell Edwards any of this?'

'I tried to. Incidentally, Roberta was there when I spoke with the keeper. He told us to use the word 'animal' as our password. Find her, ask her what the password was, and she will confirm it!'

'Mr Jones, rest assured I do not believe you complicit in this murder,' said Cox. 'But you *are* a suspect, and the police here will not release you until they are satisfied. Parkes will speak with Miss Twickham to confirm your story, and I shall speak with the professor myself. Once we can prove your innocence, you will be released.'

'I thought it was meant to be the other way round,' I muttered.

'Come, you were found in the woods with a shotgun, and one recently fired at that.'

Suddenly I had a blaze of inspiration. 'The shells!' I cried.

'What?'

'Roberta and I, we packed the shotgun shells with pellets coated with silver. It was meant to be a deterrent, since werewolves appear to be vulnerable to the metal.' Excitedly, I turned and pointed to the door. 'The police have some now, for they took them from my person when I was arrested!'

'Silver shot?' asked Cox uncertainly.

'Yes, yes! We paid the blacksmith for the use of his tools! He will confirm we were there yesterday, melting and pouring silver. And if you search the area of the shooting, I'm sure you will be able to dig stray shot of mine from the trees.' Another thought occurred to me, this even more telling. 'The gamekeeper's body! If the pellets he was shot with are ordinary lead–'

Cox stood up. 'That can be investigated right away. It's not conclusive, mind, for you might have carried plain shells as well as these silver ones, but it may be enough to cast doubt. If I can get the local police to widen their enquiries instead of being convinced they already have their man, more evidence in your favour may come to light.'

'Thank you, sir,' I said, with feeling. 'And if there's anything you can do to release me from this predicament…'

'I shall speak with Edwards,' Cox reassured me. 'It's your own damn fault you're in this mess, but you don't deserve to hang for your interference.'

'And the professor and Roberta…no doubt news of my arrest will have spread, and they will be beside themselves with worry. If you can reassure them–'

'The gamekeeper's body was examined at the nearby hospital. I will send Parkes to investigate, and I'm sure he will find out the truth of the matter in no time. Sit tight, and do nothing to antagonise Edwards and his men.'

Cox left, and I slumped on the table, head in my arms. To find such a powerful ally, at a time when all seemed lost, had left me feeling weak with relief. I only hoped that Roberta and the professor, growing tired of waiting, had not set out to capture the werewolf on their own.

I sat there in complete solitude for at least twenty minutes, listening to the noises of the police station all around me. Then, all of a sudden, the door opened once more, and I turned to see Sergeant Wallace entering the room, a look of anticipation on his battered face. 'Right, my lad,' he said grimly. 'Let's see about your confession, shall we?'

Wallace hauled me to my feet and shoved me violently against the brick wall, his face inches from mine. I could smell his breath, and his eyes glittered with emotion. With one hand he gripped my forearm, still manacled, and in the other he took my bicep, his fingers digging into the muscle like steel pins. 'First I'm going to rub your elbow up this wall,' he growled menacingly. 'I'm going to grind it to the bone, and when it's good and raw I'll start on the other.'

'Inspector Cox has just left to prove my story!' I protested. 'I did nothing wrong, I swear!'

'An' Queen Victoria herself asked me to the ball,' sneered Wallace. He slammed my arm against the wall, backwards, and I cried out as the bone in my elbow connected with the brickwork. Then he did it again, hitting it so hard that tears of pain sprang to my eyes. He appeared to be taking a savage delight in hurting me, and had I been holding the shotgun, I swear I would have emptied the charge directly into his chest.

Unfortunately I was unarmed and helpless. Fight back or put up resistance and he might literally beat me to death. But if I spoke up, confessed to the keeper's murder, Cox would find it next to impossible to release me from captivity.

At that moment the door opened, and to my enormous relief I saw Sergeant Parkes look in. He took in the situation at a glance, and he covered the ground in three strides. Sergeant Wallace was plucked away from me like a puppy, and then Parkes turned and casually threw him the length of the room. Wallace crashed onto the table and rolled across the surface before landing with a thud on the stone floor. To his credit he bounced up, and he charged at Parkes in a red mist, fists going like pistons. Parkes shrugged off the blows, seemingly oblivious, then drove his own clenched fist at Wallace with the force of a steam hammer.

The sergeant flew backwards again, and this time the solid-looking table collapsed under his weight, dissolving in a mass of broken timber and wood splinters. Wallace half-raised his head, dazed, then fell back in a dead faint.

'Inspector Cox wants to see you,' rumbled Parkes, turning to me. 'If you would care to follow me out?'

I could barely leave that room fast enough.

36

I was shown into the Station Sergeant's office, a small room with a desk and wooden filing cabinets. The windows looked out on the courtyard, where I could see a constable addressing a small group of people at the gates.

Edwards was sitting behind the desk, while Cox had taken the only other chair. Parkes stood against the wall, and I faced the two senior officers in handcuffs.

'Are those really necessary?' asked Cox, indicating my wrists.

'He's suspected of murder,' said Edwards. 'By rights, he should be locked up until we charge him, not invited into my office.'

'And yet your case against him grows weaker by the minute.' Cox took out a brass shotgun shell, the case gleaming dully. 'Your suspect was carrying several of these when you arrested him. Have you examined them yet?'

'Why? It's just an ordinary shell. If anything it weighs against him, given the victim was slain with a shotgun.'

'Parkes, your knife,' said Cox, without taking his eyes off Edwards.

The massive sergeant stepped forward, unsheathing a knife from his belt. It was a huge, wicked-looking thing, well-used, and of a size that would have put a scimitar to shame.

Cox laid the shell on the wooden desk, gripping it firmly, and with a sudden movement he brought the edge of that enormous blade down upon the very tip. There was a loud *thunk*, the knife slicing through the metal and sinking deep into Edwards' desk. A small ring of brass trimmed from the neck of the shell, wadding still attached, flew through the air to land upon the floor some eight feet away, ringing sharply as it bounced towards the wall. Then, wincing with the effort, Cox levered the knife out of the desk and passed it to Parkes. As he did so a flood of misshapen shot rolled from the damaged cartridge, spreading across the desk. The silver had dulled, but even the most unobservant could not possibly have confused it with lead.

'What the devil is this?' demanded Edwards.

'Silver coated shot,' remarked Cox. 'Mr Jones had loaded his weapon with it.'

'But why?'

'The why does not matter. What you should know, and would have known had you investigated properly, is that the murder victim had his spine blasted apart with lead shot...' Cox indicated the desk. 'Not this.'

'How do you know that?' demanded Edwards.

'I sent Parkes to the hospital, where he asked the relevant questions. I have samples of shot from the body, if you wish to see it.'

'That will not be necessary.' Edwards frowned. 'But this proves nothing. There is no telling what load Mr Jones used when he fired his gun.'

'There are witnesses who will swear Mr Jones fired but one shot. In addition, if your constables inspect the trees where this exchange of fire took place, I am convinced they will find only silver pellets embedded in the bark.' Cox sat back. 'I ask that you release Mr

Jones immediately, for it is clear to all that he is not the murderer you seek.'

'Impossible. I grant you there are questions to be answered, but I cannot free my only suspect. The chiefs would have my head.'

'Why not release Mr Jones into my custody?' suggested Cox. 'Your case against him is falling apart, and I need his help with my own case.'

'But–'

Cox leaned forward, fastening Edwards with a level gaze. 'While you hold Mr Jones, the real killer is on the loose, and might strike again at any moment. How will it look to your chiefs if there are more deaths on your watch, and all the while you claimed to have the murderer in custody?'

This gave Edwards pause, and my spirits rose as he appeared to consider Cox's request. My freedom was within reach, and so close I could all but taste it!

'Very well,' said Edwards at last. 'I will authorise the release of Mr Jones into your custody, but I need you to personally guarantee his appearance should I wish to question him at a later date.'

'Done. Let us shake on it.'

The two men did so, and then Cox glanced at Parkes before nodding towards my handcuffs. The sergeant took out a key, a mere toy in his large hands, and proceeded to free me.

We filed out of the office, only to run into Wallace. He was nursing a bruised cheek, which was rapidly turning purple, and when he spotted Parkes and myself he looked angry enough to launch another attack.

'What the devil?' demanded Edwards, who'd emerged behind us. 'Wallace, what happened to your face?'

The sergeant lowered his gaze. 'Tripped and fell, sir.'

'Are you trying to make a laughing stock out of my station? Well?'

'No sir.' Wallace glanced at my wrists, now free of the cuffs. 'Where's he going?' he demanded. 'You're not freeing him!'

'Inspector Cox asked for Mr Jones' help with some minor matter. Afterwards, Jones will be returned to us for further questioning, if need be.'

An unpleasant smile broke across Wallace's battered face. 'I look forward to that, sir.'

'Now stand aside, sergeant. And do something about that bruise!'

Outside, Cox and I climbed into the waiting carriage. Parkes went to follow, but Cox stopped him. 'Sergeant, I want you to visit the hospital and speak with the physicians there. Ask if anyone else has reported wounds from a shotgun. You can follow us to West Wickham when you have the information. In the meantime, I must inspect the professor's machine and see it working to my satisfaction.'

Parkes nodded and closed the door to our carriage. Moments later, we were on the way to West Wickham, and I sank back into my seat with relief. I expected Cox to lecture me, and chide me about amateurs getting themselves mixed up in police business, but he said nothing and for that I was grateful.

As the village of West Wickham came into view, I turned to Cox with a request. 'Sir, my parents will have heard the news of my arrest by now, and I would be eternally grateful if we could stop outside their home, just for a moment, so that I might set their minds at ease.'

'Of course. But just a second, mind! I must speak with the professor urgently, for there is no time to waste.'

The carriage stopped at my parents' house, and I stepped down and walked to the front door. Before I got there, it opened and my mother looked out, surveying the carriage with interest. 'Well, you do travel in style,' she remarked.

I gave her a big hug, holding on tight. 'Mother, you must have been so worried.'

'About what, dear?' She stiffened. 'Your father, is he all right?'

'This is not about my father!' Breaking the hug, I stood back. 'Did you not hear what happened to me?' With a shock, I realised my mother had not the faintest idea about my arrest. There I'd been, snatched from the street and confined to a cell at the Croydon police station, and she'd been blithely unaware the whole time. I almost felt cheated, for I had been looking forward to a tearful reunion and a great deal of sympathy.

'Why, where have you been?' asked my mother.

'I, er–'

My mother spied Inspector Cox sitting in the carriage. 'Who is that gentleman? He looks rather official.'

At this point Inspector Cox noticed the attention he was generating, and he stepped down from the carriage, introducing himself with a bow.

'A police Inspector in these parts!' exclaimed my mother. 'What brings you to West Wickham, or am I not supposed to ask?'

'It's a case we're working on, Mrs Jones.'

'All these murders, I suppose. Sir Lennard's gamekeeper was killed last night, the poor man. Poachers, they say.'

'We'll get to the bottom of these deaths, I assure you,' said Cox gravely. 'The police will leave no stone unturned.'

'Yes, quite.' My mother hesitated. 'Now tell me, what do you want with my Septimus?'

'Your son recently aided the London police in a serious matter, and with his help we captured a most dangerous criminal. Now, once again, we turn to Mr Jones for his vital assistance.'

'Oh my!' My mother looked from me to Cox and then back again. I saw her slightly hurt expression, and knew she was annoyed that I had not mentioned the matter in my letters home. 'Well,' she said at last. 'Lunch is all but served, and you both look like you could use a cup of tea.'

'I couldn't possibly intrude,' said Cox politely. 'Septimus and I must visit Ravenswood immediately.'

But my mother was not letting go that easily. Having an Inspector to lunch would be a major social coup, and one that she could dazzle her friends with for months. 'Nonsense,' she said, taking Cox by the hand and all but dragging him inside. 'A cup of tea and a bite to eat won't take more than a minute.'

We sat at the dining room table, Cox perched awkwardly on his chair, and my mother poured tea and served the Inspector with cold meats, crusty bread, slices of cheese and fresh pickles. As his plate filled he gradually appeared to accept his fate, and when she placed a hot cup of tea in front of him he complimented her on the spread.

'Your father is out tending to Mrs Turley's accounts,' my mother told me. 'He should be back any minute.'

'This is very good of you, but we really can't stay long,' Cox warned her. I think he suspected that my mother might parade everyone she knew through her dining room, so they might witness the Inspector come to visit, and he was eager to nip that particular idea in the bud.

Meanwhile, I was still dwelling on the fact that my mother had no idea I'd been detained and almost charged with murder. So much for the tight-knit community, I thought ruefully. I consoled myself by thinking upon my upcoming reunion with Roberta, which I was certain would be far more emotional.

A better man than I might have spoken with Roberta first, or at least dashed off at the earliest opportunity in order to set her mind at ease. I did not do so for two very good reasons. One, my mother would not have let me, and two, I was extremely hungry after my unpleasant ordeal at the police station.

37

When the carriage drew up at Ravenswood there was no sign of Emily or Ellen. I showed Cox into the hall myself, then led the Inspector upstairs to the professor's room. Here, I suffered my second major disappointment of the afternoon.

Upon opening the door I expected to be greeted with a barrage of questions, solicitations as to my well-being, and effusive delight at my return. I even harboured the hope that Roberta might run across the room towards me, her reserve vanishing as she took me in her arms and hugged me like a returning hero.

Needless to say, my hopes were dashed. The professor was picking at a plate containing the remains of his lunch, while Roberta was seated at a nearby table, playing solitaire with an old deck of cards.

'Oh, you're back at last,' grumbled Roberta, barely looking up. 'I'm so glad you didn't waste a moment returning with help.' She indicated the playing cards. 'It's just as well we found plenty of important work to do in the meantime.'

'What did you bring *him* for?' muttered the professor, catching sight of Inspector Cox. 'Couldn't you find a dozen proper policemen?'

Cox was used to the professor's ways, and ignored the slight. 'I take it this is the machine Mr Jones described to me? The machine that can locate our murderer?'

With a new audience in the offing the professor could not help himself. Abandoning the remains of his lunch, he began to point out one aspect of the machine after another, from the wires to the small mechanical devices they were connected to and everything in between. The sprites he glossed over, possibly because he had spirited them into the country on false pretences.

Roberta, meanwhile, was still engrossed in her game of patience. I approached the table, and within moments I had told her of the gamekeeper's murder, my experience with the police, and the sergeant who had decided to torture me until I confessed. As I spoke, she gradually abandoned the game, until I had her full attention. When I had finished, she leapt up and hugged me. It was brief, and nothing like the passionate embrace I had hoped for, but it was very welcome all the same. Over her shoulder I saw the professor fix me with a wary gaze, pausing in the middle of his conversation with Cox to do so.

'Is there no trace of the werewolf?' I asked Roberta.

'None whatsoever.' She indicated the sprites, which were milling about the wires in a random fashion. 'Since you left, they've not settled for more than a second or two. We are no closer to finding the werewolf than we were yesterday.'

'Perhaps it has taken refuge during daylight, and will emerge again at nightfall.' As I watched the professor and Cox examining the machine together, a sudden thought occurred to me. 'We can remain here until we catch the beast!'

'Of course.'

'I was still thinking I'd have to return to London tonight, since I gave the professor my word, but given he's here with us–'

'I am disappointed in you Septimus,' murmured Roberta, smiling impishly. 'I thought you were quick of mind, but it's taken you all morning to work out something which should have been apparent from the moment my father fell into our pit.'

'In my defense I have endured a busy few days,' I said, slightly huffily. 'What with being attacked, shot at, arrested and threatened with torture, it's no wonder my mind is slow to piece together disparate items of information.'

Roberta laughed. 'And that is why I am so fond of you,' she murmured, once she recovered. 'Even when annoyed, you are still exceedingly polite.'

I had no reply to this, and I turned to see how the professor and Cox were faring. The two of them were still inspecting the machine, the professor going into such exhaustive detail that I felt sure the poor Inspector could have built his own version. At that moment Cox caught my eye with a desperate, pleading look, and I decided to intervene. The policeman and I had not always been the greatest of allies, but he had saved me from the cells at Croydon and for that alone I would always be grateful. 'Inspector,' I called, interrupting the professor mid-flow. 'I wonder if I might have a moment?'

The relief on Cox's face was almost comical. 'Yes, yes, of course. Professor, will you excuse me?'

'Certainly, my dear fellow, but we must resume this fascinating conversation later!'

'Indeed we must,' said Cox politely.

It had been less of a conversation than a non-stop lecture, and Cox exhibited a glassy-eyed, mildly-stunned expression as he approached me. Behind him I saw the professor inspecting several strands of wire, before turning his attention to a small device with multiple gears on the surface and a small lever on one side. He ratcheted the lever several times, inspected the gears, then nodded to himself.

'Are you certain this contraption works?' Cox asked me. 'So far the professor has been long on technical detail but extremely short on practical application.'

'I saw it with my own eyes.'

'It wasn't a trick of the light, perhaps? I want to believe the professor can indeed help us to pinpoint the location of our, er, suspect, but the evidence so far has been less than convincing.'

'My father knows what he's doing,' declared Roberta. 'The creature is out of range, that is all. Once it stirs, we will have it.'

'I wish I shared your confidence.'

At that moment we heard footsteps, and we turned to see Ellen Hall in the doorway. 'I have a Sergeant Parkes below, and he insists there is an Inspector on the premises.' She spotted Cox. 'I take it you are the officer in question? I'm sorry, I did not realise we had another guest.'

Cox bowed politely. 'Inspector Cox, ma'am. Professor Twickham is helping me with a case, and I must apologise for intruding on your fabulous house without permission.'

'Fabulous once, maybe,' said Ellen, but she looked pleased at the compliment. 'Come, I will show you to your sergeant. I put him in our library.'

Cox nodded to Roberta and me, then departed in Ellen's wake.

'That man,' muttered Roberta. 'You would scarcely believe the frequency with which he begs our help, and yet still he doubts my father's knowledge and skill.'

'He's investigating a series of gruesome murders,' I reminded her. 'There will be pressure from his superiors, I'm sure, and do not forget the way he stood by me when the Croydon police wanted to keep me in captivity.'

'True. I just find it a little tiresome, that's all.' Roberta sighed. 'Let us hope we catch the beast tonight, for that will satisfy all parties.'

I glanced towards the window. It was mid-afternoon, or perhaps closer to three, and I'd been hoping we might trap our prey long before nightfall. The thought of hunting the beast in darkness, perhaps with our unknown assailant firing his rifle at us once more, did not fill me with anticipation. Then I realised Cox would bring a substantial number of police constables to help with the matter, and I brightened considerably at the thought. Why, perhaps my role, like that of Roberta and the professor, would be reduced to directing events from afar! The professor and Roberta would track the monster, and I would liaise with the police, passing them information without having to face the beast myself!

At that moment Cox returned with Sergeant Parkes. The latter was usually unflappable, with a face like a slab of granite and the disposition of a shire horse, but even his eyebrows rose a fraction as he surveyed the web of copper wires filling the room.

'Parkes made enquiries at the hospital,' Cox told us. 'The physicians assured him they have not treated any shotgun injuries recently.'

I muttered a mild curse under my breath, for the line of enquiry had been promising. But I also felt a little relieved, for it meant I had not seriously wounded someone when I had returned fire the night before. There still lingered the suspicion that the unknown assailant had only fired upon our party to warn us, or even in error or out of fear, and I had only wanted to make them stop, not hurt them.

'Tell me, Sergeant Parkes,' began the professor. 'When do your reinforcements arrive?'

The two policemen exchanged a glance before Cox spoke. 'I must verify your detector functions correctly before engaging the local police,' he said. 'I can't fill the woods with constables on a whim.'

'A whim?' growled the professor. 'You doubt my machine?'

'I have no proof that it does anything,' Cox pointed out. 'It's all very well you explaining to me, in exhaustive detail, what it *might* do, but I would like to see evidence of it *actually* working before I put my neck on the block.' He gestured at the wires. 'It's an impressive device, I grant you, but unless you demonstrate–'

'Sir, my machine is working right now!' declared the professor.

38

Cox and Parkes spun round, staring at the wires in anticipation. Roberta and I did likewise, although I confess I could not see anything about them that might have drawn the professor's attention. To me, they still looked the same, with the sprites moving aimlessly between various points.

'What is it telling you?' demanded Cox. 'Where is the beast?'

'It confirms the creature is not within range,' said the professor calmly. 'You see, by telling me nothing it is stating something.'

'Don't befuddle me with word games,' growled Cox. 'I only came to these parts because of the latest victim, and he was shot, not mauled as first reported. Unless your machine convinces me otherwise, in one hour Parkes and I will return to London. There, you can be assured I have plenty of *real* work to do.'

'Why wait an hour?' snapped the professor. 'If you don't trust me, you may leave this instant. But know this...when Septimus, my daughter and I capture this creature we will parade it before the press, and I will be the first to tell them we had little to no assistance from the police.' He gestured at me. 'Indeed, I shall recount how they snatched my assistant off the street and planned to torture him! Oh, that will read well in the morning papers, Inspector Cox. It will read very well indeed.'

I held my breath, expecting the Inspector to storm out, but instead Cox looked embarrassed, all but shuffling his feet like a schoolboy called before the headmaster. Even Parkes seemed taken aback, and I saw the policemen exchange a meaningful glance. 'Two hours then,' said Cox at last. 'Two hours, and not a minute more.'

Roberta suggested a game of whist to pass the time, which Cox and the professor readily agreed to. I was less keen, because I felt we ought to be doing something more useful, but the others convinced me. As they pointed out, there was little to do but wait, and when the professor offered to show Cox his machine instead I had no choice but to step in and save the inspector's sanity. Parkes, meanwhile, went to speak with Sam Tyler about the recent deaths.

It was fortunate there was nothing riding on the outcome of our game, for at the beginning Roberta won most hands easily, and I would have been debt-ridden and destitute in no time at all. It reinforced my opinion that cards, and other games of chance, were not the most reliable way to build one's fortune. Careful investments, prudent saving and living within one's means...those were the values I espoused.

As we played I noted Roberta's happy, outgoing demeanour, and her obvious delight at every trick she took. She enjoyed winning, and took great pleasure in playing an unexpected trump to snatch victory from her father or Inspector Cox. As for myself, I believe she went easy on me, for she allowed me to take one or two hands...but only when the round itself was already won.

However, as we played on I became more engrossed in the game, and I soon forgot my worries about the professor's machine and the forthcoming hunt in the woods at nighttime. I surprised Roberta by taking a trick she'd expected to win, and when I did it a second time the atmosphere became tense. The next hand I lost deliberately, but this only succeeded in annoying Roberta further. 'Play to win or don't play at all,' she muttered.

I did my best to comply, winning where I could, but Roberta quickly deduced my tactics and soon regained the upper hand. She won the last game easily, her earlier mood entirely restored, and Cox congratulated her as he pushed his chair back and stood up. 'I must see what Parkes has found out,' he explained. 'Thank you for a most enjoyable game.'

'And I must check the calibration of my machine,' said the professor. 'Inspector, if you'd like to view the process–'

'No, no. Parkes may have news,' said Cox hurriedly, and he all but fled the room.

'Septimus and I will go for a walk,' declared Roberta. 'I have been cooped up all day, and there is still an hour of sunshine to enjoy.'

'Don't go too far,' the professor warned her. 'If the creature is detected, we must swing into action immediately.'

'We shall remain within earshot.'

'Wait, I have just the ticket.' The professor dug around in a leather satchel, taking out two small cubes. They were fashioned from brass, with intricate patterns on the surface, and he kept one and passed the other to Roberta. 'A hundred yards, no more,' he said.

She tucked the cube away without comment, and then she and I left the room together. 'We should make the most of this,' said Roberta, as we descended the stairs to the hall. 'It might be our last opportunity for a little freedom.'

I found that remark a little thoughtless, given I was still the main suspect in the gamekeeper's murder, but I knew she did not mean it as a jibe. 'Where shall we go?'

'Yesterday I spied an enclosed garden to the rear of the house. There's a pond, although it's somewhat overgrown, and also a stone bench we can sit on.'

'It sounds delightful.'

We strolled to the side of the house, where I pulled open a creaky iron gate to gain access to a walled garden. I stood aside to let Roberta by, then followed her into a wildly-overgrown area. It looked like nobody had been there for years, and the stone bench she'd mentioned was barely visible under the ivy. Nearby, the only evidence of the pond was a statuette half-buried under a thick blanket of lily pads. 'We had better not sit here too long,' said Roberta, with a laugh. 'If we do, I fear the plants might rise up and consume us.'

I concurred, for it bore little resemblance to the cosy, sunny spot I had imagined. Indeed, as we perched on the stone bench I felt a shiver up my spine.

Caaaaw!

I looked up to see a raven perched atop the brick wall, its head tilted to one side and its beady eye fastened upon me. I gestured at it, motioning it away, but its demeanour remained haughty and unconcerned. Aside from the raven there were no other birds nor evidence of their calls, and no winged insects of any kind. It was deathly still, and more than a little oppressive.

'It looked more pleasant yesterday,' said Roberta apologetically. 'It's relaxing.'

We walked around the small garden under the watchful gaze of the raven, treading carefully lest we step right into the pond. The paving was cracked and uneven, with weeds growing through, but when I half-closed my eyes I could picture the garden as it might once have been. There a patch of herbs for the kitchen, and roses here against the wall. The statuette in the middle of the pond shiny and new, and the water in the pond itself sparking clean and teeming with fish.

Finally, our circuit complete, we sat on the bench alongside each other, and as Roberta leaned against me I put my arm around her.

Caaaaw!

I shot the bird an aggrieved look. 'Don't you have business elsewhere, my good fellow?'

The raven showed no signs of moving on, and indeed it appeared to be studying us with great interest. I found its beady eye most unnerving, and had Roberta not been sitting beside me I would have beaten a hasty retreat.

Suddenly, Roberta moved. She took out the tiny cube her father had given her, holding it between finger and thumb. 'Septimus, my father calls us. He may have located the werewolf!' Shrugging off my arm, she got up. 'Come on, quickly!'

I stood and followed, and as we departed the garden I saw the raven take flight with powerful strokes of its wings. It flew arrow-straight away from the house, and the last I heard of it was a rapidly-fading cry.

39

The professor was in a state of excitement upon our return, exhorting the tiny sparks of light to greater effort as he moved from one part of the machine to another. 'Come, my beauties,' he murmured. 'Do your jobs, and seek out our prey!'

'Father?' enquired Roberta. 'Have you located the beast?'

'It approaches, I believe, but is still at extreme range. Oh, if only there were a way to increase the sensitivity of my device!' The professor glanced about him, then frowned at the ceiling. 'Perhaps if we strung additional wires on the roof...'

'It's too dangerous,' said Roberta. 'This house is three storeys high, the slate tiles are covered in moss and many of them are most likely loose. One of us might fall to our death!'

'Septimus would only have to lean out of an attic window, my dear.'

I was only mildly surprised at the speed with which 'one of us' turned out to be myself. On the other hand, Roberta was wearing a dress, which would be most unsuitable for climbing about on attic windowsills, and the professor was not only elderly, he was needed at the machine.

'There is a crack in the ceiling over here, just near the corner,' continued the professor. 'A length of wire, carefully inserted...'

'Oh, very well,' said Roberta, giving in. 'If it will help, it's worth the risk.' Then, naturally, she turned to me. 'Will you go to the upper floor, Septimus? I shall put a chair on top of the table and attempt to pass up the wire, but you will need to identify the room directly above and take up a floorboard.'

'Take this with you,' said the professor, handing me a pocket knife. 'Firstly, it will help with the matter of the floorboards, and once you have the wire you can press the point of the knife into the windowsill, then wrap the end around the handle. Be sure to secure it well! If it comes loose, the sprites will be freed.'

I took the knife and left. In the corridor, I walked to the far end before returning, counting my steps. Then I took the narrow, rickety stairs to the upper floor, where the attic rooms were nestled beneath the roof. Originally the servant quarters, they now stood dusty and empty, with only a broken bedframe or a moth-eaten mattress to show they had ever been occupied.

I repeated my measurements, pacing evenly until I had identified the room above the machine. Entering, I hauled aside a cast iron bed frame and moved an old chamberpot–with luck, long since emptied–with the toe of my shoe. Then I crouched to inspect the floorboards. They were ill-fitting and warped in places, and it took but a moment with the professor's knife to lever one or two of them up. Underneath was a cavity, thick with dust, and to my delight I saw the bright end of the copper wire. Roberta had already pushed it through the ceiling below, and was moving it back and forth to make it more visible.

'Do you see it?' came Roberta's voice, muffled by the ceiling and the dust.

'Yes, I have it!' I cried. I took hold of the end and pulled gently, and coils of wire began to slowly build up around me. I glanced at the window, which was about twelve feet away, and once I judged

I had enough wire I got up to inspect the casement. The window had jammed but I managed to force it upwards, showering myself with flakes of dry paint in the process. Then I looked out.

The view was breathtaking, with the emerald green lawns laid out ahead of me, bisected by the gravel drive. The front gates were a hundred yards away, and I could see Emily tending to a garden bed in the shadow of a large oak. Beyond lay the village, where I could make out the roofs of the houses and shops. Others were hidden by the dip, but I could make out the hill beyond with the cluster of smaller dwellings at its foot.

I looked down to see a sloping roof immediately below the window, covered in moss as Roberta had predicted. The slate looked sound, but all the same I was glad I would not have to venture out upon those dark grey tiles, for the narrow section of roof was barely two feet wide and the fall to the ground below was terrifying.

I took out the professor's knife, and after a silent apology to the Hall sisters, I drove the point into the timber windowsill. The wood was cracked and warped, and did not offer much resistance. Once the knife was in place I took up the copper wire, passing it through the window until it stretched in a straight line from the opening in the floor, over the sill and then down across the tiles. Then I took a loop of wire and wrapped it around the knife handle, drawing it tight and testing it to ensure it would not come free.

Satisfied with my work, I took a final look out of the window. As I did so I spotted Cox and Parkes coming through the main gates, the two men deep in conversation. They greeted Emily politely, then continued on their way towards the house.

I lowered the window, pressing it down upon the wire as a precaution, then made my way downstairs once more.

'I have secured the cable,' I told the professor. 'Also, Inspector Cox and Parkes are on their way.'

'What perfect timing! With luck they will get here just as I have solid results to show them.' The professor turned to Roberta. 'Now that the upper end is fixed, you may attach yours. I suggest a junction at the midway point, in order to maximise the gain.'

Roberta was holding one end of the length of copper wire, the other running up to disappear through the crack in the ceiling. She now took the loose end and fastened it to a central part of the web, winding the wire round and round to make a firm connection. As soon as she had done so, several glowing sprites changed direction, with at least half a dozen flowing up the wire to vanish through the ceiling.

At that moment Cox entered the room with Parkes. The two men eyed the machine, and then Cox addressed the professor. 'Do you have anything?'

'Grant me a moment or two,' said the professor. 'We have just extended the range of the prognosticator, and–'

'The what?'

'My machine!' snapped the professor, gesturing. 'Already it is showing promising results, but with the additional wiring I expect to have firm data in a matter of minutes.'

Cox crossed his arms. 'The allotted time has long since passed, and still we have nothing concrete?'

'Inspector, the moment I locate your killer you will need additional men to surround and subdue it,' the professor pointed out. 'Even now, your sergeant should be rushing to Croydon for reinforcements.'

'As yet, you haven't located anything, and I'm not sending Parkes off on a wild goose chase.' Cox gestured towards the window. 'Can you imagine a dozen constables loitering around the village, waiting for a signal which never comes? They would think their superior officers had taken leave of their senses!'

'But we're on the point of discovery!' exclaimed the professor. He pointed to the sprites moving around the wires, and I had to agree the movements seemed more purposeful than before. 'Won't you look at the signs? They're trying to show us the way, I promise you, but they just don't have the range.'

'I'm sorry, professor. I gave you the time you asked for, but you've been unable to come up with the goods.'

All of a sudden I knew what I had to do. I felt my palms sweating just at the thought of it, but deep down I knew it was the only way. 'Would it help if I carried the wire further up the roof?' I asked the professor.

'I'm certain of it, my boy. But are you sure?'

'Don't even think of it!' cried Roberta. 'Septimus, you'll fall!'

'As a boy I spent half my life climbing trees,' I lied. In fact, the only trees which had interested me as a boy were those which had been turned into books. 'This will be easy by comparison,' I assured her, and although she still looked doubtful she appeared to take me at my word. Then I turned to Cox. 'Will you wait here just a few minutes longer, sir?'

'The inspector is not going anywhere,' Roberta told me firmly. Then she addressed Cox. 'Septimus is about to put his life in danger in order to speed my father's experiment along. If you leave now, I swear I shall not lift a finger to help you for the rest of my life.'

Somewhat startled by the ferocity of Roberta's tone, Cox raised his hands, placating her. 'I shall wait a while longer, Miss Twickham. As for Mr Jones, I do not ask him to risk his life on my behalf.'

'But he must, in order to detect your killer! Unless you or sergeant Parkes wish to climb about upon the roof?'

'Goodness no,' said Cox. 'It would be most unseemly for an inspector to do so, and Parkes is a giant of a man. He would plunge right through the tiles!'

With all this talk of danger I was on the point of changing my mind, but having ventured my services I did not feel I could withdraw. So it was that I mounted the stairs to the attic once again. Before I left Roberta had extracted a promise from me, a solemn vow that I would take all possible care, and the three men had clapped me on the shoulder and called me a brave fellow. To me, it seemed that each was secretly pleased they were not going in my stead.

I do not intend to portray myself as a heroic figure, for history is replete with tales of supreme sacrifice, both in wartime and in peace, and my own effort was insignificant by comparison. All I had to do was climb a roof and not fall off.

Even so, my mouth was parched and my fists were tightly clenched as I ascended those stairs, for I was neither soldier nor seasoned adventurer, but rather a bookkeeper, and my idea of dangerous behaviour was to turn in a set of accounts without checking the totals three times over.

40

The window rose in its frame with a drawn-out groan, and I leaned on the sill to take stock of the surroundings. They were not promising, for the roof just below the attic window, or dormer, was steeper and narrower than I recalled, and the drop to the ground seemed to have grown considerably.

I would have to climb out and cling to the window frame for all I was worth, using both hands to ensure I did not fall. That meant attaching the loose end of the wire to my person, for I would not have a spare hand to hold it with. And, since I could not see up the roof from my position, I had no idea what other handholds might be present. In fact, I would have no idea until I was perched outside.

At that moment I saw movement. Far below, on the lawns, stood Roberta and the two policemen, all of them looking up at me. Roberta waved, and I took one hand from the sill to reply. Then I put them out of my mind, for the idea of an audience did not thrill me in the least.

Roberta had already unhooked the far end of the cable from the machine, and so there was no risk of releasing any sprites. I undid the wire from the professor's pocket knife, which still protruded from the windowsill. The rest of the wire dangled outside, and I hauled it in hand over hand, gathering loose coils until the very end was in my grasp. With a deft movement I took two turns around my wrist, folding the sharp end over to keep it snug. It occurred to me that I might lose my hand if I fell off the roof, but at that point I guessed I would be in more danger from the fall than a few inches of wire. In addition, the wire was thin and I was convinced it would snap before injuring me badly.

Now came the moment of truth, for I could delay no longer. I swung my leg over the windowsill, straddling it, then carefully felt for the tiles below the dormer window with the tip of my shoe. The surface was gritty, and as I slid the sole of my shoe around, finding purchase, I realised it was not as slippery as I had feared. Slowly I transferred my weight, easing myself through the window whilst keeping a firm grip on the sill with both hands. If my feet slipped unexpectedly, I hoped I could take the weight on my arms and quickly pull myself back inside. Then I would return to the others and apologise for my failure.

But my feet didn't slip, and I found myself standing on that sloping roof, facing the attic window with my back to the garden and my audience. The dormer had its own eaves, with a gabled roof above, and I released the window sill one hand at a time, taking hold of a wooden trim on a level with my shoulders.

The copper wire tied to my wrist glinted in the sunlight, and I took a deep breath as I considered my next move. I knew I had to climb past the dormer window, perhaps using its gabled roof as a resting place before climbing further up. But first I wanted to spy my target. I assumed there would be chimneys aplenty, and indeed I could see several of them further along the roof.

As the highest point of the house, they would be the ideal location for my copper wire, and if there were a chimney in line with the attic window it would be ideal. Then I could climb slowly up the main roof on hands and knees, with the protruding dormer below me, ready to save me if I started to slip.

I moved to my right, shuffling my feet along the roof and adjusting my tight grip on the wooden trim. The flesh beneath my fingernails turned white from the effort, and I'd almost reached the end when the sole of my shoe slipped on the tiles. My right leg flailed in mid-air, and I clung desperately to the wooden trim, praying it was secured more firmly than the floorboards had been.

Slowly I found purchase again, and I kept going, moving slowly and testing each foot before putting all my weight on it. Eventually I reached the right-hand edge of the attic window, where overlapping wooden boards had been fixed onto the dormer's brickwork to create a weatherproof cover. A broad strip of lead flashing sealed the gap between tiles and the base of this short wall, keeping out the rainwater.

I took a firm hold and leaned to the right, looking up the roof. All the while I was keenly aware of the gulf behind me, and the long, long drop to the ground below. To my relief there was a large chimney stack directly ahead, maybe twenty feet higher up. Half a dozen chimney pots protruded from the brickwork, each capped with a rusty tin baffle against rain and wind, and any one of them would make a suitable fastening-point for my wire.

Caaaw!

I looked again, and my heart sank as I spotted a raven perched on the chimney stack. I had no idea whether it was the same one which had been observing Roberta and me in the overgrown garden earlier, but its unblinking gaze was eerily familiar. Normally the raven wouldn't have bothered me, but if the thing swooped I would need a hand to defend myself, and I suspected both left and right would already be in use.

'Go away!' I called out.

Caaaw!

The raven was unmoved, and I prayed it would remain so as I attempted to climb the roof. Slowly, I lowered myself to the slate tiles, feeling the rough surface under my hands. I tested one or two, checking they were firmly attached, and then I started creeping up the steep incline with the drip edge of the attic window overhead and the dormer wall to my left. I wondered how many years it had been since someone had tested their weight on the roof as I was, and I hoped the timbers were sturdy enough to bear me.

It was hard going, with my knees suffering the most. Soon they were crying out from the unyielding surface, but I kept going, inch by inch, with the brick wall and faded wooden boards to my left. I climbed higher, and within minutes I was sitting astride the dormer's gabled roof, my back to the rest of the climb, and as I rested there I took in several deep breaths. For the moment I was safe, and I took the opportunity to look around. The first thing I saw was the copper wire, which snaked down the roof to vanish around the side of the dormer, and from there into the attic via the window. Then I raised my gaze, and I saw Roberta and the police still watching me from far below, shielding their eyes against the sun. From their position the latter was barely above the roof, and I imagined they could barely see me outlined against its glare. Despite this I risked a quick wave, showing far more confidence than I felt, before quickly grabbing at the tiles once more.

I glanced over my shoulder to determine the easiest route to the chimney stack. There were large patches of moss directly in my path, and I could also see a shallow dip where the beams underneath had sagged over the years. To avoid these obstacles I decided to climb the roof diagonally, making for the ridge capping twenty feet above me. From there I could crawl towards the chimney, before tying off the wire and making my way down again.

I only hoped the professor did not expect me to retrieve his wire again later, for as far as I was concerned it could stay on that roof forever.

There was no point in delaying, so I turned and resumed my climb, dragging the wire behind me. The roof was warm in the sunshine, and the small patches of moss I encountered were dry and wiry. Then I imagined how treacherous that slate would be after a brief shower, and I increased my pace. There were few clouds in the sky, but an unexpected downpour would strand me there until daybreak.

Once I reached the ridge capping I was at the highest point of the roof, and I marvelled as I took in the fabulous view. Never had I seen the village from such a height, and from my vantage point the houses and trees were little more than toys.

I could have sat there for hours, but the copper wire tied to my wrist reminded me of the task at hand. The chimney stack was around ten feet away, on a level with my current position, and it would take me but a moment to reach it and complete my work. The raven watched me still, but at my approach it strutted to the opposite side of the chimney.

Two yards, one yard...and then I had made it.

Caaaw! protested the raven, and it took off with a sudden flurry of wings.

I ignored it, for I was busy unwrapping the copper wire from my wrist. I drew up a little slack, then made a loop and reached for the nearest chimney pot, intending to hook it over.

Whoosh!

Something sped by, grazing the side of my face. Startled, I drew back, barely hanging on to the wire in my sudden shock. I looked around, frantically seeking my attacker, and I saw the raven wheeling round before driving itself at me once more, wings flapping powerfully. It flew ever closer, growing huge, seemingly intent on cannoning directly into me. At the last minute I moved behind the ridge capping, clinging to the far side of the roof. Holding on to the old tiles with one hand, I ducked my head as the raven tore past, close enough to touch. I shouted at it in anger, but I might as well have bayed at the moon.

As it gained altitude, preparing for another attack, I doggedly reached for the chimney pot to hook the wire over. It took, and I gave it a gentle tug to ensure it was fastened securely. Then, before I could cover my head, the raven struck.

This time its claws gouged my scalp, the savage pain like a blast of fire. I was still holding on to the ridge capping with one hand, the other having been extended to fasten the wire, and in that instant I felt something give. The tile I was holding onto came loose, and I felt myself beginning to slide.

I released the tile and grabbed for the ridge cap with both hands, but it was too late. Already the peak of the roof was a foot out of reach, and I was sliding faster and faster. I rolled onto my back and pressed the flat of my shoes against the tiles, my arms outstretched and my hands scrabbling for something, anything, to slow my fall, but it was to no avail.

Below me, to my horror, I could see the edge of the roof approaching quickly. I was going over, no doubt about it, and then I would plunge three storeys to my death.

41

I barely had time to think before I went hurtling off the edge of the roof, my hands still clawing for a solid surface that was no longer there.

Ground and sky whirled around me, all-too-briefly, and then I landed on my back, arms and legs outstretched. I expected to be killed instantly, but instead crashed through a thick, spongy material. The air was knocked from my lungs, and I had yet to draw breath as I continued to plunge downwards. Suddenly, freezing water closed over me, and I vaguely heard the terrific splash as it reacted violently to my rapid arrival.

The thick, soupy water was filled with bubbles and stirred-up mud, and as I thrashed about in my leaden clothes I could barely tell which way was up. I fought like mad, but the more I moved the more my limbs were restrained, until they were entangled completely and I was rendered immobile. A little daylight filtered down on me, but despite only being one or two feet overhead I decided it might as well be a mile, for I could barely move a muscle. By some miracle I had survived the fall, but now it seemed I was fated to drown.

The bubbles were clearing now, and I managed to determine my situation...and the reason I had not died when falling off the roof. There was a stone pedestal nearby, underwater, and from it rose an old statuette. I recognised the thing, for Roberta and I had sat nearby an hour or so earlier. I had fallen off the roof and landed in the weed-choked pond, falling through a thick tangle of ivy and lilies!

And now that same ivy, those same lilies, were holding me fast underwater, about to end my life immediately after they had saved it. I could see specks and flashes in my vision now, as my breath, held far too long, began to run out, and my lungs felt like they were on the point of bursting.

Suddenly I saw movement, a shadow above me, and then a hand plunged into the weed-infested water and took a handful of my coat, the huge fist bunching my lapels like a sheet of paper. A sudden tug, the tearing of weeds and roots and leaves, and I was out of that water and being suspended above the pond by the huge, strong figure of Sergeant Parkes.

Desperately, I drew in a ragged breath, and then another. I must have looked like a drowned rat in my soaking clothes, with my hair plastered over my face and water streaming from me as though from a waterwheel, but I cared not a whit. I had survived, somehow, and that was all that mattered.

Parkes set me down on the edge of the pond, steadying me, and the moment I could form words I thanked him from the bottom of my heart.

'We heard you fall,' he rumbled. 'It was the least I could do.'

Then Roberta stood before me, cupping my face in her hands and studying me with concern etched in her expression. 'Septimus, are you well? Did you injure yourself?'

Remarkably, I discovered I had not. Oh, I had a few scrapes and cuts, and I was certain there would be plenty of fresh bruises, but nothing was broken. 'I am fighting fit,' I assured her. 'With a few dry clothes and a new pair of shoes, nobody will be any the wiser.'

She released my face and took my hands in hers. 'Don't frighten me like that again,' she murmured.

'I hope I don't,' I replied, in all sincerity. I still remembered the sensation of falling, of being trapped underwater, and my blood ran cold at my close escape. And that damnable raven! Had it acted out of blind instinct, or was there something far more sinister behind its attack? I glanced around, wondering whether it was observing me even now, but to my relief there was no sign of the bird.

'Father!' exclaimed Roberta. She took out the small cube the professor had given her. 'He's calling us again.'

I looked down at myself. I was dripping wet, but if I ran home to change I would miss everything. In the end I followed the others, wrapping myself in an old blanket purloined from an airing cupboard along the way. As we went up the stairs, Cox gripped my soggy shoulder. 'You had a lucky escape, lad. Don't scare us like that again.'

'I'll do my best,' I said, with a wry grin.

Given the summons, I was hoping the professor might have news for us. Had he tracked the creature by using the extended range I had risked my life to gain for him?

No, he had not.

As it turned out, the professor was impatient to learn whether I had attached the wire yet, as he was waiting to connect the other end. 'I could not extend the range until I heard, and you have been extremely tardy,' he complained.

'Septimus fell off the roof and almost died!' declared Roberta.

The professor turned his full attention to me, and I was quite taken by the concern in his expression. 'My dear boy, that's terrible! Do say you managed to connect my wire before you fell!'

I suppose I should have guessed his concern was not so much for my well-being, but for his contraption. 'I did, sir.'

'Excellent! Then let us proceed.' The professor whirled round, all thoughts of my accident quickly forgotten. He connected the loose end of the wire, the other end of which I had fastened to the chimney, then watched the meandering sprites with breathless anticipation. Cox and Roberta fastened their gaze on the machine, equally intent, and even Parkes seemed mildly curious.

As for myself, I was in need of a hot bath and dry clothes, and I was beginning to wonder what foul sickness might befall me after my ducking in the stagnant pond.

'Come on, my little beauties,' murmured the professor. 'It's time for you to light our way.' As he spoke he made ushering motions with his hands, encouraging the other-worldly beings to their task.

However, after two or three minutes of breathless anticipation, a loud snort rent the air. 'I'm sorry professor, but I've had enough of this,' growled Cox. 'You might attach that wire to the tallest tree in the land, and still this contraption would lie inert.'

'It's just a matter of time, my dear man!' exclaimed the professor. 'See how they move about, doing their utmost to–'

'They barely move at all, and Parkes and I have business elsewhere. I am grateful for your efforts, and I trust you will restore this room to its former state when you leave. The Croydon police are already offside, and they will not appreciate a complaint against you from the owners of this property.'

'Leave?' said the professor, his voice rising. 'You think I would pack my things and leave, when so many are in mortal danger?'

'You may do as you wish, but I am beholden to a higher power.'

'It would be a mistake for you to leave,' muttered the professor. He gestured at Roberta and me. 'If the three of us capture this beast, I will be sure to mention your early departure to the press.'

'Do as you will.'

'I swear to you, Cox, instead of leaving you should be fetching reinforcements. This matter may be resolved by nightfall, and you would benefit greatly from a successful conclusion. Your career–'

'My career is in jeopardy the longer I remain in this room,' said Cox flatly. 'If the Super discovers I wasted half the day watching your precious fireflies gathering upon a copper wire, I will be–'

'Gathering?' demanded the professor.

'Yes, over there.' Cox pointed. 'They clump together like wet sand.'

The professor whirled around. As Cox had observed, the random movements had ceased and the sprites had coalesced into a tight mass. 'Roberta, the readings!'

Roberta sprang into action, ducking under the wires so that she might examine the closest paper ticket to the swarming mass of sprites. I hoped she did not get too close, for the beings were highly agitated and I felt one might fly free of the wires at any moment. 'South East by East,' she called. 'Range one thousand, four hundred and...eighty yards.'

'We have it!' crowed the professor, scribbling down the coordinates. He gestured triumphantly at Cox, waving the notebook at him. 'Do you still want to leave? Eh? Do you still have urgent business elsewhere?'

We stamped down the stairs in a group, with Roberta at the head and the professor bringing up the rear. He'd paused to rummage in his equipment bag, drawing out a small magnetic compass with which to guide us.

Ellen Hall looked out from a doorway as we thundered past, watching us in astonishment.

'I apologise for the disturbance ma'am,' Inspector Cox called over his shoulder. 'Urgent police business.'

We hurried through the front door, then raced along the gravel path to the main gates. Here, we paused while the professor took a bearing. 'That way!' he pointed, and we hared off once more.

'How far have we come?' demanded Roberta, as we passed the smithy.

'Around a hundred and fifty paces,' puffed Cox.

'Wait a minute, I beg you.' The professor came to halt, panting hard. 'I cannot...run the best part...of a mile,' he wheezed. 'You must go ahead. I shall return...to the machine.'

'Yes, yes,' said Cox urgently. 'Return, and we will continue.'

The professor handed me the compass and we set off again, whilst he walked back to the house at a less frantic pace. It was at this point I noticed a flaw in our plan, for if the creature moved before we arrived at the coordinates, the professor would know immediately, but he could not communicate the information.

In addition, if the monster were in human form, and was gathered amongst others, innocents all...how in heaven's name would we identify it? We could scarcely arrest everyone we found at the professor's coordinates!

I kept my doubts to myself, partly because I was out of breath, and also because I did not want to discourage Cox. After all, we might find the monster in its foul, wolf-like state, or alone in human form with nobody else in the vicinity. I glanced at Cox and Parkes, and could not help noticing that, while Parkes had his truncheon, they lacked genuine firepower of the kind we might require. I cursed as I remembered the shotgun, for in our haste we had not thought to snatch it up. It would be a bad outcome indeed if, instead of capturing the creature, it tore us all limb from limb. As I pictured this particular ending, I decided I must, after all, speak out.

'Wait!' I cried.

The others came to a halt, staring at me.

'We are not prepared! We have no weapons, no rope to bind the beast...nothing! I have seen this monster up close, and I assure you it is very strong, and ferocious, and deadly.'

'But it might be attacking someone at this very moment,' Cox pointed out. 'Parkes and I have our duty, whatever the danger.'

'Just get me close to the thing,' muttered Parkes. 'Get me close, and I'll do the rest.'

Roberta gripped my arm. 'I will run back for the shotgun. While at the house, I will check with my father to ensure the creature is still in the same approximate location.'

She left, and the policemen and I hurried on. The sun was setting now, and the shops and houses cast long shadows on the road. A few people were about, and as we passed the inn I saw Sam Tyler coming towards us. 'Our local policeman,' I said to Cox, with a nod in Sam's direction. 'Constable Tyler.'

'I know. Parkes and I spoke with him earlier.' Cox gestured, raising his voice. 'Constable, with us!'

'Where are you going, sir?' demanded Tyler.

'You'll see soon enough,' growled Parkes. 'Now get moving or I'll drag you there myself.'

Tyler turned and ran after us.

'Any news of a disturbance?' Cox asked him. 'Any troubles in the village?'

'Nothing, sir. Quiet as the grave.' Tyler eyed us curiously. 'What's all this about?'

'We've got a lead on the killer,' said Cox. 'Straight ahead, maybe half a mile. Where would that put us?'

'The Carmichael residence,' I said, all of a sudden.

'No, it's beyond that,' said Tyler quickly. 'Somewhere in the woods behind, most like.'

I had walked the same road with my parents the day before, to the exact same destination, and I was fairly sure of my guess. However, I was also too much out of breath to argue. In any case, we would follow the trail to wherever it led, and it would make no difference whether it was Tyler or myself who had the truth of the matter.

We were all flagging after our headlong rush through the village, and I was grateful when Cox raised his hand, bringing out party to a halt. 'Hush now,' he muttered. 'We must keep our wits about us.'

Ahead, the lane ran between hedgerows, with small fields of crops on either side. To our right was a farmhouse, while ahead, further up the lane, I could see open gates leading to the grounds of the Carmichaels' house. Birds sang in the trees, and with the shafts of sunlight and the lush green hedgerows it was a most pleasant scene. Then I realised the beast might be crouched behind those self-same hedges, waiting to pounce, and the environs lost a little of their appeal.

We advanced cautiously, listening for any hint of our prey. Parkes and Tyler withdrew their truncheons, while Cox and I made do with stout branches retrieved from the side of the road. I hoped Roberta would catch up soon with the shotgun, for it was clear we were ill-prepared for a violent encounter.

Then we saw the body.

42

'Stay here,' Cox instructed me, and I was happy to obey.

The victim had been dragged under the hedge, perhaps twenty feet ahead of us, and all I could see were the soles of their boots and the lower half of their trousers. The victim was lying face down and from the size of the footwear I guessed it was a man, although I couldn't be certain. With the sun now fully set and twilight approaching fast, it was hard to see under the overhanging trees, but the boots did not look like those of a labourer. I felt a sudden chill as I thought of my father, but it passed as I told myself he always wore shoes. As a professional bookkeeper he generally wore a coat and matching trousers, and such attire did not go well with boots.

The three policemen were crouching beside the body, conferring in low voices. Then, gently, they pulled the victim from under the hedge, carefully turning the body over. I heard Tyler exclaim in shock, and then he rose, staggering away from the others. Blindly, he crossed the lane, and once he reached the opposite verge he bent double and began to retch helplessly.

'You know him, constable?' demanded Cox. 'Come on, man. Pull yourself together!'

'My god, h–his wounds!' stammered Tyler, his face as pale as a sheet.

'Yes, yes. But who is it?'

'I—it's Mr Carmichael,' replied Tyler in anguish. He pointed towards the gates, his finger shaking. 'He lives just there, with his wife and daughter!'

I could scarcely believe it. Carmichael dead? And what of Cecilie and her mother? Had the monster killed them also, slaughtering them in their very home? I ran for the gate, ignoring the sudden cries from the police, and completely uncaring of my safety. I might not wish to marry Cecilie, but I had known her for many years and the thought of her suffering a violent death left me sick with worry.

As I ran up the drive I heard Cox and Parkes behind me, their boots crashing on the loose gravel. I did not think they were trying to catch me, to restrain me, but rather my headlong rush had spurred them into similar action. They too must have realised Cecilie and her mother might be under threat at that very moment, and I only hoped we were not too late!

As for Tyler, when I glanced back I saw him lagging behind, still looking distraught. As a village policeman I guessed he'd not witnessed many violent deaths, and the sight of Carmichael had clearly shaken him.

We reached the house, where Cox knocked on the front door. It opened, and a maid looked out. 'Police matter,' said Cox, showing her his warrant card. 'Are Mrs Carmichael and her daughter present?'

'Yes sir. They're in the drawing room.'

Cox entered the house, but as I went to follow Parkes took my elbow. 'Not yet, sir. Nor you, neither,' he said to Tyler, who had finally caught up. 'Give the guv'nor a minute to break the news. We don't want a crowd.'

This was a lengthy speech for the sergeant, and I took his meaning immediately. We stood in silence, still breathing heavily from the run, and then I heard a wail of dismay that caused the hairs on my neck to rise. Poor Mrs Carmichael! And Cecilie! To hear such terrible, unexpected news would be completely devastating, and my heart went out to them.

Cox returned moments later, his face set. 'The maid has administered a tincture, which should calm the ladies somewhat. I saw no evidence of the creature that did for the husband, and any questioning will have to wait until they've overcome the initial shock. They're in no state to speak with us now, that's for certain.' He glanced over my shoulder. 'Parkes, get yourself to Croydon. I want a dozen men, quick as you can.'

'Yes sir.'

'Armed, if possible. They'll probably have two revolvers between the lot of them, I suppose, but that's better than nothing.'

Parkes hurried away, his heavy tread scattering gravel.

'We might be able to borrow a few shotguns locally,' I told Cox. 'I still have a dozen shells containing silver shot.'

'Why silver?' demanded Tyler.

'Never mind that now,' said Cox, addressing the constable. 'You know the people in these parts. Round up half a dozen shotguns. Tell them it's a police matter, and they'll be returned safely when we're done with them. When you've got them, take them to the pub. And one more thing! Tell everyone you see to go home, close their doors and windows and draw their curtains. Tell them to pass the word to their neighbours. I don't want to see anyone abroad, is that clear?'

Tyler nodded and ran off, leaving myself and Cox alone. He looked me up and down, then nodded towards the lane. 'I'll stay here in case this thing comes back. Find Miss Twickham, return with her to Ravenswood and tell her to stay put. Understood?'

'Roberta won't–'

'Mr Jones, I'm not asking, I'm telling. When she's agreed, check with the professor and bring me that shotgun of yours along with any news of the creature. I want to know where it's been and where it's going.'

'Yes sir.'

He gave me a wintry smile. 'Good lad. Off you go now, and keep an eye out. I don't want to lose you, either.'

I met Roberta outside the village, hurrying towards me with the shotgun under one arm. I took the weapon and loaded it, using one of the shells which I still carried in my pocket. They were damp from their immersion in the pond, but I hoped the wadding would have kept the powder dry.

We turned for Ravenswood once more, and on the way I told her about Carmichael's death, recounting how Cox had broken the news to the family. Of course, Roberta did not react as the others had, never having met the Carmichaels, but she was troubled all the same. 'Had we been a little quicker, we might have saved him,' she said.

'How could we possibly have got there any sooner? I risked my life climbing onto the roof, solely to increase the range of your father's machine. Without that, we might not have detected the creature at all!'

'You're right, of course. In any case, had you appeared beforehand, it might have taken a different victim. Or, indeed, it might have attacked you.' She gestured. 'It's fate, I suppose.'

I did not think the Carmichaels would be pleased to hear her say so, but I held my counsel. 'Cox has sent Parkes for help. After I've escorted you home, I shall take him the shotgun so that he can stand watch over Cecilie and her mother.'

Roberta stopped. 'Escorted me home? I thought we were going to speak with my father!'

'That too,' I said quickly.

'Septimus, my dear, if you expect me to cower indoors while this monster kills one villager after another, you can think again.'

'But Cox–'

'Hang the inspector! What does he know of this beast?'

'He knows about murders, and he's already had to break the news of one death to the family.' I held up the shotgun. 'I am to deliver this to Cox, and afterwards I am certain he will order me back to Ravenswood, to help you and the professor with the detection machine. Parkes is bringing a dozen armed constables to wrap this matter up, and they will not want us getting in the way!'

'You speak as though the case were already solved,' said Roberta. 'What if the werewolf has taken human form, and is hiding amongst the people of this village at this very moment? It might be drinking a pint in the pub, discussing the weather, and where would your dozen policemen be then? In the woods, peering behind every tree?' She shook her head. 'No, the three of us are vital to their efforts. Father will direct the search, and you and I will use our particular skills to corner the beast.'

'What beast is that? Do you hunt the werewolf?'

The voice startled us, for twilight had fallen just before we reached Ravenswood, and the area behind the garden wall was in darkness. As Roberta and I stared into the shadows, Miss Emily Hall stepped out of the garden bed with a small trowel and a wicker basket. 'Do you have news of the werewolf?' She eyed the shotgun – her father's shotgun – in my hands. 'Has it struck again?'

I nodded. 'I'm sorry to report that it killed Mr Carmichael.'

'The poor man,' she said quietly. 'I will take something to the family immediately.'

'I'm sorry, but it's not safe,' I told her. 'Inspector Cox is gathering armed police to capture the beast, and he wants everyone to stay indoors.'

Emily snorted in a most unladylike fashion. 'That monster has roamed the countryside for decades and the police have yet to find it. What makes Inspector Cox any different?'

'He will have our help,' said Roberta. 'Come now, let us go inside. You can't tend your garden in this light!'

The three of us entered the house, where Emily lit a single candle in the hall. Gas lighting had yet to reach West Wickham, and it was a shock to see people enduring such near-darkness within their homes.

Roberta and I went upstairs, where the professor had been waiting anxiously for news. He had a candelabra containing a pair of spluttering wicks, the light barely enough to reach the far walls. He groaned when he learned of the killing, and agreed that asking the villagers to remain home was an excellent idea.

'What does your machine tell us now?' I asked him.

'It's odd. Very odd indeed.' He pointed out a section of wire on the far side of the room. 'When you left, every one of the sprites was gathered in that location, presumably the spot where the body was found.'

I frowned, because I could see half a dozen sprites on the wire, glowing in the low light. 'But there are still a number there, circling about. Does that mean the monster remains?'

'No, the majority moved off, indicating the creature was moving east. Eventually, they dissipated once more, the monster having moved out of range.'

'And those?' asked Roberta, pointing to the remaining sprites.

'I don't quite understand. It's as though some part of the monster remained.'

'Like a tooth, or some of its fur?'

'Oh no. Something that small would not give off anywhere near enough paranormal energy. This is much larger.'

'Well, we only saw the body,' I told the professor. 'There was nothing else.'

He rubbed his chin, deep in thought. As he stood there, musing over the problem, I saw one of the sprites leave the others and travel along the wire, before circling aimlessly around a connection. I pointed it out, and the professor's frown grew deeper. Then, all of a sudden, he cried out in triumph. 'Decay!' he shouted.

Roberta and I stared at him, puzzled.

'Don't you see? It's the body!' shouted the professor. 'The body you found...it's the *werewolf!*'

43

'But professor, Carmichael was mauled most horribly,' I protested. 'Are you suggesting someone killed the werewolf, which happened to be Mr Carmichael of all people, and then some wild animal happened across his body and decided on a spot of lunch?'

'My dear boy, I employed you for that brain of yours, and yet you cannot leap to the obvious conclusion.'

'Perhaps it's the pond water that flooded my ears,' I muttered, not altogether happy with the professor's teasing. I was still damp from head to toe, I was hungry and I hadn't slept well. None of these were conducive to mental gymnastics, and I heartily wished he would just come out with the thing.

'There are two werewolves,' said Roberta suddenly.

The professor beamed at her, proud as Punch. 'Precisely!'

'Eh?' I said.

'Carmichael was a werewolf, that much is clear.' The professor pointed to the glowing sprites on the wire. Even as he did so, another moved slowly away, leaving only four or five circling together. 'Upon his death, the paranormal energies present in his body began to seep away, as you can see from my prognosticator. Soon they will all be gone.'

I don't know what shocked me more. First, there was the news that my potential father-in-law had been a murderous werewolf. Why, I'd been there for tea the day before, and Roberta had gone there alone to interview him! My blood ran cold as I thought of the danger she'd been in. But then came the even more troubling news that there had been two of these werewolves…and one of them yet roamed free. 'Why stop at two?' I said wildly.

'What's that?'

I gesticulated. 'Why two werewolves? Why not a dozen?' My voice rose as I became aware of the awful truth. 'By your reasoning half the village might be infected, just waiting out there to kill us all!'

'Relax, Mr Jones,' said the professor calmly. 'For one thing, my machine would have detected them. And for another, theory suggests that werewolves are territorial to a fault.'

'So, the werewolf which killed all those villagers, terrorising the area for years, has itself been killed by an even *more* vicious creature? And you expect me to *relax*?'

'You have to admit,' said Roberta, 'the second werewolf has done us no small favour.'

I stared from one to the other. In my agitated state, picturing as I was werewolves under every bed, I could not fathom their extreme calm. I half-expected Miss Emily or Miss Ellen to burst in, sprout whiskers and fangs, and set upon us all.

'Perhaps he is feverish,' murmured the professor.

Roberta placed a hand on my forehead. 'His temperature is a little high. That pond was foul indeed, though, and it may be affecting his stomach.'

'There is nothing wrong with me!' I declared. 'I just want you to understand the situation we find ourselves in! The danger!'

'We came here to hunt a werewolf,' said the professor. 'I think the danger was a given.'

Suddenly, Roberta looked at me in concern. 'Septimus, when you found the body...did you touch it? Did you get any of the blood on your hands?'

'I did not approach it. Why?'

Roberta exchanged a glance with her father. 'The traits of a werewolf are sometimes passed on through its bite, and it's rumoured that the same might happen after contact with its blood.'

'Cox and Parkes were there of course,' I said quickly. 'Tyler too, but he took one look and retreated. The others...they turned the body to inspect the wounds, but I don't recall either man touching the injuries.' I frowned. 'If they were infected, how long would this transformation take?'

'Weeks, if not months. We don't have to worry about them yet.' Roberta turned to the professor. 'When the police arrive we must set someone to move that body. It would be terrible if some innocent were to be harmed.'

The professor nodded. 'Not to mention the harm they might do to others.'

I glanced towards the doorway. Upon entering, I had leant the shotgun against the wall, and now I knew what I must do. Cox had asked me to return with that gun, and once I'd delivered it I would stand with the body, warning the police away.

'I'll come with you,' said Roberta, guessing my thoughts.

'Please, Roberta. Stay with your father, and help him track this monster. I will ask Cox to send a policeman, so that you will have a runner with which to communicate any movements our enemy might make.'

For a moment it looked like she would argue, but then she nodded. 'Take care.'

'I intend to.' I gathered up the shotgun and was about to leave when the professor cried out. 'It's here! It's right here in the village!'

I spun round, my task forgotten. 'Where?'

'The signal is weak. Roberta, your help please!'

She obeyed, checking the notes attached to the wires. 'No more than four hundred yards, and a little east of due south.'

'How the devil did it get so close?' demanded the professor.

'Is it moving?' I asked him. 'Or is it another body?'

'It was moving, but it has settled now.'

'Then we must hurry. Tyler was told to wait at the pub with spare guns...we will go there, and with luck we can round up some help.'

'Wait a moment, I will come with you,' said the professor. 'Just let me...' His voice tailed off as he took up the engraved metal jar. Carefully, he offered it up to the wire, and I saw a lone sprite leave the others and dart inside. Immediately, the professor replaced the lid, screwing it down firmly. 'Now, let us confront this beast!' he declared. 'Come, Roberta. You will be needed also!'

There was no time to argue, so I strode from the room with Roberta and the professor in my wake, the three of us taking the stairs far too quickly in the darkness. But the danger of tripping was nothing compared to the danger that werewolf represented. Why, if it were roaming the village it might break into homes and kill a dozen people in one night, my parents included!

We reached the pub in no time, traversing the deserted streets as though the werewolf itself were at our heels. As we drew close I saw a carriage outside, the same one which had brought me from Croydon earlier that day, and I realised to my delight that Parkes had arrived with reinforcements.

However, upon entering the pub I was not met by a dozen burly police constables. No, instead I saw Parkes addressing a dozen farmers and villagers, each with a shotgun over his shoulder. They looked around as I entered, and my stomach sank at the sight of their set, angry faces. Many were flushed, as though they'd been drinking, and I realised that one spark might set off the angry mob. Nearby, on a table, there were another half-dozen shotguns, and someone had brought along several boxes of shells.

'Here is Mr Jones now,' said Parkes. 'He has the special ammunition you will need, so load your guns and stand ready for my orders. Don't waste it, mind, for there's precious little to go around!'

I took the shells from my pockets, and they were quickly grabbed by the eager men. The pub echoed to the sound of guns being loaded, and I heard several men crowing that they would be the first to kill the beast. 'Parkes,' I whispered, taking the sergeant aside. 'Why have you riled them up so? They're ready to go out and shoot the first thing they see!'

'Croydon wouldn't give me a single man,' growled Parkes. 'I have to make do with whatever we've got here. I sent someone to the inspector, and he'll be along soon I'm sure.'

With a guilty start, I remembered my promise to take Cox a shotgun. Events had moved so quickly that I'd completely forgotten, and I imagined the inspector would be less than happy when he caught up with me.

Meanwhile, Parkes turned to the professor. 'Do you have any news on the beast?'

'It is nearby, and I have a way to find it.'

'Good.' Parkes nodded to the table. 'Mr Jones, grab yourself a shotgun and stand ready.' He turned to Roberta. 'You need to stay indoors, miss, and your father too.'

In reply, Roberta took a gun from the table, cracked it open and put her hand out to me for a shell. I passed her one, and she loaded the gun and snapped it closed. 'Father, will you join us?'

'Of course, my dear.' The professor selected a weapon, and after loading it quickly and efficiently, he shouldered the gun as though born to it.

Parkes shrugged. 'Very well, but I don't want any complaints if this creature tears your heads off.'

'That is all but guaranteed,' said the professor.

'So, how do we track the beast if you are not at that machine of yours?'

The professor reached into his pocket, drawing out the jar. 'Would you?' he asked me, and I took his gun in my spare hand. Then, before I could stop him, the professor unscrewed the jar and shook it violently, releasing the glowing sprite right there in the middle of the crowded pub.

44

'Are you mad?' I cried. 'That thing will be the death of us!' I still held vivid memories of Bransen, the manager at the docks, being attacked by the sprites.

Silence fell, and everyone watched the tiny spark of light. I saw nervous expressions, and fearful ones, but instead of attacking the sprite rose into the air, circling above the crowd, illuminating their upturned faces.

'It seeks its prey,' said the professor, his voice loud in the hushed silence. 'When it catches the scent, it will be away.'

As if on cue, the sprite turned and shot through the open door.

'After it!' roared someone, and the mob charged out, men elbowing and shoving each other in their haste. I expected a gun to go off in the melee, but fortunately the crowd emerged unscathed. Roberta, the professor and I followed, with Parkes hurrying past us to keep pace with the men.

'This is madness,' I muttered. 'Someone is going to get hurt, and I don't mean they'll fall to the werewolf.'

'I agree with you my boy,' said the professor. 'But you can understand their reaction, for they're scared, and they want to put an end to the killings.'

The sprite was moving ahead, zig-zagging up the road, while the mob ran after it, brandishing their guns. It was almost comical, but I was not laughing for I could almost predict the outcome. If the sprite entered a house, the men would smash down the door and charge inside, overcome by their lust for revenge. In the event, I could easily imagine the poor homeowners suffering greatly, even though they might be entirely innocent. 'Parkes, you have to control them,' I shouted. 'People could get killed!'

The sergeant was ahead of us, overhauling the running men. Parkes must have heard me because I saw him nod in agreement, and I hoped it wasn't too late for him to assert control. He had almost reached the head of the mob when the sprite began to circle overhead, with everyone ceasing their headlong rush to watch. It appeared to be seeking direction, and when I realised where I was I felt sick to my stomach. We stood at a junction, and I had barely arrived when the sprite set off to my left, down the road. Now certain I knew where it was going, I ran after it faster than I had in my entire life.

I finally caught up with the rest of the armed mob, just in time to see the glowing spark fly right through the middle of my parents' front door.

'Open up!' shouted a large, angry-looking farmer. 'Open up this second, or we'll bust in!'

Several others surrounded him, shotguns levelled at the door, and I was still fighting my way through the angry crowd when Parkes stepped in. He took the farmer and threw him bodily into the nearby garden bed, then turned to face the mob, some of whom were now pointing their weapons at him. 'Settle down, the lot of you!' he roared.

There were angry shouts, and things looked like they were about to get ugly. Even the huge figure of sergeant Parkes could not stand against so many, and I could barely make headway at all against the armed men in front of me. The crowd smelled of fear, sweat, anger and beer, and the heaving mass was almost a living, breathing animal.

Suddenly a shotgun went off behind me, the report deafening. Everyone spun round, and I saw Inspector Cox holding the professor's gun. It was pointed towards the sky, smoke curling from the barrel, and having attracted the crowd's attention he spoke in a calm but firm voice. 'My name is Inspector Cox, of the metropolitan police. I will count to ten, and after that, any man I see before me will be arrested for public affray. Do I make myself clear?'

I heard several men muttering, but Cox silenced them with a glance. 'Parkes, I want their weapons. Quickly now, set them against the wall.'

'How we going to defend ourselves?' demanded one of the men.

'The beast is mortally afraid of seawater. Get a pail, mix in a pound of salt and keep it by you at all times. If anything tries to get in, you throw that water right over it. Understood?'

I stared at him, wondering where he'd obtained such patently false information. Next to me, the professor opened his mouth to speak up, but Roberta quickly trod on his foot, silencing him with a frown.

'Better off with a gun,' muttered someone.

'Trust me, you'd only anger the beast. Now get moving!'

Still they hesitated, but the presence of a London police inspector finally swayed them, and the men began to file away, still muttering amongst themselves.

'Parkes, what were you thinking?' demanded Cox, once the five of us were alone.

'Sorry, sir. Croydon wouldn't send reinforcements, and I thought I could control that lot. Things got out of hand.'

'What was that nonsense about salt water?' demanded the professor.

Cox smiled. 'Better they soak each other than blast away with twelve-guages. Might save a life, if someone gets spooked.'

Suddenly the door opened a crack, and my mother looked out, her features illuminated by a flickering candle. 'What's going on?' she called to me. 'Why was Pete Garner hammering on my front door?'

Cox bowed. 'I apologise, Mrs Jones. People got a bit riled up, but it's settled down now. May we come in?'

'Ma'am,' said the professor, as we trooped into the hall. 'Did you by any chance see a floating spark of light?'

'What a thing to ask me!' My mother regarded him warily. 'Have you been drinking, sir?'

'No, no. I assure you, it's a legitimate question.'

'Well, this mysterious light of yours wasn't in *my* kitchen. You have my word on that.'

'Where is father?' I asked her urgently. Somehow, even with all these people in the house, I hoped there might be a way to spirit him away. Or failing that, to distract the sprite and thus avoid the revelation that my dear father was indeed the werewolf everyone sought. 'Is he here?'

At that moment my father stepped into the hall, complete with slippers and his pipe. He looked the very picture of respectability, completely normal in every way. Normal, that was, aside from the glowing sprite circling above his head.

'Oh my!' exclaimed my mother. 'What on earth is that?'

Parkes and the inspector reacted immediately, levelling their weapons with the charge silver shot that would prove fatal to my father.

I did not think, acting out of pure instinct. With no regard for my own safety, I stepped past them and shielded my father with my own body, stretching out my arms for added emphasis. 'If you want to shoot him, you'll have to kill me first,' I said quietly.

45

Staring into the flat, expressionless faces of Inspector Cox and Sergeant Parkes, I would not have been surprised if they *had* shot me down. Outside, they had saved my parents by dispersing the angry mob, but now, with the evidence plain to see as it circled directly above my father's head, they were less inclined to charity.

Then Roberta stepped forward to join me, standing by my side to shield my father. I felt a lump rise in my throat, and when the professor came to stand with the two of us, I had never felt more grateful in my entire life.

'Come now, Inspector,' said the professor. 'Cover Mr Jones if you must, but I'm sure you can see he is no threat to us. Indeed, he seems almost as surprised by this turn of events as we are.'

Cox lowered his gun, and gestured at Parkes to do likewise.

'Will someone please tell me what's going on?' demanded my mother plaintively. 'Coming in here waving those guns...it's an outrage! And you, Inspector, who sat here drinking my tea only this morning. You ought to be ashamed of yourself!'

'We're chasing a very dangerous, er, criminal,' said Cox. He shot a glance at my father. 'You, sir, are under suspicion, and I caution you not to make any sudden moves.'

'Don't be ridiculous,' snapped my mother. 'Under suspicion for what? And what *is* that...that glowing thing? It's all too much, I swear!'

Roberta left my side to comfort my mother, taking her hand and putting an arm around her shoulder. 'I'm sure it's nothing, Mrs Jones. The police just need to ask your husband some questions, that's all.'

'Bursting in here late at night,' muttered my mother. 'Murders and glowing lights and police with guns...what's this village coming to?'

'You'd better come through,' said my father, indicating the sitting room. He eyed the bulk of sergeant Parkes. 'Although it might be a bit of a squeeze for this many of us.'

The inspector thanked him, then turned to Parkes. 'Go and settle those hotheads, sergeant. I don't want an angry mob tearing through the village. And you can unload all the guns outside, too.'

'Yes sir,' said Parkes smartly, and he left, closing the front door behind him.

We gathered in the sitting room, where I couldn't help noticing that Cox sat with the shotgun lying across his lap. The sprite, meanwhile, followed my father around like a lost puppy, illuminating the top of his head with its ghostly glow. He looked up at it, then glanced around the room before settling on the professor. 'I assume your helper here is designed to seek out the supernatural?'

I felt the room tilt around me, stunned at the casual manner in which my father had broached the subject, and astonished at the way he seemed to accept the idea of a paranormal entity so readily. It was like discovering your own parents had forked tails, and they expected everyone else to have them too.

'It's a being from the shadow realms,' explained the professor. 'There was an archeological dig you see, most fascinating indeed, and when I learned–'

'The technical explanations can wait,' said Cox. 'Mr Jones, are you a...' The inspector appeared to be having difficulty with his words. 'What I mean is, do you, er, change into, a, er...'

'He means to ask if you're a werewolf,' I said, putting Cox out of his misery.

'Indeed I am, and your mother keeps a broomstick and a cauldron in the airing cupboard.'

'Father, this is serious.'

'Yes, the profusion of guns make that abundantly clear.'

'Well?' demanded Cox.

'Of course I'm not a werewolf!' declared my father. 'Neither am I a mermaid, nor a poltergeist, nor–'

Cox turned to the professor. 'Sir, do you have any way of testing Mr Jones here?'

'Indeed I do, but the kit sits upon my desk in London.'

Roberta cleared her throat. 'Not any more it doesn't.'

'You stole that too?' demanded the professor, shocked. 'Is nothing sacred.'

'Septimus and I came here to hunt the werewolf. Naturally, I brought all the equipment I thought would be useful.'

'And half my library,' muttered her father.

I stood up.

'Where are you going?' demanded Cox.

'The test kit. It's in my room.'

'Of course it is,' growled the professor, shooting Roberta an aggrieved look. 'First you steal it, then you give it away to just anybody.'

'Actually, I borrowed it from Roberta.'

The professor threw his hands up. 'I'm surrounded by thieves. I'm surprised I still have my purse!'

'Never mind that now,' said Cox. 'Will this testing reveal the truth?'

'Of course!' declared the professor. 'I designed it myself.'

Cox nodded to me, and I hurried down the hall to my room. I took the cherrywood box from my chest and opened it, gazing at the tiny vial and the glass pipette. For a second I considered emptying the vial and replacing the contents with some other liquid, but I knew the professor would be aware of the deception. No, I had to let them test my father, and I had to trust my instincts: that he was a good and decent man, someone who would never hurt another human being.

I returned with the kit, and the professor took it with a sidelong frown at Roberta. Then opened it, took out the vial and swirled it around, inspecting the contents against the light. Finally, he removed the stopper and took a careful sniff. 'It all seems in order,' he declared, and I was glad I had not attempted to doctor the thing. 'Now, we need a drop of blood if you please.'

My mother fetched a sewing needle, and my father allowed the professor to prick his finger. A drop of blood welled, and the professor took out his bound notebook and opened it to a blank page. 'Press here, if you would.'

My father obeyed, and everyone leaned forward in anticipation as the professor took a drop of fluid from the vial and held it above the page. Everyone except me, for I had tested the blood only the night before, and I already knew the outcome.

The drop fell, and slowly a reddish glow emanated from the notebook. The professor swore under his breath, and Roberta turned a sorrowful, pitying look upon me, her expression heartfelt and moving. 'I'm sorry,' she murmured.

Cox snatched up his gun, pointing it directly at my father. I could see his finger on the trigger, his knuckle whitening, and I prepared to hurl myself at him.

'Don't be so hasty, Inspector,' said the professor calmly. 'This test merely proves the presence of the supernatural, and does not indicate anything else.'

'You mean he's *not* the werewolf?' demanded Cox, lowering the gun a fraction.

'I cannot say either way.' The professor frowned at the page. 'The indicator is very weak, mind you. It's barely glowing at all.'

Roberta took the notebook and studied the page. 'Yesterday Septimus and I tested the knife he stabbed the beast with, and–'

'Septimus did what?' demanded my mother.

'Later,' I said, with a quick gesture. 'Please let her finish!'

'The blood on the knife glowed far more readily,' said Roberta. 'We tested it in a sunny room, and it was most apparent, even to the naked eye. Here, we view this result by candlelight and yet it barely shines at all.'

The professor turned to my father. 'Sir, this might seem a strange question, but have you ever tended to Mr Carmichael? Bound a wound, perhaps?'

'I'm a bookkeeper, not a physician.'

'Even so. In an emergency, anyone might bandage a wounded colleague.'

'I've known him my whole life, but nothing like that has ever happened.'

'You told me he bit you once,' said my mother suddenly.

The idea of Mr Carmichael biting my father was so comical I almost laughed aloud.

'We were just nippers!' protested my dad. He turned to us and explained. 'When we were six or seven we scrapped over something or other. During the tussle he bit my shoulder down to the bone. Caused a fuss, I can tell you, and we both got a right old walloping from our fathers.'

A kernel of hope grew within me. Roberta had explained that werewolves might pass on their disease through blood, but Carmichael was only a child when he and my father fought. What if the disease had only been nascent, weak, and not yet fully developed? If so, my father might carry the infection without being a full-blown werewolf!

'He's carrying a weakened version,' declared Roberta, echoing my own deduction. 'Inspector, this man is not the killer you seek, I'm certain of it.'

'Dammit,' growled Cox. Then he looked around the room apologetically. 'I'm sorry, I didn't mean it that way. But you understand...I thought we had him, only now I discover we've got to pick up the trail all over again!'

'Inspector Cox,' said my father evenly. 'If I thought I offered the slightest danger to anyone, I would have taken myself to the nearest police station and handed myself in. I could not have someone else's suffering on my conscience, and I'm troubled that you think me...*me!*...capable of these gruesome murders.'

Above his head, the firefly altered course, flying a wider circle than before.

'Sir, the professor has already vouched for you,' said Cox. 'None of this witchcraft and magickery makes much sense to me, and so I must defer to his superior knowledge.'

I noticed Roberta looking at me, but instead of being pleased that my father had been exonerated, she appeared to be worried about something. 'What troubles you?' I asked her quietly.

'Lycanthropy...it's hereditary. Given your father carries the infection, that means you must also be a carrier.'

This news, delivered so casually, landed in the sitting room like a mortar bomb, and I stared at her in shock. In my dazed state I barely noticed my parents exchange a meaningful look, but the significance of that glance returned tenfold later on.

'Test me,' I said, holding out my hand. 'Test me this instant, for I have to know.' A cold despair had taken hold of me, for if I carried the illness within me, my life would be altered forever. And what if it was the more powerful form, growing stronger by the day until I too became a slavering, murdering beast?

'Septimus, don't bother the professor with that now,' said my mother. 'Come, gentlemen. My boy is no monster, you can see that!'

'All the same...' began the professor.

'Test me!' I shouted, and I saw shocked faces all around at my uncharacteristic outburst.

Silently, the professor took up the needle, and I braced for the sting, and the revelation to come.

Nothing happened, and I opened one eye to see why the professor hesitated. Then I realised everyone was looking past me, to the door. I turned with them, just as the glowing sprite vanished through the wall opposite.

46

'Follow that light!' shouted Cox, and everyone got up and rushed for the hall, my parents included. The needle, the test and my own situation were forgotten in the panic, for the sprite was moving fast and that meant the *real* werewolf was abroad.

At the front door I stopped, turning to my parents. 'You must remain here,' I said. 'We have weapons, and the professor and Roberta are trained in these matters. I cannot have you endangered.'

Reluctantly they saw the sense of it. My mother gave me a quick hug and my father squeezed my shoulder, seemingly overcome, and then I turned and dashed after the others. I soon caught up, and Roberta joined me, hurrying alongside. 'I shouldn't worry about that test if I were you.'

'Of course I'm worried!'

'Septimus, you're not infected.' She indicated the sprite, which glowed in mid-air ahead of us. 'You've been around these apparitions for two days now, and not a one of them has paid you the slightest notice. My dear, you're as much a werewolf as I am.'

I staggered, my legs actually weakening with relief.

'Mind you,' said the professor, who'd overheard our conversation. 'It brings into question the matter of–'

'Quiet, father. That is a matter to be discussed at a later time.'

Then I stared at them. 'You said it was hereditary!'

'Aha,' said the professor gravely. 'I see you've realised the implications.'

'Indeed I have, for Cecilie Carmichael's father was infected! That means...'

Ahead of us, the glowing sprite altered direction. We all set off after it, and I was not entirely surprised to discover it was now heading directly for the Carmichael residence.

I ran ahead, quickly catching up with Cox. 'Sir, it might be heading for Mr Carmichael again. His body, I mean.'

'Doubt it. I had it moved.' He glanced at me. 'Don't worry, I told them not to touch any blood.'

We ran along the lane, passing the spot where we'd found the body earlier. Here the sprite hesitated, passing back and forth through the hedge once or twice, and for a moment I thought it was detecting the latent paranormal energy. But no, before I could voice my doubts it set off once more, crossing the corner of the field on a diagonal and making for the Carmichael residence ahead.

'We'll have to take the path,' said Cox. 'It'd be madness to run across a field in this light.'

The five of us hurried on, passing through the elaborate wrought-iron gates before hurrying up the driveway. Ahead, I just saw a tiny gleam of light, quickly extinguished.

'It went right through the wall,' remarked Cox. 'Check your weapons, all of you. But no shooting unless I give the order, is that clear? I'm not going to spend the next month explaining an accidental death to my superiors.'

We hurried to the front door, where Cox yanked repeatedly on the bell-pull. We waited a minute or two, but there was no sign of the maid, nor indeed any other signs of life. 'Parkes, the door,' said Cox.

The two policemen braced themselves, and were about to drive their shoulders into the sturdy front door when it swung open. Standing inside, barely visible in the darkened hallway, was Cecilie Carmichael. She appeared to be wearing a filmy nightgown of some kind, and she gazed at us in confusion. I recalled the maid had given her a tincture after the shocking news of Carmichael's death, and we'd probably woken her from a deep slumber.

'Sorry miss,' said Cox gently. 'This is urgent police business. We need to search your house this instant.'

'Oh?' Cecilie gestured languidly. 'Do come in, all of you. Come in, come in, but keep your voices down as mother is resting.'

We followed her to the parlour, where there was an unpleasant chill in the air. The fire had not been lit, and the only illumination came from an oil lamp on a side table, the glow barely enough to illuminate an area between two comfortable armchairs. As Cecilie drew closer to the light I looked away, for the nightshirt was sheer indeed and revealed far too much. But as I did so, I saw a dark, reddish patch at her elbow, and furthermore, there was something splashed across the colourful rug on the floor. A dark stain that gleamed stickily in the light.

'Inspector,' I said.

He'd already noticed the stain, and crouched to inspect it. 'Blood!' he said. Then he glanced at Cecilie, who stood with her back to us still, swaying slightly as though on the point of losing consciousness.

She was close to the oil lamp, and , 'Miss, who else is in the house. Quickly now!'

Slowly, Cecilie turned to face us, and I saw her face clearly for the first time since she'd admitted us. There was a distant, sated look in her eyes, and she seemed almost delirious. I wondered just how much of a draught the maid had given her, for Cecilie's pupils were huge and dark, and almost hypnotic.

Slowly, she smiled at us, and as her lips parted I saw to my horror that her even white teeth were coated with blood, bright red and sickly in the glow from the oil lamp. She opened her mouth further, and as the five of us stood there, transfixed by the horrible sight, the missing sprite emerged from her throat to hover directly in front of her face.

The crimson stain on Cecilie's teeth gleamed in the sprite's unholy light, and then slowly, deliberately, she licked her lips with a blood-red tongue.

47

Before any of us could react, Cecilie's hand darted out. Like lightning she snatched the sprite from mid-air, and with a snap of her fingers she dispelled it. Then she grabbed the oil lamp, enclosing the small glass cover in one hand. I heard the sizzle of her flesh on the hot glass before she crushed it in her grasp, the light winking out instantly. The last image to meet my eyes before the room was plunged into total darkness was that of Cecilie's fingernails, already grown an inch long and hooked like shark's teeth.

All of a sudden the hunters were the hunted, for we were now trapped in a pitch-dark room with a killer. A killer that could see in the dark, while we were entirely blind.

A gun boomed beside me, and in the flash I saw Cecilie outlined against the darkness, already ten feet away and moving at inhuman speed. But it was no longer Cecilie, for she was changing into the beast which had attacked me in the woods two days earlier. Another gunshot, and I saw the beast at the foot of the nearby staircase, the shredded remains of Cecilie's filmy nightgown trailing behind its gross, misshapen body.

'It's going upstairs,' growled Cox, hurriedly reloading. Beside him Parkes did likewise, for it was the two policemen who had fired.

'You can't kill her,' I said desperately. 'It's Cecilie!'

'Not any more it isn't,' said Cox. 'That's our killer, sure as I'm standing here.'

'He's right Septimus,' said the professor. 'Our chances of capturing her alive are slim, I'm afraid. After all, one bite from that creature and any one of us might be doomed to the same fate.'

'Come, we must try and corner it,' said Cox. 'Luckily for us it's trapped itself up there. It can't get away.'

Even as he spoke there came a sound of breaking glass upstairs, and a split second later I saw a shadowy form plunge past the nearby window, landing in the shrubbery. There was just enough starlight to see the monster's snarling face as it glared at us, and then it whirled round and raced towards the woods, quickly disappearing from sight.

Cox and Parkes were hard-bitten policemen, but even they were shocked at what they'd witnessed. We'd found candles, and their illumination now pushed back the darkness in the sitting room, although it had no effect on our mood.

The professor appeared saddened, while Roberta was more sanguine. As for myself, I recalled touring the gardens of that very house with Cecilie only the day before, and as I thought of her slim beauty and her sheer delight as she showed off the flowers in the afternoon sunshine I felt tears spring to my eyes. I had known Cecilie most of my life, and while I did not harbour romantic feelings towards her, the thought of anyone being overtaken by such a monstrous fate was upsetting in the extreme. It was devilishly unfair!

'We can't send the locals into the woods after that thing,' Parkes was saying. 'It'll slaughter them, sir.'

The sergeant had already been upstairs, checking the rooms, and the quick shake of his head upon his return spoke volumes. Nobody else was alive in that house.

Cox scratched his head, a most remarkable gesture for one who was usually so composed. 'Professor, I'm at a loss. How do you deal with such matters? How do you get used to them?'

'I have years of experience,' said the professor. 'But as for getting used to them, that will never happen.'

'Why did she kill her parents?' I asked suddenly, for it had been troubling me greatly.

The professor shook his head. 'In nature, creatures grow up and leave the nest. Perhaps, with werewolves, this rite of passage involves something a little more brutal.'

'Tell me, professor,' demanded Cox. 'How long will she–it, I mean–remain in the animal state?'

'I don't know. It seems she can change at will, which wasn't mentioned in any of my books.' He gestured towards the window. 'Even now, the poor girl might be fleeing to another village, there to seek refuge as a human.'

'I'd rather you didn't refer to her in that manner,' said Cox.

'What, human?'

'No. Cecilie, poor girl, that sort of thing. It just makes it worse when...when the time comes.' Cox shook himself, then became more businesslike. 'Look, we have the advantage here. The creature knows nothing of the professor's detecting machine, and it might just hide in the woods for a while before returning. If so, we can track her down and finish this.' He turned to Parkes. 'Sergeant, you and I will go to Croydon together. I will have my reinforcements, and failing that I'll put Sergeant Edwards' head on a spike and take over his damned station myself.'

'Yessir,' said Parkes, suppressing a grin.

'Be careful on the road,' I advised them. 'Your carriage might be attacked as mine was.'

Cox patted the shotgun. 'I think we can take care of ourselves. Meanwhile, the rest of you go home and feed yourselves. This night is far from over, and you've pushed yourselves hard all day.'

All of a sudden I realised just how hungry I was, and I knew he was right. It seemed callous in the extreme to enjoy a meal while all around us was violence and death, but we would be no use to anyone in a weakened state.

'Come, we'll walk to the inn together,' said Cox. 'With that monster about, it's safer in a group.'

As we left that accursed house, Roberta took my hand in the darkness. 'I'm sorry Septimus,' she murmured.

'I still can't believe it. Cecilie, a werewolf!'

'It could have been worse,' said Roberta, matter-of-factly. 'You might have found out *after* you were married.'

'For the last time–' I began hotly.

'Shh!' Roberta put a finger to my lips. 'I'm sorry, I really am. But that's twice now she might have killed you, and I will never, ever forgive her for that.'

48

On the way to the inn the group agreed to split up, with Cox and Parkes continuing to the inn while the professor and Roberta accompanied me to my parents' house. It was getting late, and I felt that Roberta and her father were unlikely to get a proper meal at Ravenswood at that hour.

'Won't it be a trifle embarrassing?' asked the professor. 'After all, it's barely an hour since we accused your father of being a werewolf.'

'That was Cox,' I said. 'You cleared his name, and should therefore be in their good books.' I hoped it would be so, and indeed, after a slightly cool reception my parents seemed to forgive the professor.

We told them about Cecilie straight away, because she represented a terrible danger to the whole village. Indeed, Cox had vowed to spread the news as widely as possible before leaving for Croydon, so that people might defend themselves if she approached them in human form.

My mother put a hand to her mouth, shocked beyond words, while my father shook his head sadly, tears in his eyes. 'I watched that poor girl grow up,' he whispered. 'What a wicked world this is!'

'It's not her fault,' I said. 'She carries an illness passed on from her father. She could do nothing to prevent it.'

Even to me, my words sounded hollow.

Soon food was laid out, and we ate mostly in silence, each lost in our thoughts. But conversations sprung up, albeit slowly at first, and soon the professor had my parents spellbound with tales of wild ghosts and vengeful spirits. I listened too, for the professor rarely discussed his past, although I confess that most of the time I was calculating how much longer it might be before Cox returned with his reinforcements.

Almost an hour had passed before I finally turned to the professor with the request that was uppermost in my mind. 'Now sir, if you don't mind I'd like to be tested with your kit.'

'Septimus...' began my mother.

'I have to know the truth!' I declared, pushing back my plate to clear a space. 'Let us settle the matter this instant.'

A moment later it was done, and the professor turned his notebook towards me, revealing the spot of blood in the middle of the page. There was no glow at all, not even a faint glimmer.

'I'm sorry, my boy,' said the professor sadly. 'It's much as I expected.'

Roberta sighed.

'What is this?' I demanded. 'Surely you cannot be upset that I am *not* a werewolf?'

'No, but–' Roberta looked at me, then at my parents.

I realised my mother looked distraught, and even my father was looking concerned. He was on the point of speaking, but my mother gripped his arm, giving him a warning look. Then he shook her hand off. 'The boy must be told, Emma.'

'We made a promise.'

'It's time to break it.'

Roberta got up. 'Come, Father. We must tend to the machine lest the werewolf comes back.'

'Eh? But–'

'Now, father. This instant.'

The professor pressed something into my hand, but they left before I could say anything, with Roberta almost pushing her father out of the front door. Briefly I saw his face at the window, peering in, and then that vanished too.

'Son...' began my father.

'Septimus, you came to us as a newborn,' said my mother. 'Tiny you were,' she said wistfully. 'Tiny, and so beautiful.'

I knew the facts of life, of course, and so this news scarcely merited the build-up, so to speak. Then I twigged, and I stared at them in surprise. In their gentle, roundabout way, they were trying to tell me I had been adopted. At first I was speechless, and I wanted to fire off question after question about my true parentage, and why I'd been brought up in this house, and many, many, more. But then I saw how anxiously they regarded me, and I pushed the questions aside. Instead, I stood up and enfolded them both in a deep, heartfelt hug. 'You're my parents,' I whispered. 'I love you both, and anything that came before...it doesn't matter a jot to me.'

'You're our one true son, and don't you forget it,' said my mother, her voice a little shaky.

My father just smiled at me, too overcome to speak.

Even so, those questions rattled around inside me like the professor's sprites within the engraved metal jar, desperately trying to get out. Now, however, was not the time.

I realised I was still holding the item the professor had given me, just before he left, and as I looked down I realised it was one of the tiny brass cubes he had used to alert Roberta.

Even as I stared at it, the device started to vibrate in my hand.

The pub was empty as I passed by, the doors closed and the lantern outside extinguished. I assumed Cox had yet to return with his men, and so I was mightily surprised at the scene which met my eyes after I passed through the gates at Ravenswood. There were two carriages drawn up, with a dozen police officers in attendance, every one of them armed with a shotgun and many carrying flaming torches or lanterns to boot. Light flickered on their polished buttons, gleaming in the darkness like a pale imitation of the professor's other-worldly sprites.

Parkes was barking instructions, giving the men their orders, and I felt conflicting emotions as I watched the overwhelming show of force. On the one hand, they looked more than capable of cornering the monster, ending its reign of terror. But then I pictured them hunting Cecilie in the woods, and the thought turned my stomach. I had to remind myself, over and over, that she was *not* Cecilie but rather a cold-blooded killer.

I only hoped that I would not be the one to corner her, a loaded gun in my hands, for I knew I would not be able to pull the trigger.

'Well well,' said an unpleasant voice behind me, interrupting my dark thoughts. 'If it isn't Mr Jones.'

I turned, and you can imagine my displeasure as I came face to face with Sergeant Wallace, my nemesis from the Croydon police station. His battered face still bore evidence of the punch Parkes had laid him out with, with his cheek now one huge purplish bruise. His eyes, though, glittered at me like cold hard diamonds, and the hatred shone from him like a beacon.

He gave me a false smile, stretching his lips over his uneven teeth, and then he leaned closer, lowering his voice. 'You'd better watch your back in those woods, my lad. I hear it's right dangerous out there, and we don't want anything nasty happening to you, do we?' He clapped me heartily on the shoulder, then dug his fingers in, making me wince. 'No, we don't want anything nasty happening to you, not at all.'

I shook myself free and hurried towards the house. With luck, the professor would ask me to help with his machine, and I could keep myself out of Wallace's clutches. It was bad enough having a vicious werewolf on the loose, let alone having the angry sergeant after my blood as well.

49

Upstairs I found the professor addressing Cox on the far side of the room, the two of them watching the machine avidly the whole while. Roberta, meanwhile, stood near the door, listening. As I entered the room she came close and enquired as to my well-being.

'I learned something unexpected,' I said quietly, 'but now is not the time to dwell on it.'

She took my hand, squeezing it, and then we turned our attention to the professor.

'Communication is the key,' he was saying to Cox, 'and it's also our weakness. Alas, there is no way to update your men on the location of the werewolf, other than sending runners into the woods.'

'Are you tracking her?' I called across the room. 'The werewolf, I mean?'

Cox shook his head. 'Damned machine doesn't have the range. It's almost like the creature has guessed what we're about.'

'Impossible,' declared the professor. 'This machine is entirely of my own invention, and aside from Parkes and the four of us, nobody is aware of its function.'

'What about the little firefly thing?' demanded Cox. 'The werewolf must have noticed a glowing light following it around everywhere it went. Otherwise, why snuff it out right before our eyes?'

I recalled how the sprite had flown out of Cecilie's mouth, and her triumphant look as she dispelled it with a snap of her fingers. *Yes,* I realised. *She knew.*

'You're right, of course,' agreed the professor. 'The machine remains a secret, but the werewolf will have suspicions.'

'Marvellous,' growled Cox. 'Either it'll go into hiding, or it'll trap my people one by one.'

'For their own safety they must search the woods in pairs.'

'I'll thank you to leave the arrangements to me,' said Cox stuffily. 'I've organised manhunts before, professor. Hunted rabid dogs too, and this is much the same.'

'Oh, but it isn't. We face a cunning, intelligent foe, and it represents a deadly challenge to your men.'

I took out the small cube the professor had given me. 'Can we use this?' I asked him. 'Signal in Morse code, perhaps?'

'An admirable idea, but the range is too short,' said the professor, shaking his head. 'In any case, it's limited to a brief vibrating effect, and it cannot handle anything more complex.'

'Can we extend the–'

'Please, Mr Jones,' said the professor, frowning at me. 'As with the Inspector here, I ask that you defer to my superior knowledge.'

Chastened, I nodded.

'Don't worry,' Roberta whispered to me. 'Despite his words, I'm sure he'll think on it.'

'Only to claim the idea as his own.'

She smiled. 'He *is* a scientist.'

Cox went to the next room and opened the window, and we heard him shouting down to Parkes. I couldn't make out the words, but it was clear the policemen were raring to get going. However, there was little point dashing around the woods without some initial direction.

'Damned thing has probably holed up for the night,' muttered Cox, as he returned. 'Parkes sent two men to guard the Carmichael house earlier, but there's no news as yet.' His hands were thrust into the pockets of his coat, his shoulders hunched, and for the first time I realised the responsibility he'd taken upon himself. The London police had no jurisdiction in the area, and yet he'd bullied the station sergeant into providing men and equipment, putting his neck on the block in the process. End the night empty-handed, and he'd be in very hot water with his superiors.

I stared at the tangled web of copper wire and the slowly-moving sprites, willing them to greater effort. 'How often would a werewolf have to feed?' I asked Roberta. 'Could it hide for days?'

'Father's books suggest they have a ravenous appetite in animal form, but as a human it would only need to eat as we do.' Roberta frowned. 'However, as I mentioned earlier they are extremely territorial, usually hunting in the same area their entire lives. Therefore it's unlikely the werewolf would roam freely.'

Cox began to pace, growing more impatient by the minute. Then he stopped before me. 'Mr Jones, you knew this girl. Was there anywhere she liked to go? A picnic spot, perhaps, or a place where the two of you–'

'I only ever met Cecilie at her house, and her parents were always within earshot,' I said stiffly, unhappy with the implication. 'My behaviour was impeccable at all times, I assure you.'

'I did not mean to impugn your character,' said Cox apologetically. 'But was there another young man, perhaps? Someone she–'

'If there was, do you think I would tramp about the woods in order to spy on them?'

'Inspector, I think you should let the matter lie,' said the professor. 'That line of questioning will get you nowhere, I assure you.'

'I have to do *something*, man!'

'Perhaps you could ask your constables to keep their voices down, for I'm convinced they can be heard all the way to Croydon. The werewolf, with it's supernatural hearing...'

Cox hurried next door, and soon after the sound of voices from below was quieted. The torchlight which had been illuminating the windows from outside, bathing the room in flickering light, was also extinguished, and in sudden darkness I could clearly see the tiny sprites moving around on the copper wires. Even as I watched, one of them detached from the rest and moved to the far end of the room, wavering between a small object shaped like an inside-out clock and a double-ended pendulum held between two brass rods. At its approach the pendulum spun once, slowly, before coming to rest again.

I turned to the others, but they had seen the movement too, and were watching in rapt fascination.

'The nearest marker is North East,' murmured Roberta. 'No word on the range, though.'

Come on, I breathed, willing the other sprites into action. *I did not brave the roof just so you can fail me now.*

All of a sudden there was a rush of movement, and I felt a joyous cry building within me as the rest of the sprites hurtled along the wire to join the first.

'Twelve hundred yards, give or take twenty,' said Roberta, checking the range. 'It's north of the Carmichael place now.' She turned to me. 'That's close to the clearing where the first victim was found.'

'And our pit,' I added. 'It might be going after the mutton.'

'It's a shame we didn't repair the cover, or we might have trapped the creature without raising a finger.'

I turned to inform Cox, but he'd already left to organise his men.

'We should go with them,' said Roberta. 'The last thing we want is for half his constables to fall into the pit.'

'Out of the question,' said the professor. 'Roberta, my dear, I need you here. I insist on it.'

'Do you need me too?' I asked hopefully.

'No, you go and warn Cox about that damned pit of yours. If a policeman does fall in, he might not be as understanding as I was.'

I ran downstairs, hoping I might deliver the message and retreat, but these hopes were quickly dashed. It was bedlam in the grounds, with armed men forming up and the torches re-lit. I saw a dozen locals amongst the police, pressed into service once more, and when Parkes saw me crossing the lawn he beckoned me over. 'We need everyone we can get hold of,' he said. 'Make sure you're armed, then seek out sergeant Wallace so he can pair you off.'

My stomach sank, but even so I advised him about the pit before adding a warning of my own. 'You should describe Cecilie to your men in case they encounter the werewolf in human form. They will not be expecting–'

'I've already briefed them,' said Parkes shortly. Then he spotted Cox gesturing at him, and he turned on his heel, raising his voice to gather the men. 'Over here, you lot. Smartly now!'

Cox waited until everyone was facing him. 'I'll keep this brief, gentlemen. I know most of you should have been home this evening, with a hot meal on the table and a pint of something good at your elbow.'

There was a half-hearted cheer, quickly stifled at a glance from Parkes.

'Well, if we all do our duty we'll be back to those hot dinners in no time.' Cox hesitated. 'I've heard some of you scoffing at the danger we face, laughing about monsters in the woods and the like. Let me be absolutely clear: the beast we're hunting has already torn several victims limb from limb with its bare hands.'

There was complete silence.

'If you get distracted, even for a moment, it will be the end of you. So keep your eyes peeled, don't stray from your partner, and be prepared to use your weapons.' Cox gestured. 'Parkes has divided you into sections, and will now direct you to your designated search areas. Good luck, gentlemen!'

There was a louder cheer, and then the crowd dispersed. I had not been assigned to a section, but as I strode towards Parkes to get my own orders, a hand gripped my elbow. 'Not so fast,' said Wallace, grinning at me from the darkness. 'You and I, we're pairing up, see?'

I had half-expected it, but even so the news sent a shiver down my spine. Desperately I looked around for Cox or Parkes, but they were striding towards the gates at the head of a large group of men, and I could only imagine their reaction should I ask them to assign me to another policeman. I would be a laughing stock.

The only consolation was the shotgun I held in the crook of my arm. As long as I was armed, surely Wallace wouldn't try anything?

We set off after the others, walking in silence. Cox's plan was to reach the clearing with the pit and then spread out, seeking any sign of the monster. The police had whistles, the sound of which carried a surprising distance, and thus anyone encountering trouble would be able to summon the rest of the search party.

Torches flickered ahead of me, light reflecting off the blank, curtained windows of the nearby houses. Now and then I saw drapes twitching as a curious inhabitant peered out at us, but they were quickly closed again.

It took us twenty minutes to reach the clearing, and as we arrived

I increased my pace. I intended to reach Parkes and point out the gaping trap, but there was little need because the haunch of mutton hanging from the tree more than advertised its presence.

'Damn thing's been chewed!' said someone.

A torch was held up and I saw it was true. Something had taken several bites of the spoiled meat, even though it hung above the gaping hole. 'Is there anything below?' I called out.

Cautiously, the man approached the edge and peered down. 'Empty.'

A policeman pointed at the overhanging branch. 'How the devil did it get to the meat?'

Cox snorted. 'It climbed the tree, came along the branch and pulled it up using the rope.'

Everyone stared at him in surprise.

'I *told* you we're not hunting some wild animal,' growled Cox. 'This creature is smart!'

A few of the men glanced over their shoulders towards the nearby trees, and I saw their nervous expressions as they peered into the shadowy, uninviting darkness. The cheerful bonhomie of earlier was gone, and now–finally–the true danger of the situation appeared to be dawning on them.

'Right men, get into your groups,' ordered Parkes. 'Stand around the clearing, backs to the centre, and when I give the word you'll move out.'

I had no choice but to accompany Wallace, who was carrying a lantern in addition to his gun. Like the others we made our way to the clearing's perimeter, with the pairs more-or-less evenly spaced out. Then, at a command from Parkes, we stepped into the undergrowth.

50

Wallace trailed me as we advanced into the woods, and I was more apprehensive about his close proximity than I was of the werewolf. He'd barely said a word since menacing me in the grounds of Ravenswood, and I was beginning to think he'd come to his senses. The man was set against me, that much was obvious, but surely it was logical to put aside his dislike while we hunted the werewolf? After all, if he attacked me, or restrained me somehow, he would only be making himself an easier target for the beast.

Unfortunately Wallace was not a sensible man.

We'd moved about fifty yards into the woods when he grabbed my shoulder and spun me round. The gun was in the crook of his left arm, the lantern in the same hand, and for a second I wondered whether to react first, punching the despicable man as hard as I could before fleeing into the darkness.

Yes Septimus, I told myself. *An excellent idea if you want to spend the next five years in jail.*

Very deliberately, Wallace set the gun against the nearby tree and put the lantern on the ground next to it. Turning to me, he gave me an evil smile, almost daring me to call for help. He knew I could not, for I was almost frozen with fear.

Slowly, he advanced on me, framed by the lantern light, his face gradually lost in shadow. I backed away, the gun held across my body, for I could not bring myself to point it at him. Why would I? I knew I could never fire upon the man. He was a sergeant in the police, and I had little doubt I would hang for such a crime.

'Put that gun down,' he told me.

I hesitated, then complied. What else could I do?

'Now put your fists up,' growled Wallace, bunching his own hands and adopting a boxer's stance.

'W–why should I?'

'If you don't I'll knock you out right where you stand.'

'But why? What did I do to you?'

Briefly, he indicated his cheek. 'I got this thanks to you, and now it's your turn.'

'I'm working this case with Inspector Cox! And when Parkes sees me battered and bruised, he's going to come after you again.'

'No he won't, because you'll tell him you walked into a tree.' He laughed. 'If you can speak at all, that is.'

'Can't this wait until later? I–I'll fight you in a boxing ring, with people watching.' It was the last thing I wanted, but I would have said anything as I played for time. The longer I put Wallace off, the more chance someone would sight the werewolf and blow their whistle. Then this madman would *have* to let me go.

Wallace shook his head. 'You'll just run away to London with your tail between your legs. No, we finish this now.'

'But–'

I flinched as Wallace stepped forward, but instead of hitting me he got close, sneering at me in disgust. 'Do you know why I can't stand people like you?' He prodded me in the chest, hard. 'You're nothing but a weak, spineless bookworm.'

I knew he was goading me, trying to get me to fight back so he could knock me down, and I was determined not to let him rile me up.

'You've never done a proper day's work in your life, and yet you think you're so much better than everyone else,' continued Wallace, prodding me again. 'Stuck-up toff, that's what you are.'

His face was close to mine now, and the jabs he was administering to my chest were getting more forceful. Then, without warning, he punched me in the stomach. It wasn't hard, but it knocked the wind from my lungs, doubling me up. Wallace wasn't done yet, for he grabbed my shoulders and pushed me against the tree, hitting the back of my head against the trunk so hard that I saw stars.

As a rule, a young man who spends his life in the company of books does not have much time for boxing, and I was ill-equipped to defend myself against this street brawler of a man. Despite that, I snapped.

It started deep inside me, a rising red tide that consumed me from within. I felt my pulse hammering in my ears as the rage took hold, and then, like lightning, I reacted. With my left I shoved Wallace away, and then I bunched my right hand and drove my fist straight at his face.

He turned his head at the last second, my fist merely grazing his already bruised cheek, and then he came at me with a triumphant snarl. My rage dissipated as I realised what a huge mistake I'd made, and I braced myself, head ducked and eyes tightly closed, as I prepared to be beaten senseless. There was nothing I could do to prevent it now, and I knew I would be helpless against the onslaught of vicious blows.

Then I heard a low, menacing growl. At first I thought it was Wallace adding to my torment, but I recognised something deep and other-worldly about the sound. Opening my eyes, I saw Wallace looking behind himself, all thoughts of my beating forgotten. His gun and lantern were about twenty feet away, while my own gun was closer, but still well out of reach.

Wallace pulled the whistle from his top pocket and put the end to his lips, but even as he drew breath to blow upon it a huge, fast-moving shape cannoned into him from the darkness to my right. One second Wallace was standing before me, framed by the distant lantern, and the next he was gone. He didn't even cry out.

I heard a *scrunch* from the woods, like a branch being snapped, and then a rustle in the leaves, getting closer. Suddenly aware of my own danger, I sprang for the gun I'd leant against the tree, but had only taken two paces when the huge, hulking figure of the werewolf leapt in front of me.

Even in the half light I could see fresh blood dripping from its jaws, and I knew instantly that Wallace had breathed his last. My first thought was complete and utter relief, which was uncharitable but perhaps forgivable under the circumstances. But this feeling lasted only a split second, for the werewolf was about to do far worse to me than the sergeant might have.

My gun was out of reach, I had no whistle and shouting for help was patently useless. I could still see flickering torches through the trees, but the nearest must have been a hundred yards away, and I wasn't even sure they'd hear me. In addition, I still hoped the werewolf might vanish back into the woods if I did not startle it. *Then* I would shout for help at the top of my lungs.

The creature and I stood there, facing each other, and then it began to advance. I knew instinctively that turning and running would be fatal, so I backed away, step by matching step, maintaining the same distance. Then my back hit the solid and unmoving trunk of an oak tree.

I went to move to my left, but the werewolf issued a deep, rumbling growl, and so I froze instead. This far from the lantern there was barely enough light to make out anything but the enormous hunched outline of the beast, and the closer it got the more it seemed to grow, until my vision was entirely filled with the dark, menacing shadow. It was like an echo of Wallace's threatening behaviour, aside from the lack of insults, but this time I had absolutely no intention of throwing a punch.

Slowly, the werewolf extended its neck, bringing its face close to mine. I could feel its hot breath on my face, and I braced myself, expecting those massive jaws to close on my neck at any second.

Instead, it sniffed at me.

I shook with fear, certain my time had come. Closing my eyes, I thought of the sorrow my parents would feel, and, somewhat incongruously, the professor's unfinished accounts, still laid out on the desk in my study. Finally, I felt a lump in my throat as I pictured Roberta. Perhaps our lives would never have entwined the way I hoped, but even so I knew that I loved her, and that she felt the same way about me. Now, thanks to Wallace's pig-headed thirst for revenge, all hope for that particular future was about to be snuffed out.

Several seconds passed, and I became aware of a strange light flickering against my closed eyelids. Upon opening them, I saw the lantern some twenty feet away, the flame wavering in an unseen breeze. It took me a moment, but I realised with a shock that the reason I could see the lantern was because I could *not* see the werewolf. It had melted back into the forest!

I took a breath, about to shout for help, and then I thought better of it. The werewolf might be nearby, and it would be madness to draw it back to me while I was still unarmed. So, first I ran to my gun, snatching it up with shaking, sweating hands. Then I hurried to the lantern, where Wallace's gun was still leaning against the tree. And then, finally, I shouted for the others, even though I was so relieved at my close escape I was scarcely able to breathe.

51

Policemen came running from every direction at my shout, and in a shaking voice I told them of the werewolf's attack and Wallace's death.

'Why didn't you shoot at the thing?' demanded a constable, as two others ran off to locate the sergeant's body.

'Don't touch any blood!' I shouted after them. 'It might be infected!'

More men arrived and soon I was surrounded, their torches and lanterns lighting the overhanging branches.

'Well?' demanded the constable. 'Couldn't you do anything to save him?'

It was a good question, but I chose not to reveal the circumstances around Wallace's death. For one they might not believe me, and in addition I did not want to speak ill of the dead to his colleagues. 'The beast came out of nowhere, grabbed the sergeant and vanished. I daren't fire in case I hit him.'

I saw a few men exchanging glances, and I could guess at their thoughts. If someone as tough and capable as Sergeant Wallace could be taken so easily, what chance did the rest of us have? A few looked at me angrily, and I knew what they were thinking too. If it weren't for the useless civilian, their sergeant might yet be alive.

Seeing their expressions, I was even more determined to keep quiet about Wallace's actions.

The two men came back, carrying Wallace's limp form between them. I turned away quickly as I saw the way his head was at an odd angle, the neck all but torn out. Nearby, someone swore.

We moved to the clearing in a group, where Cox told the men to lay Wallace out next to the pit. Someone removed his jacket, with much care, given all the blood, and covered the sergeant's face with it. Then the inspector led me aside, out of earshot. 'Well? What happened? The truth now!'

I had intended to stick with my story, but in the end I decided to trust the inspector. 'I'm sorry sir, but Wallace was more interested in settling a score than hunting the werewolf.' In a few short sentences I explained the events at Croydon police station, and Wallace's subsequent threats. 'Once we were alone he put his gun down and ordered me to do likewise, his intention being to box with me.'

'The man was a fool,' growled Cox. 'His wounded pride cost him his life, and might have ruined this entire operation.'

'You won't tell the others, sir?'

'Absolutely not. We'll keep this between ourselves.' Cox eyed me. 'You had a narrow escape. Would you like to return to Ravenswood?'

I shook my head.

'Good man.' Cox nodded towards Wallace's body. 'In any case, I think the biggest danger to your safety has passed.'

At that moment a constable ran up. 'Sir, the professor...' He took a ragged breath. 'He sent me ahead...he's on the way here.'

Cox swore under his breath. 'That's all I need,' he muttered. Then he frowned. 'Son, tell me he's got an escort.'

'Yessir.'

The professor arrived a few moments later with another constable at his side. Roberta accompanied the pair of them, and after spotting Wallace's body she looked around until she met my eyes. I saw her concern, and hurried over to meet her. 'I'm fine,' I reassured her. I recalled the werewolf's face inches from mine, and decided to keep quiet about that too.

'You may be fine for the time being, but having men running all over the woods is never going to resolve this.' She nodded towards the professor, who was conferring with the inspector. 'Father has a new plan, but he's worried it might be too risky. Come, I want to intercede if Cox has objections.'

We walked across to the pair of them, although the professor was speaking so loudly it was scarcely necessary. 'By dawn, half of your people might be dead!' he was saying, gesturing at the constables nearby.

'Easy, professor,' murmured Cox. 'Let us try to keep their morale up, eh?'

The professor gestured impatiently, and I noticed he carried the engraved metal jar. Light gleamed from the semi-polished surface, and I guessed he'd brought another of the sprites to help track our prey. 'This method is hopeless,' he said. 'I sent two runners to update you on the werewolf's location, but each time it had moved on before they'd left the grounds of Ravenswood. Then I had to wait for their return, at which point it had moved again. Hopeless, I tell you!'

'Do you have a better idea?'

'Indeed I do!' With a flourish the professor removed the lid from the metal jar, and then he tipped it over and shook it violently. Instead of one spark of light, two dozen of them poured out, quickly surrounding Cox and the professor in a whirling, cascading swarm.

I heard gasps from the watching constables, several of whom raised their weapons. 'Do not fire!' I shouted urgently, worried they might gun down the two men in their panic. 'Please, gentlemen! Trust in the professor and lower your guns!' I spoke with a confidence I did not feel, for I suspected the professor had gone completely mad. What else could have possessed him to release the swarm in the open?

But instead of attacking, the sprites began to circle in wider orbits, expanding the glowing cloud further and further. Cox was frozen like a statue, his expression stony as the tiny glowing phantasms sped by. The professor, meanwhile, had a look of anticipation, his eyes following the sprites as though awaiting a signal.

The cloud of glowing fireflies did not disappoint, for in that instant they whirled around one last time before setting off, arrow-straight, through the woods.

'Follow them!' cried the professor. 'They have the scent, and they will not lose it now!'

Everyone ran after the fast-moving cloud, and I quickly realised we were heading for the scene of my confrontation with Wallace. As we got closer the sprites changed direction, and soon we arrived at the place where the sergeant's body had been found. The leaves were trampled and sticky with blood, gleaming dully in the light of the torches, and the crowd held back, hesitating, as our other-worldly guides circled aimlessly.

Then they set off again, this time in a fresh direction, and we followed them through the dense woods as best we could. The sprites flew directly through trees, bushes and undergrowth without slowing, but the rest of us had to navigate these obstacles whilst also avoiding tree roots, hollows and half-buried rocks, any one of which might have turned an ankle most painfully.

'What direction are we heading?' Cox asked the professor.

'South east,' said the latter, pausing to check his compass.

Cox turned to me. 'You're the local. What lies in that direction?'

I thought for a moment, and then my face cleared. 'The Carmichael residence!'

52

'The Carmichael residence, eh? It should have been obvious, for where else could it go?' Warming to his theme, the professor elaborated. 'As we expected, despite the danger of discovery the monster returns to its lair. It's incapable of doing otherwise, for even with its life threatened it must obey its–oof!'

Distracted by his theorising, the professor had just run headlong into a bush.

'Father, are you all right?' Roberta asked him in concern.

The professor emerged from the shrubbery, brushing leaves from about his person. 'No harm done, my dear.'

'You were fortunate it wasn't holly, or bramble,' said Roberta, trying not to laugh.

'Give me my nice quiet study in London any time,' grumbled the professor, as we set off once more. 'If I'm entirely honest with you, I really don't hold with all this nature business.'

Soon after, we emerged from the woods behind the Carmichael house, and to my surprise there were lights in several downstairs windows. The last time we visited the entire place was in darkness, bar one small oil lamp, and I found the idea of the werewolf going about lighting candles incongruous in the extreme. Then I realised the implications. 'It's changed back,' I said. 'It must have become

Cecilie once more.'

Ahead of us, the cloud of fireflies was tearing across the lawns, and I saw them pass through a small statue before entering the house itself.

'I don't care if she's turned into the Princess Royal,' muttered Cox. 'Look at those fireflies! They have her scent!'

'It's not a scent, it's a manifestation of paranormal energy,' said the professor. 'According to my research–'

'Mind that bush,' said Cox suddenly, and despite the gravity of the situation I thought I saw a hint of a smile.

As we drew close to the residence Cox ordered his men to encircle the entire house, forming a cordon through which nothing could escape. Then he signalled to Parkes. 'Bring two men. The four of us will go in and settle this.'

The professor snorted. 'Do you really think you can handle my sprites on your own?'

'I'm sorry, but no. That house is no place for civilians.'

'Very well.' The professor handed him the empty metal jar. 'I was going to test the effect of those sprites on a corpse, but your living body will give me far more to work with. Here, you'd better take the lid as well, although I doubt you'll have time to use it.'

Cox knew when he was beaten. 'The four of us and the professor will go in,' he told Parkes.

'And my assistants,' said the professor firmly.

By now Cox was beyond arguing, and he simply threw his hands up in disgust. 'Do as you wish, but on your head be it!'

We advanced on the house in silence, with Cox and Parkes in the lead, then the professor, Roberta and myself, and finally the two constables bringing up the rear. The four policemen and myself carried shotguns, all held at the ready.

Parkes tried the back door, without success, then drove the butt of his gun through the small pane of glass nearest to the handle. He reached inside carefully to unlatch the door, then opened it wide. We trooped in behind him, broken glass crunching underfoot.

We found ourselves in a scullery, and we passed between the sinks and benches lining the small room to reach the passage beyond. None of us spoke, for we were aware that Cecilie might have changed into the werewolf once more, and the beast might pounce without warning at any second. In such close quarters the guns would be next to useless, for any shot would just as likely strike friend as foe.

I saw light spilling from an open doorway, perhaps twenty yards ahead, and the six of us advanced towards it as one. Along the way there were several other doors, all closed, and Cox bid us wait while Parkes briefly glanced into each room. There were no unpleasant surprises though, and we eventually reached the lighted room we'd been making for.

'Come in, gentlemen,' said a voice. *Cecilie's voice.* 'There was no need to break my window, for I would have let you in myself had you but knocked.'

She had arranged herself on a *chaise-longue*, with a book in her lap and a half-empty glass of wine or port at her elbow. Somehow, Cecilie had found time to don a simple summer dress, and but for her tousled hair the scene appeared normal and eminently respectable. Normal, that is, aside from the two dozen sprites swirling above her head.

The policemen behind me pushed past, spreading out to either side with their guns levelled. Parkes took out a pair of handcuffs, and Cox approached Cecilie with his own gun at the ready. 'Come quietly now. There's been enough bloodshed.'

She smiled up at him sweetly, and this time there was no trace of red on her teeth. Rinsed away, no doubt, by the glass of wine. 'Inspector, is it? Tell me, sir, what crime do you believe I've committed?'

Taken aback, it was a second or two before Cox found his voice. 'Why, murder most foul! You...you transformed into a beast, a–a werewolf, right before my very eyes, and as that same beast you killed one of my men.' Cox gestured at me. 'Mr Jones witnessed the whole thing!'

Cecilie laughed. 'Really, sir! You intend to charge me with being a werewolf? How will that sound in court?'

'We know you killed your parents! Tore them apart with your teeth and claws as though they were helpless prey.'

'I think a jury might have trouble believing you.' Cecilie smiled at him, revealing her even white teeth, then calmly held up her hands with their manicured nails. 'Do these look like the teeth and claws of a wild beast? You'll be a laughing stock, Inspector.'

My god, I thought. *She could get away with this!*

'We trapped you in this very room, where we witnessed your transformation,' said Cox doggedly. 'Parkes and I will swear to it.'

'Can you imagine telling that to a packed courtroom?' Cecilie laughed. 'Oh, the gentlemen of the press would have a field day writing about Inspector Cox and his bloodthirsty monster!' Then she was serious once more. 'Before you lock me up, consider for one moment how many I could bite.'

'Sir, let me end this now,' said Parkes, levelling his shotgun. 'It'd be a kindness, like putting down a rabid dog.'

'Could you really do it, Parkes?' Cox glanced at him. 'Are you capable of shooting an unarmed woman?'

'But she's...' Parkes wavered as Cecilie smiled at him, quite unconcerned. Then, defeated, he lowered the gun. 'I can't, sir.'

'Of course you can't.'

'Oh, you men and your misplaced chivalry,' muttered Roberta. Then, louder. 'Gentlemen, let me resolve this matter for you.'

We all turned to look at her, and for a moment I feared she might grab my shotgun and shoot Cecilie where she sat. But instead, Roberta took my face in her hands and kissed me passionately, the unexpected embrace seeming to last forever. All of a sudden I heard a terrible snarl, and I turned to see Cecilie launching herself at us, already transforming in mid-air, hands like claws and her face a tortured mask of hatred. It was clear she had but one thought on her mind: to tear Roberta into shreds.

53

The creature was almost upon us when two shotgun blasts rang out as one, hurling her backwards. The sound was deafening, but the monster's scream of rage and pain cut through it like a knife. The creature slammed into the chaise it had so recently occupied, tipping it backwards with a crash and knocking the small table and wine glass flying. I saw the werewolf's legs twitch once or twice before the creature lay still, with smoke rising gently from the terrible wounds in its chest. Parkes set aside his gun and hurried to check the grotesque body, then nodded at Cox.

Roberta was still in my arms, and I could feel the thumping of her heart against my chest. Cox turned from Parkes, regarding her with a cool, level gaze. 'That was the most callous thing I've ever seen,' he remarked. 'You knew exactly what you were doing, didn't you?'

'She couldn't live,' said Roberta simply.

'But you wanted to capture the beast alive!' I protested.

'That was our plan at first, but it turned out to be far too dangerous.' Roberta smiled at me. 'In any case, we could not have kept it indoors, for Mrs Fairacre would have had a fit. As for the back garden, it is entirely overgrown, and if I am faced with a choice between weeding in the garden and killing the werewolf, I'm afraid it was always going to end badly for the latter.'

'She's only joking,' I told Cox hastily.

Cox sighed. 'All the same, Miss Twickham, you have my gratitude.' He glanced at the monster's twisted corpse. 'I for one could never have done it.'

Roberta's arms were still around me, but now she released me and stood back. 'I'm sorry I used you as bait, my dear.'

'I–I didn't mind at all,' I said, truthfully. 'I just didn't...I didn't realise she cared for me that much.'

'She didn't. Whatever spark of jealousy she might have felt was amplified out of all proportion by the monster's rage within her.'

Roberta slapped at something, and with a start I realised we were surrounded by the sprites. Some circled above the body, but the rest were getting inquisitive...and agitated. The professor had his jar, though, and we watched as he enticed one of the tiny glowing sparks home. With one captured it became easier to trap the rest, and soon he fitted the lid on the last of the swarm, breathing a sigh of relief as he did so.

Cox left the two constables standing over the body, ordering them to keep curious onlookers away by force if necessary. The rest of us went outside, where he sent Parkes to round up the rest of his men.

'I know it's been a long night, but I'm happy to report the matter is resolved in our favour.'

There was a cheer, and I saw a lot of relieved faces.

'My sergeant will accompany you to Croydon, where arrangements will be made to collect the body.' He paused.

'Both bodies. I am sorry for the loss of Sergeant Wallace, but he died a hero and will be remembered as such.'

There was another cheer, this one far less enthusiastic, and I was not surprised to learn that Wallace had been unpopular. Clearly his behaviour towards me had not been an isolated incident, and I wondered how many of those present had been terrorised by the man over the years.

'We'll gather at the inn, where you can return the guns to their rightful owners. And if the barkeep can be found, I promise to buy every one of you a drink.'

That got a cheer, and the men departed in good spirits, their voices loud in the cool night air. Moments later, only the inspector, Roberta, the professor and myself remained. We set off after them, walking through the grounds together.

'It's going to be one hell of a police report,' muttered Cox, as he eyed the nearby mansion.

The professor gripped his shoulder. 'We will support the official version, whatever that might be. You have my word on that.'

'I'd appreciate it, sir,' said the inspector gratefully. 'If it's all right, I'll send you a copy beforehand. Keep our stories straight, so to speak.'

'Of course!'

I gestured towards the house. 'What about your constables, inspector? The two men who accompanied us inside?'

'No need to worry about them,' said Cox, with a grim smile. 'Their shots killed the thing, and they'll be in it up to their necks if word gets out the monster was really a young woman. But just in case they were thinking about blabbing, I told Parkes to have a word with them.'

I imagined Parkes 'having a word' with someone, and knew the constables would hold their tongues until their dying day.

'Will you join us at the pub?' Cox asked us.

'I must confess, I'm eager for my bed,' said the professor, shaking his head. 'With all the excitement today, I'm out on my feet.'

Roberta took my hand. 'Septimus and I have work to do. Father's machine must be taken down and the parts packed away.'

'Leave that until morning my dear,' said the professor. 'Do so, and I will be there to help.'

'That's why we're tackling the job tonight,' said Roberta, with a smile.

'Yes, about that machine of yours,' said Cox suddenly. 'Could it be modified? Used to track criminals, perhaps?'

'Sir!' said the professor, scandalised. 'That would be a gross invasion of privacy! Completely unthinkable!'

'But–'

'Do not continue down that path,' said the professor sternly. 'Why, the idea of such a thing! Who would want to live in such a world?'

By now we'd reached the lane, Roberta and I still walking hand-in-hand. Cox excused himself and left to catch up with the constables, probably fearing they'd drink the pub dry at his expense. Then I thought of something that had been troubling me for some time. 'Who killed the gamekeeper?' I asked suddenly.

'We may never know,' said Roberta. 'My guess is that Mr Carmichael was shadowing us in the woods at the time, having witnessed us organising that pit and talking about capturing the werewolf. Most likely he tried to shoot us, and the keeper intervened.'

'But–'

'My dear, the only way to find out for certain is to hold a seance, and–'

'Never again,' declared the professor firmly. 'Not after what happened last time.'

'What did happen last time?' I asked him.

Neither replied, and, realising the subject was closed, I gave up.

Upon reaching Ravenswood we found little evidence of the earlier police activity, aside from scattered gravel and boot prints in the lawn, and once inside the professor bid us both goodnight. It was another hour before I finally reached my bed, safe under my parents' roof, and after undressing I lay there in the darkness smiling at the ceiling like a witless fool. I was bone tired, exhausted both mentally and physically, but I smiled so because I could still feel the memory of Roberta's goodnight kiss upon my lips.

The smile slipped as I thought of the professor, and in that moment I decided to have things out with him first thing in the morning. Somehow, I would convince him that I was worthy of his daughter, no matter what outlandish promises I was forced to make.

But first, sleep.

54

The church was packed with people in their Sunday finest, but I was not amongst them. No, I floated near the rafters, my incorporeal form invisible to those below. The mood was ebullient, and I decided the service was not to mark the occasion of my funeral. At least, I hoped it was not, for there was a sight too much levity and good humour for my liking.

Then I saw the masses of flowers arranged in beautiful displays all around the church, resplendent in the sunshine filtering through the stained glass windows, and I realised I was dreaming of a wedding. My own, perhaps?

It seemed to me that the entire village was present, for as I moved above the guests I saw dozens of familiar faces. Among them was Cecilie, looking happy and relaxed in a pretty summer dress. She was leaning across to speak with her father, Mr Carmichael, who laughed at her comment, patting her on the hand. It was a lovely moment, and I felt a stab of remorse as I watched them.

Up front, the groom stood with his back to the crowd. He was tall with dark hair, but in my dream he was indistinct around the edges, as though my subconscious mind were unable to picture him accurately. I was half-convinced he represented me, but I could not be certain.

Then the double doors at the rear of the church swung open, and a hush fell upon the crowd. I drew a sharp breath as I saw the bride, for the sun shone down on her from behind, framing her face with a halo of glowing hair. A few strands had been curled into ringlets, and one of these brushed her cheek in a delightful, alluring fashion. She wore a simple wedding dress, elegant but not overstated, and she clutched a posy of lilies in both hands.

My heart thudded at the sight, for it was none other than Roberta, and she looked more radiant, more attractive, and more alive than I'd ever seen her before.

Beside her stood the professor, one arm linked through hers. He'd truly gone to town on his outfit, with coat and tails in jet black, a patterned waistcoat, a top hat and a gold-tipped cane. He looked to be bursting with pride, and I was moved beyond measure as the two of them swept majestically up the aisle together.

I saw lace hankies aplenty as the crowd responded to the sight, with matronly ladies smiling at each other, dabbing at their sudden tears of joy.

The bridal party reached the altar, where the professor kissed his daughter on the forehead before taking his seat in a nearby pew. Roberta smiled at the groom, but still I could not make out his identity. There was a moving, pulsing shadow where his features ought to have been, and although I willed it away, desperate to tear through the fog, it resisted my every effort.

Now the vicar stepped forward to begin the service, book in hand. It was a simple affair, brief and to the point, and then, upon declaring bride and groom a married couple, he finished with a beaming, paternal smile.

'Now you may kiss.'

The groom turned to Roberta, and she smiled warmly at him, love shining from her eyes. She tilted her head back slightly, lips pursed, eyes closed, and in that instant the fog cleared, and with a shock I finally had the groom's identity. *Sam Tyler!*

Sam smiled down at Roberta, his expression keen and hungry. Then, instead of kissing her, he bared his wolf-like teeth and went straight for her throat.

I woke in pitch darkness, tangled in bedclothes and shouting at the top of my lungs. Sitting up, I felt my heart pounding and sweat upon my brow. The dream had been so real I could still smell the flowers, see the sunlight through the stained glass windows, and hear Roberta's final, desperate scream.

I took several deep breaths, forcing myself to relax. It could not have been much past four in the morning, which meant I had barely slept three hours. My brain was fogged, my mind slow to react, but there was something lurking in my subconscious, something important which I'd forgotten. Some pertinent fact.

All I could think of was Roberta, and I winced as I relived the scene at the altar. Tyler's triumphant, crowing expression would live with me forever.

Sam Tyler.

Thinking back over the night's events, I realised what was troubling me. Sam was the local policeman, and yet I had not seen him all night. The constables searching the woods, the policemen surrounding the Carmichael residence...he had not been present for any of it.

Was he lying somewhere, dead? Or was Sam Tyler's absence far more sinister?

Throwing off the covers, I rose from my bed and dressed quickly, throwing on my clothes any old how. I had a sick, hollow feeling in my stomach the whole time, for I feared my nightmare might have been a warning. It would not have been the first time.

The shotgun was leaning against the wall, and after checking it was loaded I shouldered the weapon and left my parents' house at a run.

I hurried through the deserted village in the dead of night, and although the moon had risen it was all but obscured behind thin clouds. There was just enough light to see by, and I reached the grounds of Ravenswood without incident.

I do not know why I believed Tyler was a threat to Roberta, aside from the vivid nightmare, but I could not shake the feeling. He was a proud man, popular with young ladies, and perhaps it was because Roberta had attempted to fool him the day before. When that had failed she'd administered a sleeping draught, which could hardly have improved his opinion of her.

But Tyler was a police constable, employed to uphold the law. He might have threatened her with arrest, or used his position to make her life uncomfortable for a day or two, but I could not see him attacking her physically.

Not as a human, at least.

For I had already witnessed one lifelong acquaintance turn into a werewolf, in the person of Cecilie, and it was not inconceivable that Sam, too, might be affected. In that case, it would only be natural that he seek her out to exact his revenge. Why, Roberta herself had told me that human feelings might be magnified greatly by the werewolf's savage impulses, and as a wild beast in the grip of a murderous rage, Tyler might be drawn to Roberta like a moth to a candle.

And even if I were mistaken, the whole thing being nothing more than a transient sandcastle built upon the nebulous foundations of my nightmare, there was no harm in confirming Roberta's safety. It was not as though I were rousing the village, or calling upon the police for help.

I tried the front door but found it bolted. Normally, the residents of West Wickham left their doors unlocked at all times, but recent events had understandably led to an increase in security.

Sidling along the wall, shotgun gripped in one hand, I pushed through the low-cut, bristly bushes to try each window in turn. On my third attempt I found what I was looking for, and moments later I was standing in the library with the pale moonlight casting long shadows on the shelves of dusty books.

I crouched to remove my shoes, fearing the hard leather soles would make too much noise on the bare floorboards. My intention was not to wake the entire house, but only to look in on Roberta and confirm she was sleeping soundly. Afterwards, I would retire to old Mr Hall's study, further along the corridor, where I would spend the night dozing in the armchair I had seen therein only the day before. With the shotgun on the desk in front of me, I would be well-placed to respond to any cries for help.

In the morning I would explain myself, rather than trying to escape unseen. The others might think me foolish, but I would rather that a thousand times over than seeing Roberta harmed when I could have done something to prevent it.

A floorboard creaked loudly underfoot, and I froze. I was nearing the foot of the stairs, hidden in a pool of darkness, and I was suddenly grateful I was the only person in that house with a gun. Imagine if I woke the professor, or one of the Hall sisters, and they fired upon me after believing me to be an intruder!

For a moment I questioned my sanity, given I *was* an intruder and had no permission to be there. Tip-toeing around that cavernous old house in the darkness, clutching a gun no less? Madness!

But the thought of the possible danger to Roberta spurred me on. I had been unable to get her scream out of my mind, the horrible noise setting my teeth on edge every time I heard it.

I began to ascend the stairs, placing each foot and testing it once or twice before committing my weight. Thus I avoided most of the creakiest floorboards, chiefly by using the outside edges of each step. I reached the landing and rounded the corner, before taking the final flight to the first floor.

I had a vague idea where Roberta and the professor had their rooms. The day before, when looking for the study, she told me her room was further along the corridor, somewhere beyond the bedroom the professor had used for his detecting machine.

I decided to look into each room in turn, and so I crept along the corridor to each door, opening them with my breath held and my heart in my mouth. The handles squeaked as I turned them, the hinges crying out as though they'd not seen a drop of lubricant for decades, but while the noises seemed deafening to me in my heightened state of anxiety, they were not enough to rouse the occupants.

I found the professor first...or rather, heard him. He was fast asleep and snoring fit to wake the dead, and I quickly closed his door and moved on. That left one door facing the front of the house and two facing the rear. I checked the nearest, which led to a room packed with old boxes, chests and other goods, and then opened the one facing the front of the house. Here I saw a bed, about ten paces away and set with the head against the wall. The room was in darkness, the closed curtains blocking out the moonlight, but I could just see a figure in the bed. Listening carefully, I heard soft, regular breathing, and I felt overwhelming relief as I realised it was

Roberta, peacefully and contentedly asleep.

I began to close the door, but in that moment a breath of wind twitched the curtains. Behind them a window had to be ajar, and while we were on the first floor, the walls of the old house afforded plenty of handholds for a determined intruder. I decided to close the window, fastening it, before retreating to the study to begin my vigil.

I stepped into the room, feeling the floorboards with my toes in their woollen stockings. It took me two or three minutes, but eventually I managed to circle around the bed, avoiding tripping on the rug or knocking over any side tables or coat stands along the way. Roberta continued to breath regularly, oblivious to my presence. As I stood there with the shotgun in hand, I pictured the scene should the professor burst in at that moment, lamp or candle held high. The accusing looks, the hurt...it would be too much to bear.

However, I could still hear his snoring, despite the thick walls, and I knew that I was safe for the time being.

I reached the curtains, where the moonlight spilling around the edges seemed bright and glaring in contrast to the darkened room. I leant the shotgun against the wall, knowing I would need both hands to pull the window to and latch it, and then I stepped up to the curtains and, taking one in each hand, twitched them open to gain access to the window.

The rings rattled on the curtain rods, but it was not the unexpected sound which made me freeze, the blood turning to ice in my veins. Directly behind the curtains, with his back to the open window, stood Sam Tyler, so close he could have reached out and touched my shocked, startled face.

55

'Well well, if it isn't Septimus Jones,' murmured Sam, his voice barely above a whisper.

'What the hell are you doing here?' I hissed. 'How dare you enter a lady's bedroom without permission!'

He smiled. 'That's rich, given the way you were sneaking about.'

'Well?'

'I saw something climbing the wall,' whispered Tyler. 'Fast as lightning, it was. Straight up to the first floor, and in through this window.'

'And you just happened to see it, did you? Do you normally do your rounds at four in the morning?'

'Sergeant Parkes told me to kip all evening. Said I should get some rest, then keep an eye on the village through the night instead.'

I hesitated, for that part seemed plausible at least. Tyler *had* been missing during the night, after all, and he couldn't be expected to remain on duty for twenty-four hours straight. On the other hand, the coincidence of him being there, at that exact moment, struck a jarring note. It was as though my nightmare had predicted his presence, and I recalled all too well the tragic outcome.

I glanced towards the shotgun, still leaning against the wall nearby, and when I turned back to Tyler I saw his easy smile had vanished.

He'd noticed my gaze, the weapon, and all of a sudden he began to grow in stature. It was as though his muscles and sinew were hardening, strengthening, and I heard cloth rending as his physical being outgrew them.

'I nearly got you in the woods,' he whispered, the words distorted by the set of fangs already sprouting from his jaw. 'Would have shot all three of you...if the keeper...hadn't intervened. Nice little hunting...accident.'

His eyes reddened, and I saw hair sprouting from every pore. I was frozen, hypnotised, by the transformation, and I knew that even in this half-changed state, he could lash out with clawed fingers and end me where I stood.

'You came down here, wrecking everything.' Tyler spoke in a low, guttural growl, the words distorted and ill-formed. 'Now I'm going...to finish...this.'

'But why, Sam?' I pleaded. 'Why harm Roberta?'

A cruel smile twisted his horrifying, unnatural face. 'Because *you* want her,' he snarled.

I was desperate, but there was nothing I could do against his obvious physical superiority. That left trickery, and so I looked to my left, opening my eyes wide. 'What the–' I began.

To my surprise, it actually worked. Tyler, now more werewolf than human, spun to his right to see what had distracted me. Of course, there was nothing there whatsoever, but in that instant I threw myself at the wall, grabbing up the shotgun, desperately seeking the trigger even as I tried to bring the muzzle up.

With a snarl, Tyler lashed out, knocking the gun from my hands and sending it spinning away. There was a loud crash as it landed, and I heard it slithering across the wooden floor before fetching up against the distant wall. From where I was standing, that weapon might as well have been sitting upon my desk in London.

I barely had time to think about it, though, because Tyler grabbed my forearms with the strength of a bear, the painful grip like a pair of steel bands tightening on my extremities. So strong was he that I knew he could snap my arms like matchwood if he so chose, but instead he forced my arms behind my back, further and further until I thought they would come out of their sockets. Gasping with pain, my head went back, and then I realised the werewolf's intent. Sam's gaping jaws opened, and I knew he was going to close those huge, serrated teeth around my throat, biting it out completely. That was bad enough, but after he'd killed me, Roberta would be next.

I struggled, throwing my head from side to side even as I feared my arms would be torn from my body. I may have been shouting, screaming at him, but I don't know whether I vocalised the words or whether I was merely screaming internally. I only know that I raged at that monster like I'd never raged before, and if I could only have loosed my arms, I was convinced I would have torn its head off with my bare hands.

'Septimus! Drop!'

The shouted command came from behind me, and I recognized the voice as Roberta's. It was a voice that brooked no argument, and I obeyed without thinking. Instead of struggling I allowed myself to go completely limp, letting my weight collapse within the monster's arms. I was halfway to the ground by the time it realised what was happening, and my last sight of the werewolf's face was a puzzled look, so unexpected it was almost comical.

Then came the blast of the shotgun, and the face was obliterated in an instant. The hammer-blow hurled the creature backwards, towards the window, its claws shocked into releasing me. The back of its legs struck the wall, and then the hulking monster slowly toppled backwards, vanishing from sight. A second later there was a loud thud from below, then...nothing.

Roberta threw the gun aside and hurried towards me, and together we leaned out of the window to see the monster lying spread-eagled on the gravel drive, motionless. Then Roberta was in my arms, and I felt her warmth through the thin nightgown as I held her close. We stood there, locked in a never-ending embrace, before I eventually found the words to thank her. 'You saved my life,' I murmured.

'And you mine.'

I laughed suddenly. 'My dear, one way or another you continue to thin the werewolves' ranks at an impressive rate of knots. First Cecilie, now Sam Tyler–'

'Well it's their own silly fault,' grumbled Roberta. 'They should learn to keep their distance, shouldn't they?'

Our tender moment was soon interrupted, for the shotgun blast could hardly have gone undetected. The professor burst into Roberta's room first, clad in an old-fashioned nightgown and tassled cap, but he came to a screeching halt as he spied Roberta in my arms. 'What the devil are you doing in my daughter's bedroom?' he demanded angrily. 'And what was that loud bang?'

Behind him came Emily and Ellen, each carrying a flickering candle. They looked annoyed, understandably so, and I hurried forward to explain. 'It was another werewolf,' I said quickly. 'Sam Tyler, the local policeman. He'd climbed into Roberta's bedroom, and–'

'Oh, gracious me!' exclaimed the professor. 'Is that the best excuse you could come up with, young man?'

'Father, Septimus saved my life,' declared Roberta. 'He's the hero in this, not the villain!'

'Mr Jones speaks the truth,' said Ellen, who had come to the window to look out. She eyed me appraisingly. 'Sam Tyler, you said? I suppose it was he that did for the Carmichaels.'

I nodded. 'Something like that.'

'Hrrmph,' growled the professor. 'This village has entirely too many werewolves.'

'To be fair, their numbers dwindle rapidly,' I pointed out. I was feeling euphoric after the tight, long-lasting hug, and in addition, with the subject of my nightmare now defeated, I was convinced we had cleared the village of its hidden killers once and for all. Failing that, it would take a foolish werewolf indeed to remain in these parts, where several of their number had met such grisly ends.

'All the same,' said Roberta, 'it would be best if father and I were to provide the police with a batch of the testing fluid, just to be sure. If they apply it to everyone in the area–'

'But that would cost a fortune!' cried the professor. 'You cannot expect me to fund such a thing, for I would be left destitute.'

Ellen reassured him. 'For such a worthy cause, I'm sure your costs would be covered.'

The professor looked hopeful.

'*Just* your costs, mind,' Ellen warned him. 'This is not an opportunity for profit, sir.'

Even so, I thought I detected a gleam in the professor's eye, and I realised there was a distinct possibility that 'Professor Twickham's Patented Werewolf Detector' might soon find its way onto the market.

Meanwhile, Emily was still looking at me, and there was a certain intensity to her gaze that I did not like. 'Tell me, young man, how did you happen to be here at the precise moment you were needed?'

She indicated the discarded shotgun. 'From that, I gather this was not some illicit liaison of a romantic nature?'

'Miss Emily, you have my word!' I declared.

'So?'

I was tempted to lie, telling them I had seen Sam Tyler acting suspiciously, and had therefore followed him to Ravenswood. But Emily was not to be trifled with, and I decided to tell the truth. 'I had a nightmare,' I confessed. 'In it, I witnessed Tyler attacking Roberta, and upon waking I felt certain something of that nature was about to transpire. It was like a dread feeling I could not shake.'

'Have you experienced such things before? Dreams that came true?'

'There was a recent incident in London involving Lord Snetton. He came to me in a nightmare, and I woke with a similar feeling. It's...it's almost like I see the future.'

'He's got the second sight,' Ellen said to her sister.

Miss Emily was standing near the professor, and she now seemed on the point of saying something. Then she changed her mind, and as the candle flickered, throwing her face into sharp relief, I saw that her eyes were troubled.

'What do you know about it?' I asked, pressing them further. 'Do you both have this second sight?'

'No,' said Ellen, with a quick shake of her head. 'Our mother did, and her grandmother before her. Both were lucky they weren't burned, or drowned.' Ellen regarded me steadily. 'Even these days, you want to be careful who you tell about it.'

'But my mother never told me about...' my voice tailed off. Of *course* my mother never told me anything, for she wouldn't have known about this second sight, since I was not her natural born son!

'Anyway, it's getting on for dawn,' said Ellen. 'Don't trouble yourself over it now. We should all turn in and get a few hours sleep.'

'What about the, er–' I indicated the window. Below, on the gravel, was the body of the werewolf.

'It's not going anywhere by itself,' said Ellen. 'And if there are others about, it might serve as a warning.'

'We'll send for the police in the morning,' said Emily. She glanced at me. 'There's no point you going home at this hour, since you'll wake your parents, more likely than not. Come, I'll find you a bed for the night.'

I turned to Roberta, wishing I could give her a parting hug, but it was impossible in front of the others. Instead we shared a smile, and after bidding her and the professor a good night, I followed Miss Emily to a spare room, where I tumbled into a sagging old bed and fell asleep within moments.

56

I might have slept until early afternoon, at the very least, but instead I was shaken from my deep slumber around dawn. When I opened my eyes it was barely sunrise, and it felt like I'd dozed off some ten minutes earlier.

Above me stood Miss Ellen, and as I came round she handed me a mug of hot tea. 'Don't fret,' she said, noticing what must have been my very alarmed expression. 'Everything's peaceful, I just need your help with something before too many people are up and about.'

She was referring to the werewolf's body, as I soon discovered. Using a rickety wooden barrow, we hauled the inert form to a garden shed, where we hid it beneath an old canvas sailcloth. It was a most distasteful task, and I was glad when it was finished. Afterwards, the only sign of the struggle was an indentation in the gravel driveway, and some minor patches of dried blood.

'I'll send someone for the police,' Ellen told me. 'Best if you head home now, before you have to explain your absence to your parents. I shall tell the others where you've gone.'

'Miss Ellen, this second sight you mentioned–'

'Come back at lunch and we'll discuss it then.'

I hurried home, where I sneaked in through the back door and made it to my own bed. I didn't bother to undress, merely lay down and closed my eyes. I did not think I would be able to sleep, but I managed at least an hour, perhaps two, and this time my sleep was untroubled by nightmares. Finally, a shaft of sunlight woke me once more, and I revelled in the warmth and cosiness of my familiar bed.

Getting up, I followed my nose and ears to the dining room, where my parents were sitting down to breakfast.

'Septimus!' said my mother. 'I called you to breakfast an hour ago, but you were dead to the world.' She eyed my clothes, which were crumpled and dirty, but said nothing. In fact, my parents appeared reserved, which was hardly surprising given the revelation of the night before. Having told me I was adopted, they seemed to be expecting a barrage of questions.

However, within minutes the normalcy of breakfast, which proceeded like so many others we had shared throughout my life, sufficed to soothe their worries.

'Isn't it awful about the poor Carmichaels?' my mother asked me. 'They say a vagrant broke in and killed them all in the night! Even Cecilie, the darling!'

'It's a terrible world we live in,' said my father gravely.

'Inspector Cox got the killer,' I told them. 'There was an exchange of fire, and…well, let us just say that the monster that did this won't be troubling any more innocents.'

My mother fanned herself with her hand. 'It's too distressing, it really is. Why, if you'd only married the girl–'

'Emma, don't,' said my father sharply.

I looked at him in surprise, for he rarely raised his voice to anyone. He regarded me steadily, and in that moment I realised he'd learned the truth about the Carmichaels. Don't ask me how, for the constables wouldn't have opened their mouths to save their lives, but I knew deep down that my father was *au fait* with the true events of the case. Then he lowered his brows, giving me a warning look whose meaning was all too clear: don't tell your mother!

'I thought we might plant out some daisies this afternoon,' my mother told me. 'There's a patch in the back garden which would look lovely with a mass of flowers.'

'I'd love to help you,' I told her. 'I'm expected at Ravenswood soon, but perhaps after lunch?'

As I spoke the mansion's name my parents started, and I saw a look pass between them. I thought nothing of it at the time, being more worried about my upcoming conversation with the Hall sisters, regarding this second sight business, and with the professor, concerning Roberta. Later on, however, I certainly became aware of the significance.

Soon after I was striding through the village, and as I headed towards Ravenswood once more, I could not shake the feeling that one way or another, my life was about to change forever.

The first person I saw at Ravenswood was Miss Ellen, who was in the garden with her working clothes and a pair of hand shears. She saw me looking along the driveway, to the spot where the werewolf had lain, and informed me the police had already taken the body away. 'They'll want to question you eventually, but they said the Kensington police can handle the matter upon your return to London. Right now, it appears they have more than enough paperwork to be going on with.'

I thanked her, then looked towards the house once more. 'Are the others awake yet?'

'Not when I left. I could hear the professor's snoring from the kitchen.'

I smiled.

'I want to thank you, Septimus. Emily and I need our paying guests to make ends meet, and quite apart from the tragedy of the thing, if anything had happened to the Twickhams under our roof…well, the outcome might have ruined us. As it is, we're hoping the newspapers don't get hold of the story. You know how they exaggerate things.'

'They won't hear it from me,' I promised her. 'As for the professor and Roberta, I will swear them to secrecy.'

She smiled at me gratefully. 'And how are your parents? Are they glad all this nonsense is over?'

'They don't know about Tyler yet. They're still getting over news of the Carmichaels.' I hesitated. 'This second sight you mentioned–'

'Not here,' said Ellen, glancing about her as though someone might overhear. 'Come indoors. My father's study.'

Upstairs, we entered the dusty room with its shelves, large desk and glass-fronted cupboard, which now held the old shotgun once again. Ellen had said nothing as we climbed the stairs, and now she stood looking out the window, lost in thought.

I was unwilling to disturb her, for I guessed she was working out the best way to explain the matter to me.

'What I'm about to tell you goes no further,' she said at last.

'You can trust me.'

'Years ago, my sister was intimate with a gentleman visitor,' said Ellen, matter-of-factly. 'I do not blame her, for it could just have easily been me. Cooped up alone we were, with father ill and neither of us used to the company of men.' She glanced at me. 'Soon after, this gentleman went off to war, and like so many young men, he failed to return. In the meantime, it became obvious that Emily had conceived. The scandal would have broken my father, so my sister was packed off to an aunt on the coast for a few months. Ill health, that was the excuse. While she was away I made enquiries, and eventually the baby was placed with a local couple who so desperately wanted a child. As is usually the way, they found they could not have one despite many years of trying, while Emily had succeeded admirably at her first attempt.'

'My parents?' I guessed. It did not come as a shock, and instead only confirmed what I already knew, deep down. The matter of the second sight, apparently hereditary, had sealed it, although the implication hadn't dawned on me right away.

'You knew.'

'I found out only last night. The test of the professor's...' my voice tailed off. 'It's not important how, but it was proved beyond doubt that my parents...well, that they couldn't be my natural parents.'

'A small payment was offered to help with rearing you, but they refused. And thus, you became the centre of their lives.'

A lump rose in my throat. 'Well do I know it,' I whispered. 'I never wanted for loving care nor devotion.'

'You are their son in all but blood,' said Ellen. Then she smiled. 'Of course, when my sister and I depart this earth, you will be our sole heir and descendant. Ravenswood will be yours, although I'm sad to say there is no money to go along with the house.'

While I was digesting this astonishing news, she turned to gaze out of the window. 'This village will continue to grow, of course, and one day all this land will be worth its weight in gold. There are many developers in London who will snatch your arm off for this haven, but I suggest you sell it in small lots, piecemeal, so as not to flood the market.'

'Why do you not sell the land now, when you can use the money?'

'My father,' she said simply. 'He's long gone, rest his soul, but I know it would have broken his heart. However, once Em and I have followed him to the next life, there will be nobody to remember us.' She looked at me. 'Do not reveal to Emily that you know her deepest secret, for she's carried it most of her life now.'

'And the second sight?'

'A family trait, as I told you yesterday. Not every dream is a foretelling, but most deliver up hints to the future. There's no way to tell truth from fiction, and so your only recourse is to treat every warning as the truth, no matter how outlandish.'

At that moment we heard footsteps. The door opened and Emily looked in, and upon seeing us by the window, she smiled inquisitively. 'Ellen, are you monopolising our young guest?'

'I must go and peel the carrots,' said Ellen. She turned to leave, giving me a warning glance. 'I'm preparing a nice hearty stew for dinner tonight. It will do us all good, assuming you're not rushing back to London right away.'

I smiled and nodded my thanks, still shocked by her revelations. Then Emily came to join me at the window, gazing out upon the broad swathe of green and the woods beyond. I turned to study her profile, trying to detect any hint of a family resemblance in this woman who, I now knew, had given birth to me. 'She told you, didn't she?' asked Emily quietly.

Silently, I nodded.

'My sister never could keep her mouth shut,' said Emily fondly. She reached for my hand as we stood facing the window, squeezing my fingers. 'Sometimes I wish things might have been different, Septimus, but I refuse to dwell on the past. There's a will registered with our solicitors, and Ravenswood will pass to you in due course, but until then I ask that you forget everything you've learned today.' She released my hand. 'Will you promise? We live a quiet, peaceful life, and I would not have my reputation in the village tarnished by ancient history. The whispers and pitying looks would be too much to bear. After I'm gone, of course, none of it matters.'

I nodded wordlessly.

'Thank you,' breathed Emily. 'Now, let us see if your friends have awoken. That young lady of yours is a corker, and I've enjoyed some lively conversations with her during her stay.'

57

I encountered Roberta in the hall, and after a quick hug we went through to the dining room, where the professor was seated at the table with a boiled egg and toast on the plate in front of him. The food was untouched, and at first he appeared to be writing in his notebook, until I recognised the repeated diagonal strokes. He was sketching something.

'Ah, Septimus! Good morning, my boy!'

'And to you too, professor.'

'Come, I have something to show you.'

As I drew close, the professor angled his notebook to show me a rather well-done sketch. In it, I saw a handsome gentlemen of about forty, with dark hair, a bushy moustache and a noble, intelligent face. Underneath were the words 'Professor Twickham's Patented Werewolf Prognosticator', which was almost as I'd imagined the night before, word-for-word. 'Who is this gentleman in the picture?' I asked him.

The professor looked affronted. 'Why, it's me of course!'

I studied the lined face before me, framed by white whiskers and topped with a wayward mop of snowy white hair. Then I regarded the sketch once more. 'The resemblance is somewhat, er, fleeting,' I suggested.

'It's marketing, my boy,' he said, with an airy wave of the hand. 'You would not understand.'

'Father,' said Roberta. 'Your lunch grows colder by the minute.'

The professor eyed his boiled egg. 'What I wouldn't give for some sausage, and perhaps a rasher or three of bacon.'

At that, I had a sudden idea. 'Roberta, would you mind if I borrowed your father for an hour?'

She looked surprised. 'How mysterious! But if I'm honest, it would suit me just fine, as I have yet to finish packing.'

'What's all this about?' asked the professor. 'If you're going to ask me for a loan, just come out with it. There's no need–'

'Sir, they serve a hearty lunch at the inn, and it would be my pleasure to treat you.'

'Oh well, in that case...lead on, my boy! Over sausage and bacon you may ask me whatever you like.' He hesitated. 'Do they have black pudding as well? I'm partial to black pudding.'

'I'm not certain, but we can certainly find out.'

The professor and I left together, Roberta watching us go with a slightly bemused look.

'This little werewolf incident might lead to a very lucrative line of business,' the professor said, as we strolled along the gravel path to the gates.

'I thought you were only getting reimbursed for your costs?' I pointed out.

'Yes, yes, but that's here, in West Wickham. These werewolves might have infested half the villages in England, don't you see?' He spread his hands. 'I can see the advertisements now. Test your family before they eat you!' He thought for a moment. 'Is your neighbour a monster in disguise?'

'Peace of mind for half a guinea,' I suggested.

'Tame, my boy. Far too tame.'

We reached the inn, where the barkeep served us a working man's lunch, the plates piled high with good, solid food. The professor made his delight known by means of grunts and appreciative nods, although as for myself I was so nervous I could barely stomach a mouthful.

There was an ulterior motive to the lunch, of course, but now the moment had arrived I was as terrified as I had been during my recent confrontations with killer werewolves out for my blood.

Finally, the professor pushed his empty plate aside, sitting back with a look of supreme contentment. 'Now that, Mr Jones, *that* is what I call a decent lunch.'

I just sat there. I wanted to speak, to broach the subject which was tormenting me, but I found I could not. Then I saw the professor's eye upon me, a hint of a smile on his lips. If anything, that made things worse.

'I cannot endure this any longer,' he said, with a chuckle. 'Septimus, you are not as devious as you think you are, for I have guessed that this luncheon comes with strings attached.'

More like the anchor rope of a Navy frigate, I thought desperately. 'It's...it's about Roberta,' I blurted out.

His face fell, the smile disappearing like magic. 'I see.' He took a deep breath. 'Well, I've seen you both together, of course, and I've noticed you growing closer. You cannot deny it.'

'I won't, sir. I respect you too much for that.'

'You know my wishes, Septimus. I want the best for my daughter.'

I nodded miserably.

The professor gripped my shoulder. 'My boy, you lack even the most modest of means, reliant as you are upon the meagre wages I pay you.'

In that instant I was tempted...no, *desperate*...to tell him of Ravenswood. Of my secret family ties, and the unexpected inheritance which would one day see the house become mine. If I revealed this startling fact to the professor, swearing him to secrecy, that alone would convince him I would one day have the means to support Roberta. It was the answer to all my problems. A trump card *par excellence*.

And a secret I'd sworn to keep.

I knew then that I could not break my promise to Emily and Ellen, whatever the temptation. Instead, I looked the professor directly in the eyes. 'Sir, if I were to promise you, upon my honour, that one day–'

He gestured. 'I do not need your promises, Septimus. I want the best for my daughter, my boy, and I am telling you that I could not hope for a better man than you.'

It took a moment or two for the words to sink in, and then, astounded, I stared at him.

'Yes, Septimus, you heard correctly. You have my permission to ask Roberta for her hand in marriage. My objections, such as they are, cannot stand in the way of your obvious attraction to each other. To ask otherwise would consign all three of us to a life of misery and despair. Of course,' he added, smiling, 'knowing my daughter as I do, she is just as likely to refuse you.'

Scarcely believing the sudden change in my fortunes, I could only sit there, gazing into space. Then I realised I'd only succeeded in scaling one impossible cliff, and I now faced another. What if I broached the subject with Roberta, and she laughed it off as a joke?

The professor noticed my nervous expression. 'I'd ask her sooner rather than later,' he told me kindly. 'Don't let it fester.'

I got up, determined. 'Thank you, sir. I'll never forget this.'

'I dare say you won't.'

Upon returning to Ravenswood, the professor gripped my hand and slapped me on the shoulder. I thought he was going to speak, but to my surprise I saw tears spring to his eyes, and he resorted to a quick nod before turning and hurrying away.

I was still overcome by this rare show of emotion when I saw Roberta descending the stairs from the upper floor. She was wearing a flower print dress, her long hair tied up anyhow, and she looked at me curiously as I stood in the hall, just watching her. 'Did you have a good lunch?'

'The best,' I declared, finding my voice. 'Would you...shall we go for a walk?'

'Of course!'

We crossed the back garden, hand in hand, and in the distance I saw the sisters tending to their vegetable patch. One of them, Ellen I think, waved, and I returned the gesture.

'They're both quite lovely,' said Roberta. 'I'm surprised they never married.'

I almost looked at her, but I kept my gaze averted as I knew my expression would have revealed my innermost thoughts. Roberta was highly intelligent and very perceptive, and it scarcely seemed possible she would mention marriage so casually, not when I had returned tongue-tied and brimming with suppressed excitement after a secretive lunch with her father. Even so, I was determined to see things through properly. 'The professor and I spoke over lunch,' I told her.

'Yes,' said Roberta, with a nod.

'In the past there were certain obstacles, er, in the way of the question of, um–' I paused, because it was going even worse than I'd feared. 'Your father told me that certain conditions, once insurmountable, no longer have to be met.'

'Yes,' murmured Roberta.

'And so, he's given me permission, to, ah–'

'Yes.'

'Why do you keep saying yes?'

'Because that's the answer, you fool.' So saying, Roberta turned to me, smiling. 'It was always going to be yes.'

I was so surprised I could only stare at her. 'But I was going to go down on bended knee!'

She surveyed the ground, poking it with the toe of her shoe. 'I shouldn't bother if I were you. You'll just get mud on your trousers.'

'It'll brush off,' I growled. So saying, I turned to face her, taking her hand in mine and dropping to one knee…mud and all. 'Roberta Twickham, will you do me the honour of being my wife?'

'Yes, of course. But you're washing those trousers.'

It was later that afternoon, and Roberta and I were enjoying tea and biscuits in the library. I was still floating on a cloud, somewhere above the ground, and I had to keep pinching myself to confirm this was no dream, but real life.

We'd revealed the happy news to the professor, and then my parents, and there had been congratulations and joy all round. The Hall sisters were delighted, and Emily, more invested in me than anyone else realised, had burst into tears of happiness. Now, after all the excitement, I confess I was thoroughly enjoying the peace and quiet in the library.

'I heard father talking with one of the sisters yesterday evening,' said Roberta casually.

'Oh yes?'

'I shouldn't have listened, of course, and I retreated as soon as I heard what they were talking about.'

I smiled at her fondly. 'And what was that, my dear?'

'I don't suppose I ought to repeat it.'

'You cannot withhold it from me now,' I said, my smile getting a little strained. 'It would be cruel in the extreme.'

'Oh, very well. I heard Emily telling my father that you and I were meant for each other. She expressed surprise that we were not already betrothed, and *he* said it was a matter of your prospects.'

It seemed to me that Roberta had overheard a great deal before moving out of earshot, but I wisely said nothing. As for the professor's reply, that was a well-trodden path, and hardly a surprise revelation.

'So, the next thing I knew, Emily told my father she gave birth to you, and that one day you would inherit Ravenswood.'

I choked on my tea, spraying myself with the hot liquid. 'She said *what?*'

'Why the surprise? I assumed that's what the two of you were talking about upstairs, since she told my father you'd be informed this morning.'

As I sat there with hot tea soaking through my shirt, two contrasting emotions took hold of me. The first was my undying gratitude to Emily, who had apparently revealed her deepest secret to the professor, and by doing so had risked her own reputation and standing to ensure my happiness. As for the second emotion, let us just say that a wry smile came to my lips. The professor's magnanimity during lunch, when he'd informed me I was right for his daughter, despite being penniless and having no prospects...his speech about my good character, and the obvious attraction...his entire performance had been a sham!

Because all the way through that painful lunch, *the professor had already known I would inherit Ravenswood.*

'That wily old goat!' I exclaimed.

The End

Historical Notes

A few remarks from the author.

Several locations mentioned in this novel are real, as are some of the people.

West Wickham is the town where I grew up. Croydon is where I was born, at St Mary's hospital. Thornton Heath is where my grandmother had a clothing factory in the late sixties and early seventies. Later, around 1971, my father, his brothers and *their* father (my grandad) built some of the earliest hang gliders in England in that very same factory under the Waspair brand.

My grandparents lived in Addington and then Biggin Hill – both a stone's throw from West Wickham – and my grandfather Ken served in the Eighth Army during World War II. At one stage he was posted missing believed dead, but fortunately he turned up alive and well.

Back to Croydon for a moment: this is where my other grandparents lived. Roland, my grandfather, served in World War I, lying about his age to join the Royal Flying Corps. I still have a photo of him as a despatch rider: trim uniform, barely seventeen, proud as punch astride his huge motorbike. Much later, during World War II, a bomb fell on their street, destroying the house next-door-but-one and killing the family that lived there. My mum was only a toddler at the time, and it was lucky for her (and me!) that bomb didn't fall thirty or forty feet to the left.

The Hall sisters, Emily and Ellen, were real, and lived at Ravenswood until their deaths in 1911. During that time they wrote extensive diaries on life in West Wickham, and these diaries are preserved in the Bromley library. In my novel I have only borrowed their names, intended as a tribute of sorts, and everything I've written about them is a fiction.

Ravenswood was demolished in 1957 to make way for a petrol station and then a supermarket. A few years earlier it was used as a cinema, and when I told my parents I was researching the house for my novel, they revealed that they used to catch a bus together as teenagers in order to visit that very same cinema.

Wickham Court is a grand manor, almost a castle, originally situated on five acres of lawns and gardens, and was the ancestral home of the Heydon and Boleyn families. (Yep, *that* Boleyn). Sir Lennard was lord of the manor at the time of my novel, but again, I have only used his name and everything else is a figment of my overactive imagination. The Lennard family owned Wickham Court until the early 1900s, when the son emigrated to Canada. The property was used by the Army in the Second World War, and is now home to a school.

In the nineteenth century West Wickham was a sleepy country village with several grand houses on acres of rolling countryside. Despite being very close to London, even today there are large tracts of countryside which are protected from development. As a boy I delivered newspapers in the area, pedalling my trusty bicycle through the snow before sunrise, and I still recall the huge, two-storey houses with their paved driveways and magnificent trees.

A hundred and fifty years earlier Septimus may have walked under some of those very same trees. I might have looked closer on my paper round, hoping to see the faint marks from his shotgun practice, but then he wasn't a very good shot, was he?

Simon Haynes, Perth, Western Australia

About the Author

Simon Haynes was born in England and grew up in Spain. His family moved to Australia when he was 16.

In addition to novels, Simon writes computer software. In fact, he writes computer software to help him write novels faster, which leaves him more time to improve his writing software. And write novels faster. (spacejock.com/yWriter.html)

Simon's goal is to write fifteen novels before someone takes his keyboard away.

Update 2019: goal achieved and I still have my keyboard!

New goal: write thirty novels.

Update 2020: Enigma in Silver is #29...

Stay in touch!

Simon's website is spacejock.com.au

Author's newsletter: spacejock.com.au/ML.html

Facebook: facebook.com/halspacejock

Twitter: @spacejock

Acknowledgements

Bill, Corey, Dave, Gary, Helen, Kim, Larrie, Laurence, Lynne, Mike, Nathan, Nick, Paulette, Peter, Phil, Phillip, Ray, Ryan, Sankar, Sean, Selene, Steve, Susan, Terry, Tim, Val and Vince thanks for the awesome help and support!

THE
HAL SPACEJOCK
SERIES

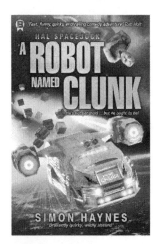

"Brilliantly quirky, wildly absurd"

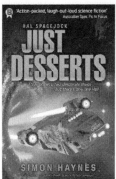

"The perfect blend of adventure, conflict and laughable moments"

but wait...
there's more!

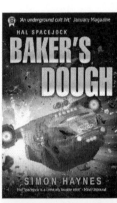

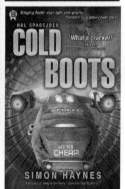

Available in Ebook and Trade Paperback

THE MYSTERIES IN METAL SERIES

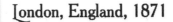

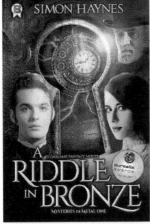

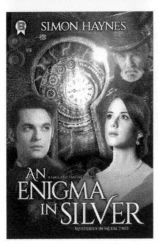

London, England, 1871

When I applied for the position of book-keeper with Professor Twickham and his daughter, I lied about my qualifications.

As it turns out, they lied about the job for which I was applying.

Had we not been so untruthful with each other, there might have been fewer night terrors stalking the inhabitants of the City.

Fewer unexplained disappearances. Fewer deaths.

Now, nobody is safe from the creeping horrors we've unleashed.

With no time to spare, we face an impossible task: we must discover the mysteries in metal in order to right this wrong.

But is it already too late?

Ebook and Trade Paperback

THE
SECRET WAR
SERIES

What happens when you're worth more dead... than alive?

When a decorated fighter pilot goes missing, his death is quickly turned into propaganda, inspiring fresh recruits to feed the war's voracious appetite.

Sam Willet is one such recruit, but she's different.

Different because the missing hero is her brother, and Sam has questions.

Questions nobody wants asked.

Questions that will probably get her killed.

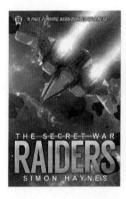
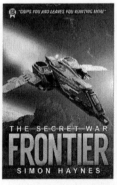

Ebook and Trade Paperback

THE HARRIET WALSH SERIES

It's Harriet Walsh's first day as a Peace Force trainee, and she's given a simulated case to solve. Simulated, because Dismolle is a peaceful planet and there's absolutely no crime.

Well, almost no crime.

You see, Harriet's found a genuine case to investigate, and she's hot on the trail of a real live suspect.

Which is a shame, because her crime-fighting computer is so basic it doesn't even have solitaire.

Coming 2020

Ebook and Trade Paperback

THe
HAL JUNIOR
SERIES

"A thoroughly enjoyable read for 10-year-olds and adults alike"
The West Australian

Hal Junior lives aboard a futuristic space station. His mum is chief scientist, his dad cleans air filters and his best mate is Stephen 'Stinky' Binn.

As for Hal ... he's a bit of a trouble magnet. He means well, but his wild schemes and crazy plans never turn out as expected!

Hal Junior: The Secret Signal features mayhem and laughs, daring and intrigue ... plus a home-made space cannon!

THE DRAGON & CHIPS TRILOGY

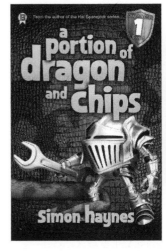

Ebook and Trade Paperback

A mild-mannered old robot has just been transported to a medieval kingdom, and things are quickly going from bad to worse:

A homicidal knight is after his blood - or the robot equivalent.

A greedy queen wants to bend him to her will.

A conniving Master of Spies is hatching his own devious plan for the mechanical marvel.

And worst of all, there's nowhere to get a recharge!

"Laugh after laugh, dark in places but the humour punches through. Amazing!"

Made in the USA
Monee, IL
16 May 2021

68767743R00231